DOUBLE TWIST

A MIA MURPHY MYSTERY

STEPHANIE ROWE

AUTHENTICITY PLAYGROUND

COPYRIGHT

Print ISBN: 978-1-940968-94-0

Publisher: Authenticity Playground, LLC

are excerpts from other books by the author in the back of the book.

ACKNOWLEDGMENTS

Special thanks to my beta readers. You guys are the best! Alyssa Bird, Ashlee Murphy, Bridget Koan, Britannia Hill, Deb Julienne, Denise Fluhr, Dottie Jones, Heidi Hoffman, Helen Loyal, Jackie Moore Kranz, Jean Bowden, Jeanne Stone, Jeanie Jackson, Jodi Moore, Judi Pflughoeft, Kasey Richardson, Linda Watson, Regina Thomas, Summer Steelman, Suzanne Mayer, Shell Bryce, and Trish Douglas. Special thanks to my family, who I love with every fiber of my heart and soul. And to AER, who is my world. Love you so much, baby girl! And to Joe, who keeps me believing myself. I love you all!

Thank you to Elizabeth Turner Stokes for the most AMAZING cover. I am in awe of your vision and your talent. Plus, you're the coolest chick ever.

Thank you also to Nina and the team at Valentine PR for all your advice, support, and hard work to help my books dance out into the delighted hands of the readers who will love them.

Thank you to Melanie Downing for fantastic editing.

Huge, mega thanks to Lee Conary, the owner of Kezar Lake Marina, for the inside scoop on marina life on a Maine lake. Anything I got wrong about boats, boating, lakes etc is definitely on me, not him. You rock, Lee! I hope you get a chuckle when you see some of your tidbits show up in this story!

WHAT READERS THINK

ABOUT DOUBLE TWIST

"OMG, I love Mia Murphy…What a fun-loving, non-stop, action-packed whodunit that I could not put down." Dru's Book Musings

"This book was spectacular! The writing was so witty and funny, the characters were quirky and fun, and the whole story was action-packed and never boring even for a minute!" ~Five-star Goodreads Review (Rachel M.)

"Mia Murphy is my new favorite character! She is fun, witty and slightly cracked." Five-star Goodreads Review (April M.)

"I want King Tut…because who doesn't want a guard cat that looks like a bobcat? I love it and can't wait for the second entry to hit. THIS IS THE COZY SERIES TO READ AND FOLLOW!" Five-star Goodreads Review (LittleRead)

"Strong early Stephanie Plum vibes, and that is certainly a compliment…I will absolutely keep reading this delightful series." Five-star Goodreads Review (Karen H.)

"A laugh-out-loud, nail-biting, page-turning read." ~Riding Reviewer

"The book is so funny (I mean SO funny!)...the twists and turns they get into, there's no predicting it! I loved the story." ~Five-star Goodreads review (Maureen W)

"This is one of the funniest books I've read in a long time...I loved this book so much that I want to read the next in the series right now. Kudos to the author. Highly recommended." ~Joanna's Books Blog (Five Stars)

"*Double Twist* is a delightfully witty, fast paced whodunit with incredibly likeable characters whose hair-raising schemes trying to solve a murder to prove their friend innocent are priceless... A can't put down book you will read with a smile on your face from start to finish." Lisa's Cubby, Five Stars

CHAPTER 1

A SHADOW MOVED across my fifth-floor window.

Assassin.

I yelped and launched myself out of bed. My foot caught in the sheet, and I crashed to the floor. I rolled onto my back, frantically kicking to get free. I scrambled up and lunged for the doorknob—

Then I heard a meow.

I whirled around and saw King Tut, my neighbor's rude and massive black cat, staring at me through the glass, with his unblinking yellow eyes, thick gray mane, and unruly tufts of fur in his ears.

A cat. Not a hit man. *I wasn't going to die tonight.*

My legs gave out. I landed hard, and then pressed the heels of my hands to my eyes, trying to slow my frantic heart rate.

Breathe in. Breathe out. Breathe in. Breathe out. *I'm not going to die tonight.*

It was hard to believe I used to be fairly chill. Relaxed. Resilient.

Being raised and trained by a con artist mother had made me pretty unflappable, even after I'd ditched that life when I was seventeen.

Now? A grumpy *cat* had sent me running for my life. Two years being undercover against my drug lord ex-husband, Stanley Herrera, had totally screwed with my tolerance level for stress.

I'd made one little anonymous tip to the FBI hotline after finding bags of white powder in our china cabinet. One tiny, socially conscious gesture. That was all it had taken to get me dragged into a two-year sting run by an FBI control freak I'd nick-named Griselda.

Agent Straus didn't appreciate my pet name for him, which made me call him Griselda as often as I could. I'd needed to find some way to amuse myself, because spying on the man I was sharing a bed with had been surprisingly stressful, especially once I learned how much he liked to have traitors chopped up into little pieces and used as an example to others.

Con artists were non-violent. Non-confrontational. Clever law-benders who delighted in the artistry of deception. My childhood hadn't prepared me for thriving in a world of hit men, murder, and violence.

The night Stanley had figured it out and pointed a gun at my forehead? If Griselda hadn't been literally breaking in the front door at that second—

But he had. So it had worked out fine.

Except for the apparent wee bit of lingering jumpiness on my part.

King Tut meowed again, tapping his left paw impatiently on the glass.

I took a deep, calming breath, and rolled to my feet. "All right. Cool your jets."

I walked over to him and fought with the window until I was able to get the crooked casing to move. As soon as it was open, King Tut hopped off the sill and strolled into my cardboard-box-sized bedroom, the one I'd been stashed in during Stanley's trial so a hit man couldn't keep me from testifying.

I'd always thought it would be fun to have my ex sending killers after me. Childhood dreams right there, right?

Tonight, no FBI agents were lurking in my hallways, and no one cared what I did. Why? Because ten hours ago, Stanley had been convicted, and he was now heading off to his new home behind bars.

Since I had nowhere else to go, Griselda had let me stay in the safe house for one more night, which gave me a chance to say good-bye to the cat who had been my only decent company for months. My only friend, actually, but who wants to sound like a loser?

The FBI had offered me witness relocation, but I'd turned it down. The last thing I wanted was to turn my life over to yet another person. I'd been forced into crime by my mother. I'd been tangled up with Stanley for years. And then I'd been used by Griselda as his little spy.

I was done letting someone else control me.

No more. Never. Ever. Again.

Tomorrow, I was packing up and moving on. To where? I had no idea. But I had about twelve hours to figure it out, so plenty of time.

The air drifting through King Tut's window was cold and crisp, an early May chill that made me shiver. The spring air felt alive and clean, like the fresh start I was claiming for myself. I braced my hands on the window and leaned out, inhaling the night air.

My next-door neighbor's window was open, and I marveled once again at how King Tut managed to jump the gap between our windows without being fazed by the five-story drop to the unforgiving pavement. Granted, I'd met my very sketchy neighbor a couple times, and if I lived with him, I'd probably risk plummeting to my death to get away from him, too.

The sound of a police siren drifted up from below, and I leaned out to check the street. It looked more like Griselda's ride than a Boston police car.

It stopped in front of my building as the theme from *The Greatest American Hero* burst from my phone.

Habit borne from two years of taking every call in case Griselda had news that would save my life made me hurry over to the nightstand and check the screen. *Griselda.*

This was supposed to be over. He wasn't supposed to call me in the middle of the night anymore. Ever again. Alarm prickling at the back of my neck, I hit the send button. "What's up?"

"Mia! Assassin. Get out!" he shouted. "Now!"

Terror shot through me, and I grabbed King Tut. But just as I started to run for the front door, I heard the whoosh of a silenced gun, and the lock on my front door exploded.

I skidded to a stop, scrambling backwards as I gripped the phone. "He's at the door!" I whispered. "He's here!"

Griselda swore. "Hide in the bathroom. Lock the door and get in the tub. I'm on my way up."

The front door splintered, and King Tut yowled in fury and tried to leap out of my arms.

Struggling to keep my grip on him, I raced into the bathroom, locked the door, and then dove into the tub, clutching the wriggling feline in my arms. I yanked the mildewed shower curtain closed, and then curled onto my side in the fetal position so all my body parts were below the rim.

The floorboards creaked outside the door, and I tried to hold my panicked breath, but it echoed off the yellowed tiles. Loud. So freaking loud. I really had to learn how to stop breathing in times of crisis.

I couldn't believe this. After all I'd survived for the last two years, *now* I was going to get whacked in a tub?

There was so much indignity in being murdered in a bathtub.

King Tut purred and began kneading my chest, through my tank top. I bit my lip and slid my hand beneath his claws to protect my skin.

His purring got louder, and the footsteps paused just outside the bathroom door.

Seriously? I was going to get busted by a cat?

I raised my head enough to peer around the edge of the

curtain at the door. The wood was so flimsy there were already cracks in it. Literally one bullet is all it would take to get in. It probably would take no more than a gentle nudge with a pinkie finger, actually.

I was pretty sure my late-night visitor could muster up at least that much force, which meant I had maybe a millisecond at most until the only thing between me and a hired killer was a moldy shower curtain.

Griselda was, at that very moment, sweating his way up four flights of stairs. He was almost as fit as he liked to tell everyone he was, but he wasn't *that* fast.

In retrospect, maybe it would have been better to lock the bathroom as a red herring, and then hide somewhere else, like hang out the window by my fingertips. I would admire myself so much more if I died that way, instead of cowering in a tub.

My mom would be so disappointed in me for cowering in my last moments of life.

Truth? I would also be disappointed in myself for cowering in my last moments of life. I needed to die as more than a bathtub victim.

My phone rang again, but it was outside the bathroom. I must have dropped it during my sprint for safety. The floor creaked, and I heard my personal Grim Reaper move away from the door in pursuit of my phone.

Frantically, I scanned the bathroom for a weapon. Toothbrush? Towel? Mascara? Hairdryer?

Hairdryer.

I tucked King Tut under my arm, scrambled out of the tub as quietly as I could, and climbed up onto the sink. I tucked myself up against the corner closest to the door, set King Tut on my lap, and picked up the hairdryer.

I tested the weight of the hairdryer, swung it from the cord, and then heard the creak in the hall again, outside the bathroom.

I went still.

My assassin waited.

King Tut purred.

My quads started to cramp. My arm ached from holding up the hairdryer. Sweat dripped down my eyebrow and stung my right eye.

The doorknob rattled.

Fear shot through me, obliterating all thought of leg cramps.

The gun fired, and then the door handle exploded. I leapt back and my foot slipped on the porcelain. King Tut dug his claws into my thighs for balance, as I grabbed the towel rack to keep from tumbling off my perch right to my assassin's feet.

Two more shots and the door drifted ajar while I perched precariously, clinging to life by one old towel rack and a stained sink. I'd never wanted to see Griselda as badly as I did in that moment.

But he didn't show up.

Instead, the gleaming barrel of a gun poked through the gap in the door and then bullets flashed out of the end of it, right at the tub. Where I'd just been. Because that had clearly been a great place to hide. *Thanks, Griselda.*

A man moved into my line of vision. He was angled away from me, his gun and his attention focused on the tub. His all-black attire and ski mask escalated my terror level to near-debilitating heights.

He fired several more shots into the shower curtain, then reached out with his gun to push the shower curtain aside and inspect the bullet-ridden body he wasn't going to find.

This was it. My chance.

I braced myself, then tightened my grip on the cord. "Hey!" As I shouted, I swung as hard as I could.

He spun around just as the hairdryer smashed him across the face, shattering his nose with a loud crunch. He dropped like an old lady shocked by her first sight of porn.

I leapt over him, landed on the hall floor, and then raced for the front door. I ran out into the hall corridor, and then something hit me between the shoulder blades and flung me forward. I hit the carpet and dropped King Tut, who yowled with protest as he landed gracefully on his feet.

I scrambled up, but before I could get off my knees, something cold and hard pressed into the back of my head. A gun?

I froze.

"Mia Murphy. You two-faced, lying, little snake."

I blinked at the sound of my ex-mother-in-law's voice. "Joyce?"

The gun pressed harder into the back of my head. "We took you in as family. We loved you. I called you my daughter. And then you turned on my son and ripped him from me. And now you want to steal his business."

"Steal his business?" If I hadn't been so stressed about the gun pressed up against the back of my head, I would have started laughing at the ridiculousness of that idea. "There's literally nothing I want less than becoming a drug lord—"

"For that, you die." Joyce kicked me in the hamstring, and my leg immediately cramped, making me lurch to the right.

Except dying. *That* was something I wanted less than running a major drug operation.

"Turn around," Joyce snarled. "I want to watch your agony and pain as the life drains from your pathetic, unworthy body."

Wow. That was alarmingly sociopathic.

I slowly turned, frantically trying to figure out how to get out of this one. Then I saw her face. It was bright red. Twisted with rage. Mottled with anger. Her eyes were almost glazed. Crazy eyes. And she was aiming a machine gun at my face.

She met my gaze with unflinching hatred. "Without your testimony, Stanley won't get convicted on his appeal."

Witness protection? Who needs witness protection? Clearly it had been a great choice to turn that down. "Listen, Joyce, there's been a misunderstanding." I tried to summon the quick-thinking that had saved me so many times as a kid, but the assault weapon aimed at my face was making it difficult to concentrate. "I'm not going to testify against Stanley again or take over his business."

"Exactly. You'll be dead." Her flushed face twisted into a triumphant grin. "Say good-bye, you snot-nosed, thieving rat."

"Wait!" I held up my hands, which were shaking so badly I could practically feel the breeze on my face. "If you shoot me, you'll go to prison. Put the gun down. We'll both walk away and pretend we never met—"

She called me a name that would have had nuns fainting (or cheering, depending on the nun), and then her finger moved on the trigger.

I had no time to duck before the deafening sound of gunshot exploded in the hallway.

I yelped, but I didn't collapse in a bullet-ridden death.

Her mouth opened in surprise, a red stain blossomed on the front of her shirt, and then she toppled over. She hit the floor with a thump, and behind her stood Griselda. He was dripping with sweat, panting, and aiming his gun right where she'd been.

CHAPTER 2

King Tut was nice enough to wait with me for the four hours it took the cleanup squad to erase all signs of Joyce's untimely demise.

Fortunately, I had not killed my hit man, so there wasn't much paperwork for me. It was pretty cool, however, when the paramedic had complimented my hairdryer prowess while loading the prostrate bathroom-invader onto the stretcher.

Never underestimate a woman with a hairdryer.

It was nearly dawn by the time Griselda appeared in the doorway of my bedroom. I was sitting on the bed with the cat and my computer, stretching out my final farewell to the faded, slightly musty, navy bedspread and the sparsely decorated, worn-out shoebox I'd come to call home.

"You didn't have to stay," he said. Griselda was wearing jeans, sneakers, and a T-shirt, not the uptight coat and tie he usually wore. He also had stubble on his jaw, instead of that baby-soft close shave he usually sported. It made him look younger, closer to the mid-thirtyish I suspected he was. Maybe even slightly rugged, for those who liked the stoic, inflexible FBI type.

More importantly, it almost made him look human, which was

not the agent I'd grown to love. Or hate. Hate might be a little strong. Or it might not. I was still deciding.

"I stayed because I don't have a place to go," I reminded him as King Tut glared at him for interrupting our bonding moment. "You guys confiscated everything except my computer, my phone, and my clothes."

"All your marital assets were connected to drug money," Griselda reminded me.

I ignored his sensible logic. "I didn't even know I was working for the family drug business, but I lost it all anyway." I wasn't bitter. Really, I wasn't. Well, I was working on not being bitter, because bitterness never served anyone. I patted King Tut as a reminder of the importance of friendship and love. *Nice kitty.*

Griselda walked in and stood at the end of the bed, casting his shadow across my screen in a stalkerish way.

I shut my computer and glared at the looming hulk of muscle "What?"

He paused, then inclined his chin. "Sorry about tonight."

"You are?" Griselda had never apologized for anything. Not a single thing, even while carefully taking apart every last bit of my life.

"Yeah. I didn't see that coming with Joyce. My mistake."

I eyed him. "Well, at least you got here before I *really* needed you."

He grinned. "I like to make you sweat. It's entertaining."

"One of the many reasons I'm not going to miss you." I gave him my most exasperated tone. "Did you see the bullets lodged in the bathtub? Don't give that advice to anyone else trying to evade a professional killer."

"Noted." His smile faded. "Good job, Mia."

"On what?"

"All of it. The hairdryer. The trial. And everything the last two years. Great work." His gaze was steady, and I felt the genuineness of his words.

His compliment warmed me. "We got him, didn't we?"

"We did." Griselda looked pleased. Satisfied. Not as serious as usual. Almost like he might someday learn to relax a little. "I'm being moved to the New York office. I leave today."

"Promotion?" Stanley had been a big win. Griselda deserved it.

"Yeah."

I realized I wasn't going to see Griselda again. Ever, most likely. The thought felt weird. He'd been a part of my life pretty much every moment for the last two years. He'd put me in danger, but he'd also been the one in charge of making sure I stayed safe. He'd been the only person I could talk to honestly. The only one who I knew wouldn't abandon me.

I cocked my head. "Are we friends?"

He hesitated, then shrugged. "Maybe."

Maybe. That felt right.

"What are you going to do next?" he asked. "Pick up another accounting job in Boston?"

"No." I opened my computer, then turned it around so he could see the screen. "I'm going to a place like this."

The bed sagged as he braced his hands on the mattress and leaned in for a better look at my computer. "A lake in Maine?"

"Diamond Lake." It was a gorgeous, mountain-flanked lake, with a charming town full of tourists in the summer and skiers in the winter, plus a healthy supply of year-round locals. I knew that because I'd Googled it. Repeatedly.

Well, only when I couldn't sleep.

Which meant every night of the last two years.

But maybe tonight, I would finally sleep. A girl had to have hope that normalcy would someday return, right? "It's in the town of Bass Derby."

He gave me a speculative look. "You don't seem like a small-town Maine person."

"Au contraire, Griselda." I smiled when his eyes narrowed at my pet name for him. We really did love that name, didn't we? Or maybe just me. Who knew? "When I was in high school, a friend of mine invited me to a lake in Maine with her family. I've been dreaming about it ever since."

Well, it wasn't quite how it happened. My mom had conned her way into a trip with some people we'd just met, but the impact of the week on the lake was the same.

He knew about my childhood, including my mom. That was part of the threat they'd been holding over me to make me work for them.

"I've always wanted to go, and now I will." Peace. Quiet. Beauty. Things I'd never had in my life. I pulled up another picture and showed it to him.

His brows nearly shot off his forehead when he saw the real estate listing that I'd been stalking for months. "You want to buy a marina? With what money?"

I turned the computer away from his rude response. "It's a fantasy, Griselda. Hopes and dreams fuel the soul."

"Do you know *anything* about boats?"

"No, but I take umbrage at that tone." His doubt made me want to buy the marina just to prove him wrong. "It has two commercial tenants and an apartment over the marina. I'd have income, a place to live, and Stanley's family would never drive that far north just to murder me."

Griselda snorted. "They might drive even further to kill you." Concern flickered across his face. "Are you sure you don't want to do Witness Relocation?" He jerked his chin in the direction of where Joyce had cornered me, apparently worried that I'd already forgotten that she'd tried to murder me tonight. There was an edge of genuine concern in his voice, which warmed the cockles of my pickpocketing little heart.

"I'll be fine." I shut my laptop for dramatic emphasis. "I'm like that game with the gopher and the mallets. I can't be stopped."

"The gophers get hit all the time. There are just a lot of them, and they're made of metal under all that fur. I'm pretty sure you're not made of metal." He paused, his face grim. "If I hadn't gotten here in time to stop Joyce, you'd be dead."

"But I'm not dead, and that's really the point." Or, at least, it was the one I was choosing to stay focused on, mostly because if I thought about how close I'd come to dying, I might have to curl into the fetal position for the rest of my life, and who wanted to live like that? I was reclaiming my confident, irreverent self, end of story.

Griselda raised his brows. "Is that *really* the point?"

I narrowed my eyes. "Look, Griselda. You taught me all about staying alive during my indentured servitude to you. Between you and my mom, I'm not exactly helpless. I want to live my life on my terms, and not be trapped into whatever identity some government numbnut decides to give me." I tapped my index finger pointedly on my laptop. "I'll buy my marina. You just watch. Maybe not today. Maybe not tomorrow. Maybe not that specific marina. But I'll get it."

The corner of his mouth quirked. "*Maybe* not today?"

I glared at him. "Okay, so it's definitely not going to be today. Do you want me to share more of my dreams you can try to crush? Because it won't work. I'm not giving up."

"You never do." There was a hint of admiration in Griselda's tone that made me pause.

"Is that a compliment?" I asked, not quite able to keep the surprise out of my voice.

"It's an observation." Griselda dug into his pocket and pulled out a crumpled piece of paper about the size of a sticky note. "When I got the call about Joyce, I was already pulling up outside because I had something to give you before I left."

I eyed it suspiciously, making no move to take the folded paper. "A love note? Because I have to tell you now, I don't date men named Griselda."

"No." Amusement glinted in his blue eyes. "The FBI was able to release some of the confiscated funds to you. I just got word last night, and I wanted to deliver the news in person, before I left town."

My fingers tightened on my computer. "Funds? As in money?"

"Yep." He sat down next to me and held out the wrinkled note. "I wrote the amount on there, but it's already been wired to your bank account." He gave me a triumphant smile. "Buy the marina, Mia. If anyone can make it work, you can."

"Buy the marina?" I snatched the paper and opened it. *It was enough.* Tears filled my eyes before I could quickly blink them back. "Holy cow." I couldn't even breathe.

Griselda patted my knee and stood up. "If you run into any more criminals, give me a call. You have my number."

I looked up at him, still unable to believe it. "You did this, didn't you? You made it happen."

He shrugged. "Maybe."

I leapt off the bed, ran over, and hugged him. For a moment, he stood stiffly, then he relaxed slightly and gave me a little hug back. "Okay, I gotta go." He pulled free and for a second, some sort of actual emotion flashed across his face.

Stunned, I stared at him. "You're going to miss me, aren't you?"

"Never." He gave me a serious look, then walked out of the bedroom.

I shrieked and flopped back on the bed with King Tut, dragging him into my arms. "We're going to Maine!"

"*We*? You can't take him with you." Griselda strode back into the room, looking irritated. "He's not your cat."

I hugged the overweight beast to my chest. "Ssh! He doesn't know that. I'm not telling him until he's older and can understand better."

"Whatever." He held out his hand. "My phone, please."

I blinked at him innocently. "Your phone? Why would I have your phone?"

"Because you're a pickpocket."

"Former pickpocket, unwillingly forced into child labor by my mother." I pulled the phone out of my sleeve and tossed it to him.

He caught it easily, not cracking even a little smile.

In two years, he'd never been able to catch me with my fingers in his pocket. It was our little game, and we both loved it. Or maybe it was only me who loved it.

It had been difficult to find things to keep me going over the last couple years, but seeing Griselda's face when he realized I'd gotten his phone again had been one of them.

He put the phone in his back pocket. "You're one of a kind, Mia."

I grinned at him as I snuggled King Tut. "Admit it. You're going to miss me a little."

He rolled his eyes, turned around, and strode out the door. After a moment, his thumb and index finger appeared around the doorframe, in the universal signal for "just a little bit."

I grinned. "Me, too!"

His hand disappeared. "He's not your cat, Mia," he called out. "Don't take him to Maine."

I held up a purring King Tut and peered into his yellow eyes. "Do you want to live in this gross little apartment building with an owner so bad that you leap a five-story gap to get away from him? Or would you like to go to Maine and keep an outdated, failing marina free of mice while I try to resurrect it with zero knowledge of lakes, boats, or running a business?"

He blinked at me.

I nodded. "That's what I thought."

CHAPTER 3

I PULLED over to the side of the barely-two-lane road and parked my car on the sandy shoulder. "We need to take a picture of that, don't you think?"

My co-pilot, who might or might not have been a rude, overweight black and gray cat with a lion-worthy mane, massive tail, and hairy ears, who I might or might not have purloined for the good of all involved, shot me a baleful look from the back window of my Subaru.

"I'll take that as yes." I hopped out of my car and slammed the door shut, grinning at the weathered wooden sign on the side of the road. The lettering was faded, and the sign listed slightly to the right, but it was small-town adorable.

On the top of the sign was a loon with black and white checkered feathers and the words, "WELCOME TO THE TOWN OF BASS DERBY." Below was a poem, clearly hand-carved, that proclaimed:

WE FISH.
We swim.
We eat good meals.

And we always welcome new friends.
Unless we don't like you. Then keep driving.
Just kidding. Maybe.

BASS DERBY. My new home. The town even had a sense of humor. "How great is this?"

It had been only two weeks since Joyce had tried to kill me, but my new bestie, Ruby Lee Hanrahan, real estate agent extraordinaire, had been delighted to arrange for a quick closing on Eagle's Nest Marina, so there I was.

Ready for my new life.

I crouched down next to the sign and posed for a selfie. I was just hitting the button to take the picture when I heard the screech of tires from behind me.

I glanced over my shoulder and saw a dark blue SUV speeding around the corner, smoke rising from the pavement. I frowned as it careened across the center line toward me.

As in, *directly* toward me.

Had Joyce come back from the grave to finish the job?

Dammit. I had totally underestimated her.

The vehicle sped up, barreling straight at me. Alarm shot through me as I realized that it was actually going to hit me. Yelping, I dove to my right and hit the dirt, rolling out of the way as the SUV crashed through the sign. I covered my head as the tires sprayed road dirt all over me. The SUV skidded to a stop a few yards from me, but before I had time to celebrate my life-saving agility, the backup lights came on and the driver hit the gas, coming at me so fast I didn't have time to get out of the way.

With a litany of curses that would have made my mom proud, I flattened myself into the dirt, hoping the high undercarriage would save me. A split second before I became roadkill, the vehicle skidded to a stop, inches from my head.

Could I dive to the side before the tires started moving? I

didn't think I could. I was trapped. At their mercy. And that really pissed me off.

So, I stayed in the dirt, waiting, terrified.

The bumper sat there, inches from my face, taunting me with life or death.

It felt like an eternity that I lay there, afraid to move in any direction, because every move I could make would put me in the path of the SUV. If Joyce were alive, I'd believe it was her, basking in the joy of watching me hover on the edge of death.

But I was pretty sure Joyce hadn't faked her death, so what was going on?

As I lay there, frozen, frantically trying to figure out how to not die, a black pickup truck rounded the corner. The moment it appeared, the SUV leapt forward, lurched back onto the road, and disappeared around the bend, leaving me gloriously alive.

Holy cow. What had that been about? Assassin? Or daytime drinking and driving? What the heck?

I scrambled up as the black truck drove past. The driver was rough-looking, with a ragged beard, a black ball cap, and a barn jacket with the collar pulled up. His eyes were cold as he looked at me. He didn't exhibit any small-town warmth by leaping out of the truck to make sure I was okay.

Which was fine. I didn't need his help. So, hah. But it would have been nice.

For a moment, we locked gazes, and I felt a prickle of unease down the back of my neck. Then he hit the gas and was gone before I could worry he was going to vault out of the truck and kill me. He disappeared around the corner in the direction the SUV had gone.

I looked both ways to make sure no one else was coming for me, but the road was empty. Threat over.

"Well, that was fun." I let out my breath and clasped my hands on my head as I spat out dirt and blinked the road grit out of my eyes. The beautiful welcome sign was in about a thousand pieces, strewn across the road. All that was left were two stumps where the legs had stood. Prophetic? I really hoped not.

The hood of my car had a huge dent in it. So did the roof. And the loon had impaled itself through my windshield.

"King Tut!" I raced over to my car and yanked the back door open. The cat hadn't moved even an inch from his pedestal. He blinked and meowed once, as if to tell me to leave him alone.

I didn't, because who takes orders from cats?

I dragged him off his throne, hugged him, and then carefully searched for any pieces of wood jammed into his fluffy body. I had just concluded that he had survived far better than my car when I heard the brief surge of a police siren and saw the flash of blue lights. A black and white SUV hung a U-turn and pulled up behind me.

I had a split second of alarm, then I remembered that I was an upstanding citizen now, so I forced myself to relax and smile as the driver's door opened. A well-fed and decidedly unathletic police officer climbed out. He looked to be about ten years younger than Griselda, but I was pretty sure my least (and most) favorite FBI agent could outrun him while wearing the cement boots that Stanley had never had the chance to use on me.

Despite his lack of cat-like athleticism, however, the officer was sharply put together.

His hair was short, his uniform was pressed, and his car was polished to a high sheen.

I put King Tut back in my car and then smiled at the officer. "Hello." I could feel sand in my bra, down my pants, in my mouth, in my hair, and on my face. My palms were burning, and my knee hurt.

But as the other option was for me to be dead, I was pretty thrilled with my current state.

The police officer didn't smile at me. Instead, he trudged around the decimated sign, evaluating it from about a dozen directions, looking more and more annoyed before he finally came to a stop in front of me.

I tried again. "Hi. I'm Mia Murphy—"

"Did you do this?"

I blinked. "No, I was taking a selfie with it, and a car came around the corner and plowed it over."

"A selfie?" He looked past me to the loon sticking out of my windshield. "Is that your vehicle with the loon in the windshield?"

"Yeah. I'm the new owner of the—"

"What kind of car hit it?"

"An SUV. Mid-sized. Blue, I think." I was pretty proud I'd managed to notice that much given how focused I'd been on not dying.

He nudged the rubble with the toe of his very polished black boot. "That describes a lot of vehicles in town. Did you get a license plate? A look at the driver? Were there any defining attributes to the vehicle, like words on the side?"

Given that the license plate had been about six inches from my face, I probably should have taken note of it. Next time I almost died from being crushed by a car, I would try to pay better attention. But for this one, I had nothing. "No, I was diving for my life when it almost ran me over, so I was a little busy." I couldn't quite keep the sarcasm out of my voice. Sigh. Police officers really didn't bring out the best in me.

"Were you?" His tone said that he didn't believe I hadn't killed his sign, which made me a little prickly.

Cops had that effect on me. "How could I have done it? My car is intact, except for the loon and a few dents. I'm definitely not strong enough to knock it over with sheer arm strength." I flexed my biceps for him to prove it.

He looked at me like I was literally insane. "You're from Massachusetts?" He pulled out his little notepad and started writing on it. "Visiting or driving through?"

At least he was taking notes. Progress was everything. "Actually, I'm moving here. Today. I bought the marina." How amazing did that sound? *I bought the marina.*

His eyebrows shot up. "Rusty's?"

"No, the Eagle's Nest Marina."

A slow smile spread across his face, becoming wider by the moment. "We call it Rusty's around here." He sized me up, and then his grin got even bigger. "Good luck with that."

I frowned at his barely suppressed glee. "What does that mean?"

"Just welcoming you to Bass Derby, voted Best Lake Town in Maine for eleven years in a row."

I grinned. "I know. I saw that when I was researching the town." I owned a marina in the best lake town in Maine. How cool was that?

"We're going for win number twelve this week. The final judges are visiting this weekend, and that sign would have been a real help." He handed me a piece of paper. "It's a hundred dollar fine for driving with a cracked windshield."

"What?" I looked down at the paper. "You're giving me a ticket?" He hadn't been taking notes on my story. He'd been writing me a citation for the loon that I hadn't put in my windshield.

"Yep." He handed me another one. "And this is for destruction of town property."

I gaped at it. "Five hundred dollars?"

"It's a historical monument. Costs more. We take Apple Pay and credit cards. Out-of-towners need to pay on the spot, but since you're a local, you can come to the station and pay within twenty-four hours. Which do you prefer?"

"But I didn't hit the sign." I pointed to black tread marks on the road. "Look. Skid marks that clearly aren't from my car."

"They could have been there for days." He put his notepad away. "You're welcome to file a complaint at the station about the vehicle you say almost hit you."

"It did almost hit me." I waved the tickets. "I'm not paying these."

"Really?" He brightened. "Then I'll arrest you."

I paused. "Arrest me? Really? That feels like overkill, don't you think?"

"We keep a clean ship in this town." He set his hands on his hips and looked at me. "This sign has defined Bass Derby for forty-seven years, and you're the only witness to its destruction. Someone is going to pay for it, and it's you, until and unless you provide proof that it wasn't. And if we lose Best Lake Town this year because we don't have that sign, you'll have even more to answer for."

Seriously? I gave him a tension-diffusing smile of pure charm. "Look, Officer—"

"Chief," he corrected me. "Chief Stone."

Chief? He was the top dog in my new town? That was a bummer in all sorts of ways.

"You can be on your way." He grinned. "Unless you want a police escort to Rusty's?" he asked hopefully.

I'd had enough police escorts to last me a lifetime. "I have GPS on my phone. I'm all set."

"Okay then." He pulled out his phone, clearly disappointed. "Welcome to Bass Derby, Ms. Murphy. I'll be seeing you soon."

"You will? Why?" Me, paranoid about cops? Totally.

His brows went up. "When you come to the station to pay your fines."

"Oh…right." Not that I would be paying anything, of course. Protesting? Definitely. I managed a let's-be-friends smile. "Nice to meet you, then."

He didn't reply, but his nod as he turned away was almost in the ballpark of cordial. I managed to maintain my tension-diffusing smile long enough to navigate the sign carnage and make it back to my car.

I tried to get the loon out of my windshield, but Chief Stone kept looking over and checking on me. It was a little unnerving, so I quickly decided to leave the loon where it was and hit the road with it in there, so I could fight with the bird in private. He was still watching me when I pulled out, his eyes narrowed suspiciously.

I had a feeling that it would be in my best interest to make sure

Chief Stone never found out that the infamous, still-at-large Tatum Murphy was my mother, and that I'd been married to a drug lord. He'd do something with that info, I could feel it.

This was my new start. My new life. My past wasn't coming with me. Period.

But when I glanced back in my rear-view mirror, I saw Chief Stone taking a picture.

Not of the carnage around him.

Of my license plate.

He wanted my secrets.

And he could probably get them.

CHAPTER 4

Fifteen minutes later, when I arrived at the Eagle's Nest Marina, I realized that Ruby Lee Hanrahan was much more than a real estate agent.

She was also a con artist.

I'd bought the marina sight-unseen with the understanding it would require a little revitalization. But this? It needed a complete resurrection. It was, almost literally, a dump.

My heart sinking, I parked my car, then compared the photographs on the real estate listing to the buildings in front of me.

Same shape. Same size. Same sign. Same place. But the marina had at least a decade more of neglect now than it had when the pictures had been taken. Rust. Peeling paint. A covered front deck that had no railings. Abandoned junk in the bushes.

No wonder Chief Stone had been so amused.

There were four docks, one of which had what looked like an antique gas pump on it, with fading black paint and rusted chrome. There were a grand total of two boats: a very old, very small motorboat half-filled with water, and a gleaming green canoe with a little motor attached. There was an ugly warehouse-type building out back, which I was guessing was where the boats got fixed and stored, if there were boats to be worked on, that was.

The main building had three storefronts, plus the second-floor apartment I was planning to live in. There was a café in the middle, and beside that was a tattoo parlor. I'd been assured both spaces had paying tenants, but they were both shut down tight.

All of it was decrepit and depressing. A life that someone had forgotten about a long time ago.

This wasn't anything like what I'd imagined. I was already on the radar of the police chief, and the marina resonated with the hopelessness and loneliness that I'd been trying to escape.

Could I really fix this?

I wasn't so sure anymore that I could, or that I even wanted to. I leaned back against the seat and clasped my hands on my head. *Crud.*

Before I had a chance to descend into an abyss of self-pity and misery, a horn tooted. I turned as a shiny, royal metallic blue Mercedes SUV sped into my parking lot. The driver pulled right up to my bumper, the door opened, and out popped a perky woman with pitch-black hair, six-inch heels, and more glittery purple eye shadow than an ordinary face could reasonably support. She was so tiny that the makeup probably doubled her body weight. "Mia! Yoo-hoo! Mia!"

I barely got my window down before she was leaning into my car. She smelled like she'd had a perfume accident on her way to the marina, and looked like she hadn't seen the sun in about a thousand years. "Hi," I said cautiously.

"You don't recognize me?" She beamed at me. "I'm Ruby Lee Hanrahan!"

"Ruby Lee?" The real estate agent? She was at least thirty years older than her photo, in which she'd been blond, curvy, and tanned.

"Yes, it's me! I need to update my professional photo, but honestly, youth sells, so why would I change it?" She rested her arms on the window frame, showing off the sparkly purple polish on her perfectly shaped nails. "Isn't the marina fantastic? Don't you just love it?"

"It's not in very good condition," I said as tactfully as I could. "The pictures made it look a lot better."

"Did they?" She peered at the marina as if she had no idea what I was talking about. "Must have been the lighting. Good thing I told you that it was in rough shape, right? No surprises there."

"Well, yeah, you did tell me, but the pictures—"

"Who cares about the pictures? It's yours now!" She patted my shoulder. "I mean, yes, it's not as luxurious as your husband's drug mansion, but it's all yours!"

I waved my hand to shush her. "You didn't tell anyone about Stanley, did you?" The papers had referred to me as Mia Herrera even though I'd never actually taken his name, so I was hoping that no one in Bass Derby would connect Mia Murphy, brunette marina owner, with Mia Herrera, blond drug spy. Granted, Ruby Lee had figured it out in about two seconds, but she hadn't seemed to care.

Ruby Lee pretended to lock her lips and throw away the key. "No worries. I told Rusty because he had to okay the deal, but no one else." She looked around, and then leaned closer. "Are you really planning to keep it going up here?" she whispered.

I had no idea what she was talking about. "Keep what going?" I whispered back.

"Stanley's drug empire. The papers said that you were taking it over." She wiggled her brows at me.

Was she besties with Joyce? Because who else would believe that? "There's literally no chance of that. I'm not bringing any of that into Bass Derby."

She nodded and wiped the back of her hand across her forehead in a dramatic show of relief. "Thank heaven for that. I needed to be sure. We can't let drugs into our little town, can we?"

"No," I agreed emphatically. "I want to get as far away from that as I can."

"Great then. I'm thrilled we got that sorted out." She patted my shoulder again and glanced at her sparkly gold watch. "I saw your car and popped in to say hello, but I need to jet. Call if you need anything or have any questions." She winked. "I can get you anything. *Anything* at all."

That sounded a little too much like a mafia go-to promise. "Thanks. I'll keep that in mind."

"Perfect!" She practically sprinted back to her car, managing the high heels on the dirt parking lot with astonishing agility. She hopped into her Mercedes, gave another round of enthusiastic honking, and tore out of the parking lot.

She was gone before I realized I'd forgotten to lodge a significant complaint about the decrepit state of the marina.

Wow. I used to be good at the "distract and redirect" myself, but Ruby Lee was a master. Not only had she sold me the marina under clear misrepresentation, but she'd gotten me to like her anyway. Impressive.

I let out my breath, feeling a little better. Her energy had been infectious. Meeting a charming, ebullient con artist was like coming home. "Well," I said to King Tut, who had relocated to the front seat and was finally sitting in the basket I'd made him, after rejecting it for almost two hundred miles. "Let's go check it out, at least." I put on his harness, attached his new red leash, and then climbed out.

He hopped out after me, his massive tail flicking as he surveyed his new realm.

As soon as I stepped out of the car, I caught the energizing scent of fresh water. It was the smell I remembered from that trip to Maine so many years ago.

Excitement leapt through me, and I hurried toward the lake, King Tut happily racing along beside me.

As I reached the end of the dock, I could hear the gentle sound of the water lapping at the pilings. Then I turned to the right and gasped.

It was the lake of my dreams, stretching out ahead of me, a

glistening body of crystal-clear water. The marina was in a little cove, but the south end of Diamond Lake was right there. Mountains stretched up in the distance behind the opposite shore.

The water was so clear I could see a school of inch-long fish dart out of sight beneath the dock. There were adorable houses lining the lake. Around the corner from my cove, across the lake, was the town center, with stores, a town dock, boats, and activity. The community I'd dreamed of. *Yes.*

Stunned, I sat down, my legs giving out as the enormity of the moment hit.

I had a home now. I owned a business. On a lake. *I had a life.* One that didn't involve crime, police, sting operations, or anything else that had defined me since the day I was born. "We're staying, King Tut. We'll make this work—"

He yowled suddenly and leapt off the dock, yanking the leash out of my hand. He hit the water with a massive splash and disappeared below the surface.

"Hey!" I jumped in after him in a panic. The shock of the cold water knocked the breath from me, and I gasped for air as I surged back to the surface.

King Tut popped up ten feet from me, a squirming fish clenched in his teeth as he swam straight for shore, his ears flat against his head from the weight of the water.

"You swim? *Underwater*?" I shouted after him. "I'm pretty sure cats don't do that."

Completely ignoring me, King Tut made it to shore before I'd managed to slog more than a few feet. He hopped up out of the lake, shook the water off, and then trotted off to a shady spot under a tree to dine.

I'd rescued a feline anomaly. No wonder he'd wanted to come with me. Not a lot of swimming opportunities in an apartment building in Boston. But, honestly, how cool was that? I loved that cat so much already.

"Hello? Hello?"

I looked toward the parking lot and saw an old pickup truck in the lot. A woman about my age was climbing out of it, waving at me. She had light brown skin, dark kinky hair in a bushy ponytail, and she moved like an athlete.

A customer? That would be fantastic. "Hi!" I waved and waded more quickly toward the shore. "Just a minute." I detoured toward King Tut, but he bared his teeth and growled, a low, aggressive sound that reminded me of exactly how sharp his claws were.

So, instead of grabbing him, I snagged an abandoned cement block and dragged it on top of his leash. "Enjoy."

He flicked his tail at me and purred.

Wiping the dirt off my hands, I headed toward the parking lot. The woman had already rolled back the cover that was over the truck bed and climbed into the back of the vehicle.

I walked up to the truck, noting that the bed was filled with packages and bins of letters. "Hi. Can I help you?"

"You bet." She had huge brown eyes, gold hoop earrings, and several rope bracelets on her left wrist. She was wearing jeans, sneakers, and a lightweight jacket, every bit the casual, resourceful Mainer I wanted to become. Her eyes were dancing with warmth, and her smile was genuine, making me grin back. "I noticed the Massachusetts plate. Are you Mia Murphy? The new owner?"

The new owner. I loved how that sounded. "Yes, I am."

"Wonderful! I'm Lucy Grande. I have mail for you."

I looked at her truck, which said George's Lobster Shack on the side of it, in letters so old they were barely readable. "You're the mail carrier?"

She pointed to a small U.S. Mail sign on the top of the vehicle. "We drive our own vehicles up here." She bent over, sorting through the bins of mail. "It's only my second week on this route, so I'm still trying to get up to speed. I used to have a different route, but they had me take over this route for Ellis."

"Ellis?"

"Ellis Stratton. The former mail carrier. He was fired for mishandling packages and taking bribes."

I raised my brows. "What is there to bribe a mail carrier for?"

"Stealing packages. Diverting mail. Lots of things." Lucy hefted a big box up and set it on the edge of the truck bed. It was stamped with "Refrigerated Items" and "Keep Cold" warnings all over it. "Take this first. It's been sitting around for a few days. Might want to get it in the cooler."

Did I have a cooler? I had no idea. "Sure thing." I grabbed it and pulled it off.

It was so heavy that I lost my balance, stumbled backward, and then fell, landing on my back with the box crushing my chest.

Lucy peered down at me as she set a crate of mail on the edge of the truck bed. "Are you all right? That looked super awkward."

"No, I'm fine. It's all good." I grabbed the edge of the box, braced my foot, and shoved my whole body over, rolling the box off my chest. I managed to catch it before it tipped over. "How long has the mail been accumulating?"

Lucy shrugged. "I'm guessing for ten years, since that's when Rusty moved to Florida. There's a lot here."

"No one's been running the marina for *ten* years?" That explained a lot. I wondered what else Ruby Lee had failed to tell me. I was both increasingly impressed and annoyed by her.

"Technically, Rusty's been keeping it open, but not very well, obviously." She leaned on the boxes, studying me. "You're very wet."

I nodded. "I was excited to try out the lake."

"Fully clothed?"

"Isn't that how it's done in Maine?"

She grinned as she held out the bin of Rusty's mail. "I like you, Mia Murphy. You're all right."

I smiled back. "Thanks." I'd spent so long with only Stanley and Griselda for company that I'd forgotten what girl talk was like. It felt good. "Back at ya." I took the mail bin carefully, using my chest to try to brace it, but the moment Lucy let go, it skidded right down my body, gouging a path out of my poor skin before it crashed to the dirt. "Are you extremely strong, or am I that weak?"

"Lucy's freakishly strong. Baton twirling and installing docks will do that." The voice came from right behind me, scaring the bejeebers out of me.

Startled, I jumped to the side, scrambling over the boxes to get away.

"You're very jumpy." The amusement in the voice broke through my panic, and I spun around.

Leaning on the truck, one arm propped up on the back, was a woman with enough wrinkles to pass for mid-seventies, but that was the only elderly thing about her. Her hair was a vibrant royal blue, and the six studs in her right ear looked like an ocean wave of blue and green. She was wearing jeans, boots, and a black T-shirt that said, "I'll show you what old is."

Not an assassin, but she definitely had attitude. I liked her immediately. "Baton twirling?" I echoed.

Lucy nodded. "I was a competitive twirler for years, and my family owns a business installing docks. I can sledgehammer a post into the lake bottom in three minutes, and do a quad illusion spin with flames at the same time."

I tried to picture Lucy in a sparkly leotard, but failed entirely. "Sledgehammer?"

She grinned. "I love sledgehammers. They're great for getting out frustrations."

Okay, so now I liked Lucy even more. How could you not like a woman who loved sledgehammers? "That sounds like fun."

"It is. You should try it. I can bring a couple by for you to play with."

"Why not?" Imagine how much damage I could do to an assassin with a sledgehammer instead of a hairdryer, right?

Feeling better by the moment, I grinned cheerfully at the newcomer, who was studying me with open curiosity. "I'm Mia Murphy, the new owner."

"Mia Murphy." She surveyed me carefully. She had the gaze of a woman used to causing damage using nothing more than her thoughts. I suspected she could probably kill me with her pinkie finger. She had that kind of vibe. "Ruby Lee wouldn't tell us anything about you," she said, "except that you were coming up from Boston."

Ruby Lee was back in my good graces for not telling them about Stanley. "I've wanted to live on a lake in Maine since I was sixteen. This is my dream."

She cocked an eyebrow at me.

I tried to cock one back, but just managed to sort of leer at her.

She burst into a big smile and slapped her hand down on the truck, making me jump. "You'll do, Mia Murphy. You'll do just fine."

I grinned. "Great. Glad to hear it. Now, who are you?"

"Hattie Lawless." She jerked her chin at the building behind us.

I noticed then that the faded sign over the door next to the marina store said, "Hattie's Café" in brightly colored antique, flowery letters. "You're my tenant?"

"Tenant?" Hattie raised her brows, putting a little edge into the word.

I hesitated. "No?"

"No." She drummed her fingers on Lucy's truck. "'Tenant' is diminutive and disempowering. You contribute the building, and I contribute the only thing about this place that draws in customers, so we'll go with business partners. Equality for women everywhere. Sound good?"

Lucy grinned. "Say yes, Mia. No one argues with Hattie and lives to tell about it."

I suspected she wasn't talking literally, but my recent experiences with a gun-wielding mother-in-law and homicidal SUV driver made me take a little step back from the senior citizen standing in my parking lot.

Hattie nodded. "Rusty argued with me and left town. Never came back."

Lucy crouched down so she was closer to our level, resting her arms on the truck. "No one local would buy the place because Hattie comes with it."

I looked back and forth between them. "Really?"

They both erupted in laughter. "We need to work on your gullibility, city girl," Hattie said. "Rusty left because he found a woman who'd put up with him."

"No one bought the place because Rusty let it fall apart and kept the price too high." Lucy grinned at me. "You probably overpaid for the marina, but Hattie won't kill you in your sleep."

"As long as you don't irritate me," Hattie added, "you're perfectly safe."

I looked back and forth between them, and suddenly, I understood. "You're a little bit of a con artist, aren't you?" I asked Hattie. "Making people afraid of you?"

Hattie gave me a wide-eyed innocent look. "Me? Never."

"You guys are both liars." Lucy and Hattie were the kind of women I was going to like. Not because they were liars, but because they had the same irreverence I'd never been able to quite suppress. "You guys aren't part of an organized crime ring, are you? Drug dealers? That kind of thing?"

Their laughter went silent, and they both stared at me.

"Drug dealer?" Hattie finally asked.

"Not that I want any. I just wanted to make sure you weren't in that business." Now that I thought about it, it was kind of a strange question to ask a couple of women I'd just met. "I have issues."

"We all have issues," Lucy said cheerfully.

"I don't." Hattie cocked her head to study me. "You look familiar. Do I know you?"

Oh... I hoped she hadn't read the papers. I shouldn't have brought up the drug dealer thing. I grabbed the refrigerated box, staggering under its weight as I braced it on my thighs and began stumping my way toward the store. "People say I have a famous face," I called over my shoulder, as I took my famous face away from her.

"Huh." I felt her watching me for another moment, then she turned to Lucy. "Why are you driving George's truck to deliver the mail? Where's yours?"

Lucy sighed. "Rex stole it."

Theft? That caught my attention. "Who's Rex?" I regripped, trying to keep from dropping the box.

"Rex Giannetti," Lucy said. "My ex. He stole it over the weekend."

Hattie grabbed a mail bin and tucked it under one arm. "Well, go get it back."

Lucy sighed. "I tried. He has it locked in his garage. I filed a claim with Chief Stone, but he's afraid of Rex and won't go get it."

"No problem," Hattie said. "I'll shoot the lock out."

Shoot the lock? I turned around to see if Hattie was joking.

She looked completely serious.

To her credit, Lucy looked skeptical. "What if you hit my car?"

"It'll be fine," Hattie said. "Bullet holes can be fixed, but if you never get your car back, then what's the good of having it intact?"

Good heavens. I needed to save them from themselves. "What kind of lock is it?" I set the box down, trying to uncramp my fingers. "Key? Doorknob? Deadbolt? Electronic?"

"Doorknob. Key." Lucy hopped out of the truck and began rolling the tarp back over the contents. "Why?"

Sweet. That was easy. "Just pick the lock. That kind is easy."

Hattie snorted. "We don't have lock picks." She turned to Lucy, who was locking down the cover. "I'll pick you up at eight. I'll bring my gun and—"

"You can borrow mine," I interrupted quickly. I couldn't see how it was remotely possible it would go well to have Hattie firing a gun at Rex's garage.

Hattie looked over at me, shooting me a look that made it clear she was contemplating whether I might be a complete idiot. "I don't need to borrow a gun. I have several."

Um. No. "My lock picks," I clarified. "You can borrow my lock picks."

"You have lock picks?" Hattie frowned at me. "Why? Are you a locksmith?"

"A locksmith?" I laughed. "No. I'm a former petty…" I stopped myself just before I could say thief. I picked up the box again, staggering under its weight. "This box is very heavy." Distract and redirect, just like Ruby Lee.

Hattie caught up to me. She had a mail bin under each arm, and she was eyeing me with interest. "Do you know how to pick locks?"

I grimaced. "It depends on the lock. Some are easier than others. Where do you get your hair done? I love that blue."

"Dutch's Salon in the center of town. Do you have any plans tonight?"

I shifted the box, trying to make it the last few feet without dropping it. "I'm going to unpack and—"

"That can wait." Hattie trotted ahead of me and set the two mail bins by the front door. "Lucy, Mia's going to go with us and pick the lock for you."

"What?" I let my box drop next to the front door, and bent over, bracing my hands on my thighs as I panted, trying to catch my breath. "No, I'm not—"

"That's awesome!" Lucy gave me a fist pump as she climbed into the driver's seat. "You're the best, guys. My route will go so much faster with my vehicle instead of George's."

"But—" My protest died as she peeled away, the truck sputtering and protesting as it bounced over the rutted parking lot.

Hattie dusted off her hands. "I'll be here a little before eight to pick you up. I'm off."

"No. Absolutely not." I wasn't going to get sucked into criminal activity, even if it did sound like fun to jimmy a few locks in the name of girl power. "I don't get involved with illegal activities—"

"It's only illegal if you get caught." Hattie trotted across the parking lot to a massive black pickup truck with huge tires and floodlights on the top.

"That's not even remotely true—"

"Of course it's true." She opened the door with a wink. "Welcome to Bass Derby."

"Wait! Aren't you going to run the café today?"

"Not on Mondays." She waved her hand as she swung herself up into the truck that was easily a good three feet off the ground. "Wear dark clothing."

Dark clothing? "I'm not going to break in—"

"I can't hear you!" She pulled the door shut, and the truck roared to life with a purr. She rolled down the window and pointed at my car. "Have you gotten any death threats for killing that sign?"

I'd totally forgotten about the impaled loon. "Death threats? For a sign?" I couldn't help but laugh, even though Hattie didn't seem to be kidding. "No. Should I expect some?"

"Maybe. Yeah."

Oh, goody. "Sounds like a great time."

"I'm serious." She raised her brows. "You better get that loon out of your windshield. If the locals see that, they'll hunt you down for destroying a town landmark."

Some of my amusement faded. "Hunt me down and do what?"

"Depends on who it is..." She paused. "Just get it out of there!" She thumped her fist on the horn, nearly deafening me, and then pulled out, the rear tires skidding out on the dirt. She was still honking and waving her arm out the window until she was out of sight.

CHAPTER 5

As Hattie disappeared from sight, the truth was clear: if I had any chance of a crime-free life, I had to stay away from her.

Which meant, at eight tonight, I wasn't going to be home, no matter how much fun it sounded. And if someone came by to threaten to kill me for breaking the sign that I didn't break, I would definitely not be home.

Granted, I felt for Lucy. Scumbag exes sucked. And it had been too long since I'd had the fun of picking a lock for nefarious purposes. Plus, I liked both women, and it would be easy to help them.

But no. *No.* I wasn't going to screw up my chance at the life I wanted. I was a law-abiding citizen. End of story—

I heard a meow by my ankle. I looked down to see my purloined cat staring up at me, the remains of his chewed leash dragging in the dirt. He licked his lips, then meowed again, completely unapologetic for destroying the leash I'd spent almost thirty minutes picking out.

"I didn't steal you," I told him. "I rescued you. There's a difference." Nothing illegal to see here, folks.

King Tut walked over to the door of the marina store, stared up at the doorknob, and meowed again.

Right. My store. I took a deep breath, suddenly excited again. "Let's check it out." I fished my key out of my pocket, and slid it into the deadbolt. My heart leapt when it went in easily, making me realize I'd been harboring secret fear that I didn't actually own the marina, and it was all a cruel, cruel joke.

But nope, the key worked, so it was the real deal.

I looked down at King Tut. "You ready?"

He meowed impatiently, so I turned the key and opened the door to my very own store.

The minute I stepped inside, I sighed with relief. It was so much better than I'd expected.

Yes, it was a little musty. A lot cluttered. Very disorganized. But there were life jackets hanging on racks. Fishing poles. Water skis. Brightly colored nylon ropes. Inflatable rafts and lake toys. "We have product to sell! How awesome is that?"

King Tut bounded ahead of me, tackled a pile of ropes, and began dragging them around the store as I walked through. There was a display case that contained small things, like little floaty things for boat keys, flashlights, and fishing lures.

There was a refrigerated case at the back of the store, like the drink section in a convenient store, only it had a lock on it with a key sticking out of it. There were a few sodas in there, but the bottom section was empty. Plenty of space for the box.

I hurried outside, retrieved the box, and lugged it inside. I managed to slide the box into the cooler, then re-locked the door. Just in case there was a reason to keep it locked that I didn't know about, I pulled the key out and shoved it in my pocket.

It was then that I saw the door at the back of the store. I ran over to it, my heart skipping when I flung the door open and found a staircase.

It led to the apartment. To my new home. My *first* home that was all mine. King Tut charged past me up the stairs, and I followed him, taking the steps two at a time.

There was another lock at the top of the stairs, and the other key Ruby Lee had given me opened it easily. I pushed it open, and instantly gagged at the stench that flooded out the door. It smelled like a thousand dead fish had been gutted, ground into the walls and floors, and left there to rot.

King Tut yowled with delight and bounded into the apartment.

I ran to the window, threw up the sash, and leaned out, gasping for air. After I caught my breath, I pulled my shirt up over my face and twisted around to look back at the apartment.

A large, stained butcher-block table sat in the middle of the living room. There was plastic sheeting on the floor, sharp knives resting on the kitchen counter, and a stack of metal buckets on the linoleum. It was the perfect set up for a backwoods serial killer.

Fear prickled down my spine, and I quickly shook my head. "No serial killers here," I said out loud, my voice echoing through the empty room. It was probably used to gut and clean fish. That's why it smelled so bad. No bodies. No human remains. It was fine.

I forced my gaze away from the table and looked around. The living room was big, and the kitchen was old-fashioned but decent sized. A hall led to what should be two bedrooms and the bathroom. There were big windows looking out onto the lake, and the high ceilings made it feel spacious and bright. Everything I'd hoped for.

Except for the stench and serial killer paraphernalia, of course.

King Tut leapt onto the table, sniffed it, and then flopped onto his back and started to grind himself into it.

"Don't do that!" I lunged for him, but he jumped off, ducked past me, and darted out the open window. I raced over to the window and leaned out. He was sitting on the edge of the slanted roof, his tail flicking as he surveyed his new kingdom.

"Hey, kitty. Come here." I held out my hand and wiggled my fingers, but all he did was turn his head and give me a haughty sigh, as if to remind me that he was capable of leaping five-story gaps over cement. A second-floor roof was nothing for him.

I eyed the slanted roof. Did I dare go out and get him? Or would he just mock my sub-feline climbing skills and jump off the moment I stranded myself? While I was debating, a motorboat turned into the cove. It slowed as it neared my docks, as if it were going to turn in. A customer?

The man driving it was standing at the wheel, wearing a navy jacket, jeans, and sunglasses. His hair was short, and there was an energy to him that reminded me a little bit of Griselda's don't-mess-with-me attitude.

Then I saw the words "Lake Police" on the side of the boat, and my heart sank.

Was I in trouble already?

He drove into one of the slips at my dock, and then waved at me to come down as he reached over to grab a piling. It was too late to run.

But I didn't need to run, right? I wasn't a criminal. It was going to be fine.

Really.

It was.

I mustered up a friendly smile. "I'll be right down," I shouted. "Just a sec."

I took a deep inhale, held my breath, and ran through the fumes to the stairs. My sneakers squished out lake water as I jogged outside, and I slowed to an innocent-person saunter as I reached the dock. As I stepped out onto the ramp, I waved. "Hi. I'm the new owner."

He leaned on the piling, using one hand to hold the boat to my dock. "Mia Murphy, right?"

"Yep." I walked over to the boat, surprised by how tall he was. Muscular. Sculpted. As fit as Griselda tried to be, I'd be putting my money on Lake Police.

I couldn't see his eyes behind his shades, but his hair was a closely cut dark brown, his skin a slightly lighter shade of brown than his hair, and his cheekbones were just defined enough to make him look more dangerous than charming.

He was both alarming and interesting, neither of which I needed or wanted in my life right now.

"I'm Officer Hunt," he said. "Devlin Hunt."

I shook his hand, careful not to lean too far over the gap between the dock and the boat. His grip was strong, and his wrist was sexy.

I didn't want to notice his wrist. I'd just gotten liberated from a marriage from hell, and I wasn't ever getting back in the dating game. "Nice to meet you," I said, trying to keep my voice neutral.

"How's everything going?" His question was too casual. I didn't believe it for a moment.

I immediately tensed. "The apartment smells like a thousand fish died a horrible death in there," I offered neutrally.

He raised his brows. "Rusty had a bait shop for a while. As I hear, he'd use the upstairs to prepare the bait and clean the fish his customers caught in the lake."

"He murdered fish in my living room?" That was so much better than human sacrifice, but still pretty unappealing.

Devlin grinned, showcasing dimples that were much too adorable. "Murder is a little strong. Maybe 'prepare for feasting' instead?"

I relaxed slightly and even managed a smile. "I like that. Thanks." Officer Hunt might be Lake Police, but he seemed to be relatively sane and normal. Maybe I could hit him up for information. "Do you know if there are any employees working for me?"

He nodded at the bright green canoe tied to my dock. "That's Cargo's boat. He's your mechanic. He's probably in the garage."

"Really?" Someone had been there the whole time? "Are there boats to work on?"

Officer Hunt considered me. "Do you know anything about your business?"

"No, not really, but I'm trying to learn. Got any helpful hints?"

"Sure." He studied me as his boat rocked gently on the water. "The thirty-second skinny is that you bought into the low-end of the lake. Your marina services the locals who don't trust anyone but Cargo to work on their boats. All the summer folk?" He jerked his thumb across the water to the cluster of stores and shops along the lake. "They go to the Diamond Lake Yacht Club, which is owned by Jake Nash. The locals or day-trippers who want a cheap day on the lake go to Eagle's Nest."

"So, I'm the cheap date in town?" Not surprising. "That's fine. I like a challenge."

He grinned, this time with a hint of amusement that made me relax even more. "Now that I think about it, I don't see much of anyone over here at all anymore. They might all go to Jake at the Yacht Club now. You actually might be dateless."

"A social pariah, then? Cool. That's always been a lifelong goal of mine."

His smile widened. "Gotta have dreams, right?"

"Totally." Trying not to notice that Devlin's smile was extremely charming and appealing, I studied the cluster of buildings across the lake. Jake had won *all* the lake business? "I guess I'm going to have to do a little recon over at the Yacht Club to see what's so special."

Officer Hunt raised his brows. "Jake and Rusty never got along." He sounded thoroughly entertained by the idea of me showing up at Jake's.

"Rusty contaminated my home, so I don't get along with him either." I grinned, feeling more chipper. Hot lake police officer had a sense of humor and didn't want to arrest me. I had an employee and a tenant, aka business partner. And there were customers to be had. It was just a matter of stealing them from Jake. Purloining? Wooing? Proving my awesome? I liked the last one best. Life was looking up. "Anything else I should know?"

Devlin nodded, dug a business card out of his back pocket, and handed it to me. "If you need anything. I added my personal cell number."

I looked at the card. It listed the Bass Derby police department office number, as well as a mobile number. He'd also scrawled a phone number on there. My stomach did a little flutter. I'd known I was charming, but seriously? "I think it's a little early in our relationship to be handing out phone numbers."

He didn't crack a smile. "Hawk said you might run into trouble. Use any of the numbers on the card until you find me."

I stared at him blankly. "Hawk?"

"Agent Straus."

He was talking about my favorite FBI agent? "His first name is *Hawk*? That's so much cooler than I would have expected."

Devlin shrugged. "It's what we call him. His real name is Rob."

That made more sense, but his answer created a whole new set of questions. "We? Who is we?" Hawk was such a badass name. How did Griselda get a name that cool? And why hadn't he ever told me?

Devlin had given me his first name within ten seconds of meeting me. Point for him.

"Our team. Former team," Devlin said evasively. "Anyway, I stopped by because he asked me to check on you. Other than the fish odor, it's good?"

I finally realized what Devlin was saying, and my amusement disappeared. "Griselda *sent* you to keep an eye on me? Why?"

"You call him Griselda?" He grinned, showing off his ridiculously appealing dimples. "He didn't tell me that."

"What *did* he tell you?"

Devlin's smile faded. "He said it was possible, but unlikely, that your ex-husband's family or business associates would try to eliminate you. He asked me to keep an eye out for you."

The use of the world "eliminate" instead of "murder" didn't make his comment any less concerning. Suddenly, my lake nirvana felt much more nefarious than it had felt thirty seconds ago. "He really thinks someone is going to try to kill me?"

"Probably not, but since I'm here, he asked me to keep an eye out." His phone buzzed, and he looked down at it. "I need to go. Let me know if you need anything." He let go of the piling, shifted gears, and began to back out of the slip. "And by the way?"

I was still reeling from the revelations that Griselda had sent Officer Hunt after me. "What?"

"If you try to pickpocket me, I *will* arrest you. I don't have Hawk's sense of humor."

I looked up sharply, but he wasn't smiling. Not at all.

Griselda must have told him everything. About Stanley. About my mother. About all the things I wanted to leave behind.

And just like that, they were here with me in Bass Derby.

"Wait! " I ran to the end of the dock and grabbed the front of his boat, leaning back to stop the backwards movement of the boat.

"Don't do that—"

His warning came too late. The boat's backwards force was much stronger than I was, and it yanked me forward. I lost my balance and plunged into the lake for the second time that morning. I came up spluttering, stumbling as I wiped the water out of my eyes.

Devlin's boat was still floating backwards. "Are you all right?" He looked like he was fighting not to laugh.

"Yes." I took a breath, trying to calm down as I wiped the water out of my eyes. "Listen, can you not tell anyone about my past? I want to be normal here. Low-key. Blend in."

He grinned. "Ms. Murphy, from what Hawk says about you, there isn't a chance in hell that you're going to blend in."

"What? That's not true—"

He tipped his cap. "Welcome to Bass Derby. Call me if you need me." Then he hit the gas and the boat roared away, leaving me standing chest-deep in water that was much too frigid for swimming.

I was wet. I was cold. Griselda's name was Hawk. He had a distractingly hot friend who was my sort of bodyguard. And I was possibly on a hit list.

I needed my hairdryer, for a multitude of reasons.

CHAPTER 6

Thanks to Devlin's visit, I spent the rest of my first day at the marina with half my attention focused on looking for places a hit man might lie in wait, and checking every passing vehicle for a gun barrel aimed at me. It was a little draining, I'm not going to lie.

The maintenance garage, where I didn't find my one and only employee, was rife with potential weapons and hiding places. It was amazing how many lethal implements are involved in boat maintenance. On a bonus note, I did find a bunch of kayaks and canoes, several paddle boards, two sailboats without sails, and three motorboats with their engines in assorted states of disrepair. It looked old and decrepit, but not *completely* abandoned.

I had no idea how to contact Cargo, so I hoped he was planning to return to work at some point. Today, tomorrow, eventually.

No one showed up to open the tattoo parlor, and I had a bad feeling that there was no current tenant. I could see tattooing paraphernalia through the window, so I decided to hold out for a few days before trying to rent it.

No customers stopped by the marina, which I was hoping was

because of the big "Closed Mondays" sign on the door, and not because there was literally no business.

On the plus side, no one showed up to kill me, and I started to relax a bit. I used the customer-free time to tackle a few essential tasks.

First, unable to completely dismiss Hattie's warning about murderous locals avenging the town sign's death and destruction, I fought with that stubborn loon until I finally got it out of my windshield. Basking in my victory, I then headed off to buy furniture for my apartment, which was pretty exciting. Delivery in five days, which was sooner than I'd hoped. It also meant I had to get my apartment habitable by then…which I had a feeling was going to be a challenge.

King Tut spent the day on the dock, diving after fish and swimming to shore. He was the most sopping wet, bedraggled, pathetic-looking, and happiest creature I'd ever seen in my life. See? Kidnapping him had been a gift. I was a hero.

By evening, I was in my third hour of battling with my stinky apartment. I was on my hands and knees, my arms aching as I dragged a scrub brush across the wood.

The cleaner I'd found in the garage could probably double as a lethal inhalant, which would be great if someone tried to kill me. However, since I didn't want to incinerate my lungs, I'd snagged a snorkel and mask from the store, which was helping slightly. I was pretty sure I was making progress with the odor, though. Either that, or the cleaner was slowly starting to kill me. Time would tell.

I had just finished the section where the butcher block table had been when I heard a creak from the stairwell.

I froze.

King Tut? But he was sitting in the window watching me.

Assassin? *Please no.*

I heard another creak, and then there were footsteps racing up the stairs toward the door…which I'd left ajar to allow the fumes to escape.

I looked around frantically, but there was nowhere to hide. My hairdryer was on the kitchen counter, too far away.

The door opened and a head poked around the corner. I shrieked and hurled my scrub brush at the intruder as I lunged to my feet—

Hattie swore and dove to the floor, ducking out of the path of the brush just in time. She hit the floor in a perfectly executed dive roll that took her across the room. She came to a stop by the opposite wall, up on one knee, her arms out in an offensive posture, like she was ready to karate chop my head clean from my body.

We stared at each other.

I was panting, struggling to recover my equilibrium after the jaw-dropping terror of thinking I was about to be murdered.

Hattie looked much calmer.

She'd ditched the "I'll Show You What Old Is" T-shirt and replaced it with a long-sleeved black shirt, black leggings, and a black baseball cap.

Add a ski mask and she'd look like an assassin.

Which I needed to not be thinking about.

"Going swimming?" she finally asked.

I stared at her blankly. "Swimming?"

"The snorkel?"

Oh. I spit out the snorkel and pulled the mask off my head. "Toxic fumes."

"Of course. Snorkels are handy for things like that. I use them all the time."

She didn't sound like she was mocking me, but I could have been wrong, so I decided to move on. "Why are you here?"

She lowered her hands from karate chop mode. "Girls' night, remember? A little breaking and entering, car theft, fun stuff like that."

"Ohhhh, right. I forgot."

"That's good to know. I wasn't sure if that was simply your own special way of saying hello, because if it is, I was going to try to explain to you the many ways in which that's lacking." She wrinkled her nose. "This place smells awful."

"I know, right? I've been working on it for hours."

"Hours? That's a long time to make so little progress."

I stared at her. "That's not really helpful and supportive."

"I am being helpful. Clearly you haven't figured it out on your own that you need a different approach. I'm pretty sure you won't survive the night if you continue to breathe this air, which you've apparently managed to make even more toxic than it was originally." She stood up, hopping to her feet with an ease and grace I'd never managed in my life. "Let's get out of here. We're picking up Lucy on the way. We only have a small window where Rex won't be home."

I retrieved my scrub brush from the landing of the stairs. "I would love to help you guys, but I can't."

She set her hands on her hips. "Why? Did you forget how to pick a lock?"

"No." I held up the brush. "I need to work on the floor—"

"Didn't you find your lock picks?"

I inadvertently glanced over at the kitchen counter where I'd set them next to the sharp knives and my hairdryer. "Yes, but the floor—"

"Great!" She grabbed the lock picks and shoved them in her pocket. "Let's do this." She jogged to the door, then paused to look back at me, when I didn't move to follow her. "What?"

"Look, I want to help Lucy. I feel for her. But I…" I didn't know how to explain it without revealing my sketchy history. "I don't want to get involved with illegal activities. I'm here to make a fresh start."

"A fresh start?" Hattie studied me for a long moment, then understanding dawned. "Are you a criminal on the run from a checkered past that will be revealed if they run your prints?"

I blinked. "Well, no, not exactly—" But also, kind of exactly.

She winked. "No problem. We'll take the heat if anything happens, which it won't."

Her reaction surprised me. "You wouldn't care if—" I couldn't finish. She didn't care if I had a questionable life history? People always cared when they found out I was an accomplished criminal.

"Stop." Hattie sighed and marched over to me, staring me down. "Mia, any woman who owns lock picks and knows how to use them is a woman worth admiring."

I stared at her, shocked by her speech, and warmed by it. There was no guile. No judgment. Just honest truth. "You think it's *admirable* that I have lock picks?"

She nodded. "Too many women are taught to play small and subjugate themselves to men. That's a bunch of crap that I don't have time for. Women have to pull each other up, which means supporting each other when we show we have strength. Lock picks used to help a friend who's been jerked over by her ex is strength all day long. Love it. Love yourself. And let's go take care of business."

"Wow." I was pretty sure I'd just fallen a little in love with her. "That's awesome."

"Right? You coming?"

"Heck yeah, I'm coming." I'd pick locks all night long to get a chance at another speech like that. I ran to the window and peered out at King Tut, who was now sitting on the roof watching the bats that were starting to take to the sky. "I'll be back, sweetie."

He ignored me, but it still made me smile to think that I had something, someone, to come home to. I grabbed a sweatshirt, my keys, and my phone, then followed Hattie down the stairs.

Tonight would be fine.

Fun, even.

It was going to go great.

CHAPTER 7

PICKUP TRUCKS WEREN'T MEANT for speed, but Hattie, apparently, didn't care. She drove like a mad woman.

By the time she skidded to a stop in front of a little white house on a cute neighborhood street, my stomach was maybe two more big ruts in the road away from being completely severed in half by my seatbelt.

She landed on the horn and hollered, then turned to grin at me. "Now that we're business partners, I'll eventually know all your secrets. I'll defend you to the end, because that's what I do. So, let's go, and start letting it all hang out, because it will be that much easier to cover it all up in the end if I know what's coming for you."

I stared at her. "What?"

She gestured impatiently at me. "I've been thinking about your 'fresh start' comment on the drive over. I decided the only way to handle this is to work together on it. You need to let that weight off you, and I'm the one you need to unload onto."

"Hey!" The back door of the cab opened before I could invent a reason not to pour out my life's story, and Lucy slid into the back seat. I was happy to see that she was wearing blue jeans and a gray sweatshirt, instead of hit man attire like Hattie. She grinned at me. "Thank you so much for coming, Mia." She held up a set of car keys. "These do me no good if I can't get in there to get my car."

My resistance faded at her genuine appreciation. "No problem. Happy to help."

Hattie hit the gas, and Lucy slid across the seat as she scrambled for her seatbelt.

"Lucy," Hattie said, as we hurtled down the quiet, residential street. "Mia's got some dark secrets she's ashamed of and wants to leave behind. I told her she needs to unload. Mia, Lucy's as good as I am at keeping secrets, so let 'em out."

"Oh..." Lucy leaned forward, resting her arms on the seat. "Does this have to do with the fact you know how to use lock picks?"

I looked back and forth between them. "Is this how the female bonding thing works?"

Lucy raised her brows. "You don't know how to girl bond?"

"No. My mom and I moved around a lot when I was growing up. I didn't really have time to make friends." I grimaced. Did that make me sound like a loser? "It was fine, though," I quickly added. "I was fine. It was fine."

Hattie glanced in her rearview mirror at Lucy. "Does it sound fine?"

"Doesn't sound fine." Lucy tapped my shoulder. "Hattie and I are great at female bonding. We'll teach you."

If female bonding meant I had to tell them all about the past I didn't want to share, I wasn't sure I was cut out for it. I'd come here for roots and a community, but spilling my secrets had been the exact opposite of what I wanted. "Shouldn't we focus on the plan?"

"Plan?" Lucy frowned. "What's to plan? We'll pull up, you'll pick the lock, I'll drive my car away. Seems easy."

Hattie nodded. "Pretty straightforward."

"Have neither of you done anything like this in your life?" I couldn't keep the surprise out of my voice. "The most basic rule, the one that's an absolute necessity, is to have an exit strategy."

Lucy raised her brows. "Basic rule of what? Stealing your own car?"

"Thievery?" Hattie asked.

"Breaking and entering?" Lucy added.

"Righting a wrong against an ex?" Hattie asked.

"Trespassing?"

I held up my hands to stop them. "All of the above! Any time you do anything that has any chance of going south, you need to have already thought of how you're going to escape."

"That seems like pretty negative thinking," Hattie said. "Why assume the worst?"

"I'm not assuming the worst. I'm just making sure I can get out if I need to. It's basic survival strategy."

"So, you've had to fight for your survival?" Hattie asked. "That's tough. What did you need to survive?"

"I—" I stopped. How had this conversation gotten completely out of my control? "All I want is a plan in case the cops show up. Or Rex comes home."

Lucy hesitated. "If Rex comes home, that will be bad."

The tone in her voice got my attention, and I twisted around to face her. "How bad?"

She bit her lip. "Pretty bad."

Hattie nodded. "Rex Giannetti is a bad guy," she said. "Involved in a lot of sketchy things."

Lucy sighed. "I had no idea what he was like when I met him."

I knew how that went. "Good-looking? Charming?"

She nodded. "He was Mr. January in Maine's volunteer firefighter calendar. Let's just say he looked great in snowshoes and not much else."

"That he did," Hattie said. "Nothing like a six pack to distract a woman from what matters."

"Right?" Lucy flashed Hattie an appreciative smile.

"How bad a guy could he be if he's a volunteer firefighter?" I asked. "That's kind of heroic."

"He lasted a week in their training program. Fired for failing the drug test," Lucy said. "It didn't say that in his calendar bio, of course."

"I think they accepted him for training just for the calendar." Hattie shrugged. "It sold a lot of copies so it was a good move. But let's not get distracted by his pecs. Tell Mia how you met him."

"He was on my old mail route," Lucy said. "Or rather, his dad, Marco Giannetti, was."

"A rude little toadstool that man was," Hattie said as the truck skidded around the corner. "He was best friends with Rusty, and the two of them cheated pretty much anyone who ever tried to do business with them."

I grimaced. So many great things associated with my marina, right?

Lucy nodded. "Marco had just died. Rex was there with an old twirling teammate of mine going through Marco's belongings when I dropped off the mail. My friend introduced us, so I figured he had to be all right, but clearly, I missed the boat on that one—"

"He's hot," Hattie interrupted. "The man has muscles worthy of every woman's fantasy. There was no way for you to resist once he turned his charms on you. I mean, who could turn down that shoulder tattoo?"

"His tattoo?" Lucy raised her brows. "Were you stalking him? Because you couldn't see his tattoo in the calendar."

"I drove by the house a few times when he was working in the yard without his shirt." Hattie grinned. "I might be old, but I'm not dead."

"Yeah, well, maybe *you* should have slept with him instead." Lucy sighed. "I feel so stupid. Everyone knows what Marco was like. Why would Rex be any different?"

"Rex was a charmer and good-looking," Hattie said gently. "You got out as soon as you knew he was like his dad. We'll get your car back, and you can write him off as a growth opportunity to find your inner badass."

Lucy hesitated. "There's one other thing he still has. A necklace my mom gave me before she died. It's in the nightstand."

I looked at Hattie, and she glanced at me and raised her brows.

"I can try to get into the house, too," I said grudgingly. Reclaim her dead mom's necklace from a scumbag? There was literally no way I could say no.

Relief lit up Lucy's face. "Really?"

"I'll try. It depends on the lock—"

"We're here." Hattie whipped into a driveway of a small, nondescript gray house with a red, metal roof. The brown yard was overgrown, the landscaping sparse. To the right of the house was the garage. It was a standalone building that looked like it had been an afterthought. It also appeared to be relatively new, which wasn't always a good thing when it came to lock picking.

"I'll keep an eye out." Hattie looked at her dashboard. "You guys have less than thirty minutes until he'll be back from Keno night. Get on it."

"Right." Lucy leapt out.

I paused. "Can you position your truck so that we're blocked from the view of anyone driving by?"

"You bet." Hattie started backing up immediately.

I had to scramble out of her way as I stepped out of the truck. "Seriously, Hattie. You can't give me one second to get out of range?"

"You're young and agile. You can handle it." She winked at me, and then flew backwards. I jumped back and barely managed to avoid being plowed over.

Lucy was already by the side door of the garage, trying the doorknob. As I ran up, she shook her head. "It's locked."

I crouched down to study the lock. There was no deadbolt, and it was a simple doorknob lock. I was almost disappointed it was so easy. "Is there an alarm?"

"No one uses alarms around here." She looked over her shoulder as Hattie's truck screeched backward toward us.

I jumped sideways, nearly knocking over Lucy to get out of Hattie's way. The truck skidded to a stop six inches from my hip. I let out my breath. "How many people has she run over?"

"Hattie? None. She's a race car driver. She's excellent."

I glanced at Lucy as I edged back to the door. "She races cars?"

"Yep, there's a track over in Montgomery. She's been racing there for fifty years. She still beats men in their twenties. It's pretty cool."

Huh. Maybe I could hire her as a driver in case Stanley's family found me. "I think our exit plan may be Hattie's driving." Relieved, I pulled my lock pick kit out of my pocket.

It had been a long time since I'd used them, but the picks felt natural in my hands. It was like coming home again, only this time, for the first time ever, I was using my skills to help someone. It made it even more fun than it normally would be. "I missed doing this," I said as I went to work on the lock.

"It's fun?"

I nodded. "It's like a brain teaser. A puzzle. This one's easy, though." As I said it, the lock clicked, and I sat back on my heels. "All yours."

She grabbed the knob, opened the door, and peered inside. "It's there! Thank you!"

"No problem." I glanced over at the house, on a roll. "Do we have time for the house?"

She looked at her phone. "Yeah, that took less than two minutes." She raised her brows. "You're good."

I grinned. "Thanks. It's been a while. I'm glad my skills are still there. Let's go." We jogged around the house to the back door. Hattie's headlights had lit up the front pretty well, but in back, it was very dark.

Like creepy dark.

A stick cracked in the woods off to my right.

I paused as the hair on my arms prickled in warning. I remembered one of my mom's rules. *Never get greedy.* We'd liberated the car. Was it time to go?

"What's wrong?" Lucy whispered.

I pressed my lips together, listening. I heard another stick crack. I peered into the woods, and for a split second, I thought I saw antlers, but then it was gone. "Something's in the woods."

She snorted. "Of course there's something in the woods. It's Maine. Black bears, moose, deer, bobcats, squirrels. You name it, we've got it."

"Oh…right. I forgot about animals." It made sense, but I still took a moment to try to identify the sounds. The cracking had stopped, and the night became quiet. "How far do the woods go?"

"It's about a five-minute walk to the lake from here," she said. "The house has lake frontage. The dock went in a few weeks ago."

I couldn't see the water from where we were. I listened, but I didn't hear anything else to alarm me, but there was no mistaking the sensation of danger. I'd spent enough time creeping around with my mom that I'd learned to listen to my instincts. As much as I was looking forward to having my way with another lock, I felt like something was wrong. "I think we should go."

Lucy paused for a long moment. "Really?" There was no mistaking the disappointment in her voice.

Her dead mother's necklace.

Her mom. Who was dead.

I'd bailed on my mom, and yet I still missed her every day. The lock picks had been my favorite gift from her on my tenth birthday, and I kept them because they reminded me of her. What if Stanley had kept them when we split up?

I would have gone back for them. At any cost.

Maybe I was being paranoid about the danger. Maybe I was on edge because of my conversation with Devlin earlier about hit men. Two years undercover had definitely made me a little jumpier than I used to be.

I didn't want to be like that anymore. It was time to find my footing again. "Okay, let's do it." I ran across the yard and crouched by the back door. Out of habit, I grabbed the knob to see if it was actually locked, and the door drifted open of its own accord. I sighed with disappointment. "It's already open."

"Really? That's weird. He never leaves it unlocked. His dad was always paranoid about keeping doors locked, and Rex picked it up from him."

The alarm bells started ringing again, even louder this time. Dammit. I had no idea if we were walking into something dangerous, or if I was becoming completely paranoid. My mom always believed that when in doubt, the best option was to bail. Better to miss out on an opportunity than to throw yourself into trouble. "I think we should—"

"I'll be right back." Lucy darted past me and disappeared into the house.

"—leave," I finished saying to no one. Muttering under my breath, I turned and pressed my back up against the wall of the house, so I could see the yard. It was pitch-black, but it felt alive. As if something was watching us. Me.

Griselda was making me paranoid. This was Bass Derby, Maine. It had bears, not sharpshooters with guns. Nothing was in the woods—

I heard a crash from inside, and then Lucy shrieked.

I lunged for the door and was just rushing inside when someone burst out the door, slamming into me. My lock picks caught on his clothes, twisting them painfully in my fingers for a split second before he shoved me to the side, tearing the lock picks free as I fell off the steps and landed in the yard. I gasped from the impact, rolling onto my side to try to see who had hit me. He sprinted across the yard and bolted into the woods. It was too dark to identify anything about him, but it was definitely a person, wearing some sort of hat.

Hattie came tearing around the corner with a flashlight. "What's happening? Who screamed?"

"Lucy!" I scrambled to my feet. "Someone ran into the woods."

Hattie shined her flashlight on the trees, while I ran up the steps and into the house. I made it only about five steps before the light came on, blinding me. I immediately tripped over something and pitched forward into the linoleum.

When I looked up, Lucy was standing in the hallway, a fireplace poker clutched in her hand like she was ready to swing it, staring past me. "Rex," she whispered, her face stricken.

I spun around to see what I'd tripped on.

A shirtless man was on the floor behind me, sprawled face down, not moving. He was well-muscled, with gorgeous hair, delectable five o'clock shadow on his jaw, and shoulders that were droolworthy. His head was turned to the side, showing a perfect nose and gorgeous cheekbones. Less attractively, his vibrant green eyes were open and staring blankly, as if he'd just seen the love of his life for the first time ever.

Or, open and staring as if he were dead.

Given the size of the puddle of blood currently oozing from the gaping wound in the back of his head, I was going with the latter.

Rex Giannetti was dead.

CHAPTER 8

"WHAT DO WE DO?" Lucy asked, clutching the poker.

Years of training kicked in hard and fast. "We need to get out. Now." My adrenaline spiked, galvanizing me into the energized, hyper-alertness that had defined my youth. I spun in a quick circle, making sure no one else was there to catch us, kill us, or throw us in prison. "Is anyone here? Did anyone see us?"

Lucy stared at me as if I'd lost my mind. "Get out? Why?"

"You never stick around the scene of someone else's crime, unless you have ironclad proof of your innocence. We don't have that, which means we need to vacate." I looked around and saw a dishtowel on the kitchen floor. I grabbed it and threw it to her. "Wipe your prints."

It landed about two feet short, and she made no move to pick it up. "Why would I wipe my prints?"

Didn't she ever watch television? "Because we don't want any evidence linking his death back to us. We gotta go!" I started for the door in a hurry, but Hattie appeared in the doorway, blocking my exit.

She took one look at my face, then stood taller. "What's happening—" She stopped when she saw Rex on the floor. "Holy crap." She looked right at Lucy. "Did you kill him?"

Lucy's eyes widened. "What? No. Of course not."

"Because if you did, you need to tell me so we can fix it." Hattie's gaze bore into her. "So, I'll ask again. Did you kill him?"

It was my turn to gawk. "You wouldn't turn her in for killing him?"

She shot me a quelling look. "Why on earth would I turn her in?"

"Because she murdered someone. I feel like that's generally a valid reason for someone to be arrested."

"Hey!" Lucy waved the poker to get our attention. "I didn't kill anyone! Someone threw the poker at me, and I caught it so I didn't get brained."

"Lucy didn't murder *someone.*" Hattie continued, unfazed by Lucy's protest. "We're talking about *Rex*. It was simply a matter of time before someone killed *him*."

"Hey!" Lucy shouted this time, and we both looked at her.

She gave us both a look that said we were complete idiots. "I didn't kill him!" Lucy pointed at us with the poker that was a pretty perfect implement for creating the wound in Rex's head. "Don't you guys listen? I walked into the kitchen, didn't turn on the light because I was sneaking in, then when I reached the living room, someone jumped out, threw the poker at me, and then ran out the back door. I didn't see Rex until I turned around."

"Someone ran past me," I confirmed. "My lock picks got caught in his sweater."

"Perfect. We'll stick with that story." Hattie pulled out her phone.

"It's not a story." Lucy let the poker drop to her side. "It's literally the truth."

"Right." Hattie winked at Lucy as she started to dial.

"Wait." I held up my hand to stop her. "What are you doing?"

"Calling the police."

"Oh, no, no, no." I shook my head and waved my hands in the universal sign for "hell, no." "This is a murder scene. We need to leave before the police get here."

"Guilty people run. Innocent people call the police." She held the phone up to her ear in blatant disregard of my great advice.

"It's not about being innocent. It's about whether you *look* innocent!" I tried to duck around Hattie, but she moved with me to block the exit. I set my hands on my hips and glared at her as I pointed at Lucy. "She's gripping a possible murder weapon like she knows how to use it. She's strong enough to kill a man, *and* she had a grudge against Rex."

Lucy dropped the poker immediately, and it thudded to the tile. "I'm not holding anything."

"See? It's fine." Hattie peered out the window at the backyard. "I'm guessing our murderer took off in a boat, so he's probably not coming back, but guard the door anyway. If he thinks we can identify him, he'd be smart to come back and kill us all."

Guard the door? From a killer? That felt like a plan I didn't want to have any part of. Con artists were clever, bold, and resourceful. We were not violent criminals. Spying on Stanley had helped me fully grasp the depth of my aversion to violent crime, so, I was not liking the direction the night was heading.

Hattie shoved me toward the back door and handed me the flashlight. "Stay."

Stay? "I'm not a dog." The flashlight didn't have a cord like the hairdryer, so I felt a little handicapped in using it to save my life. "How do you know there aren't more people in the house? Killers work in pairs." I had actual proof of this fact, thanks to Joyce.

"Good point." Hattie grabbed a butter knife from the counter and tossed it to me. "Go check the house. I'll guard the door."

I made no move to catch it, letting it clatter to the floor next to the poker. "Check the house? You've got to be kidding. That's what they do in horror movies before they all get chopped up by a chain saw." I'd seen things in Stanley's organization that I could never unsee, and with Rex dead on the floor, my mind was going to all sorts of creative and inventive ways to die.

"Marco probably had several chain saws," Hattie mused as she held the phone to her ear. "Everyone around here does."

"How is that helpful?" I could hear her phone ringing, making me even more agitated. My need to get us out of there was so strong I could barely make myself stand still.

"It's good to know all your options." Hattie held up her hand to shush us and spoke into her phone. "This is Hattie Lawless. I'm at Rex Giannetti's place, and he appears to have been murdered. Yep, sure we'll stick around." She hung up. "Chief Stone will be here in a few minutes."

"Chief Stone?" I might trust Griselda not to blame me for the carnage surrounding us, but a lifetime of distrust of police couldn't be erased by one decent cop, especially when I already knew which category Chief Stone fell into. "He ticketed me for destroying the sign simply because I was present. Do you guys really want to give him the chance to pin a murder on us? Because I don't."

Hattie and Lucy stared at me for a moment, and I relaxed slightly. How could they argue with that logic? Then Hattie shrugged. "He already knows I'm here."

"I want my necklace." Lucy spun around and raced upstairs, taking the steps two at a time, in blatant disregard of my warning about multiple killers and Chief Stone's incompetence.

"Lucy!" I ran to the bottom of the stairs. "Get back down here!"

"I'll be right back!" I heard her slamming drawers, putting material goods ahead of life, limb, and freedom from incarceration.

You never did that. Ever. Always make sure you can walk away if you need to. Did these women have *no* common sense when it came to committing illegal activities? "At least wipe your fingerprints!" I shouted.

"My fingerprints are already everywhere," she yelled back. "He was great in bed so I stayed over a lot."

"Good sex. A woman's downfall," Hattie lamented. "Honestly, that's why she stayed with him. He charmed her with his wanker."

I set my hands on my hips. "Wanker? Really?"

"Yep. He wanker-charmed her. Haven't we all been wanker-charmed a few times in our lives?"

I thought of Stanley. Full-on wanker-charming until he'd gotten the ring on my finger. Then it had been a dry, arid desert of denial. "It's been a while since I've had any wankering in my life, charming or not."

"Really?" She raised her brows. "That surprises me. You're pretty hot."

I felt my cheeks turn red, but who was I to turn down a hotness compliment? "Um, thanks. You're...um...pretty smokin' as well. That blue hair looks fantastic."

"Of course it does. Men love me. It's difficult to keep them away from this bundle of lusciousness." Hattie picked up the butter knife, wiped it clean with her shirt, and set it back on the counter. "In the meantime, learn from Lucy. That's what you do when you're waiting for the police to show up at a murder scene. Make the most of it." Hattie flicked the light switch by the door and the backyard light went on.

We both peered out the window, but I didn't see anyone skulking back to kill off the witnesses.

"Every moment in life is an opportunity," Hattie said. "What are you going to do with this one?"

I shoved my lock picks into my pocket. "Leave." Rex was the second dead body I'd been up close and personal with recently. I didn't like the direction my life was going. "We broke in here, Lucy grabbed a fireplace poker, Rex is now dead from a head wound, we have no proof that anyone else was here, and the Chief of Police has already proven his willingness to arrest the nearest bystander, regardless of guilt. How does this go well for us?"

Hattie folded her arms across her chest. "You're very tense, Mia."

"I'm not tense. I'm being smart. Self-preservation is one of my gifts."

"No. You're definitely tense." She studied me for a moment,

then understanding dawned on her face. "You're worried that your checkered past will get you into trouble if Chief Stone turns his beady little eyes onto you, aren't you? I get it. Go. I'll cover, but tomorrow, you have to tell me what you're on the run from."

"I'm not on the run!" But the checkered past? Yeah, a little bit of that. "I haven't done anything illegal—"

She glanced at her watch. "Do you want to argue or leave? Because Chief Stone doesn't live that far from here."

"Leave. I want to leave." I knew I was innocent, but I was too smart to stick around. The instinct to flee was almost overwhelming.

"Then go. Fast."

"Okay. Thanks for covering for me. I'll see you later." I bolted for the back door and raced out into the yard.

Into the darkness.

And I stopped.

Where was I going to go? Hike through the same woods that Rex's murderer had just fled into? Walk down the side of the street, so the cops would drive past me? Run to the lake where the murderer was probably climbing into his boat? I had no idea how to get home from here. And the trees were incredibly, impenetrably dark.

I looked back at the house, with its blazing light in the kitchen. Hattie and Lucy were in there. They were witnesses that I hadn't broken the law. I'd had no witnesses at the sign, but I did now.

Aside from my criminal, untrustworthy mom, I'd never had witnesses that would stand by me, but as I stood there in the pitch black, all alone, I knew that I had them now.

I'd just met these two women, but somehow I knew they wouldn't throw me under the bus. Heck, I was pretty certain that Hattie would hide the crime if Lucy *had* murdered Rex, and that was pretty big.

I wasn't sure I'd defend a murderer.

Unless...maybe if the victim was someone really, really bad.

Rex had clearly fit that definition. I didn't even know the guy, and I was pretty sure the world was a better place without him in it.

Did we owe the murderer a thanks?

The door slammed open, and I whirled around, my flashlight raised for battle as Hattie leaned out. "If you're going to go, you need to jet, Mia."

I looked into her blazing brown eyes, with her blue hair peeking out from under her black cap, and resolution flooded me. Hattie Lawless was a woman who would stand by her friends, and I wanted to be a part of that. By staying, I could help clear their names, as they were doing for me. I wanted to defend them as well. "I'll stay."

Her face lit up with a smile. "That's my girl. Come on in."

"I will." I thought of the one illegal activity I *had* engaged in. "Let me just make sure my fingerprints are off the garage door—"

"Why would your fingerprints be on the garage door?"

I jumped as Chief Stone strode around the corner of the building. His boots were polished, he was wearing his uniform, and he looked as if he'd been sitting at his desk, waiting for a chance to show off the creases in his pants. He looked right at me. "Ms. Murphy? Why would your fingerprints be on the garage door?"

Completely uncharacteristically, I drew a complete blank, probably caused by the stress of being only a few yards from a murder victim which Chief Stone might decide to arrest me for. "Umm..."

Hattie stepped in. "We came here to reclaim Lucy's car and her necklace. We got the garage door open, but the back door to the house was ajar. When we went to walk inside, someone rushed past Mia and into the woods. We found Rex dead on the floor."

Chief Stone looked sharply at Hattie. "I heard correctly? He's been murdered? I thought you must have said burned or spurned or—" He paused, looking slightly aghast. "Really murdered?"

"Pool of blood under his head, and all," Hattie said. She gestured to the door, where Lucy was now standing, shoving something into her front pocket. "Go check it out."

Chief Stone didn't move. "I don't want to see that."

Hattie raised her brows. "You're the Chief of Police. That's your job."

"I'm not going in there." He pulled out his phone. "Mom? I'm here at Rex Giannetti's house with Hattie Lawless. She said Rex has been murdered. What do I do?"

I looked at Hattie. "Mom?" I mouthed the word.

She rolled her eyes and nodded, holding up her finger to tell me to wait.

Chief Stone's face became more and more ashen as he listened. Finally, he hung up. He let the phone drop to his side, looking defeated.

I was never good with awkward silences, so I tried to fill the gap. "Is this your first murder?"

He shot me a glare. "No," he lied, his voice cracking. "I got this." He took another deep breath and pulled his shoulders back. "Okay, then, let's do this." He marched ahead of Hattie, his body stiff as he strode across the grass and into the house.

Hattie grinned at me as Lucy hurried over. "This is going to be good," she said. "Let's wait here."

"What are we waiting for?" I flexed my hands restlessly and stood next to Hattie.

"Give it a minute." There was no mistaking the gleeful anticipation in her voice.

I counted only to three before Chief Stone ran out the door, leaned over the edge of the stairs, and tossed up his cookies.

"Wow." Lucy said. "That's not a sight you really want to see."

"It sure isn't." It was like a train wreck. I wanted to look away, but it was impossible. "Is he crying?"

"I think he might be," Lucy said.

"His mom, Eloise Stone, is the mayor," Hattie whispered giddily. "She hires the police officers. He couldn't get a job anywhere else."

Ah…things were clearer now.

Chief Stone looked up, and he met my gaze. I immediately

wiped the grin off my face, but it was too late. His eyes narrowed when he realized the three of us had just seen him in a very undignified position. "I need statements from all of you." He looked right at me. "Especially you."

"Me?" I stiffened. "Why especially me?"

"You have that shifty look," Hattie said. "I noticed it right away."

"Me, too," Lucy offered. "Definitely suspicious."

I glared at them. "Is that what you consider helping? Because I'm pretty sure it's not."

"It's good to know your weaknesses." Hattie beamed at me, putting on a very sweet, very innocent, senior citizen expression. "See? No one ever thinks I'm guilty of anything."

I stared at her. "I'm impressed." Because I suspected Hattie didn't have an innocent bone in her body.

"Right?"

Chief Stone stood up, trying to pretend he hadn't just unloaded his entire dinner onto Rex's lawn. I doubted Rex would mind, so it was all good. "You." He pointed at me. "You first."

Did no one in this town understand the concept of multiple assailants? "Although someone did run out of the house," I said, "we didn't check the rest of the building. There could be a second murderer still in there."

Chief Stone became even more ashen, and he looked like he was going to throw up again. I had a feeling he wanted to call his mom back, but to give the man credit, he pulled out his gun, holding it like a man who was pretty sure, but not absolutely certain, he knew how to use it, then he turned and headed back into the house.

He made it as far as the threshold, and then stopped.

We waited.

He stood there for several minutes, clearly trying to make up his mind about whether to go into the house. Finally, he glanced surreptitiously over at us, then swore under his breath when he saw we were all standing there, watching him.

Finally, he pointed at me. "You. Come with me."

"Me?" I felt my stomach drop. "I'm not a cop."

"I want you to walk me through what you found—" At that moment, we heard a truck pull up.

We all froze. I mean, seriously, froze. Who was it?

Chief Stone looked like he was going to pass out, and even Hattie edged backwards, toward the woods, pulling me and Lucy with her. "If there's a shootout," she whispered. "Run."

I rolled my eyes. "You think?"

"Stop being a smartass. It's always good to communicate." Footsteps crushed on the gravel, and Hattie pulled us all another step backwards.

Toward the woods.

The woods Rex's killer had run into only a few moments ago.

Yes, those woods.

Someone came racing around the corner, and I saw the outline of a weapon. "Gun!" I shouted.

Chief Stone dove into the house.

I bolted for the woods, with Lucy and Hattie on either side. They were both faster than I was, so they each grabbed an arm and dragged me along with them. Awkward at best, but effective.

We'd just reached the woods when I heard a shout. A shout that sounded faintly familiar.

I glanced back over my shoulder just as Lake Police hotness Devlin Hunt stepped under the floodlight, his weapon out as if he actually *did* know how to use it. "Guys, it's Devlin—"

I ran straight into a tree, hitting it so hard that I thought I'd broken every bone in my chest. The impact flung me backward, and I crashed into the hard ground, landing flat on my back.

I lay there, stunned.

"Mia!" Lucy crouched next to me. "Are you okay?"

I nodded, and tried to answer, but I couldn't get any air.

Panic hit me, and I tried to inhale again, but I couldn't. Holy crap! I was dying! I grabbed Lucy's arm and tried to tell her to call 9-1-1, but I couldn't breathe. I couldn't talk—

"Calm down." Hattie crouched next to me. "You knocked the wind out of your lungs. You'll be able to breathe in a minute."

A minute? I would suffocate in a minute!

I tried to suck in air, and my lungs clamped down, expelling the tiny breath of air before I could get it into my body. I tried again, and again my lungs blocked it. My breath was stuttering, and I couldn't get any air into my lungs.

I was dying. I'd killed myself without any hit man being needed—

"Slow it down," Hattie said. "Stop panicking."

Stop panicking? I couldn't breathe! But even as I thought it, I was able to take a slightly deeper breath.

And then another.

And slowly, agonizingly slowly, my lungs stopped stuttering and finally, I was able to take a deep breath. A little shuddering, but an actual breath nonetheless.

And then another.

I was going to live.

I scrunched my eyes shut, trying to calm down as tears of relief caked my cheeks. I was pretty sure those two minutes of not being able to breathe had just been the most terrifying moments of my life. At least when I'd been hunted in the safe house, I'd had adrenaline and a hairdryer. This time, I'd had no weapons. Just a terrifying suffocation that had lasted an eternity. "That was so much worse than being stalked by a hit man."

My words sounded suspiciously loud to my ears, even though I had silently thought them.

I opened my eyes and saw surprised looks on Hattie and Lucy's faces. "Did I say that out loud?"

They both nodded. "Are you in witness protection?" Lucy whispered.

"No." Oh, man. I tried to sit up, and they helped me. "But I'm beginning to think maybe I should be."

"Holy mother of mackerel." Hattie suddenly snapped her fingers. "You're the woman in the news. You went undercover against that drug lord you married. You changed your last name and swapped out your blond hair for brown, but it's you."

Crud.

"The drug lord wife?" Lucy frowned, looking back and forth between me and Hattie. "That's you?"

The drug lord wife. That was my identity? *The drug lord wife.* I propped myself up on my elbows. "Listen, I came here to start over. To reclaim my own life. I don't want people to know. I just want to be Mia." I couldn't quite keep the desperation out of my voice. "Can we keep it just between us?"

They looked at each other, and something passed between them.

I wasn't sure what it was until they both turned back to me with big grins, nodding. "Girl, your secret couldn't be in better hands," Hattie said. "I'm like a vault."

"And I'm sworn to protect the secrets of citizens as a US mail carrier," Lucy said. "You wouldn't believe what I know about everyone on my route."

Relief and gratitude made tears well up and my throat tighten. They really weren't going to judge me. "Thank you," I whispered. "Truly."

Hattie punched me lightly in the shoulder. "No need to thank us. We should be thanking you. You're going to be a fun addition to Bass Derby."

Lucy nodded. "I can't wait to hear the stories."

"No stories." I shook off my emotional response and sat the rest of the way up, my lungs still a little sketchy. "I'm putting it behind me. I'm a marina owner now."

"And also a witness to a murder. Funny how things like that keep following you around, eh?" Hattie beamed at me.

I scowled at her. "They don't follow me around." But even as I said it, I felt a glimmer of worry that she was right. I was less than twenty-four hours into my new life, and I'd already picked a lock, been party to about six dozen traffic violations, been knocked over by a fleeing murderer, and had the good fortune to gawk at a super-hot, newly murdered jerk who took fantastic care of his body.

Or he had, until he let it get bludgeoned.

Hattie raised her brows. "No one can ignore her past, Mia. It's a part of who we are."

"I can, thanks." I stood up and brushed the dirt off my butt. "This incident tonight was not my fault. It was your problem, and you dragged me into it."

Lucy's face fell. "Are you mad?"

I looked over at her. Her eyes were big and weepy. Her mouth was turned down, and she looked like she was about to cry. "You look like a puppy dog that someone forgot to feed. How can I be mad?"

Her face lit up much too quickly, and she beamed at me. "See? Hattie's not the only one who can look pathetic. You really need to learn that expression, Mia. It's quite handy."

I didn't want to tell them the number of personas I'd learned to don over the seventeen years I'd lived with a very successful con artist. I could fake innocent. I just chose not to. Because *I was not going back to that life.*

The back door opened, and Devlin came out onto the steps. The floodlight cast him into silhouette, but I could see from the set of his shoulders and his confident stance that he was not going to vomit at the sight of a dead body.

In fact, he looked relaxed, ready, and focused. I tried not to think about how distractingly good he looked in his jeans, because that was not at all helpful. He was all cop right now, which meant he was the enemy.

It might have been Chief Stone's first murder scene, but I was willing to bet it wasn't Devlin's. Not by a long shot. He was too calm.

I thought back to the fact Griselda had contacted him. How they'd had their little team with nicknames like Hawk. Devlin Hunt was not simply a lake police officer in Maine. He was something else. Something more. Something like my favorite FBI agent.

Griselda was the type who always got his criminal. When he'd set his sights on Stanley, Stanley had had no chance.

What if Devlin targeted Lucy? Chief Stone we could handle, but Devlin?

At that moment, the cop in question looked directly at Lucy. "You're the girlfriend, right?"

She nodded. "Ex," she clarified.

"I want to talk to you first. Come with me."

My gut sank as Lucy shot us a worried look, then headed toward him.

Hattie glanced at me, her brows knit with concern.

I had my answer.

Devlin was going to be a problem for us. For Lucy.

A really big problem.

CHAPTER 9

"THEY'RE GOING to pin it on you," Hattie said as soon as I got into her truck, an hour later.

"Me?" Alarm shot through me. "Why do you say that?"

"No. Not you." She looked into her rearview mirror at Lucy, who was in the back seat, because they hadn't let her take her car. Crime scene and all that. I knew how that worked. "Lucy."

Relief shot through me, quickly followed by a sinking feeling in my gut. I didn't want to be on the shortlist for murder, but I didn't want Lucy there either. I looked back at Lucy. "I got the same vibe. Did you?"

"Yeah, but I'd hoped I was wrong." Lucy bit her lip. "I thought I was being paranoid. You guys thought the same thing?"

Hattie and I both nodded as she hit the gas and tore out of Rex's driveway.

"You make sense," Hattie said. "You're the ex-girlfriend. Rex treated you badly, stole your truck, and held your mother's legacy hostage. Plenty of motive."

"I'm pretty sure the fireplace poker you were holding was the murder weapon," I added, trying to extract the shoulder belt from my throat. I realized suddenly that I hadn't seen her use the dishtowel I'd tossed to her. I twisted around in my seat. "You did wipe your fingerprints off it, right?"

Lucy opened her mouth, then shut it silently and shook her head. "I got distracted."

"Bad miss there," Hattie said.

Crud. The fact it had been a long time since I'd done any breaking and entering didn't excuse the fact that I'd let both of us leave our fingerprints behind. It was one of the top five best practices for petty thievery. Everyone knew that, even people whose entire criminal career consisted of binge-watching *Law & Order*.

"They'll figure you stumbled across Rex when you invaded his house, a struggle ensued, and you got lucky with the poker," Hattie said. "Everyone knows you're strong enough."

Lucy grimaced. "What about the guy who ran over Mia—"

"No proof he exists," Hattie said. "Unless either of you whipped out your phone and took a video?"

We both shook our heads. "That would have been handy," I admitted.

"Devlin went down to the lake, but there was no sign of a boat. No other car was on site. No mystery killer, as far as the police are concerned." She hit the brakes, screeching to a halt at a stop sign. "There you go. Slap Lucy in handcuffs, and the case is solved."

See? That was why I'd wanted us all to bail. Next time we stumbled across a murder, I was taking charge.

"Chief Stone has known me my whole life," Lucy protested. "He'd never believe I killed Rex."

Hattie drummed her fingers on the steering wheel. "Chief Stone needs to solve this murder before it ruins Bass Derby's chances to be named Best Lake Town in Maine for the twelfth consecutive year. He'll sacrifice you in an instant for the sake of the title."

I recalled Chief Stone mentioning that title. "Seriously?"

Hattie nodded. "As I said earlier, Eloise Stone, our mayor, is Chief Stone's mother. She's obsessed with that title. Everything she does is designed to retain it for the next year. Winning brings in tourists, and keeps the price of everything high. She's probably already figuring out how to spin Rex's murder to minimize damage."

Lucy swore under her breath and leaned back against the seat, her hands clasped on top of her head. "I didn't think of that, but you're right. They can't afford a murder."

I frowned. "A title is more important than justice?"

They both nodded. "Absolutely," Lucy said.

"Especially this year. The town of Bugscuffle has come in second to Bass Derby for the last five years," Hattie explained. "The mayor, Viola Rollins, is determined to win this year. She and the city council made massive upgrades to the town center and jacked up the charm factor all around Lady Slipper Lake. It'll be close, especially since the welcome sign got destroyed."

"Why on earth does it matter so much?" I couldn't wrap my head around making a title that important.

"Pride," Hattie said. "Bragging rights are a big deal around here."

"That's not all," Lucy added. "The winner gets the cover of *Charming Maine* magazine, a big plaque, a challenge trophy they keep for a year, and a ten-thousand-dollar prize."

Ten thousand dollars would be a lot of money for a town this size, but worth convicting an innocent person? No. Never.

Hattie came to a barely rolling stop at an intersection, then hit the gas again. "If Chief Stone doesn't wrap this up and get it off the radar in a hurry, the murder could cost Bass Derby the title. His mom, and the entire town council, will kill him. She could lose her job over it."

"What about Devlin?" Lucy said. "He's only been here for six months. He won't care about the title."

I let out my breath, and Hattie glanced at me. "What do you think?"

"Devlin's going to be a problem," I said. "More than Chief Stone."

Hattie nodded her agreement. "How many times did he ask Lucy to go over what happened when she walked in?"

"Seven." I knew all about that police tactic. "He was trying to catch her slipping up with the story."

"Did I mess up?" Lucy leaned over the seat. "Did I sound like I was telling the truth?"

"You sounded nervous," I said honestly. I'd tried hard to direct the conversation, but either I was out of practice leading cops where I wanted them to go, or Devlin was too well-trained to succumb. Either way, he'd been much too focused on Lucy for my comfort.

"You made it clear how mad you were at Rex for stealing your car and being an all-around jerk to you," Hattie added. "Motive is big."

"But you guys were with me. You're my witnesses," she said.

"You went in first," Hattie said. "You were in there by yourself long enough to kill him, and you admitted that to the police. We can't even lie to protect you, because you told them the truth."

She looked back and forth between us, desperation etched on her face. "Innocent people tell the truth!"

"Not when it's going to get them arrested for murder." I sighed. "The truth is really overrated sometimes." How had this gotten so messed up so quickly? "Cops are like that," I said. "They twist everything around so fast you can't think."

"I'm sunk, then," Lucy said. She sounded on the verge of tears. "Once they match my fingerprints on the poker, I'm done." She sat back and clasped her hands on her head. "I'm going to prison."

"Not necessarily." Hattie looked at both of us. "Not if we find the murderer ourselves."

Lucy brightened. "Really? Do you think we can?"

"What?" My stomach lurched. I didn't want to track a murderer. They killed people. Nice, sweet people like me. Granted, they also killed jerks like Rex, but that was on Rex.

Hattie nodded. "Between the three of us, yeah, I think we can."

Between the *three* of us? No, no, and no. "I can't get involved."

"We need you." Lucy didn't give me her puppy face. Instead, she looked at me expectantly, like she had no doubt I was going to deliver. "You spent two years undercover for the FBI. You know things we could never know."

"Whoa." I held up my hands to stop her. "I spied on my husband, under duress, I might add. That's not the same thing as poking a murderer until he gets mad—"

"They're translatable skills, I'm sure." Hattie grinned as she turned into the marina parking lot. "Plus, you can pick locks. What other skills do you have?"

"None." I said it too quickly, and I saw the flash of skepticism on their faces. I had a lot of skills. Small-time, unimpressive skills that were no match for taking down a killer. "Seriously. Lock picking was a hobby I had as a kid. Nothing more."

Spying on Stanley for two years had almost done me in. I would never forget the moment he figured it out and pulled the gun on me. If Griselda hadn't been breaking down the door right at that moment, I would be dead, and I knew it. Stanley and Joyce had traumatized me forever, I was pretty sure. "I'm ordinary. I'm nothing special. I don't know how to hunt murderers." *Hunt murderers?* That sounded like maybe the worst idea in the world.

Lucy's face fell, and Hattie slammed on the brakes, skidding to a stop in front of my door.

Hattie shifted into park, rested her arms on the steering wheel, and gave me a disapproving look.

Neither of them said anything.

They just looked at me.

And kept looking at me.

I glared at them. "You guys are merciless."

Hattie chuckled. "I was going for relentless, but merciless will do," she said. "Did it work to convince you to help out a sweet, innocent young thing from spending the rest of her life in prison for a crime she didn't commit?"

"No." Then I saw the apprehension in Lucy's eyes, and I knew I could never walk away and let that happen to her. I sighed and threw up my hands in capitulation. "Fine, yes, it worked. I'll pick locks for you, but that's it. Okay?"

Hattie grinned, and the two women gave each other a high five. "What do we do first?" Lucy asked.

Hattie rubbed her jaw. "Well, Rex and his dad have cheated a lot of people over the years. We could make a list of what we know and start there."

Lucy nodded. "I can start that tonight."

"Let's do lunch at the café tomorrow," Hattie said. "We'll compare lists and try to narrow it down."

"We need to find out what drove him," I said. "If we figure out what mattered to him and what his vulnerabilities and motivations were, then we can figure out how to tap into that and—" I stopped before I said something asinine like, set up a con where we can bilk him out of all his money.

"And what?" Hattie raised her brows.

"Figure out what he was involved in that might have gotten him killed," I finished. It sounded a little lame. "And then we can tell Devlin, and he can investigate it. Because we're not actually going *after* Rex's killer, right?"

Hattie made a non-committal noise that worried me, but before I could clarify, she reached across me and opened my door. "See you in the morning," she said. "I get there early to bake, so don't try to decapitate me with a scrub brush when I walk in."

I felt my cheeks heat up as I climbed down from the monster truck. "Don't scare me, and I won't try to kill you."

Lucy scrambled over the back seat into the passenger seat as I started to close the door. "Mia?"

I paused. "What?"

"Thanks for helping." She managed a smile, but I could see the genuine worry in her eyes. "I don't want to go to prison."

It was that half-smile that did it. She was scared, and for good reason. She had motive, opportunity, and her fingerprints were on the weapon. I'd spent two years undercover because I hadn't been able to stand back and let a bad man do bad things.

And now? I couldn't let bad things happen to a good person, especially when it meant that a murderer got to go free.

New life. Same old me. I sighed. "I'm in. All the way."

Lucy shrieked and hugged me, and Hattie beamed at me. "Tomorrow lunch," she said. "Bring ideas, Spy Girl."

"I'm not—" Hattie hit the gas, and Lucy yanked the door shut, scrambling not to fall out as they tore out of the parking lot. "—Spy Girl," I finished, my words dropping uselessly into the dark night of the empty parking lot.

I knew I was going to regret this.

But I had to admit, it sounded like it could be fun. Girl bonding, lockpicking, and outsmarting police officers? It definitely had potential.

As long as we didn't get ourselves killed, of course.

CHAPTER 10

Several hours later, right in the middle of a dream in which Joyce was cackling with maniacal laughter and chasing me with a chainsaw, I jolted awake to angry shouts and the high-pitched whine of machinery.

For a split second, I froze in terror. The chainsaw had been real? Not just in my dreams? King Tut leapt up, digging his beastly claws into my chest as he launched himself off me. He tore out of the marina store and sprinted up the stairs to my apartment.

I scrambled over the life jackets I'd used for a mattress, my heart thundering as I lunged for my hairdryer. I wrapped the cord around my wrist, grabbed my keys, and ran for my car.

I burst outside, and then stopped in surprise when I saw half a dozen Jet Skis churning the lake into a frenzy in front of my docks.

Jet Skis? Not chain saws?

Not a serial killer with a chainsaw. Just a bunch of obnoxious idiots, doing donuts in the water, yelling, and swamping my dock and my one little boat.

I let the hairdryer drop to my side, totally annoyed with my reaction. I was so over this new Paranoid Mia. I needed to chill out. Get back to my unflappable self.

It was freaking Jet Skis.

It was still dark out, with just the faintest hint of dawn streaking the sky but as my eyes began to adjust, I realized that the Jet Skis were being driven by moose.

Big, furry, antlered moose.

Because who else would be driving a Jet Ski at dawn, right? That made complete sense.

I edged toward the lake to get a better look, and saw that it wasn't actually moose (big surprise there, right?), but people dressed in moose costumes. Six people, to be exact. They had antlers, hooves, head-coverings, and full-body fur costumes that looked disturbingly realistic in the dark streaks of barely dawn. One of them was even wearing a big, red-and-white-striped bow on the right antler, like it was my welcome to Bass Derby gift.

They were shouting obscenities and throwing things onto my dock.

Obscenities didn't bother me, but tossing junk at the marina? Not so amusing. This was my home. "Hey!" I ran down toward the lake. "Stop!" As soon as my feet hit the ramp, they spun around and raced away, their Jet Skis bouncing over the wakes they'd left in the water. They sped out into the main lake, turned right, and then disappeared from sight as they headed up the lake, the whine of the Jet Skis hanging in the air long after they were out of sight.

I ran down to the dock, and picked up one of the items that had been thrown there.

It was a broken piece of wood. Why would they throw that on my dock?

Then I saw "keep driving" written on it, and I realized it was part of the sign that my windshield loon belonged to.

It was hard to see in the dark, but I could tell that all the other items on the dock and floating in the water were more sign parts.

Holy cow. Hattie had been right. I was being harassed by moose for the destruction of a sign I hadn't even touched.

I let out my breath as I surveyed the extent of the carnage. Welcome to Bass Derby, right?

Much of the wood was in the lake. It had old paint on it that could have lead in it. I couldn't let it sit there. But the water was cold, and the night was dark. I didn't want to go on a fishing expedition.

King Tut meowed at me from his safe vantage point on the marina roof, and I waved at him. "Thanks for your support, dude." He'd run away from the threat. I'd run toward it. Good to know his priorities when things got dangerous. "I'm not taking you on our murderer hunt," I hollered at him.

It was kind of unfortunate to know he couldn't be counted on to be a secret weapon. Cat claws were pretty offensive when used correctly.

I suddenly heard the whine of an engine, and I tensed, gripping the "keep driving" board more tightly. It wasn't a hairdryer, but if any of those moose came after me. I wasn't going down easily.

I strode down to the end of the dock, armed, ready, and waiting. Bullies liked to prey on the weak, and I had no interest in taking on victim status. *Bring it on, Moose Freaks!*

But what came around the corner wasn't a herd of passive-aggressive moose.

It was a little motorboat, which almost looked like a rowboat with a motor tacked to the back. The increasing light of dawn gave me enough visibility to see that the man driving it had a gray ponytail, a beige baseball hat, and a matching vest over a plaid shirt. He had several fishing rods propped up, and a large cooler at his feet.

He cruised up to the dock and caught a piling to stop himself, just as Devlin had. "Good mornin' to ya."

I lowered the board. "Good morning," I said cautiously.

He looked around the docks. "Cargo not in yet?"

I looked around as well, and didn't see his canoe. "No. Does he usually come in this early?"

"When he wants to." The man looked back at me, studying me with open curiosity. "You're the flatlandah, eh?"

"The flatlandah?" I repeated. "What does that mean?"

"You're from away."

"Away?"

"Not from Maine. Flat. Land. Uh."

"Oh. *Flatlander.* Yes, I'm from away." I paused. "Is that bad?"

"Most folk don't care, but there are some." He looked slowly around the dock and the water. His attention lingered on the floating wood, and his eyes were much more judgmental when he looked back at me. "We don't use this here lake for garbage."

"It wasn't me," I said quickly. "I was attacked by moose on Jet Skis. They threw it." I frowned. "Didn't you see them? They were literally just here."

He paused. "I heard some Jet Skis, but didn't think nothing of it." His bushy gray eyebrows went up as he considered me. "The Derby Moose, musta been."

"The Derby Moose? That's a thing?"

He nodded and let out a low whistle. "They haven't been seen in a long time. This ain't good. They're trouble, big trouble." This time, his gaze held sympathy when he looked at me. "When they target someone, they don't stop until they get their way. I'd pack up now if I were you. Get on your way."

"On my way?" I set my hands on my hips. "This is my home. I'm not leaving. Besides, I could never live with myself if I let myself get driven away by grown men who dress up as forest animals and yell obscenities. Seriously."

He studied me, then nodded. "I heard about you. Sounds about right."

"Heard about me?" I tried not to grimace. "What did you hear?"

He lowered his voice. "You going to start up here?"

I matched his tone. "Start up what?" I whispered.

"The business."

Oh, for heaven's sake. Really? "The marina?" I asked innocently, just in case that was what he'd meant.

He wiggled his brows.

I wiggled mine back.

He inclined his chin.

I inclined mine back.

Finally, he grinned. "Tricky thing, aren't you?"

"I don't know what you're talking about."

He looked around then leaned forward. "The drug business. You bringing that to town?"

I set my hands on my hips and sighed in exasperation. "What did Ruby Lee tell you? She said she hadn't told anyone. I'm not dealing drugs. I'm not taking over his business. I'm a law-abiding citizen who gave up her entire life to do what was right, so back off!"

He studied me for a moment. I met his gaze and glared at him, letting him see that I meant it.

Finally, he nodded. "All right, then. I'll take some gas."

I blinked at the abrupt change in topic. "Gas?"

"For my boat." He pointed at the antique pump about six inches from my leg.

"Oh, well, okay. Great." I felt strangely pleased that he was willing to buy from me. Maybe my outrage had convinced him of my upstanding moral code. I eyed the pump beside me. It was very old, but it had a hose and nozzle. Seemed basic enough. "Where do I put the gas?"

"I'll show you." He tossed me a rope. "Tie 'er up."

"Okay." I watched as he tied the rear of the boat, then I quickly looped mine around the piling like he had. "I'm Mia Murphy."

"Bryan Quinn." He climbed out of the boat and shook my hand, a strong, rugged grip that made me stand taller. He was very tall, over six feet, and there was a wiry strength to his frame. "This is how it works." He unearthed the gas tank in his boat, quickly flipped a few things, dragged the hose, and then stuck it in the tank. "Notice how the numbers on the pump don't work."

The white numbers weren't moving. They were stuck at $777.77. "Yep."

"Been like that for twenty years. Rusty just tells ya what you owe him. Overcharges every time."

My heart sank. "Really?"

"Until Jake moved in, Rusty was the only choice on the lake. People paid. Put up with his lowlife attitude and business. Now they don't have to. They go to Jake." He met my gaze. "No one comes here anymore, 'cept if they want Cargo." He studied me. "I came by to check you out. See if you were like Rusty or not." He paused. "It seems as though you're not." He sounded almost disappointed by that revelation, as if it were a crushing blow not to have the drama of a crook running the marina.

Apparently, it wasn't only the run-down building that I was going to have to rehab. It was the marina's reputation. I was an ex-pickpocket and thief who'd been married to a drug runner. Yet, I was the one who had to prove to the community that the marina that used to steal from them was now honest.

The irony was not lost on me.

Unfortunately, I was pretty certain that shouting my innocence at every potential customer wasn't a sustainable path toward prosperity and trust, even if it had worked with Bryan, at least enough to sell him a tank of gas.

We stood in awkward silence as we waited for the tank to fill.

"You moved in?" Bryan finally asked. "Living at the marina?"

"I am." I wrinkled my nose. "The upstairs smells terrible, though. I heard Rusty cleaned fish up there."

"Ayuh, he did." Bryan replaced the nozzle on the tank. "How much do I owe you?"

I shrugged. "I have no idea. You tell me."

He studied me for a long moment. "It takes about thirty seconds a gallon. So, about twenty bucks."

Excellent. Now I knew how to total the gas. That was progress right there. "Give me ten. You get a fifty percent discount for loyalty and helpful tips. I appreciate it."

He grinned and handed me a ten. "You met Cargo yet?"

"No."

"I think he'll keep working for you. That's a good thing." He untied the rear rope. "Get the bowline, will ya?"

The bowline. Right. "On it." I untied the rope and tossed it into the boat like he did. "Hope you catch some fish today."

He grinned as he yanked on the cord and started the engine back up. "Always do. I've got a gift." He gestured to the debris. "You going to clean up this mess?"

"The wood? Of course. I'm not leaving it in the lake."

He nodded approvingly. "I think there are some wet suits in the store. Rusty used to rent them for water skiing. One of those might fit. The water feels real cold this time of year."

"Thanks. I'll check it out." If I found a new one, I was confiscating it for my own use. Used and probably unwashed wet suits didn't sound great, but death by hypothermia wasn't something I had time for.

"No problem." He paused. "I'm happy to help you sort through stuff in the store, if you want. I do that for Cargo now and then. Go through the mail, things like that. I heard you got a bunch. Did a box of live bait come in? I can take that off your hands."

Small town gossip was so strange. Who gossiped about the amount of mail people got? But the offer was super thoughtful. Maybe yelling at potential customers was the way to go, after all. "Thanks, that's really nice of you. I haven't gone through it yet. I'll let you know if I need help." Live bait? Was that the refrigerated box? I was going to have to toss that without opening it, I was pretty sure.

"I don't mind at all. I could stop by later today, if you like."

The mail was way far down on my list of priorities, behind getting the apartment habitable, learning as much as I could about the business, and keeping Lucy out of prison. "I'm pretty busy today, but I'll definitely let you know."

"All right, then." He let the boat drift back from the dock. "The town needs this place. Don't give up."

"I won't." I pulled my shoulders back. "Oh, and Bryan?"

"Yeah?"

I grinned. "If you catch fish, there will be no cleaning them upstairs anymore. That's my living room now. Just wanted to set expectations. Loyalty doesn't extend that far."

He laughed. "I never let that crook touch my fish anyway. Your living room is safe from me." He tipped his hat to me, then turned his boat and chugged away, a slow, relaxed speed that made me think that Bryan might have the best life on the lake.

Then I looked around at the carnage strewn around me, and my happiness faded. I wasn't going to let the Derby Moose ruin my lake or my marina.

I was going to fight back.

CHAPTER 11

An hour later, I was shivering with cold, soaking wet, and trapped in cracked, crusty neoprene that smelled like other people's body odor. I had splinters in both hands. And the pile of broken wood on my dock had barely made a dent in the debris floating in the lake.

Discouraged? Yes.

Cranky? Absolutely.

Regretting my decision to flee to Bass Derby? On the razor-sharp edge.

I was on the precipice of plunging into a soggy swamp of self-pity when Hattie's truck shot into the parking lot, skidded across the dirt, and fishtailed perfectly into the corner spot down by the water.

She leapt out of the truck, took one look at me, and trotted down the ramp. She was wearing jeans, a pink T-shirt with "Hattie's Café" written on it in curvy, blue letters, and black boots that looked like she meant business. And, noticeably, she was dry and not shivering, which meant I was immediately jealous.

"I don't even know what to ask first," she said, putting her hands on her hips as she surveyed the scene. "Where on earth did you get that outfit?"

"From the store. I think Rusty rented it out. To a lot of people. And never washed it. But joyfully, I was able to get it on once I stripped off all my clothes except my sports bra and underwear, so it's touching my bare skin pretty much everywhere."

I tried really hard not to think about that. Success rate? Moderate at best.

"Dare I ask *why* you decided on that particular attire for the morning?"

"Because I wanted to clean up the lake."

Her gaze darted to the pile of wood on the dock, and the pieces still floating in the water. "What happened?"

"Derby Moose." I was pretty proud of myself that I could rattle that off like a local.

"Well, you go, girl." She set her hands on her hips. "You awoke the beast when you killed that sign."

"Oh, come on." I heaved part of a post onto the dock, where it landed with an ungrateful thud. "I didn't hit the sign. You know that."

"Of course I know. It's fun to see you get all defensive." Hattie crouched down on the dock, her face suddenly serious. "Are you okay? The Derby Moose can be aggressive."

The concern in her voice almost made me laugh. "They're moose who ride Jet Skis. How scary can they be?"

"Hard to say. Some of the people they harassed may have just moved."

I waved impatiently. "As opposed to—?"

"Who knows why people vanish, right? Sometimes they have good reason."

"Vanish?" I paused, considering the implications. "You mean they kidnap people? Or kill them?"

"Never proven. I'm sure you're fine." She eyed the broken fragments. "It's been a long time since they've been on the lake. Maybe they've mellowed a bit."

Her lack of conviction made me slightly concerned, but honestly, I had much bigger things to deal with than moose bullies. "I'm sure they're harmless. But how was Lucy when you dropped her off?" I heaved another board onto the dock.

"Worried but cool. She's good." Hattie took the next board from me and set it beside the others. "Any more thoughts on the case?"

"Actually yes." My brain had refused to shut off after they'd left, and I'd been trying to put pieces together. Some had seemed to fit. I rested my arms on the dock. I was afraid if I got out of the cold water that I'd never get back in. So I stayed where I was. "You know how Lucy said the killer threw the poker at her?"

She nodded. "Yep."

"He clearly knew how to take someone out with it. Why would he just toss it at her, instead of hitting her?"

"Because he didn't want to kill her. Obviously."

"But why wouldn't he want to kill her? She was a witness." These were all the questions that had kept hammering at my brain all night, until I'd finally started to come up with some answers.

"He didn't want to add another body to his count, I assume." Hattie frowned. "Not all murderers like to go on killing rampages."

"Yeah, maybe." I paused for dramatic flair, because I was pretty proud of what I'd come up with. "Or maybe it was because he wanted to set her up for the murder."

"Oh..." Hattie rocked back on her heels. "*Oh.*"

"Right?" My time with my mom and spying on Stanley had taught me a lot about the importance of details, and what stories they told. "What if he knew she had baton experience? What if he knew she would catch it and get her fingerprints on it?"

Hattie narrowed her eyes. "You mean he specifically chose *her*?"

I shrugged. "Maybe. She had motive, so she was a good choice, as we already know. If Chief Stone thinks he has his murderer, he won't look any further." I paused. "How many people knew we were going there last night?"

"I didn't tell anyone. Let me text Lucy and see if she did." She pulled out her phone and typed a quick message.

I leaned my arms on the dock and rested my chin on my hands. "If he didn't plan it, then, he took advantage of her arrival. Which meant he recognized her immediately and knew she would make a solid suspect."

Hattie sat down cross-legged. "So, it had to be someone who knows Lucy well enough to know that she did baton twirling. And that she's strong enough to have killed Rex. And that she dated him."

"How long is that list?"

"Not everyone in town knows that, but many people do. But if you cross-reference it with the people who Rex cheated, not as long." She grinned and patted my shoulder. "Good start, Mia. I knew that FBI spy stuff would come in handy."

"Hattie! That never happened, remember?"

She winked. "Never happened. But I'm glad it did." Her phone dinged, and she looked down at it. "Lucy didn't tell anyone we were going over there last night."

"Bummer." I sighed. "It's so much more fun when it's easy."

"Nonsense. Challenge makes us grow." She stood up. "I need to start cooking. Be there for lunch." She didn't wait for an answer. She just hurried off, racing up the dock with a speed that most twenty-year-olds would envy.

I wanted to be like her when I was her age. She was such a great example that age is mental. I had a feeling Hattie would probably outlive me.

I couldn't help but grin as I sank back into the cold water. It was fun to be using my brain again for the things I'd trained for.

But I'd have to be careful.

I couldn't afford to get involved in anything illegal.

My marina needed an owner of the utmost upstanding and moral character. It was bad enough that I had an illicit past. If I added to that with new illegal activities? I'd have no chance at rebuilding community trust.

I had to stay legit. For my future. For my home.

No matter what Hattie tried to drag me into, I had to make sure I didn't cross that line.

I had a feeling she wasn't going to make that easy for me. The thought made me grin. It would be fun to battle with Hattie.

No. No grinning.

Being pushed across legal lines would be bad.

Not fun.

Bad, the kind of bad that would derail my last chance at happiness.

I needed to remember that. The old Mia could *not* come back to life. She simply couldn't.

BY THE TIME I finished my cold-water cleanup, the sun was high in the sky, my skin was permanently attached to the crusted neoprene that had done a masterful job keeping me from dying of hypothermia, and the parking lot was filled with cars.

Well, maybe not filled, but there'd been a constant stream of vehicles since six.

How many of them had gone into the Eagle's Nest?

Zero, plus or minus zero.

Everyone had been going into Hattie's café.

Some people had walked out within a few minutes, holding steaming coffee.

Others had carried out bags of food.

And a fair number of them had taken up residence at her tables. I could see them through the window, chatting, eating, and pointing at me as I waded through chest-deep water. I gave them friendly waves, but when all I got in return were stares, I realized that it was going to take a lot more than that to gain their trust.

Maybe I should yell at them like I'd done with Bryan? Or maybe not.

I finally threw the last board onto the dock and leaned on it, trying to catch my breath. My arms and legs were shaking from the effort of slogging through the water for hours, but I also felt vibrantly alive. Taking care of the water had been personal. My lake. My marina. An investment in my forever.

I loved it so much.

I scanned the water around the docks for any last remnants of the sign. To my surprise, Cargo's beautiful green canoe/motorboat was tied up in the last slip. When had he arrived? I hadn't even seen him come in.

It sounded as if I was going to like Cargo. I was excited to get to meet him today.

King Tut was sitting on the dock next to the gas pump, soaking wet from his morning swim. He stretched out in front of me, staring at me as the water dripped from his fur, through cracks between the boards, and into the lake with a steady drip-drip-drip.

I rested my chin on my forearms and grinned at him. "This is the life, right?"

He flicked his tail and purred, not seeming to mind that his ears were so heavy with water that they drooped.

"I hear you. It's great out there, isn't it?" The cold water was invigorating. It was awesome watching the fish dart out of my way as I moved. I enjoyed seeing the boats cruising by on the main part of the lake. The air smelled crisp and clean, and I could almost feel the years of grime washing off my soul.

The pile of sign fragments was impressively large. The Moose Crazies had managed to throw pretty much every sliver into the water, including those with nails, paint, and stain. The Derby Moose were industrious and thorough, despite the ridiculous costumes.

Eventually satisfied I'd finally salvaged everything, I braced my hands on the dock and tried to boost myself out of the water. I made it only about four inches off the bottom of the lake, nowhere near enough to get onto the dock. Arm strength? Not my forté.

No problem. I'd install a ladder. Despite what Hattie said, easy solutions were great. We needed a few more in a hurry, and hopefully we'd get them today.

I ignored King Tut's disdainful stare and started wading toward shore instead. I'd made it only a few yards when an SUV pulled into the parking lot.

It was blue.

Familiar.

And the entire left side of the front fender was crushed.

It was the SUV that had run over the sign and almost killed me.

CHAPTER 12

"HEY! HEY!" I stumbled as I slogged my way to shore, waving my arms. "Hey! Hattie! That's the car! That's the car!"

A few people in the parking lot turned to look at me, but no one seemed at all concerned about a soggy woman splashing toward shore shouting. They just continued on to their cars, sipping their coffee and chatting. Maybe that was a normal sight in Bass Derby.

King Tut ran along the ramp beside me, meowing encouragement as I struggled through the water.

The SUV pulled up in front of the marina. I saw feet appear, and the driver ran into the café. The vehicle was blocking my view so I couldn't see who it was, but they'd definitely gone into Hattie's.

Holy cow. I was impressed with the audacity of the driver to show up here, when I was being blamed and harassed for killing the sign.

I reached shore, climbed up the bank, and then ran through the parking lot, King Tut bounding delightedly by my side. The wet suit made a weird rubbing noise as I ran, and my feet were squishing in the little booties. It was insanely awkward to run in, but there was no way I was letting the driver get away.

I lurched up the steps to the café, shuffled across the deck, flung the door open, and then blocked the doorway with my body. "Stop!"

The entire place went silent as everyone turned to look at me. There were at least twenty tables, with forty or fifty customers. All of them had paused, some of them with their fork halfway to their mouths as they gaped at me.

Whoops.

I'd totally forgotten about customers when I'd charged in here to find the sign killer. That probably wasn't the best way to introduce myself to the people I wanted to win over.

Time to pivot. I replaced my fierce expression with a friendly smile and an amiable wave. "Heeeyy." I gave my voice a cheerful singsong. "I'm Mia Murphy. I own the marina now. I'm really looking forward to getting to know everyone."

Silence. Except for the drip, drip, drip off my wetsuit.

King Tut sat on my foot and meowed.

I tried again. "I'm running a special this week. Fifty percent off all services and gas."

Again, silence.

Where was Hattie? I needed her to put in a good word for me.

But Hattie wasn't there. It was just me, and a bunch of folks who didn't seem impressed that a flatlander in a crusty, too-tight wetsuit, and a soggy cat had interrupted their breakfast, which actually looked really good. I could see a couple quiches on plates, along with a few stacks of pancakes, and even what looked like Eggs Benedict.

I really loved Eggs Benedict.

The café smelled delicious, as if fresh bread was in the oven. A white, antique wood-fired oven was at the back of the room. Was Hattie actually baking bread in it? That was genius. I'd eat here every day for the rest of my life just to breathe that in.

The café had charm. The ceiling beams were low, exposed wood, and there were white metal poles placed strategically, prob-

tle	DOUBLE TWIST (A MIA MURPHY MYSTE
ondition	Good
ocation	Walden Aisle J Bay 07 Item 11327
escription	May have some shelf-wear due to normal use. Your purchase funds free job training and education in the greater Seattle area. Thank you for supporting Goodwill's nonprofit mission!
ource	Prescanned
KU	0KVOG10015XY
SIN	1940968941
ode	9781940968940
nployee	1nmanzoni
ate Added	4/3/2024 5:30:55 PM

itle	DOUBLE TWIST (A MIA MURPHY MYSTE
ondition	Good
ocation	Walden Aisle 1 Bay 07 Item 11327
escription	May have some shelf wear due to normal use. Your purchase funds free job training and education in the greater Seattle area. Thank you for supporting Goodwill's nonprofit mission!
ource	Prescanned
KU	0KVOG.001SX
SIN	1940968941
ode	9781940968940
mployee	Jimmunzon
ate Added	4/3/2024 5:30:55 PM

ably holding up the ceiling. It was a little dingy, but definitely homey and welcoming.

It was way nicer than the marina store.

At that moment, the door to the kitchen opened. I expected to see Hattie, but instead, a set of matching, muscular, tall guys in their early twenties came rushing through, flashing dimpled smiles at the room as they balanced trays of food. They were both wearing T-shirts that said "Hattie's Café" on them. One had a purple shirt, and the other had a turquoise one, but other than that, they looked identical. Their dark hair and features made me pretty certain they were actual Greek gods who had blessed this little corner of the world with their presence.

One of them glided toward the back corner of the café with an athletic grace that eluded all but the most gifted of humans.

The one with the purple shirt headed straight for me. "Welcome to Hattie's Café," he said, not even blinking an eye at my dripping wetsuit or the cat by my ankle. "I'll be right with you."

He effortlessly handed out the meals, chatting cheerfully with all the patrons, calling each of them by name, asking them about their kids, their work, or their boat, with detail that was beyond impressive. Everyone beamed at him, and the café seemed to wrap around me with its warmth.

I never wanted to leave.

He finished handing out Hattie's brilliant creations, and then walked back over to me. "My name is Niko Stefanopoulous. We require street clothes inside, but I'd be happy to seat you on the deck. Are you new to town?"

His white teeth were nearly blinding in their perfection, and his dark eyelashes were so long and thick that he could almost be a cover model for a makeup company. I blinked, trying to stay focused. "I'm Mia Murphy. The new—"

"Our new landlord! Of course!" He flashed adorable dimples at me and shook my hand vigorously, his grip strong and manly. He was about ten years too young for me, but he was the eye candy that every woman needs in her day. "It's fantastic to meet you," he said. "Hattie said you're awesome. Who do you think murdered Rex? She said you were there last night with her."

I blinked, startled by his question. I hadn't been thinking about the murder at that moment. "I don't know—"

"Oh, you were there, too!" A younger couple in their mid-twenties at a nearby table leaned in. "Was it true there was blood everywhere?"

I grimaced. "It was more like a little pool."

An old dude in jeans, a faded T-shirt, and sneakers that had to be at least twenty years old tapped my elbow. "Did Chief Stone really flash the hash in Rex's yard?"

"Flash the hash?" I had no idea what that meant.

"Yeah. I heard he took one look at the body and that was it." He waved his hands by his mouth, indicating projectile food. "Salute to the Technicolor gods."

Ah…I got it. "He might have," I hedged, not really wanting it to get back to Chief Stone that I was telling people about his inglorious moment.

"Hey." A woman near the window waved her hands to get my attention. She was wearing a bright red headscarf, a red blouse, and jeans. Her dark hair was streaked with enough gray to make her look regal. "Hattie said that the murderer trampled you when he was escaping. That he threw you into a tree, and you almost died. Did you see who it was?"

Everyone stopped eating to wait for my answer. I cleared my throat. "Actually, I kinda threw myself into the tree, and I did *not* see who it was." I spoke very clearly, so Rex's killer would not decide he had to come back to eliminate the witness.

There was a resounding sigh of disappointment.

Niko grinned at the woman. "Hattie already said they didn't know, Yaya."

I raised my brows. "She's your grandma?"

Niko nodded as his grandma waved her arm in greeting. "Angelina Stefanopoulous," she shouted. "Hattie said you're trouble in a thousand ways, Mia. Great to meet you!"

Hattie. She would tell people that, wouldn't she? I gave her a non-troublesome smile and waved back. "Nice to meet you, too!"

"Did you smell him?" It was the old, ratty-looking dude again.

I glanced at him. "Smell who?"

"Rex's killer, when he ran into you." He nodded. "Did he smell like he fished? Worked with wood? Steel? Smoke a pipe? Cigar?"

Wow. Those were actually really good questions. "I didn't notice."

He shook his head in visible disappointment. "You have to notice things like that. What about sound?"

"Sound?"

"Was he wheezing? Did he run lightly? Tread heavily? Footsteps tell a lot about weight and size."

I stared at him. "Those are excellent questions."

A smile flashed across his face. "I know. What about the answers?"

"I get an F. I didn't notice anything." But now I almost wanted to go back to that moment so I could. I definitely hadn't taken advantage of the opportunity. "His sweater caught in my lock…in my keys, though. Maybe there's a hole in his sleeve."

"A hole?"

"Maybe."

He laughed. "Next time you run into a killer fleeing a scene, now you'll be better prepared."

"Next time?"

He grinned. "You never know."

"God, I hope not." I liked him, though. I stuck out my hand. "Mia Murphy. I'm the new owner of the Eagle's Nest."

"I know." He took my hand, his grip solid and strong despite his age. "Beau Hammerly. Nice to meet you, Mia Murphy."

"Beau Hammerly?" I inspected him more closely. "Not, *the* Beau Hammerly?" Beau Hammerly was the name of a very, *very* successful mystery writer. Many of his books had been made into movies, and two of the hottest streaming shows were based on his books as well. His new releases were a fixture at the top of the

New York Times bestseller list. His net worth was probably at least 100 million dollars.

This Beau Hammerly looked like he'd never set foot outside of the town, or spent more than twenty dollars on a pair of jeans.

This Beau raised his brows at my question. "I'm just a resident of Bass Derby, same as you."

Holy cow. That wasn't a denial, which meant it definitely was a yes. But if he wanted to stay low key, I could relate. I took a breath and tried to squash my fangirl. I could be chill about meeting him. "Right then. I get it. May I join you for a moment?"

He raised his brows. "You're wet."

"I know, but I own the place, so it's fine." I pulled out a chair and sat down across from him. "How long have you lived in this town?"

Niko made a strangled noise, hovering over us with those cute dimples. "We don't bother Mr. Hammerly when he comes to eat here. House rules."

"It's my house, so I can change the rules." I beamed at Beau as King Tut sauntered over and curled up on my foot. "You don't mind, do you? I want to channel your expertise for a few minutes."

Beau leaned back in his seat and hooked his thumbs through his belt loops. "I can't say I do mind," he said with an easy drawl. "We're good, Niko."

Niko looked close to apoplectic, but he nodded and left us alone.

Beau raised his brows at me. "Are you a writer?"

"Me? No way. That's not one of my skills."

"What are your skills?"

I gave him a thoughtful look. "I could take anything out of your pockets, and you'd never know it."

Interest flashed across his face, and he leaned forward. "Do tell."

Hah. I had a feeling I would interest him. "I'd love to, but I'm on a mission."

"What kind of mission?"

"To catch Rex's killer."

More interest flashed in his eyes. "Isn't that what the police are for?"

"The police have limitations." I waved my hand dismissively. "What do you know about Rex? Who would have wanted to kill him? I bet you keep track of this town. I bet you know things."

His smile widened. "I do know things. Many things." He lowered his voice. "For example, I know you're the daughter of Tatum Murphy."

My smile froze. "What?"

"People interest me. I keep track. Your mother sounds fascinating. I'd like to meet her. I watched the documentary on her three times."

The made-for-TV documentary had spent some time talking about the mother-daughter team of Tatum and her bold and audacious little girl, Mia. I cleared my throat. "I haven't seen her in a decade. You'll have to make do with me."

Beau studied me, clearly contemplating whether that was a satisfactory option.

"I want info about Rex," I said, forging onward. "What do you know?" I needed to get a picture of Rex in my mind. I barely knew anything about him. Beau had to know something. He was one of the greatest puzzle-minds ever to type a word. People like Beau did exactly what he'd claimed to do when he'd said he kept track of people.

He shrugged. "Rex didn't interest me. I didn't bother with him."

I could tell he was telling the truth. Shoot.

"He had a girlfriend, you know." The woman at the next table leaned over. "I'm Opal Turner, and I'm not talking about Lucy. He had another pie in his pantry, if you get my drift."

I spun around to face her. She had brown hair up in a ponytail, a pink sweater, and jeans. Her face was slightly lined, suggesting she was maybe in her early fifties, but it was difficult to tell for sure. "Who?"

"I don't know, but my husband Ralph is an electrician. He went to Marco's house to collect money Rex owed him, and he heard them riding the hobby horse. Lucy was on her route, so it wasn't her."

A cheating lover? That gave Lucy motive, which was not the helpful information I'd been hoping for. *Crud.*

Beau grinned and leaned back in his seat to listen, so I did the same.

"That Rex was a cheater all around," Opal continued. "He owed my husband almost five hundred dollars to fix up the electrical so he could put his dad's house on the market, but then he decided not to sell it and canceled the project. Rex wouldn't pay my husband for what he'd already done, and then he went and died."

"Your husband died?" I asked.

She and Beau both gave me a look that said I was an idiot. "Rex," she said. "Rex died. You remember you were at his murder last night?"

Oh, right. Duh. "Did Rex do that a lot?"

"Die?"

"Cheat people."

Opal nodded. "All the time. To everyone."

"He sounds charming," I said, hoping to urge her on.

"Charming?" She snorted, then sighed. "Okay, so yes, Rex could be very charming."

"And easy on the eyes," someone else chimed in.

"Definitely easy on the eyes," Opal acknowledged. "But still a cheat. It's incredibly inconvenient that someone got to him before we all got our money from him. My sister Wanda works for the law firm handling Marco's death, and she heard that Rex was going to get a hefty sum from his dad's estate. But now Rex is dead, so who knows where that will go?"

Well, that was a very good question. Where was that money

going to go? Suddenly, it made a lot of sense to follow that money trail, instead of looking for the people Rex had cheated. No one could get money from a dead man, so people like Opal's husband wouldn't have killed him. But whoever was getting the inheritance had a very good reason to knock him off. "Does Wanda know who's going to get it now?"

She shook her head. "Nope. It's all locked up and hush hush."

Huh. "Did he have any relatives?"

The woman shrugged. "Marco's wife took off about twenty years ago, and there are no other kids. Rex never married or knocked anyone up. If there's family around, I don't know it. Anyone know who's getting their money?"

The folks nearby, who had all stopped eating to listen, shook their heads.

"There you have it." She waved her hands. "Cheaters die, and no one benefits."

Someone had benefited.

"Mia!" Hattie shouted my name, and I looked up. She was standing in the doorway to her kitchen, her hands on her hips. "What is wrong with you? You're dripping on my floor. And you brought a *cat* into my café? I could lose my license for that!"

Beau chuckled under his breath as I shot to my feet. "Sorry." I extricated my foot from under King Tut's soggy bottom, hefted the hairy beast into my arms, and scurried back over the threshold so I was standing on the deck. The sign-destroying SUV was still outside, taunting me. Somewhere in that café was the person who'd almost driven over me. "I came here because I wanted to ask you about—"

Her eyes widened, and she cut me off. "Everyone, I'd like you to give a warm welcome to Mia Murphy. She's my new business partner at the marina." She met my gaze. "She's a good one."

Several of the people in the café raised their coffee mugs at me, and I heard a few "Welcomes" and "Great to meet yous" drift my way. I even got a smile from one woman.

The awesome power of Hattie.

She clapped her hands. "The muffins will be out of the oven in three minutes, so if you're waiting on them, they're coming. Mia, meet me around back." She gave me a look and then turned and went back around the corner.

Right. "Nice to meet you all!" I jiggled King Tut as my best effort at waving. "Thanks, Beau," I added.

He nodded. "I still want to meet your mother."

"I'll let her know if I ever hear from her." I quickly darted out of the café, noting the dented fender and the streaks of paint and slivers of wood in the grill of the Jeep parked out front.

Definitely the SUV that had killed that poor sign.

I was willing to bet Hattie knew who it belonged to, which meant I was about to find out who had nearly run me down.

Someone in that café had almost killed me.

I hoped it wasn't Beau.

CHAPTER 13

Still holding King Tut, I squished around the building as quickly as I could until I found the back door to the café. I pulled open the wooden screen door and peered inside.

The kitchen was smaller than I'd expected. It was old and well-used, but it was impeccably clean. There were bins of veggies on the counter, and they looked fresh and crisp. It was the kitchen of a professional, an interior that far outclassed the run-down building that housed it.

I wasn't sure what I'd expected, but I was impressed.

Hattie was moving swiftly at the counter, putting together breakfast sandwiches. The turquoise-shirted hot Greek was with her, chopping carrots into little flowers with impressive speed and dexterity. He didn't even look up when I walked in, and I could hear him humming to himself as he worked.

"Hattie," I whispered.

She looked over her shoulder. "What are you doing, about to ask me about the murder in front of everyone?" she hissed. "I could see it on your face."

"It wasn't about the murder. It was about the Jeep out front. Who owns it?" I stepped into the kitchen.

"Halt." She pointed a spatula at me. "No cat. I'll lose my permit."

King Tut had purred himself into a soggy nap in my arms. I kissed his head, and then set him down on top of a wooden crate behind the building. He stretched out in the sun, not even bothering to open his eyes.

Life was good for the purloined cat. I was glad I'd given him a chance at a better life.

I tried to enter the kitchen a second time, but again, Hattie pointed at me, this time with a butter knife covered in what looked like basil aioli. My mouth started watering just a little bit.

"No puddles. Ditch the wetsuit."

"You have no idea how much I'd love to do that, but I'm wearing only my underwear under this thing."

The carrot-chopping Greek looked up at that, glanced over at me, then quickly went back to work, his cheeks turning pink.

How cute was he? I wanted to collect him and enshrine him.

"Then stay outside." Hattie hurried over to the griddle and started flipping pancakes. "Why do you want to know whose Jeep that is?"

"Because it's the one that almost ran me down and destroyed the Bass Derby sign."

"What?" She paused, the hot pink spatula hovering over the griddle. "Are you certain?"

"Absolutely. Who owns it?"

She held up her hand to silence me, and then turned to her sous chef. "Cris, can you run out front and see if Niko needs help? He's been out there a while."

He glanced at me, then nodded. "Sure thing, Hattie. Be right back." He left his knife in place and headed out.

The minute the door shut behind him, Hattie turned toward me. "Cris is quiet and a good kid, but it's better to keep him out of this."

I'd been right. Hattie knew who owned the Jeep, and it was big. "Who owns it?"

Before she could speak, the door to the restaurant section opened again and Lucy popped her head through the doorway. "Your bathroom is almost out of toilet paper, Hattie." Her face brightened when she saw me, giving me a warm smile. "Oh, hey, Mia. Hattie told me about the Derby Moose. You need to call Chief Stone about that. They're bad news."

"They're moose. I'm not worried." Annoyed, yes? Worried? It was difficult to muster fear of people dressed like moose after spending two years waiting for my ex to chop me up into little pieces. Perspective, and all that. I was so glad to see Lucy hadn't been arrested yet. "Did you get your car back?"

"I did." Her smile faded. "He wrecked it. Obviously, I'm not going to get any money from him to fix it." She paused. "Is that crass? Complaining that he can't pay me because he's dead? It felt a little crass."

"The guy was a pig," Hattie said. "It's fine, right, Mia?"

"Yeah, I agree." I'd never met Rex, but I had my own share of issues around my ex, so who was I to judge? Then I realized what she'd said. "Wait a sec. He *wrecked* it? Is the blue Jeep out front *yours?*"

Lucy nodded. "Sure is. Did you see the dent? How do you even do that to a car?"

"By driving it into the Welcome to Bass Derby sign," I said. "That would do it quite nicely."

Lucy stared at me, and then I saw awareness dawn. "It was *my* car that hit the sign?"

"It was that Jeep, so if that's yours, yes."

"Holy cow." She walked into the kitchen and let the door drop shut behind her, looking stunned. "No one will believe I wasn't driving it. I don't want Derby Moose at my house!"

"Of course you weren't driving it," I said. "It was in Rex's garage. Devlin and Chief Stone both saw it."

"It was there in the evening. I could have been the one driving it earlier. Maybe I hit the sign and then got caught by Rex when I was hiding it in his garage. Maybe he threatened to report me, so I killed him."

I stared at her. "Why would you kill him over a sign?" Who on earth would believe that?

"People murder for less than that," Hattie said. "You know that."

She had a point. I did know that. I knew more than I wanted to know about the seedier side of humanity.

"It's Bass Derby," Lucy added. "That sign is a big deal. People would definitely murder over it. I mean, the Derby Moose came back to life to avenge it, right?"

"You think the Derby Moose are planning a revenge murder to avenge the sign?" Because it was my car that had had the loon in the windshield. Evidence never lies, right? At least to a posse of murderous moose.

Had I literally just thought "murderous moose?"

I was losing my mind. No one was going to kill me over the sign. But as I looked at Hattie and Lucy's solemn faces, some of my conviction ebbed away. They looked genuinely worried about the longevity of whoever had killed the sign.

I decided to change the subject and focus on more cheerful things, like Rex's murder. "I was talking to Opal Turner, and she mentioned that Rex was supposed to inherit a bunch of money from his dad before he died. Do either of you know about that?"

"He wouldn't talk about it," Lucy said. "But I got the sense it was a lot."

Hattie tapped her spatula on the grill, eyeing me thoughtfully. "You think Rex was murdered for the inheritance? I can't believe I didn't think of that."

"Maybe. Any chance you guys know who inherits Marco's estate now that Rex is dead?"

"No." Hattie's eyes gleamed. "But that's an excellent question."

Lucy shook her head. "I don't know either."

I rubbed my jaw. "Do you know the name of the law firm his dad was using?" I asked reluctantly. I couldn't believe I was getting this involved. I'd sworn I wouldn't, but I couldn't stay away.

Lucy nodded. "Dutch, Dutch, & Smith. They have an office in town, next to Dutch's Supply."

Hattie grinned. "Let's sneak in there tonight. You can pick the lock, and we'll find out."

I had to admit, it sounded like fun, but breaking into a lawyer's office to steal confidential files wasn't the same as breaking into Rex's garage to repossess Lucy's car. "I'm not picking the lock." I paused at their disappointed faces, then sighed. "There are easier ways that aren't going to get us arrested."

They both looked intrigued. "Like what?" Lucy asked.

I cleared my throat. "We could talk our way in." I grimaced as I said it. Conning my way into those files was treading dangerously close to waking up the old Mia, who wasn't allowed to come back to life.

"*Talk* our way in?" Lucy sounded a little skeptical.

"What, like pretend you want to write a new will now that you're divorced?" Hattie asked.

"Something like that," I hedged. That wasn't *exactly* what I'd had in mind.

"Hah. I see the look on your face," Hattie barked. "You're trouble, Mia Murphy. I love that so much."

I couldn't help but grin, then remembered that I wasn't trouble anymore. "I'm not helping with the illegal stuff," I reminded her.

"For now." Hattie winked at me.

"Ever." I set my hands on my hips and tried to focus. "How did Marco get all his money?" The more I knew, the better chance I had at figuring out the right approach.

Lucy shrugged. "Cheating people, probably."

"Male prostitute," Hattie declared. "It's the only possibility. He was too stupid and too good-looking for anything else." She raised her brows at Lucy. "Did Rex ever ask you to pay him for sex?"

"What?" Lucy threw a roll at Hattie. "Don't be crass. I'd never pay for sex."

Hattie snatched it effortlessly out of the air. "I would, if he was hot enough. Why not?"

"Because that's gross."

"It keeps things simple." Hattie patted her breasts. "Once a man gets a chance with the girls, he can never move on. It's like emotional quicksand."

I grinned suddenly. She'd just given me an idea on how to find out who inherited Rex's inheritance. All I needed was a little more info. "Opal said Rex was selling Marco's house and then changed his mind. Do you know why?"

"He was going to move to Florida and buy a house on the beach," Lucy said. "That's why he was selling."

"Florida?" I frowned. "Why Florida?"

"Marco and Rusty used to rent a place in Florida during the winter and split time there," Hattie said. "That's where Rusty met the woman he's been shacking up with for the last decade while he abandoned the marina."

Lucy nodded. "Marco would take Rex there on school vacations sometimes. Rex wanted to go there permanently."

Ah…I understood about the allure of following in your parent's footsteps. "Do you know why Rex changed his mind?"

"No." Lucy shook her head. "Even Ruby Lee couldn't get it out of him. She was the one who had listed the house. He changed his mind the day before the buyers were supposed to close on the house."

"Ruby Lee? The woman who sold me the marina?" I was surprised Rex had managed to say no to her. She was like a tsunami masquerading as an innocent puddle.

"Yeah." Lucy nodded. "Even Ruby Lee couldn't get him to change his mind."

Hmm… "You think Ruby Lee would have killed him?"

"How would she have killed him? She weighs about two pounds and struggles to lift a pencil," Hattie said as she finished plating some delicious-looking egg sandwiches. "He wouldn't even have felt it if she hit him with a poker, let alone died from it."

Good point. I'd met Ruby Lee. I knew she was tiny. I also knew that she was morally flexible, although I didn't know how far she was willing to bend.

Niko, the purple shirt, came back into the kitchen, and Hattie handed him the plates. He gave us all an adorable smile, then headed back out. "Are they twins?" I knew I should be focused on Rex, but I couldn't stop from asking. They were just such an unexpected gift to the world.

"Yep," Hattie said. "Bunch of trouble, but their grandma pays me to keep them employed."

"You're such a liar," Lucy scoffed, putting her hands on her hips as she turned to me. "The Stefanopoulous twins were complete terrors when they were little, but when they came to live with Angelina after their parents disappeared in the Brazilian jungle, Hattie gave them work and trained them. They're both in college on football scholarships now, but Cris is planning to be a chef like Hattie, and Niko is planning to go for his Ph.D. in biophysics."

"Wow." As beautiful as they were, they weren't relying on their looks to get them through life. "That's so impressive."

Hattie rolled her eyes and went back to cooking, but Lucy nodded. "They wouldn't have done it without Hattie. I also worked for her for years while I was going to college, until I started delivering mail. She helped me so much, too." She grinned at me. "She cares. She pretends to be all tough, but our Hattie has a heart of gold. "

"I can see that." No wonder Hattie had been willing to hide the body for Lucy. I understood more about her now, and I liked what I saw. She might be a little dismissive of the law, but her passion was awesome.

Hattie grumped under her breath as she pulled muffins out of the oven, but Lucy ignored her. "I need to get going," Lucy said. "What's our plan?"

Hattie opened the oven to check on some quiche that smelled amazing. "Mia? What's your idea for the law firm?"

I quickly filled them in. By the time I finished, they were both laughing so hard tears were rolling down their cheeks.

"I would love to see that so much," Lucy said. "Holy cow."

"You can't be there. You'd give it away," Hattie said.

"I know, but dear heavens. Mia, you're amazing."

I grinned. "Well, let's see if it works first." It had been so long since I'd tried something like what I'd just told them. It sounded so fun. Or, it would be fun if Lucy's freedom didn't raise the stakes so high. That was a little sobering.

"I'll go with you," Hattie said.

"You?" I frowned. "They'll recognize you."

"No chance. I got it covered. Please let me go with you." Hattie grinned. "I'm extremely versatile, I swear."

"You're literally a landmark in this town," Lucy said. "There's no chance you wouldn't be recognized. You can't go either."

I couldn't take the feel of the neoprene anymore, so while they argued, I grabbed the Velcro holding the shoulder straps on and unfastened them. I dragged the bib down to my waist, not even caring that I was wearing only a sports bra. The cool air was glorious against my skin, and I half-considered dragging the rest of it right off.

Hattie eyed my bare upper body. "It's illegal to walk around in a sports bra in Bass Derby."

I paused. "Really?"

"No, not really. What do you think we are? A bunch of prudes?"

I opened my mouth and then closed it. I wasn't sure what I thought about the residents of Bass Derby yet. "We need to search Lucy's Jeep. Just in case Rex left anything in there."

"I can't do it now," Hattie said as Cris came back in, dumped a bunch of plates in the sink, and started working on the carrots again. "This is my busy time." She said something to Cris, and then disappeared into her walk-in freezer.

"I can't either," Lucy said. "My next stop is the town office, and my aunt gives me grief if I'm late."

"Your aunt?"

"Eloise Stone. The mayor. Chief Stone's mom. "

"She's your *aunt?*" I did the math with impressive speed. "So Chief Stone is your cousin?"

"Cousin Clyde and Aunt Eloise," Lucy nodded.

"Well, that's good, right? If Chief Stone, I mean Clyde, is your cousin, then why wouldn't he try to keep you out of prison?"

"Heavens, no." She made a face. "They pretend we aren't related."

My gut sank. "As in, they would *want* you to go to prison for murder?"

"I think it would give them a fair amount of joy, yes."

"Why?"

"Family drama. Revenge, spurned love, broken dreams, accidental pregnancy. Fun stuff like that." She waved her hand dismissively. "Nothing interesting."

"That's totally interesting." I definitely wanted to hear about it. "What happened?"

She grimaced. "We try not to talk about it."

"My ex-mother-in-law tried to kill me with a machine gun and a professional hit man, so I get family drama."

She raised her brows. "You're kidding."

"Swear. I liked her until then, but you know, that kind of thing is a buzzkill on relationships."

"Totally." She relaxed a bit. "So, my aunt Eloise wanted to become a movie star. She went to Hollywood to make it, but she failed, got knocked up with Clyde, and had to come skulking home. When she arrived, Eloise found my mom had married the boyfriend that Eloise had dumped to go to Hollywood. My aunt said my mom had stolen him, there was a big family brouhaha, and now she and Clyde, Chief Stone, want me to suffer for all my mom's sins."

"Chief Stone has to be in his twenties. That's some long-standing hatred." Holy cow. The stakes had just shot up for the looming murder charge that had suddenly turned into an opportunity for a personal vendetta. "We need to search your Jeep as soon as we can."

"I stop serving at two," Hattie said as she returned from the walk-in freezer. "The doors close when the last person leaves." She handed Lucy a takeout bag that made me a little jealous. "We can meet then."

I looked at Lucy. "Does that timing work for you?"

She nodded as she took the food. "I can adjust my route." She stood up and gave Hattie some money. "I'll see you guys then."

"Try not to touch much in the car," I said. "You don't want to accidentally mess up some detail that will be significant." My mom and I had survived on details. I'd survived StanleyGate on details. And Beau Hammerly, mystery writer superstar, had reminded me how important they were.

"I'll be careful. See you guys in a few hours!" Lucy hurried out the back door, leaving me in the kitchen with Hattie, who had just pulled the quiche out of the oven.

My stomach rumbled as I caught a whiff of it. I was a terrible chef, but I could appreciate good food all day long. "How much for a piece?"

"For you? $6.99."

"How much is it normally?"

"$6.99. Friends don't ask friends for freebies. Friends offer to pay extra to support each other." She cut a generous piece, put it in a takeout container, and held it out to me with a wink. "You can take it out of my monthly rent."

I took it happily. "How much do you pay in rent?"

"Nothing. It's free. We do profit-sharing."

"Really?"

"No, not really. Of course not really." She set her hands on her hips and faced me. "We need to talk."

Uh oh. "Am I in trouble?"

Cris looked over at me and grinned, making me wonder how many times she'd said that to him.

Hattie ignored him. "You need to step up, Mia. Giving away marina services for half-off in some random, unplanned announcement? Not even looking at your contract with me? How do you expect to run a business if you don't get smarter?"

"Hey." I stood taller. "I've been a little busy being stalked by moose, witnessing a murder, and trying to get a dead fish smell out of my apartment," I retorted. "I'll get to it."

"You need vision to be a success," she continued, as if she hadn't heard my protest. "You need to see the big picture, focus on what you want, and then fill in the details to support it. Without a vision, you'll just wind up fishing boards out of the lake until you run out of money." She grabbed a loaf of still-steaming bread and began slicing it. "Get a vision. Work on it. Make it happen."

My fingers tightened on the takeout box. "That was a great speech."

She looked over at me, and her face softened. "I like you, Mia," she said gently. "I can't even tell you how much better you are than Rusty. You need to succeed so I don't have to work for some rude, obnoxious, cheating scumbag again."

"He was a real jerk," Niko said as he walked into the kitchen. "He sucked to work for."

"Hattie's teaching me to be a chef," Cris added. "I need this job."

I let out a breath I didn't know I'd been holding as I looked at the three earnest faces. "Okay."

"Good." Hattie handed me a slice of the fresh, still steaming bread. "Here. On the house, but don't get used to it. Even Niko and Cris have to pay for their own food. I fed them when they were in middle school, but once they hit high school, they had to earn it."

I could have cried I was so happy to have that bread. "Thanks."

She nodded. "Get out of here. We need to work." She snapped

her fingers at the twins. "Back to work, gentlemen. We have a full house."

"I'll see you in a few hours." I took a bite of the bread as I walked out. It literally melted in my mouth, flavors rich with wheat and honey. "You are a bread goddess."

She laughed. "I know. Now go away." She turned to Niko and put him to work dishing up the quiche.

"See ya." I let myself out, leaving behind the delicious smells of the kitchen as I stepped over the threshold onto the rear of my property.

I stopped as reality sunk in.

The dusty dirt was filled with weeds. Old crates were piled up under the trees off to the side. Dented barrels were stacked in a pile behind the kitchen. A cracked and faded hose was sitting randomly in the middle of the parking area. There was also a tractor, several rusted boat trailers, and a picnic table on its side.

It was abandoned and old. The only life in the place was Hattie's café, which was vibrant and energized, filled with the passion she brought to a property that had been trying to die for a long time.

I thought of Hattie's speech. It had taken ten years for Rusty to find a buyer. If I failed, who would buy it?

No one.

The bank would take it, and someone would turn it into a luxury house.

Or Jake would add onto his land grab.

Either way, Hattie would lose her space.

It wasn't just my dream at stake. My success or failure impacted more than just me. Hattie. Niko. Cris. And even the elusive Cargo, who clearly preferred it here, or he would have gone over to the Yacht Club and worked for Jake.

When I'd bought the marina, it had been my dream. My journey. My life. I hadn't thought about the people counting on me for a job. For their livelihood. For their happiness.

But I was thinking about it now.

CHAPTER 14

I CALLED the law firm of Dutch, Dutch, & Smith as soon as I figured out the details of my plan, securing an appointment for four o'clock. It took me about a half hour to get all my gear together, and then, I was stuck in the toughest part of the con life: waiting.

I was too rusty to handle the tension, so I did the only thing I knew how to do, and that was to get busy doing something else.

That something else was getting my marina off the precipice of death.

But how?

I'd stopped by the garage after a quick shower in my slightly less stinky apartment, but all I'd found of Cargo was a still steaming cup of coffee from Hattie's Café, and the crumbs of a blueberry muffin. I'd left him a note to come see me, and then King Tut and I had headed back to the marina store.

"Vision," I said aloud. "Hattie said I need vision."

I stood in the doorway and surveyed the contents, trying to look at it objectively. Optimistically.

The store was a pile of grunge and disorder. The walls were solid wood, but they were covered with wrinkled, faded paper with hand-written signs thumbtacked to the wall.

The glass in the display counter was so thick with dust that I'd actually written "wash me" with my finger in it. Because there was no way to let that level of dust go unrecognized.

There was a sign above the register that listed the types of boats available to rent, and how much the daily rentals were. Apparently, I rented canoes, kayaks, pontoon boats, ski boats, fishing boats, and some little motorboats, but I'd seen only some of those boats on the property.

Under the register were shelves packed with papers and logs. There were no product details, just dates and random notes that I couldn't decipher. I couldn’t even find a list of suppliers, an employment contract with Cargo, or a lease agreement with Hattie. I did find a few other empty "keep cold" cartons like the one that Lucy had delivered. They smelled of fish, which made me not at all interested in dealing with the one currently in the store fridge.

I'd tossed the boxes in the dumpster, added a couple bags of the most egregious trash, but when I walked back in, I didn't know what to do next.

"What can this become?" I kept thinking of Hattie's welcoming café, but I couldn't make this a café. It was a marina.

So, what could I do with it? How could I make it come alive again?

I turned around and looked across the water to the Diamond Lake Yacht Club. There were many docks with slips. Gleaming boats. Blue and white striped umbrellas. White tables set outside with brightly colored flower boxes everywhere. Even from this distance, it looked bright and cheerful. I could see people moving, and boats going in and out. "King Tut?"

The cat chose not to interrupt his nap on the front deck by acknowledging me.

"We need to visit the yacht club." If I could spy on Stanley without getting caught, surely, I could manage to spy on Jake, right? Not that I was going to try anything nefarious. I just needed some sort of inspiration about what this place could become.

Already, the umbrellas and tables had caught my eye. If I could create an interesting space and public Wi-Fi, I could work with Hattie to create a hangout spot on the water. It wouldn't sell boats, but with her food, it would create a positive vibe for people to enjoy after a day on the lake. Quieter than Jake's. More aligned with the tranquility of the lake.

As I inspected the yacht club for ideas, I saw a boat backing out of one of his slips. It was a motorboat with the words Lake Police on it.

Devlin. Maybe he had some info about Rex that I could pry out of him without him realizing it. "Hey!" I broke into a run and jogged down to my dock, waving my arms to get Devlin's attention.

He turned his boat toward me immediately, making me wonder if he'd been planning to come over anyway.

I was glad Lucy had already left.

King Tut sat down beside me, his fluffy tail flicking as we waited for Devlin to pull up. It was late morning, and the sun was bright, making me wish I'd worn my sunglasses.

As it was, I had to shade my eyes and squint as Devlin drifted up to the dock.

He tossed me a bowline, but it hit me in the stomach and then fell into the water before I could react. He grinned, clearly trying to contain his amusement. "When people drive up to your dock, they'll often toss you the line for you to help pull them in."

"Oh. Right." I knelt on the dock and leaned over to fish it out of the water—

"No, don't—"

The boat bumped my shoulder, knocking me off balance. I plunged headfirst into the water, scraping my shin down the side of my dock as I went in. I managed to get my hands over my head before I hit the bottom in the shallow-ish water. My head hit, but the sandy mud was soft, giving under the impact. The force of the collision still shook me, and I scrambled for the surface, swimming straight up…into the bottom of Devlin's boat.

It was completely over me. I couldn't even see the surface of the water anywhere. I couldn't get out. I didn't even know which way to swim. All I could see above me was the white bottom of the boat—

I needed to breathe, but I couldn't get out of the water—

Panic hit me, but before I could freak out, Devlin grabbed me around the waist and dragged me to the side in a swift, hard move. He shoved me to the surface, and my head burst out of the water.

I dragged in a shaky breath.

"It's okay." Devlin's arm was still around my waist, holding me up. "Slow your breathing. You're okay."

I gripped his forearm, fighting against the fear wrapping around me. *I'm okay. I'm not drowning.*

It took another couple minutes of Devlin's coaching and my own iron will to survive before I finally was able to take a calm breath. And then another. And then finally, I became aware of the fact that I was in Devlin's arms, leaning back against his chest, with his arm locked around my waist, just under my breasts.

And then I realized that it felt pretty fantastic to be wrapped up against him.

There had been zero physical affection with Stanley for a very long time. I'd had no idea how badly I missed the touch of another human being until right now.

"You all right?" he asked, his voice low and much too sexy as it rolled over me.

"Yes. Good." I didn't want to have this reaction to Devlin. I was desperate to be independent, to never be trapped again, not with a man, not with my mom, not with anyone. I needed freedom, not this. "I'm all set." I patted his forearm, trying not to notice how muscular it was.

He took the hint and released me.

I immediately stepped away from him, putting distance between us as I turned to face him. "Thanks."

"No problem." His brow was furrowed, and water was still

cascading in rivulets down his forehead. His lake police jacket was plastered to his body, and his sunglasses had disappeared, showcasing very dark brown eyes that were a little too captivating.

Curse him for being so attractive and saving my life. Seriously. That was an unfair combination.

He touched his own forehead. "You're bleeding. I think you hit your head."

I brushed my fingers over my hairline, flinching when my fingers brushed over a cut. I pulled my finger away and saw I was bleeding. Did I have first aid supplies? I was pretty sure I didn't. "Do you have any Band-Aids in your boat?"

"Yep. Give me a sec. Do you need help getting out?"

"No, I'm all set." I saw that his boat had drifted to the shore, and was bumping gently against the spot King Tut had chosen as his egress from the lake. "I'll meet you on dry land."

He shot me a skeptical look that said he wasn't as convinced as I was of my good health and prosperity, but he obediently waded away to retrieve his boat.

King Tut was standing at the very edge of the dock, his tail flicking restlessly as he meowed. I looked over at him as I half-walked, half-swam toward the dock. "I'm all right, thanks—"

As I said it, King Tut launched himself off the dock right at me, his claws bared to prepare for a secure landing. I yelped in terror, but there was nothing to do but brace myself as the massive animal slammed against my chest. I caught him, but his lack of faith in my competence made him dig his claws all the way through my shoulders so he wouldn't fall.

"Ow, ow, ow." I pulled the little daggers out of my body as he purred and pressed his face into my chest, burying himself against me. My heart softened. "Did you think I was dead? Because I did."

My second time in two weeks when I'd thought I was dead. Third if my encounter with Rex's tree counted.

I didn't want to make a habit of it, but at the same time, maybe repeated exposure to almost dying would increase my resilience. That would be good, right?

King Tut wiggled in my arms, trying to get even closer to me. "You were worried about me?" Totally sweet, but at the same time, it raised the stakes. I didn't just have Hattie and Cargo counting on me. I also had an emotionally dependent cat.

The pressure kept mounting with every passing moment.

My mom had always believed that attitude was everything. Confidence had always been the difference between spending the night on a bench in the park or securing a month-long invite to a beautiful home in the Hamptons with a private chef and a butler.

Without confidence, nothing good ever happened.

With confidence? Sometimes it was possible to force a win.

I could do this. *I could do this.*

Less than ten minutes later, I was sitting in Devlin's reclaimed boat, being nursed by a man who had more muscles than should be legal.

I knew exactly how muscular he was because he'd taken off his wet jacket and shirt and laid them out over the boat to dry.

Which meant he was now shirtless.

Right in front of me.

Impossible to avoid looking at.

"I don't think you need stitches." He was efficient and professional as he worked on my forehead, which made it easier for me to focus on things like the fact he might be close to wanting to arrest Lucy for murder instead of the way his pecs flexed when he moved.

"Good to know." I had a pretty decent headache from the impact, but I wasn't going to admit it to myself. "So, the reason I waved you over is that I had a situation last night." I decided to slide in the Rex questions on the backside, when he was focused on the moose.

His hand paused for a split second, and he stiffened almost imperceptibly. "You mean after you left Rex's?"

"Yes." I supposed the events at Rex's could have qualified as a situation, so clarification was good. "Just before dawn, I was awakened by six moose on Jet Skis yelling obscenities at the marina, and throwing remnants of the Welcome to Bass Derby sign at my dock." I decided not to call them the Derby Moose. I wanted to see what he thought.

He stepped back from me so he could see my face. "Really?"

I was surprised by his surprise. "Really." He didn't sound as concerned as everyone else had been, which took some of the fun out of my drama. Plus, it interfered with my plan to distract him from my questioning. I tried to amp him up. "Hattie said it was the Derby Moose. And that they were trouble."

He frowned. "I've never heard of them. I'll ask around."

Never heard of them? I recalled then that he'd been in town for only six months. But at the same time, Devlin seemed so competent. How did he not know about them? The Derby Moose seemed to be a rather sordid and infamous element of Bass Derby's history.

I felt strangely deflated at his lack of reaction.

Being stalked by deadly moose that had come out of hibernation for me had been sort of exciting. Possibly dangerous, yes, but also exciting. Was that weird? Maybe. I thought of Griselda asking if I'd be bored in Bass Derby because I was so good at hunting drug dealers. I immediately decided to unthink that comment, because I did not want to have some sort of life-threatening need for danger. "Hattie said that Chief Stone should be told. Should I call him?"

"I'll talk to him." Devlin folded his arms over his chest and studied me. "Did you really see someone leave Rex's house last night?"

I stiffened at his abrupt change in subject matter. His tone was not friendly anymore. Not hostile exactly, but friendly? Not so much. Investigative was a better word. But that was fine.

He'd opened the door to the subject I wanted to talk about anyway.

I sat a little taller and lifted my chin. "Yes, I did. He knocked me off the deck and ran into the woods." I paused, trying to consider how best to ask, then decided to just go for it. Maybe it would get him off the Lucy angle. "I heard Rex was going to inherit a lot of money from his dad's estate. Any idea who gets it now?"

"Marco's wife, who's been MIA for twenty years. No one can find her, so it's going to sit around for now. Of course I checked that."

Oh, bummer. I sighed. I guess I didn't have to go to the law firm and work my magic. I was relieved not to have to jump back in the game, but also a little bummed. I'd been sort of excited about my idea.

No, it was good. I was already treading close to the line. It was so much better not to go full-fledged con on an attorney, right? Right.

Devlin continued right on. "We didn't find any evidence of anyone else having been in the house at the time of the murder." He was watching my face carefully, and I realized that he was trying to figure out if I was covering up for Lucy.

Holy cow. He thought I was lying to the police, as I had done many times during my formative years. After all I'd endured for the last two years to help the police, I still had to fight the battle to prove I could be trusted?

Anger swelled inside me, anger that had long, deep roots. I bolted to my feet. "Just because I grew up as a petty thief and made the mistake of marrying a criminal, you think that's who I am? That I'd lie to the police to protect a murderer?"

He didn't back down. He just watched me, with that same relentless focus that had defined Griselda.

Screw his over-abundance of tightly corded muscle. "You're just like Griselda. I should start calling you Griselda Number

Two," I snapped as I snatched King Tut off the bow of the boat, where he'd been sunning himself.

I should call him "No. 2." Perfect, actually. Succinct. Powerful. On point. A clever reminder to myself not to ever forget that his loyalty was to his work, not to me. Never to me. Devlin's boat might be lovely, but I'd rather sit in a sinking canoe than be on there with him.

Devlin raised his brows. "How am I like Hawk?"

"You're both so focused on the win that you don't even take the time to feel the humanity of the situation. I gave up everything to take Stanley down. Griselda never cared. Ever. And you're just like him." I climbed out of the boat to the dock, clutching the cat to my chest.

How could Devlin know what I'd done for Griselda and still think I was a liar? And not trust me?

Because my past defined me, that's why. It haunted me everywhere I went.

"I see the humanity," he said evenly. "I see you."

"Do you?" What? Me sounding sassy and sarcastic? Never. "What do you see?"

"I see a woman who was taught to skirt the law for her own agenda."

"Of course that's what you'd see." This was why I'd wanted to leave my past in Boston. I didn't want to be judged. I wanted to reinvent myself as *me*. If I ever needed a better reason why the old Mia had to stay dead, I was facing it right now.

Devlin wasn't finished. "I also see a woman so driven to do what's right that she'll cross any line to make it happen."

"I—" I stopped, surprised by his words. By "cross any line" did he mean perform acts of impressive courage, moral fortitude, and devastating self-sacrifice in the name of what was good and right? Because I did pretty much meet those standards. Maybe I would forgive him. "That's a good thing."

"Is it?"

I frowned. "It's not?" Retracting his compliment in less than one second? That felt rude.

"Your standards of right and wrong aren't defined by the law or what anyone else says. They're defined by your own unshakeable inner code of personal ethics." He raised his brows. "*That's* what I see when I look at you."

I stared at him, startled by his words. I'd always believed my standards of right and wrong were in accordance with the law. That's why I'd left my mom. That's why I'd reported Stanley. That's why I'd given up everything to take him down.

I played by the rules.

Didn't I?

Devlin then delivered the crowning blow. "I believe that if you thought Lucy had done the right thing in murdering Rex, you'd protect her."

"There was someone else there," I said, meeting his gaze steadily.

He watched me very closely, waiting for my eye to twitch or my nostrils to flare.

Hah.

I didn't have any tells. I was a very good liar. Plus, I wasn't lying, so there was that.

"Huh," he said.

Yeah, that's right. Huh, indeed.

But if I *did* think Lucy had killed Rex for good reason, would I protect her?

No.

No.

Maybe.

Maybe? I honestly might protect a murderer? If it was Lucy… Yes. I might. Depending.

The realization staggered me. Was I not the good person I'd fought so hard to become? There was no denying my plans for the lawyer's office this afternoon hadn't been exactly angelic, but to give me credit, I'd found another way to get the info, so I'd avoided having to revisit my past.

But I couldn't lie to myself: I'd been willing to jump back in without hesitation.

An unwelcome revelation.

Devlin started his engine. "If you think of any more details about last night, let me know."

I was too busy having a shocking inner identity crisis to answer him.

"And Mia?"

I glared at him. "What?"

"Next time you miss catching a dock line, let the boat drift closer and grab the boat itself." Unlike last time when I'd fallen in, he wasn't laughing. "Every year, people die on this lake. Don't be one of them."

CHAPTER 15

BY TWO-THIRTY, I'd worked myself into a state.

Purging eleven bags of trash from the store, the garage, and the surrounding area hadn't calmed me down. Going through the marina store with a trash bag and a mop hadn't been as therapeutic as I'd hoped. Maybe because the shop hadn't looked much better after a couple hours of work. It just felt...old. Abandoned. Lifeless.

Even the voices and smells coming from Hattie's Café all morning hadn't been enough to make me want to stay in my shop. I had managed to schedule a professional cleaning service to have their wicked way with the stench in my apartment, but that wouldn't help the depressing vibe that the store was giving off. How on earth could I entice strangers to come by if I didn't even want to be there?

I was stumped.

During that entire time, not a single customer had come by the marina. The grim truth was becoming apparent: I hadn't bought a business. I'd bought the coffin that a dead business had been buried in.

I was frustrated with the marina's future and present well-being.

I was mad at Devlin for questioning my moral character.

I was worried because I thought he might be right.

I finally decided I had no choice but to walk away from helping Lucy before I crossed a line I didn't want to cross.

And immediately after that, I realized that there was no chance I was going to do that. I was in, and I was stuck.

But I had to set boundaries, or I would be lost forever in the thrill of the life I'd walked away from.

Unfortunately, I still hadn't figured out where those lines were by the time we met by Lucy's car at two-thirty. We chose to perform the inspection behind the main marina building near the tractor. Our parking spot wasn't visible from the road, and only delivery trucks ever went back there, according to Hattie. Perfect for a clandestine operation.

It was time to find out if Rex had hidden anything in it. I hoped it was a video recording of his own death, but I wasn't all that optimistic.

Hattie was armed with iced tea, sandwiches, and more of her magical bread. "Eat first."

"Eat first?" I was too antsy to wait any longer. "You guys eat. I'll start looking."

Hattie stopped me with the takeout box. "Relax for thirty seconds. I know you didn't eat lunch."

"I ate." But even as I said it, I realized she was right. Aside from her quiche, the only food I'd come near had been the snacks I'd tossed from the store, most of which had expired six years ago.

"Oh, yay! Pesto chicken!" Lucy sat down on a crate. "I'm starved." She lifted up the sandwich with its grilled homemade bread, and then took a bite.

The rapture on her face convinced me. I took the box from Hattie. "Thanks."

"No problem. It's $9.99. I'll keep a tab so you can deduct it from my rent." Hattie sat next to Lucy, and I perched on another crate. "So, what's up?"

"Chief Stone searched my house this morning," Lucy said. "I wasn't home, but my neighbor called me."

"Oh..." My gut sank. If Chief Stone had gotten a search warrant, that meant they had significant evidence against Lucy. "Did they find anything?"

"What's there to find?" She shrugged. "I didn't do it."

I knew that innocence didn't always mean there was no evidence to find that they could use to indict you. But maybe best not to say that. "Did Rex have stuff there?"

"I threw it all out a month ago," she said. "I don't think I missed anything." She paused as she looked at my face and Hattie's. "I should be worried?"

"No—"

Hattie interrupted me. "Hell, yeah, you should be worried. If Chief Stone doesn't arrest someone soon, his mom will fire him. All he cares about is getting her off his back, and quickly. You're the fastest route."

Lucy stared at us. "So, this might be my last good meal of my life? Prison food for eternity? Because that sucks."

"We'll figure it out." Hattie looked over at me. "What about Devlin? I saw he stopped by. You guys were getting a little cozy in his boat there."

"What?" Lucy sat up. "What happened? Do we get to have sex talk?"

"No!" I felt my cheeks turn red. "I almost drowned, he saved my life, accused me of lying to cover up Lucy's homicidal tendencies, and then told me to try not to die on the lake. It was super romantic, and we're getting married on Saturday." I took a bite of my sandwich, and almost died right there. "Holy cow. This is incredible."

"Of course it is." Hattie grinned. "I noticed he took his shirt off for you."

I swallowed. "He was wet from saving me. Because I almost drowned. Did you not hear that part?" I took another bite, barely able to stop myself from sobbing with joy. Hattie's pesto chicken had a good chance of being the best sandwich I'd ever eaten.

"Devlin is pretty hot," Lucy teased. "Plus, I don't think he's a drug dealer. You're probably safe to go out with him."

"You could use sex to manipulate him into abandoning the case against Lucy," Hattie said.

My cheeks got even hotter. "I'm not going to sleep with him!"

"Not even to save me?" Lucy asked. "I thought we were friends."

"It *is* a murder charge," Hattie added. "Sex is a small price to pay for Lucy's lifelong freedom."

I stared at them. "Are you guys serious?"

They both burst out laughing. "You need to learn how to have girlfriends," Hattie said.

That didn't answer my question. "So, a good friend would have sex to save Lucy, or good friends tease about sex all the time, and it's not serious?"

They looked at each other, then spoke at the same time. "Both."

This time, I saw the sparkle in their eyes, and I relaxed and even smiled. "Got it. He does have nice muscles. I guess I could sacrifice." I thought of Devlin's assumption of my character. How far *would* I go to keep Lucy, or Hattie for that matter, out of prison?

I was beginning to think I didn't want to know the answer to the question. I'd done a lot of things as a kid to keep myself and my mom out of jail. I didn't want to be that same person.

Maybe that was why I'd turned Stanley in. To make up for my past life.

So, where did that leave Lucy and Hattie? I liked them. They felt like friends, even though I hadn't known them long. Loyalty was already taking root, loyalty that felt safe and good. Loyalty that I'd wanted in my life for a very long time.

But at what cost? I looked at Lucy as she finished her sandwich, and I saw the worry in her eyes. Laughter aside, she was in real trouble, and we all knew it.

Hattie finished her sandwich and dusted the crumbs off her hands. "Okay, in case Mia doesn't have the bedroom skills to keep Lucy out of prison, we need to get on with this search. Everyone ready?"

"Yep." I was surprised to see that I had an empty box in my lap. I'd literally scarfed down the sandwich. I quickly downed my iced tea and stood up. "Let's do it."

"I'll take the front," Lucy said.

"I got the back seat," Hattie claimed.

"No one take the cargo area," I said. "I want it." They both rolled their eyes at my cleverness, and then we split up.

I lowered the tailgate to the Jeep and blanched at the sight of all the mail bins. Then I realized they were mostly empty, and well within my capabilities to manhandle. It took only a moment to relocate them to the dirt, and then I turned my attention back to the vehicle.

It didn't take long to search, because it was pretty clean. Lucy clearly took her work seriously, because all that was in there besides the mail was a black blanket, a set of jumper cables, and a first aid kit.

I set my hands on my hips and studied the interior of the vehicle. If Rex had been doing something illegal, he would have hidden it. Every place my mom and I had lived, we'd found a way to stash the items we didn't want found.

There was always a way.

A man like Rex would have things to hide. And he'd been in this car the day he'd hit the sign, when he'd been driving with incentive.

I scanned the interior again, then noticed the knobs at the corner of the mat. I quickly unscrewed them and lifted the carpet. Beneath it was a built-in compartment, the one that was meant to contain the jack and maybe even the spare tire itself.

I'd hidden in compartments like that when I was little. The memory still gave me the heebie-jeebies, but I grabbed the handle and hauled it open. There was a dark mound inside. "Hey, guys, there's something in here."

"What is it?" Hattie asked as she dug around in the back seat.

"I can't tell." I reached forward to grab it, then jerked my hand back when it squished under my touch. "I think it's a dead animal —" I stopped mid-sentence as my eyes adjusted.

And then I realized what it was. "Holy cow," I breathed, stunned, but also not stunned.

"Hey! I found some receipts!" Lucy waved a few slips of paper. "He went to the Ugly Man Tavern a few times." She paused. "Including the night before he was killed."

"The Ugly Man Tavern?" Hattie popped her head up. "That place is bad news. Did he go there when you were dating?"

"Hey guys," I said. "You need to see this."

"Not that I knew of," Lucy said. "Why do you think he was going there?"

"I don't know." Hattie tossed some trash out onto the ground. "But I think we'll be going there tonight to see what we can find out."

"People get killed there," Lucy said.

"Only once, and it was a bar fight. We won't get in a bar fight," Hattie said.

"Hey!" I raised my voice, and they both finally looked at me.

"What?" Hattie frowned at me.

I dragged the item out of the spare tire compartment and held it up. The brown, synthetic fur was damp and matted, the antlers were sagging, and there was mud all over the plastic hooves, but there was no doubt about what it was. "Does anyone want to dress up like a moose and swamp the Yacht Club on Jet Skis tonight?"

CHAPTER 16

HATTIE'S MOUTH opened in astonishment. "Is that a Derby Moose outfit? I've never seen one up close before."

"It looks like the ones I saw," I said. "Same brown. The horns look the same. The head is the same shape." I didn't know how much variety there could be in moose costumes, but I seriously doubted there were a lot of wet, full-coverage moose costumes running around Bass Derby. Then I saw a squashed, red-and-white-striped bow tied around the right antler. "Yep. This one was there."

"I want to see!" Both women scrambled out of the Jeep and hurried over to me.

"That's one of them, for sure. Those beady eyes never lie." Hattie peered at it. "Is it yours, Lucy?"

"Mine?" Lucy poked at it gingerly with her index finger. "Of course not. You know I would have washed it. Only a guy would let it get that gross."

Good point. Women had standards.

"You think Rex was a Derby Moose?" Hattie asked. "Because I would have thought he was too much of a loner for a team outing like that."

"He was dead before they visited the marina, so he wasn't in that group, but yeah, this outfit being in the Jeep certainly seems to connect him, and maybe his murder, with the Moose." As I said it, a tiny chill shimmied down my spine. I hadn't been taking the Derby Moose seriously, but if they had anything to do with Rex's murder, that changed my opinion of them in a hurry.

Suddenly, I was glad I'd mentioned them to Devlin.

Hattie clasped her hands on her head. "This doesn't make any sense."

"It does make sense. We just don't see how yet." I recalled the advice Beau had given me to look for details, so I shook the costume. It made no sound. I pressed my face into it and inhaled. It smelled a little musty, but mostly just wet. "It hasn't been in there long, or it would smell worse." Hah! Look at me being a sleuth! I was so impressive.

"Someone else must have worn it last night." Hattie looked over at Lucy. "When did you get your car back?"

"This morning."

"Which means there was time to get it stashed in the Jeep after they visited the marina." Hattie was frowning. "But why put it there?"

"To frame Lucy?" I paused, considering that idea. "Maybe it wasn't a fluke it was Lucy's car that hit the sign." I looked over at her. "Maybe this has been all about you from the start."

Hattie and Lucy stared at me, stunned surprise evident on their faces.

"Why?" Lucy finally said. "What in the world have I done?"

Hattie frowned. "Lucy doesn't have enemies."

"Maybe not that she's aware of, but maybe she's involved through Rex." I turned the costume around, looking for any clues that would solve the case immediately. Sadly, there were none. Just mud, fuzz, and little sparkles embedded deep in the fur. "Is that glitter?"

"Let me see." Hattie grabbed the moose and tilted it, making it sparkle. "Definitely glitter. That stuff never dies."

"Glitter?" Lucy took it from Hattie and peered at it, and her face fell. "Glitter."

I raised my brows at her dejected tone. "What's wrong with glitter?" Yeah, Bass Derby didn't really seem to be the glitter-central type place, but Ruby Lee had been all in on her glitter eye shadow, so it probably wasn't illegal.

"I used to twirl, remember?" When we nodded, she continued. "We used glitter all the time for our performances. In our hair, on our costumes, on everything. I still have boxes of it in my spare bedroom. Glitter is like a neon sign pointing right at me."

For a moment, we all stared at each other, digesting that little nugget. Had it been intentional to incriminate Lucy? If so, well done. I thought of the other woman that Rex had been sleeping with, and how it gave Lucy motive as the scorned lover.

I decided not to mention that, but she was in trouble, and we all knew it.

Hattie cleared her throat. "Rex was on the run only hours before he was murdered," she said in a low, haunting voice. "Driving your car, loaded with glitter and fake fur, only to be killed by a poker that you're completely capable of handling." She wiggled her fingers in a creepy, melodramatic gesture, her voice becoming even more ominous. "What have you been up to, Lucy Grande? Because it's coming back to haunt you." She whistled eerily, sending chills down my spine.

We both looked at her. "Really with that?" I asked.

"It was needed." She grinned. "Tension relief. Everyone feels better, right?"

"No." Lucy looked like she was going to pass out.

"Tension escalator," I corrected Hattie. "Not tension relief."

"Either way, it was fun."

"Was it?" I asked. "Was it really?"

"It wasn't," Lucy said. "Not fun at all."

Hattie waved her hand dismissively. "You kids have no idea how to keep things light. You're lucky you have me around to show you. With age comes great wisdom, and you two get to be my protégés." She looked right at me. "You get it, don't you, Mia? Never take things too seriously. I saw you having fun out there picking those locks, right?"

"Picking locks is fun. Murder is a much bigger deal."

"All the more reason to lighten up." She patted the moose's floppy head. "This big guy will lead us right to the truth. Let's name him something cheerful to remind us not to take life so seriously. How about Fluffy?"

I brightened. "Oh, I like that. I vote for Fluffy."

Lucy set her hands on her hips. "I'm the one at risk for a murder rap. I think that gives me naming authority."

Hattie and I exchanged glances. Who was going to argue with that? "Go for it," Hattie said.

"Fluffy's not quite right. How about Sylvester?"

"Too long," Hattie said. "We need quick and dirty."

"Good point." Lucy held him up and gave him the stare down. "Wally," she said decisively.

Hattie clapped her hands, and I grinned. "Perfect."

Lucy held Wally up by the scruff and stared into his beady eyes. "Talk to us, Wally. Who killed Rex, who stuffed you in my car, and what's with the glitter?"

Wally remained stoically silent.

"Damn moose," Hattie muttered. "Holding out on us."

Lucy giggled. "Right? Moose are notoriously unhelpful."

"Especially ones who wear glitter," I said with a grin. "It's all about them. Never about the greater good."

"Selfish lot, all of them," Hattie said.

At that moment, the crunch of tires on gravel caught our attention, and we turned to see a police cruiser pull into the marina parking lot.

"It's Clyde," Lucy said.

Having Chief Stone catch us with Wally would not look good for Lucy, or any of us. I grabbed him from Lucy and shoved him at Hattie. "Put him in the kitchen."

"No way. My kitchen is an oasis of cleanliness." She shoved

him back at Lucy. "Put Wally in the Jeep."

"Not my Jeep!" Lucy threw him at me. "If Clyde finds Wally in there, he'll think he's mine."

"I don't want him either!" I heard his footsteps coming around the corner. I sprinted over to the abandoned tractor and shoved Wally under the back tire, nudging him with my foot until he was out of sight. I'd just made it back beside the women when Chief Stone strode around the corner.

He looked a little pale and shaky, not the arrogant jerk who'd welcomed me to Bass Derby with such charm and fairness only twenty-four hours ago. He stopped when he saw the three of us loitering beside Lucy's extensive stash of mail, his eyes narrowing in suspicion. "What's going on here?"

"We're helping Lucy organize," Hattie said, cheerfully. "Almost done. Let's go, Lucy."

The two women immediately started packing the Jeep again, leaving me to deal with the chief. "Can I help you?" I asked.

He ran a hand through his hair, looking weary. "You haven't come by the police station to pay your fines. I'm taking you in."

I blinked. "What? You're arresting me?"

"The twenty-four-hour window to pay your fine passed ten minutes ago." He held up handcuffs, and I instinctively took several steps back.

It was critically important never to get in the hands of the police. Once you did, they had the power. A thief never did well when turning power over to the police. "I can pay right now. I'll get my credit card—"

"Too late. I'm getting grief about that sign. I need to make an example of you." He waved the metal wrist cuffs at me. "Turn around."

"No. Absolutely not," I snapped, changing tactics to the offensive. "I'm not taking responsibility for it."

His eyebrows shot up, and his fingers tightened around the cuffs. "No? Did you just say *no*?"

Crud. My refusal hadn't made him back down. I needed to

pivot. "I'm a little distracted," I said quickly. Had I gotten Wally completely out of sight? I didn't dare check. "Rex's murder was very upsetting. I kept dreaming about the pool of blood around his head."

Chief Stone turned slightly green, as I'd hoped he might. But it didn't derail him. "I'm arresting you for resisting arrest. Keep pushing me, and I'll add more."

I folded my arms across my chest. "That's abuse of power."

"It's the law." His voice was getting higher with urgency. "Turn around now."

"His mom must have chewed him out," Hattie muttered under her breath as she bent to pick up the bins by my feet.

His mom. Shoot. I'd forgotten about the mayor with the eleven-years-running title obsession. I'd already seen her power over him last night, when she'd made him haul his terrified self into the murder scene. "Listen—"

Clyde put his hand on his gun. "Turn around and put your hands behind your back."

"A gun? You're literally pulling a gun because of a sign?" Sweat on my brow, and my chest got tight as memories of my little encounter with homicidal Joyce popped in my mind. *No guns pointed at me, please.* "It wasn't my car that hit it. It was—"

I stopped suddenly. There was no way to prove that Rex had been driving Lucy's car when it had hit the sign. Pointing out the damage to Lucy's Jeep might clear me, but it would incriminate her in a hurry.

She was already in enough trouble.

I heard Hattie and Lucy go still behind me, waiting to see what I was going to say.

Clyde was walking toward me with the handcuffs now, getting closer. I took a few more steps back. "It was—" I wanted to save myself. I wanted to so badly. But I couldn't betray Lucy. "My marina was attacked last night by six moose riding Jet Skis and throwing the remnants of the sign at my dock," I blurted out instead.

If I'd been underwhelmed by Devlin's reaction to the moose story, Chief Stone more than made up for it.

His face turned gray, he sucked in his breath, and stumbled, barely keeping his balance. "*What?*"

"They were shouting obscenities."

"Were they singing?"

"Singing?" I shook my head. "No, they were yelling and shouting, but it definitely wasn't a song."

"Thank God." He sat down on a crate, fumbling to guide himself down on it. "Oh, dear heaven. Derby Moose."

I began to feel concerned for his health. "Are you all right?"

"You're sure they weren't singing?" His hands were shaking.

"I'm sure. Why?"

"Then it was just a warning." He pressed his face to his hands. "They haven't sung in decades. When I was ten, they sang in front of my next-door neighbor's house. I watched them from my window. Scariest noise I ever heard. The way their voices carried over the still water. Echoing. Vibrating."

I swallowed. "What happened to your neighbor?

"He was found floating in the lake the next morning. Dead."

Real alarm set in now, so that I barely noticed when Lucy peeled out of the parking lot and Hattie edged back to the door of her kitchen. "They've really killed people?" The moose-Rex connection was looking more and more macabre now.

"They've never been caught. No one knows who they are. One time..." He paused. "Ten years ago, one of the police officers investigating them disappeared. No one ever found him. All they found were the moose costumes piled up on Eagle's Nest dock."

I sat up. "*My* dock?"

"Rusty had already left town, so it wasn't him, but that was the only trace anyone found of them. The night they sang in front of that cop's house was the last time they were ever seen on the lake. Until now."

Ok...I understood why he was terrified. Now that we'd found Wally in Lucy's car, potentially linking the moose to Rex's death, I was less inclined to mock Chief Stone for being afraid of people dressed up as moose.

I mean, I still felt slightly ridiculous giving them any credit, but dead men don't lie. "I thought this town was a charming, lovely small-town oasis."

"It is. It definitely is. Best in the state." He sat up straighter, summoning fortitude I wouldn't have suspected he had. "But we'll never win the title if the press finds out about the Derby Moose. Murder is bad enough, but the Derby Moose? Old legends like that have tremendous power."

Good point. Iron-grips on meaningless titles were definitely more important than people being murdered.

He suddenly stiffened. "What's that?" He was looking toward the tractor.

I quickly turned and saw a tuft of brown, synthetic fur sticking out from under the left rear tire. Oh...*no.* "It's an animal my cat killed. A..." What kind of animals lived on the lake that had brown fur? "A muskrat." Did muskrats live in the lake? Maybe not. "A beaver. An otter? I'm not sure what it was, but—"

"No cat can kill something that big." He leapt to his feet and edged forward, his hand on his gun.

I hurried after him. How could I stop him from looking too closely? "My cat's quite large. And he's an aggressive hunter. He's been eating it. Trust me, you don't want to get close to it."

Chief Stone didn't even appear to hear me. "That looks like..." He swallowed his words, but I heard the fear in it. He knew exactly what it was. The image of the moose costumes had probably been burned into his brain since he was ten.

If he found it stashed under my tire, there was no way to explain it away. I was very certain that being associated with the Derby Moose wouldn't go well for me, especially with the connection to Rex's murder. "Wait—"

He bent over and reached for the fur. Instantly, a massive black paw shot out from under the tractor, claws bared, and slashed at his hand.

He yelped and jerked his hand back, cradling it to his chest.

As we both watched, a very dry, very fluffy, very large King Tut belly-crawled out from under the tractor. As he emerged, he rose to his feet moving with pure menace. His fur was puffed out, his tail was stiff, and he bared his teeth in a low growl. He looked like he weighed at least fifty pounds and was as long as my entire wingspan.

"Holy mother of pearl." Chief Stone stumbled backward, his hand going for his gun. "It's a bobcat!"

"Don't shoot him! It's my cat!" I jumped between them instinctively.

His hand was still on his gun. "*That's* your cat?"

"Yes. His name is King Tut. He's very protective about his prey." And, apparently, fake fur moose costumes that made for cozy places to nap in the shade.

"That's the biggest cat I've ever seen." He continued to back slowly away. "I've seen Maine Coon cats before, but that thing is a beast."

King Tut was a Maine Coon cat? I'd have to Google it and see if Chief Stone was correct. "He's not a beast. He's my sweetie pie." Although he did look pretty terrifying. And that low growl. I almost wanted to back away as well. "He's a little feral, though, so I don't recommend trying to take away his dinner. Don't touch that dead animal, or you might lose a hand."

"He can have it." The Chief was still clutching his hand to his chest, and I could see rivulets of blood leaking out between his fingers.

King Tut sat down next to my ankle.

"I need to go talk to the mayor about the Derby Moose," the Chief said. "I'll come back and arrest you later."

I waved cheerfully. "No problem. I'll be waiting." Not.

The minute Chief Stone was around the corner, I heard him break into a run.

I looked down at King Tut, who was staring up at me, a loud purr rumbling in his chest. "And you, my darling, deserve the dinner of your choice for that move." I held out my arms and he vaulted straight up into them, barely digging his claws into me as he landed.

I decided to leave Wally where he was for the moment.

I didn't want to lose my hand either.

CHAPTER 17

FOUR HOURS LATER, we were heading toward a place I was increasingly certain I didn't want to go. But I was going anyway.

"You brought Wally?" Hattie scowled at me as she peeled around the dark bend in the road on the way to Ugly Man Tavern later that evening. "What if we get stopped?"

I tucked the garbage bag containing Wally the Moose more securely behind the boxes stacked in Hattie's backseat. The labels claimed they were from a place called Francine's Mill, which gave Wally a nice, innocuous place to hide. "What would we get stopped for? Other than the fact you drive like a maniac?"

She hit the gas and drove even faster. "I never get stopped. I am in harmonic unity with the universe. But that moose costume could screw with it. It has bad karma bleeding from it."

"Was I going to leave it at home for Chief Stone to find if he snuck in with a search warrant?" He'd never made it back to arrest me, and as soon as King Tut had gone for his afternoon swim, I'd retrieved the moose costume and hidden it in my freezer.

But that didn't really feel like a fantastic option, even with King Tut sitting on the kitchen counter on guard duty. Mostly because King Tut had no loyalty, and I'd caught him skulking around in the grasses hunting small rodents when he was supposed to be guarding the moose.

So much power and aggression in that feline.

So little motivation or long-term commitment to becoming a personal bodyguard.

Cats, right?

Lucy was in the front seat this time, and I was the one leaning over the seats, squished between huge, heavy cardboard boxes.

Both of us had offered to drive, but Hattie hadn't even entertained the thought.

No one takes the keys from Hattie.

I shuddered to think of what would happen when Hattie became too old to drive safely. Who would dare sideline her? No one. She'd have to be allowed to roam free, and the rest of the world would have to take cover.

"Good point," Hattie said. "I like your thinking. Clyde is a sneaky little twit who would definitely come back after you left."

"If we get caught with Wally," Lucy said, "I'm not claiming him."

"Me either," Hattie said.

I sighed. "We won't get caught." But they were getting me a little concerned. It had seemed like a good idea at the time to stash Wally in a trash bag and bring him along, but now… not so sure. "So, what's the plan tonight?"

"Three girlfriends out for a drink," Hattie said. "We'll flirt a little. Gain some trust. Then go from there."

I sat back in my seat, grimacing when the corner of a Francine's Mill box poked me in the ribs. "That's not a plan."

"Of course it's a plan. It has the flexibility to adapt to whatever situation arises," Hattie retorted.

Seriously. These women needed to take a class or two from my mom. "Do you even know what we're trying to accomplish?"

"Finding Rex's murderer," Hattie said. "Don't you pay any attention at all?"

I threw up my hands. "Obviously, I know that's the long-term goal. But what are we trying to do *tonight*?"

"See what there is to see," Hattie said. "How can we set a plan? We have no idea what Rex was involved in. We need to be agile and light on our feet, so we can pivot at a moment's notice."

"Even pivots need to be anticipated." No wonder my mom had stayed solo professionally. This kind of thing required a surgeon's precision, not a fly-by-the-seat-of-your-pants approach.

Lucy twisted around to look at me. "Do *you* have a better plan?"

I let out my breath. "No, but let me think for a sec." I drummed my fingers on the seat. "What's this place like?"

"Seedy," Hattie said.

"Scary," added Lucy.

"Trashy."

"It smells."

"Have either of you ever been there?" I asked.

They both shook their heads. "Never," Lucy said. "It's a cauldron of backwoods testosterone."

Hmm… "That sounds exactly like the kind of place that numbnuts who dress as homicidal moose would hang out," I said. "And it seems like Derby Moose could be the kind of upstanding citizens who might murder Rex."

There was silence in the car for a moment. "Does anyone want to turn around?" Lucy finally said, echoing my own thoughts.

"Yes." I was pretty sure I spoke for all of us.

"Except for the Lucy in prison thing," Hattie said.

"And the Derby Moose killing Mia thing," Lucy said.

I wrinkled my nose. "I hate things like that." I didn't like that I was taking the moose more seriously as a threat now, but with the appearance of Wally in the car of a murder victim, I had to be a little more respectful of their capability.

"So?" Lucy asked. "How do we handle this without inciting the moose or Rex's murderer, or both?"

I thought about it. "We could pretend we wanted to join the

Derby Moose. Or Lucy could ask about returning Rex's costume," I said, thinking out loud. But what did we want? I wanted the names behind those moose costumes. I wanted to find out what else Rex was involved in. I wanted to find out who else he'd been sleeping with. "We need to get people talking about Rex."

"How do we do that?"

I sighed. I knew what we needed to do. The Double Twist was one of my mom's most utilized cons, but my least favorite. It felt so disempowering to women everywhere. "It's a testosterone hotspot, right?"

They both nodded.

"So, we make them come to us."

By the time we emerged from the two-mile dirt road that led to the hidden gem of the metal-roofed shack known as the Ugly Man Tavern, Hattie and Lucy had graduated from a crash course on Double Twist.

All of my mom's cons had names, so it was easy to call a pivot, and we'd both know what we needed to do. The Double Twist was pretty basic: reel the prey in by giving a man the chance to utilize his gender bias to see a woman as weak, needy, and vulnerable. Then, if he takes the bait, let him find out the hard way that not all women are weak. I always thought it should be called something like *If he's jerky enough to try to take advantage of a woman in need, then he deserves all he gets.* But that was a little wordy and maybe a little bit bitter, so we called it the Double Twist, which made it more fun anyway.

If you don't keep a sense of humor about life, then what's the point, right?

Double Twist was now in progress. It was the first named event I'd been involved with since I was seventeen. I wasn't going to lie. I was a little uncomfortable getting back in the game. And I was even more unsettled by how energized and excited I felt.

I didn't tell Hattie and Lucy that they'd just been inducted into the world of the con. As far as they knew, it was simply a good idea that I'd had, with a clever title just because I was creative and adorable.

Despite their acceptance of my lock-picking skills, I wasn't going to risk telling the girls the true extent of my past. Not tonight. Not ever.

Hattie pulled into the parking lot that was packed with pickup trucks. Literally, the only type of vehicle in the lot were pickups. Some of them old and beaten. Some of them as flashy and souped-up as Hattie's. The Ugly Man was tucked up on the shore of a lake, and a number of boats were tied up. "Is that Diamond Lake?"

"No. There's a whole series of lakes, rivers, and ponds in the region that connect to Diamond Lake. This one is called Little Diamond Lake."

"Why didn't we boat here?"

"I haven't put my boats in the water yet. They're going in this week." She swung her monster truck around with deft precision and flew backwards into a spot by the emergency exit door, driving over the "do not park here" sign to do it. "Exit plan, right?"

I grinned. It was the perfect placement for egress whether we were flying out the front door or running for our lives out the emergency exit. We had a clear shot at the dirt driveway, which was the only way back to the main road. "You learn fast."

"I'm a sponge for information that interests me." She shifted into park, then looked back at both of us. "You girls ready?"

Lucy nodded. "You got it."

I grinned. "Yep." We climbed out of the truck. I glanced down at the dirt parking lot and found a perfect rock. I gave it to Lucy. "Grind this over the end of your nose."

She grimaced. "Really?"

"Trust me, it works. Make sure you get it all around your nostrils especially."

Lucy did as instructed, and each time she tried to stop, I made her keep going. Finally, when the end of her nose was red and blotchy, I let her stop. "Perfect. Now cheeks."

"I found eyedrops in my purse." Hattie held out a small bottle. "I think they expired a few centuries ago."

"Perfect." I took them and gave them to Lucy.

"I hope these don't blind me." But she didn't hesitate. She just poured them into her eyes until they spilled down her cheeks. She did pause then. "You really want me to pour this up my nose?"

"It helps with credibility."

"Then let's do it." She immediately tipped her head back and squirted the eyedrops up her nose. She sniffled. "Do I look like I've been crying?"

"You look like a wreck who can be saved only by rebound sex." I put my arm around her. "Let's go, ladies."

Lucy leaned into me, and we headed up the steps.

My heart was pounding. It had been a long time since I'd done something like this, and in the past, I'd only done it to part a jerk from his money. I'd never done it to ferret out a murderer.

The thought made me pause.

A *murderer* could be in the very building we were about to walk into.

I might enjoy the art of the con, but violence? No. No. And no.

But I was doing it anyway.

I swallowed. "Ready?"

Lucy and Hattie nodded.

I managed to grin at her. "Then start crying."

CHAPTER 18

Lucy was a sniveling, sobbing mess as I pulled open the door of the Ugly Man Tavern. The minute I opened it, the smell of cigar smoke, old beer, and sweaty bodies hit me in the face.

"Oh, man." Hattie took a step backward. "Places like this give a bad name to responsible food purveyors everywhere."

I stepped on her foot to remind her that we were playing a role, then I dragged a wailing Lucy inside, doing a lightning-fast assessment of the place. Except for a few booths along the side, there were no private tables, just long ones with benches that could seat maybe twenty people along each side. They were as long as the room was wide, four on the right and three on our left.

I could see a big deck out back, but no one was at the tables. I suspected it was a summer hotspot, but the evenings were still cold.

The clientele was surprisingly well-balanced between men and women, except for the table closest to the kitchen. It was all men, and they looked rough. And wow, there were six of them. How many Derby Moose had there been? Six. What a random, odd coincidence.

I headed toward the empty seats at the near end of their table, because where else would we want to sit except next to the roughest looking group of men in the seediest tavern in town? Nowhere. Ever. That was the only place I wanted to be right now.

Especially without Griselda sitting in his little car just around the corner, ready to swoop in and save me.

As it was turning out, it was a lot easier to be brave when I had the FBI monitoring my every move, than it was when my only backup were a seventy-something race car driver and a freakishly strong mail carrier.

I wished King Tut had come with me.

Or that I'd brought a hairdryer.

Or, better yet, that I'd stolen one of Stanley's guns. Except I would have probably shot my foot off, so maybe not.

"I miss Rex," Lucy sobbed, leaning on my shoulder.

"I know." I patted her and guided her through the maze to the end of the table occupied by men I'd never want to be near. Hattie sat across from Lucy, and I sat next to her, closer to the men.

"Okay, turn it on," I whispered.

Lucy let out an unearthly wail unlike anything I'd ever heard. Hattie's eyes widened, and we stared at each other as Lucy howled.

Everyone in the place turned to look at her, with varying expressions of concern, irritation, and pure disgust.

I knew it was a matter of minutes, maybe seconds, until we were asked to leave. This was a rough-neck, dude-drinking hide-away, a place they went to find women who were willing to make their night better, not shrieking, hysterical women.

"Tone it down about a hundred notches," I muttered as I patted Lucy's shoulder. "You want to be rescued by one of these guys, not kicked out for disturbing the peace."

Lucy cut herself off mid-scream and sat back in her chair with a sigh. "I need a beer," she announced, almost bellowing it.

Subtlety clearly wasn't Lucy's best asset. Again, a little too extreme to be believable.

I'd never tried a con with anyone other than my mom. I had new respect for all the skills she'd taught me. Sure, we'd blown plenty of opportunities, but fake crying was a basic skill. Putting on the role of the tragic woman who is an easy target to fall into the arms of a guy who will listen to her tears was pretty simple. Or so I'd thought.

"You need to get laid," I said, trying to inject just the right amount of volume for the adjacent group to hear us, but for it to look like an accident. I hit the perfect note on my first try.

Nice.

The guy nearest us looked over. I barely kept myself from grinning. Yeah, I was pretty perfect. Of course, he was so unappealing that I wasn't sure we could actually fake it long enough to make this work, but that was a different problem.

Hattie rolled her eyes. "I don't think having sex with some random guy is going to help her get over Rex," she said, using the same tone I had.

She was good. I supposed that didn't surprise me.

"It's not like Rex was that good of a guy," I protested. "All Lucy needs is to sleep with some guy who's decent in bed, and she'll realize that she's better off without him." I had debated whether to diss Rex, but I was pretty sure anyone who'd come into contact with Rex would conclude he wasn't a decent chap.

That was good for us, because his dude friends wouldn't feel any compunction about moving in on his territory after his unfortunate demise.

Lucy folded her arms over her chest. "I'm not having sex with anyone ever again. If I ever see a penis again, I'll pull out my axe and chop that little sucker right off—"

Hattie squawked and hit Lucy in the shoulder with her purse, knocking her right off the chair mid-sentence.

But it was too late. The big, rough-looking, backwoods drinking and hunting buddies at the end of our table were all staring at Lucy with varying degrees of raw, unbridled terror on their faces.

Laughter started to bubble up in my throat as Lucy sat up,

picking old French fries out of her hair. "Are you okay?" I asked, my voice stuttering as I tried not to crack up.

"This floor is sticky. Is it old beer? I hope it's old beer, and not something worse."

Hattie had her head down on her arms on the table, and her shoulders were shaking with the effort of not laughing. "Penis-chopping?" she whispered, gasping as she tried to keep herself together. "You'll hack off his *penis*?"

Lucy looked back and forth between us. "I was going for the angle that guys use when they say that they can't get it up anymore, and then women take it as a challenge."

Hattie squawked again. "Men don't like to have their penises hacked off with an axe," she said. "I can't believe you just said that."

Lucy's brows went up. "Too much? I was trying to really get into the role."

I bit my lip. "The level of hate for penises of all kinds was so visceral that every man who heard you is now covering his family jewels and trembling," I whispered.

Lucy glanced over at the men beside us.

Every guy had both hands out of sight beneath the table, and most of them were hunched over in a protective posture. From her vantage point on the floor, Lucy was able to see beneath the table. As soon as she looked, her lips pressed together as she tried not to laugh. "I don't hate penises," she said, raising her voice. "I think they're really great additions to life."

"Is that why you hack them off?" Hattie asked. "So you can add them to your penis collection? How do you store them? Al-dente or over-cooked macaroni style?"

I pulled my T-shirt over my face as I started laughing again. "Stop it," I hissed. "We're on a mission."

Lucy put on a look of mock horror. "I don't collect them. I worship them. I pray to the penis god every night to deliver me a perfect specimen I can ride into the sunset."

"The penis god?" I tried to hold in my laughter.

Hattie paused, her breath coming in rasps as she tried to get the next words out. "Do you keep the altar in your bedroom or in your butcher shop?"

Oh, God. "A penis altar?" I couldn't help it. I knew we were on a mission, but I was gone. The image of a shiny gold penis sculpture with penises in little bottles hanging off it like a Christmas tree with ornaments popped into my mind, and I couldn't get it out.

The men at the next table called for their check. The one nearest to me, a big, terrifying man with a heavy beard gave me a dirty look, which made me laugh even harder.

Hattie was sitting up now, laughing so hard that she couldn't even keep her eyes open. "You're so evil," she said. "Penis-hacking wenches."

"I'm not a penis-hacking wench," I protested. "Lucy is."

Lucy crawled back onto the bench, her face red from laughing so hard. "Hey, don't call me that," she managed. "I'm not a wench."

That did it.

We completely lost it.

I'd never laughed so hard in my life. It was that silent laugh that's so uncontrollable that our whole bodies were shaking, but no noise was coming out. Lucy bent over, bracing her hands on her knees, laughing too hard to sit up.

One of the men at our table got up and walked to the bathroom. As he passed me, he bumped me, sloshing beer over my head and down my shirt.

I was laughing too hard to care, and it sent Lucy and Hattie into fresh gales of laughter.

Hattie's face was in her arms on the table, laughing so hard that her whole body was shaking. No sound. Just that silent, unstoppable laughter.

Tears were pouring down my face, and my stomach hurt from laughing so hard.

Hattie held up a butter knife and a fork. "Do you…use…" She

couldn't even get the words out, but made a little stabbing motion with the fork while she sawed with the knife.

"Stop," I gasped, as Lucy went into fresh gales. "I can't take it. You have to stop—"

"Excuse me." A woman walked up to the table.

No one even looked at her. We couldn't. We were laughing too hard to even make eye contact.

"I'm going to have to ask you to leave," the woman said.

"I can't stand," Hattie gasped. "I'll never make it to the door."

"I need beer," Lucy managed. "We came here for beer. I need a guy. I need to get laid. Rex died. I'm so sad."

I started laughing again. We were so far off script, it was a lost cause. "We failed," I gasped. "It's over. It's a complete fail."

"Lucy?" The woman trying to kick us out sounded startled. "Is that you?"

We looked up. She was wearing jeans, a black T-shirt, and a little nametag that said "Jillian." Beneath her name it said "Server." She was a tiny little thing, maybe around ninety pounds and under five feet. She had puny little arms, and her shoulders were about the width of my wrist. I'd thought Ruby Lee was the smallest woman I'd ever met, but Jillian was a close second.

Lucy sat up quickly, her laughter fading. "Jillian? I didn't know you worked here."

"Rex is dead. Why are you laughing? He was your boyfriend." She almost spit the last word.

We all tried to swallow our laughter in the face of Jillian's outrage.

"We weren't dating anymore, but you're right." Lucy cleared her throat. "I know he was your friend. I'm sorry for your loss."

"Are you? You seem pretty upset." Jillian's eyes were glistening with tears. "He's *dead*, Lucy. And you're laughing about it?"

We weren't laughing any more. Suddenly, I felt like a complete jerk.

She glared at all of us. "I think you all should leave. Get out and don't come back—"

"Jillian." A lumber-jack-type-muscular, rough, and rugged dude wearing a black T-shirt that said "Ugly Man Tavern" on it, with a caricature of a man with a hunting cap, a rifle, and a freakishly large nose on it, tapped her shoulder. "Why don't you take a break?"

She pressed her lips together and nodded, throwing Lucy another glare before stomping back toward the kitchen.

"Sorry about that." The man who'd sent her away tossed some menus on the table. "My name's Diesel Knox. I'm the owner. We never evict anyone unless they're breaking furniture or each other. Dessert is on us. I'll send another server out to you."

Huh. Diesel was the owner? He was not nearly ugly enough to have named the tavern after himself. In fact, he was pretty decent looking, with just enough scruffiness to make him a fit for some sort of small-town romantic comedy set in the old west.

I gave him a bright smile, relieved that we hadn't been escorted from the premises before we'd gotten any info. "Thanks so much. It's no problem at all. She's sad about Rex. We get it."

"Nothing to get." He rolled his eyes. "Rex Giannetti was scum. Had to kick him out two days ago for fighting." His gaze slanted toward the other end of our table. "Hey, Hugo! You going to make me regret letting you back in?"

We all turned to watch a bearded, scary dude at the end of our table raise his beer. "Rex is dead. I got no one else to fight anymore."

"Keep it that way." Diesel gave us a nod and then headed toward the door, welcoming a newcomer, leaving us to our menus.

I glanced back over my shoulder at Hugo, the guy who'd gotten in a fight with Rex. He was hunched over in deep conversation with his drinking buddies. Now that I was looking at him more closely, I realized he looked vaguely familiar, which didn't make sense. I didn't know many people in town. "Do you guys recognize him?" I asked.

"Hugo?" Hattie gave him a thorough inspection. "I think I've seen him with Ruby Lee."

"Ruby Lee?" I sat back in my seat. Hugo was backwoods scary. Tall, lanky, shifty-looking, with a dirty T-shirt and a ratty ball cap. Ruby Lee was a hair-sprayed, high-heeled sales phenomenon about twenty years older than he was. I hadn't seen him with Ruby Lee, so that wasn't how I knew him. "Why would she hang out with him?"

"I think he's some distant cousin. He showed up in town a few months ago to sponge money off her. I think he's living in a tent on her family's property or something," Lucy said. "Apparently, she can't get rid of him. He refuses to leave."

"Ah." That made more sense. "Family is the best."

Lucy grinned. "Totally, right?"

Ignoring our little bonding moment over family, Hattie leaned over to Lucy. "What was up with that waitress? You know her?"

Lucy checked the door to the kitchen to make sure our hostile server was still banished, then she lowered her voice. "You remember how I told you that an old twirling teammate of mine had been at Rex's the day I met him?"

"The woman you said you didn't actually like," Hattie said.

Lucy nodded. "That was her. Jillian Rollins."

"Wait a sec," I said. "Jillian works at the same place Rex was hanging out?"

"Maybe that's how she knew him." Lucy grimaced. "I guess it was a little insensitive to be so happy, but I had no idea she worked here."

"It's not insensitive at all," Hattie said, putting her arm around Lucy. "Everyone's feelings are valid and perfect." But as she said it, she looked over at me.

I knew what she was thinking. Jillian was now a connection between Rex and Lucy. Not that Jillian could have killed Rex. He'd been a big, muscular guy, and Jillian was so tiny she probably couldn't kill an ant if her life depended on it. Plus, her grief had been real. But her presence at the Ugly Man definitely made the tavern a potential focal point in Rex's death.

"Why don't you like her?" I asked.

"It's more like, why she doesn't like me." Lucy shrugged. "I was always better at twirling than she was, and she didn't appreciate it much. She was a little brat." She looked over at Hattie. "Her mom is Viola Rollins, the mayor of Bugscuffle."

"Bugscuffle?" I asked. "The town trying to steal the title from Bass Derby?"

Lucy nodded. "Bugscuffle is on Lady Slipper Lake, which is about five times the size of our lake. It's really a nice lake. They have four marinas."

"Four?" Hmm...maybe I should head over to Bugscuffle and see what I could learn from their marina emporium.

"It's not surprising Jillian was a bratty kid," Hattie mused. "Viola is one of the most obnoxious women I've ever met. Jillian must have been tormented by her."

"Her mom used to enter her in toddler beauty contests before Jillian took up twirling," Lucy said. "She was one of *those* moms."

Hearing stories about Jillian's mom made me think of mine, who I hadn't seen or even heard from in so long. In comparison, my mom didn't seem so bad. She'd encouraged me to be smart, savvy, and bold, and she'd made sure I understood that my value in life had nothing to do with my looks.

Suddenly, I missed her. I didn't even know if she was still alive.

As I listened to Hattie and Lucy discuss Jillian and her mom, the back of my neck began to tingle. Instinctively, I looked over my shoulder. The tavern was dark and shadowy, and it took me a moment to figure out what I was feeling, but I finally found him.

At the far end of the bar, one of the bartenders was watching us intently.

Too intently.

He met my gaze and then jerked his chin toward me. I jerked

my chin at the bar, and he nodded slightly before turning away. "You guys," I said quickly. "I think that guy wants to talk to me."

They both twisted around to see. "The one with the mullet?"

"Or the one with the skull and crossbones tattoo?" Lucy grimaced. "Because I don't think you should talk to him. He might murder you on the spot."

"Or the hot one in the corner with lumberjack muscles?" Hattie asked. "Because I'll go talk to him for you."

"Or do you mean the one in the—"

"The bartender," I clarified. "The young one." I stood. "Anyone want a beer? I'll go get them." I lowered my voice. "If I get abducted, save me."

"Save yourself," Hattie said. "You can do it."

I shot her a look, then headed across the tavern toward the bar lined with rough-looking men and their biker-chick women. I squeezed in at the far end of the bar, tucking myself up against the wall so I was a good ten feet from the nearest patron. I gestured to the young bartender for a drink.

He strolled over immediately. His name tag said his name was Tyrone, and he was younger than I'd thought, barely legal to serve alcohol. His skin was a beautiful brown, and the topline of his hair was bleached twists, the sides shaved short. He looked way too cool and clean cut to be hanging out at the Ugly Man Tavern. He leaned on the bar. "What are you here for?"

I paused. "Um…a beer? Or three?"

Tyrone shook his head. "No. *Why are you here*?" He turned away and began pouring a draft beer.

Something about the way he said it made me sit up. "I want to find out who killed Rex Giannetti."

He didn't look at me. If anything, he made even more of a point not to look at me. "Why?"

I hesitated, not sure whether to mention that there was a perfect scapegoat about to go to jail for his death. Tyrone glanced up at my face, and I saw fear in his eyes. Suspicion.

I decided to go with the truth. "An innocent person is about to go to prison for his murder. I want to clear her name."

He searched my face for a moment, then his shoulders relaxed infinitesimally, apparently satisfied by what he saw there. He shoved the beer at me. "Go to 22 Main Street in Bugscuffle between two and five tomorrow afternoon."

I repeated the information to myself so I'd remember. "Why?"

"Just do it." He poured another beer, still not looking at me.

"Okay." I paused. "Do you know who killed Rex?"

He didn't look up. "No."

I felt the truth of his words. He didn't know. But he knew something. "Do you know anything about the Derby Moose?"

He set a bowl of peanuts on the bar in front of me. "Rex was in here a couple months ago, recruiting people to ride with them."

I frowned. "Really?" That was long before I'd shown up. "Why?"

"I don't know. Diesel shut him down, though. Said that the Derby Moose weren't allowed in this place."

I wasn't so sure about that. "Why did Rex and Hugo get in a fight the other night?"

His shoulders tightened, and his gaze flicked toward Hugo's table. "I don't know."

He was lying! Oh, he knew. "If you did know, what could you tell me?" It was amazing how often it worked to rephrase the question that way. People who were lying were rarely on top of their game.

He topped off the beer and proved me right. "Ruby Lee Hanrahan came in here a few nights ago. Rex and Hugo were at a far table huddled up. She came in, sat down with them for about ten minutes, and then left. As soon as she left, they got into it. Turned into a drunken brawl."

Ruby Lee again? I frowned. "Does she come here much?" I couldn't imagine her hanging out here for any reason.

"No."

That was the answer I would have expected. "What did she want that night?"

He didn't say anything for a moment. He just watched the beer as he filled it.

I leaned forward. "What did Ruby Lee say to Rex?"

His gaze slid to mine. "She told him he had two days."

I frowned. "Two days? Two days until what?" To accept the offer on his house? Would Ruby Lee track Rex down to a place like this for a real estate sale? Yeah. Probably. I could see her having that level of zeal for the mighty dollar.

"I don't know. Something about the house. Rex got mad. Hugo got pissed, too, but she shut him down." He managed a half grin. "I guess even her cousin won't cross Ruby Lee, huh?"

So much fire in that tiny body of hairspray and lacquer. "Apparently. But Rex didn't back off?" It sounded like it was an innocuous real estate issue. But what if it wasn't? What if it was more? What else could be up about that house?

"No, Rex kept arguing with her." Tyrone finished pouring the third beer, and then shoved it across the wood to me.

He was clearly nervous to be speaking to me. "Why are you helping me?"

Tyrone kept his gaze on the bar as he pulled out a cloth and wiped the already clean surface. "Rex was a cheater and a crook," he said, "but I owe him. So find out who killed him."

"You owe him? For what?" Money? Drugs? Gambling debt? Tyrone seemed way too clean-cut for that.

For the first time since I'd sat down, Tyrone looked right at me, his brown eyes focused and intent. "Rex saved my life two months ago."

Huh. That was the first good thing I'd heard about Rex, other than that he was great eye candy. "What happened?"

"Doesn't matter." Tyrone tossed the towel under the bar, but I didn't miss the flash of fear across his face. Or the fact he glanced across the bar at Hugo before ducking his gaze. "If anyone asks, you and I talked about beer and the best fishing spots on the lake. That's it."

He didn't want to tell me about Rex saving his life? Oh...that sounded so juicy. I wanted to know what Rex's sole claim to human decency was. "Okay, but—"

"22 Main Street tomorrow. I'll have your server add the beer to your bill. Have a great night." Then he hurried away, not looking back at me as he tended to other customers.

Huh. I stared after him, then glanced over at Hugo. He was in deep conversation with his cronies, only a few feet from Lucy and Hattie. What had he done that had scared Tyrone so badly?

CHAPTER 19

I WAS JUST PICKING up the beers when someone leaned on the bar beside me. I jumped to the side before I saw the familiar face of my favorite, and only, customer. "Bryan!"

He grinned. "Hey, Mia. What brings you here?" He'd spruced up a bit from his dawn fishing gear, wearing a black V-neck sweater, a pair of jeans, and shiny black boots that were almost dressy. The white collar of his shirt was tucked in neatly, and he had just enough swagger to be impressive. The wrinkles on his face made him look distinguished, and he'd ditched his ponytail so his gray hair drifted down around his shoulders. He was wearing a ball cap again, but this one was white and clean. A man ready for a night on the town.

"Hattie wanted to go drinking," I said. "You know how she is."

"Hattie's here?" He looked over his shoulder. Hattie saw him and waved. "Looking good as always."

I raised my brows at his evident appreciation of my getaway driver. "Would you like to join us?"

"Turn down a chance to hang with Hattie? Never. Let me help you with that." He picked up one of the beers, plus the one he already had, and headed back to our table.

I grabbed the last two and hurried after him. He was already squeezing in next to Hattie when I got there. Hattie was giving him a hard time, but looking delighted to see him.

Huh. I sat down next to Lucy. "Do they have a thing?" I whispered to her.

"They flirt," she said as she accepted the beer. "I don't think they've ever hooked up, though."

"Hooked up" seemed to be the wrong phrase for a seventy-something flirt-a-thon, but if any senior could pull it off, it would be Hattie. "What'd you learn?" Lucy asked.

Hattie was too busy chatting with Bryan to pay attention, so I quietly filled Lucy in. She glanced down at the end of the table, where Hugo was still sitting. He seemed to feel her gaze, because he turned suddenly and looked right at us, his gaze hard and aggressive.

Lucy immediately pulled her attention off him, but I didn't. Hugo felt like a bully, and I knew the only way to deal with bullies was to not be a victim. So I stared him down. He stared right back without flinching, and I quickly realized that I'd just picked a battle I didn't really feel like spending the next two hours playing.

Hattie kicked me under the table. "What are you doing?"

"Staring contest. It's fun." Hugo took a long drink of beer, still not taking his gaze off me. I wasn't even sure if he was blinking.

"Really?"

"No. Save me." He leaned toward me, his shoulders wide, his eyes relentless and unwavering. "I can't back down, but I'm afraid my eyeballs are going to start bleeding from looking at him for so long."

"He looks angry," Lucy said.

"Yeah, like he's going to explode over the table and strangle me." I shifted in my seat, my eyes literally starting to twitch. The other men at the table had turned to see what Hugo was staring at, so now I had all six of them looking at me. "This isn't going at all like I'd hoped."

I remembered Tyrone's fear of Hugo and decided it maybe

wasn't in my best interest to plant myself so squarely on his radar. "Help—"

I suddenly got a faceful of cold beer. I gasped, coughing as the beer dripped down my face and over my clothes. "What was that?" I dragged my forearm over my face, trying to wipe it out of my eyes.

Hattie was grinning, Bryan looked startled, and Lucy was trying not to laugh. "I gave you an excuse to look away," Hattie said. "You're welcome."

"You literally threw your beer in my face."

"I'm an agile and quick problem solver. You're welcome." She handed me her napkin. "Here."

I snatched the napkin and wiped my eyes. It was grossly inadequate for handling the amount of beer drenching my shirt and dripping down my neck.

Bryan and Lucy were both laughing now, making me start to laugh, too. "Hattie, you're officially insane," I said.

"Why thank you, my dear." She filched my beer and raised it in a toast. "To bold women. May we take over the world."

I raised my empty hand, and Lucy toasted with her beer. "To bold women. May we take over the world."

Bryan added to the toast. "I love bold women. Someday, Hattie, you're going to go out with me."

Hattie rolled her eyes. "Never. You're too nice, Bryan. I'd crush your soul like a gnat."

"Too *nice*?" Bryan's brows went up. "I'm more than you think, Hattie. Try me."

"Nope." She propped her elbows on the table. "I'm never settling down again, Bryan. I've told you this before. Tony showed me what it's like to tie yourself to a man, and I'm not doing that again."

"Tony?" This was the first I'd heard of Tony.

"Tony York. My ex," Hattie said. "Married him when I was twenty-two. Divorced him when I was twenty-four. Lovely human being."

Before I could ask for clarification on the sarcasm dripping from every letter, Hugo and his pals walked past the table and headed out the door. He gave each person at our table a long look, finishing with me.

We all watched them go, and I had to admit to a feeling of relief when the door shut behind them. "Bryan? Do you know them?" Maybe Bryan had info.

"Seen 'em around a couple times, but I don't bother with the likes of them. Trouble, they are." Bryan settled back, taking a long sip of his beer. "How's the new mail route going, Lucy?"

She grinned at him. "Great. Hattie and Mia are on my route now, so it's awesome."

"You going to keep it, or you going back to your old one?"

"I hope I keep it. I heard Ellis got fired, so he's not getting the route back."

Bryan grunted, and I jumped in. "Do you come here much, Bryan?"

He shook his head. "Just a few times a month with my boys. We've been doing it for years." He nodded across the tavern, indicating a table occupied by three gray-haired men about his age. In their plaid shirts and ball caps, they looked sweet and outdoorsy, almost like the grandpas everyone wishes they had. "Used to come with Marco, but it's down to the four of us now."

I heard the wistfulness in his voice, and I recalled that he and Rex's dad had been friends. "You miss him, huh?"

"Yeah. He was an ornery bastard, but friends are friends. I need to go." He nodded at me. "Offer still stands to help you clean out the marina, Mia. I'd love to see it get back on its feet. I can come by tomorrow?" He glanced toward Hattie, and suddenly I understood.

He didn't want to help me with the marina. He wanted a chance to see Hattie.

I grinned as I wiped a fresh napkin across my brow, trying to get the beer that was still dripping off my hair. "You know, I just might take you up on that."

Hattie rolled her eyes at me, but Lucy cleared her throat to cover up a sudden burst of laughter.

"All right, then." Bryan stood up. "I'll see you all later." He winked at Hattie as he started to walk away.

"Wait!" When he turned, I tried to look casual. "Rex was here looking for people to join the Derby Moose. Do you know anyone who joined him?"

Bryan frowned. "Rex? The only time I saw him in here was the night Ruby Lee came after him, yelling about that house." He lowered his voice. "Looked to me like she had that no-good cousin of hers rough up Rex to get him to sign the deal on the house. Don't know what she has on Hugo, but he does whatever she asks."

"Hugo?" Lucy asked. "Tiny Ruby Lee controls *him*?"

Bryan shrugged. "Just making observations." He looked at me. "You know what she's like. Talked you into paying too much for the marina, I'll wager."

I inclined my head. I did know the tsunami-level force of Ruby Lee's personality. "I do know what she's like."

"I got no place spreading rumors, so I'll be heading off now," he said, tipping his hat. "Have a lovely evening, ladies. Maybe I'll swing by the marina tomorrow and see if anyone needs help."

Hattie waved him away as he sauntered off.

"He seems so nice," Lucy said. "Why do you keep turning him down?"

"I'm a single woman," Hattie announced. "No man gets to tame this warrior woman." But her gaze was following Bryan as he sat down with his friends.

"Maybe he doesn't want to tame you," I said. "Maybe he knows exactly who you are and wants to let you stay free."

Hattie raised her brows. "No man can keep up with me."

Lucy grinned. "Maybe there's one out there somewhere. Maybe not Bryan, but someone else."

"I think we need to focus." I leaned back in my seat as I watched Bryan sit down with his friends. "We need to talk to

Ruby Lee. She might not be strong enough to kill Rex, but Hugo is." As I said it, my gut tightened. I didn't want Ruby Lee to be involved. I liked her. She reminded me a little bit of my mom.

Hattie frowned. "Ruby Lee a killer?"

"Maybe not on purpose," I said. "What if she didn't mean to have Rex killed? What if they went there to rough him up, like Bryan said, and things got out of control?" I thought of how the killer had run toward the woods. "Does she have a boat?"

Hattie nodded. "She has a big pontoon. Luxury. She uses it to take potential clients on tours of the lake." She handed me another napkin. "She's tiny, but no one messes with her."

I patted the beer off my chest, but my shirt was hopelessly soaked. "She could have been waiting at the dock after she sent Hugo in to pressure Rex."

"Or maybe she took off when she heard our truck pull up, and left Hugo to set up Lucy," Hattie said. "She's pretty clever like that, as you know."

A chill ran down my spine. Had I been in a stare-down with Rex's killer? Had I bought the marina from a woman who'd orchestrated it? I swallowed. "You guys. We need to talk to Ruby Lee."

Hattie raised her brows. "Now?"

"Now."

Hattie clapped her hands. "Oh, goody."

CHAPTER 20

It took ten minutes to get the bill, but then we were finally outside. Lucy was giving Hattie grief about breaking poor Bryan's heart, and Hattie was defending her right as a warrior woman to never be tamed by a man.

I was obsessing over Ruby Lee being a murderer, or at least directing it. Why would she do it? Over a commission? It didn't make sense. There had to be something else about Rex's house. Something that started with Marco.

As soon as I thought about Marco, the back of my neck started to tingle. It took a moment to realize that the tension was coming from my environment, not from my own thoughts. I started scanning to see what my subconscious was picking up. At the other end of the parking lot were Hugo and two of his table buddies, standing around a large pick-up truck.

Their shoulders were hunched, and they were pacing restlessly. Tense. Angry hand gestures. Dark looks in our direction.

They were watching us.

And all of them were holding rifles.

Hattie and Lucy had migrated to discussing Lucy's bloodthirsty penis tendencies, so I tapped Hattie's arm. "Um, guys? They have guns."

Hattie absently dismissed me with a flutter of her hand. "Everyone in Maine has a gun. It's fine."

"I don't think it's fine that *they* have guns. We need to leave." As I said it, I pulled out my phone and casually took a picture of the license plate on the truck they were standing around.

Lucy and Hattie might be amateurs, but they both instantly picked up on the urgency in my voice. Their laughter faded, and they both looked past me to the men at the end of the dark, woodsy parking lot.

The men were watching us too carefully.

Three men. Three rifles.

Three of us. No rifles. Or hairdryers.

We had a two-mile dirt driveway to navigate before we would be out of the isolated woods. Hattie's mad driving skills wouldn't be much use if a bullet took out her tire.

Hattie let out a low whistle. "Yep, time to go." She jogged around to the driver's side, and Lucy and I climbed into the truck. We had to get out ahead of them and stay out of bullet range. If we did, they'd never catch us, not with Hattie behind the wheel.

They fanned out into two trucks, and their headlights came on as Hattie's truck roared to life.

Hattie hit the gas, and our truck shot forward.

And then a raccoon stepped out of the darkness right in front of us.

Lucy shrieked, I squawked and pointed, and Hattie swore. She hit the brakes and swerved.

I braced myself as the truck went into a skid, careening across the lot, in a full spin out. We went around twice, and then Hattie somehow managed to pull us to a stop with her truck facing the driveway.

I couldn't believe we were still alive. I swallowed, trying to get some sort of saliva working again. "That was nicely done."

"Thanks. That was so much fun."

"Yeah. Totally." I was still peeling my heart out of my throat, so I wasn't on the love bandwagon quite as much, but I was highly pleased that we weren't peeling an animal out of the grill of her truck.

Lucy's hands were still braced on the dashboard, and I wasn't sure she'd ever let go. Her face was ashen. "I think I almost died," she whispered. "Are we dead?"

We didn't have time to illuminate her on her mortal status, because the pickup trucks behind us sped forward, their engines roaring.

"Go!" I shouted.

Hattie let out a whoop, and then our truck exploded forward so fast that I was flung back against the seat, and one of the Francine's Mill boxes fell off and landed on me. I swore, gasping as it gouged its way down my body. "What the heck is in these things? They weigh a ton." I shoved it off me, and it thudded to the floor.

"Bread flour. It's the best around." She peeled out of the lot into the driveway, tires spinning as she straightened out. We made it about thirty yards before our truck's cab suddenly lit up like the midday sun.

I twisted around and was almost blinded by bright floodlights right behind us. "Um, Hattie?"

"I see them." She hit the gas, and our truck flew through the air as it hit a rut in the road.

Lucy turned around to look behind us, her frown evident in the blast of interrogation-level floodlights invading the cab. "How did they catch up? I thought you had the fastest truck in the state."

"I did, too. Apparently, I'm going to have to have a little chat with my dealer about that." Hattie whipped around a corner, and I grabbed the door as the right tires came off the ground.

Holy cow. I was going to die. "You have to slow down."

"So they can shoot us?"

"They aren't shooting—" There was a loud crack, and then the back window spiderwebbed into a thousand pieces. "Holy cow. They're *shooting* at us. Does that happen in Maine all the time, too?"

"It does at the Ugly Man. Usually only on Saturday nights, but sometimes you get lucky midweek." Hattie swore as the floodlights swerved to the right, and a second truck pulled up beside it, so the two of them were side by side behind us. "They're going to try to bump us," Hattie shouted. "I have a gun under the back seat. Shoot them."

"What? No!" I wasn't getting in a shooting match. "That is not the way to handle this—" I heard the ping of more bullets hitting the truck. "What is *wrong* with them?" I turned around to see that the trucks had split up, and they were speeding up to flank us.

"If you won't shoot them, then do something!" Hattie peeled around another corner. "I didn't spring for bulletproof glass."

I looked around frantically. All I could see were the Francine's Mill boxes stacked beside me, and Wally's furry butt sticking out from between them. I wasn't going to sacrifice Wally. "Can I use the flour?"

Hattie sighed. "Fine, but I'd rather you shoot them."

"I'm not going to shoot them! Does anyone have a knife?"

"I got one!" Lucy handed a massive hunting knife over the seat. It had a serrated edge and a blade big enough to take down a tiger.

I stared at it. "What's that?"

"It's a knife. Hattie keeps it in her glove box."

"It's not a knife. It's a horror movie in the making." I grabbed it, but just as I went to jab it in the box, Hattie swerved, and I stabbed the middle of the box, instead of the tape. It went in so easily that I decided that keeping my precious body parts out of the way would be a good plan. "Who uses a knife like this when they're being thrown around in a truck?" Another bullet pinged off the truck, and I dragged the knife down the middle of the box and ripped the flaps open.

Inside were brown paper bags of flour. I grabbed one, made a few small cuts in the paper, and handed it to Lucy. "Throw it on their windshield, but don't get shot."

"I'm on it." Lucy grabbed it and rolled down her window as I grabbed another one. She hurled it out her window, and it hit the windshield of the truck creeping up on her side. The bag exploded in a glorious poof of white powder. Flour went everywhere, a total white-out of the windshield.

The driver hit the brakes and spun out, skidding across the road and off into a ditch in a cloud of white dust. "Woohoo!" Lucy held up her arms in victory as Hattie cheered.

The truck on the left side wasn't deterred. It was still inching up. "I got this one," I announced as I grabbed another bag. I leaned out the driver's side, hefting the five-pounder. Trying to keep my head inside the car so it didn't get a bullet in it, I threw the bag.

It dropped almost straight down, landed on the ground in front of the truck, and disappeared under the grill.

"You need to throw harder," Lucy said. "Give it some muscle."

This was a strength activity? That didn't bode well for us. A bullet pinged off Hattie's rearview mirror, and it shattered.

I grabbed another bag. "I really don't like these people. On any level."

"Just get the bag!" Hattie said. "Now!"

I leaned out this time, and I threw the bag upward in a beautiful arc. It stayed airborne long enough for the truck to catch up. It landed with a thump on the hood and rolled off without exploding.

"You have to throw it harder," Lucy said. "Let me do it."

I was afraid Lucy would get shot or turn into a windshield projectile if she unstrapped herself to climb into the backseat. "I got it." I grabbed another bag and jammed the knife into it, ripping it partially open. Flour flew up in clouds as I cradled it to my chest. I leaned out Hattie's window, then almost ducked back inside when I saw how close the truck was.

I could almost touch the hood.

I could see the driver's face. It was Hugo. He looked right at me, and I felt my gut tighten as I suddenly recognized him.

He was the driver of the truck that had passed me right after

Lucy's Jeep had destroyed the sign. Seeing him behind the wheel had made it click. What the heck? What did he have to do with the sign?

Then I noticed the guy sitting next to him, and the long barrel of a gun easing out the passenger window right toward me. *Yikes.* "You're insane!" I hurled the broken bag of flour right at the windshield as hard as I could.

It hit square on the glass. The ripped bag tore open, and flour flew up everywhere.

"Nice work!" Hattie cheered as flour cascaded all over Hugo's windshield. I waved my hands to clear the dust around my face, watching as Hugo hit the brakes. The truck skidded out, then careened off the road, down an embankment, and into a thick stand of bushes. The angle was so sharp I knew he'd need a tow truck to get it out.

Hugo jumped out of the truck, shouting at us, but Hattie hit the gas, and we were around the corner and out of sight in a split second.

"Holy cow." I collapsed back against the seat. "Why were they trying to kill us?"

"Kill might be overly aggressive," Hattie said. "I think they were just trying to stop us. Everyone knows about my driving. It would take a lot to stop me."

"They were trying to stop us so they could kill us, then. Why?" I closed my eyes, trying to calm down. The ping of bullets hitting the back of the truck was permanently wedged in my memory next to the sound of Joyce's hit man shooting the shower curtain, only a few inches from my face.

Good sounds. Good memories. Life was full of blessings.

"Because you challenged his dominance," Hattie said. "Men like that get all dramatic when a woman out-alphas him."

"The staring contest? That can't be it."

"Stupid, drunken men with anger issues don't require a lot to get them worked up," Hattie said. "Throw in your staring contest with Lucy's penis-hacking, and that was enough to set him off."

"Let's not go back there." No wonder Tyrone had been afraid of him. Heck, I was afraid of him now. "He's crazy."

"Insane, yes, probably." Hattie glanced in the mirror at me. "But nice work, Mia. Really nice."

"I agree. That was great." Lucy beamed at me. "What a fantastic idea with the flour."

I grinned at her compliment. "It was a good call, wasn't it?"

"See? I knew you'd be helpful." Hattie grinned at me over her shoulder. "You're coming with us every time, Mia."

"No way. Never again." But I couldn't help smiling. If I hadn't been there, Hattie and Lucy might have ended up in jail for shooting someone. My mom had been a big advocate of non-violent solutions, and she'd taught me to always look for opportunities to problem-solve without violence. Yay for flour, right?

"By 'never again,' I assume you mean, until tomorrow? We have a date in the afternoon at 22 Main Street," Lucy said as Hattie pulled out onto the main road.

"22 Main Street? What's at 22 Main Street?" Hattie asked.

I'd forgotten about that. I glanced at Hattie's shattered mirror as Lucy filled Hattie in. Real bullets had been flying today. Who knew what we would find tomorrow?

I didn't want to go to Bugscuffle tomorrow. Playing sleuth had been all fun and games when it had been about picking locks and running the Double Twist. But actual bullets aimed at my head?

No. I didn't want to do it. I didn't want to keep going with this.

"Sounds great," Hattie said. "I'm in."

"I'll start my route early and meet you at the marina at two." Lucy looked over at me. "You're coming, right?"

"I don't know," I hedged. The gun thing had really knocked me back a few steps with my commitment.

"Step up, Mia," Hattie snapped. "A few bullets won't kill you."

"Actually, they will."

Lucy twisted around in the seat to look at me. "Please. I don't want to go to prison."

"I—" I paused at the expression on her face. "You literally have puppy dog eyes. How do you do that?"

Lucy grinned. "Is that a yes?"

Hattie looked back at me when I didn't answer. "Mia?"

There was no way I could leave them to handle it alone. They needed me. I sighed. "No more shooting."

Hattie and Lucy exchanged glances.

"Sure," Hattie said.

"No problem," chimed in Lucy.

I stared at them. "You guys are completely lying right now. You're not even trying to make me believe it."

"This is true," Hattie agreed. "We were giving you the answer that would make you sleep better tonight, since we all know you're coming regardless of whether there are bullets involved."

Lucy grinned. "Yeah, we kinda do." Her smile faded. "Have I told you how grateful I am for your help? I don't want to go to prison."

My throat tightened at her sincerity. I liked these women. They were the first friends I'd had in a very long time, maybe ever. I leaned back against the seat. They were right. I wasn't going to let them go alone, and I wasn't going to let Lucy go to prison.

"Fine. I'm in."

"Great," Hattie said, "because we just arrived at Ruby Lee's house."

CHAPTER 21

Ruby Lee was not remotely helpful.

Mostly because she wasn't there.

She didn't answer the door of her very large, absolutely gorgeous, lakeside mansion.

Her car wasn't in the driveway, and we didn't see it when we looked in the windows of the three-car garage. I hadn't brought my lock picks, so we had to satisfy ourselves with walking around her massive house and peering in all the windows.

Not that I would have broken into her house, though. Hopefully.

Since I didn't bring my tools, it wasn't an issue, but I was a little afraid of what Hattie and Lucy might have been able to talk me into.

Ruby Lee had a lot of beautiful furniture, a massive fireplace, and original artwork, but we didn't see her. Granted, most of the house wasn't visible from the few windows we could see into, but I refused to let Hattie break into the garage and look for a ladder.

We did see a tent off to the right of her house in the woods, which made us decide not to hang around very long. Who wanted to be there when Hugo got his truck out of the ditch and came back?

None of us.

We made it out of Ruby Lee's without running into Hugo and headed back to town, going over everything we'd learned so far, but unable to fit the pieces together.

We were almost back to the marina when I noticed the sign for the Bass Derby police station as we hurtled past.

The light was on, and there was an SUV out front, the same one that Devlin had been driving when he'd scared the heck out of all of us at Rex's house.

I had a sudden idea. "Hattie. Turn around. I want to stop at the police station."

She immediately yanked the steering wheel to the left and whipped us into the parking lot, the tires screeching to a stop right in front of the door. "What's up?"

"Chief Stone's car isn't here. I want to run in and pay my fine so he doesn't arrest me."

She raised her brows. "Now?"

"He's not here. What better time?" I loved the idea of depriving Chief Stone of the chance to arrest me. "I'll just take a sec."

"Fine. Hurry up." Hattie put the truck in park.

I glanced at Lucy, who was watching the police station nervously. "Why don't you take Lucy home, and then come pick me up?"

Lucy frowned. "I'm fine to wait here."

"What if Chief Stone shows up?" It was one thing for him to arrest me for sign destruction. It was another to have him arrest Lucy for murder. I was really worried about what he might have found at her house.

Everyone who had seen any movie knew how easy it would be to plant evidence, especially since I was increasingly certain that Lucy had been intentionally set up as a suspect. I couldn't stop thinking about the fact Hugo had driven by only moments after Lucy's car had hit the sign.

I felt like this had to revolve around Hugo somehow. I liked Ruby Lee. I didn't want her to be a murderer, or be involved with one. The fact that Hugo apparently lived on her property created a connection that I didn't want, I needed to find out more about who he was. "Run Lucy home. I'll be fine."

Lucy flashed me a smile, visibly relieved. "Thanks, Mia."

"You got it." I climbed out of the back door. When my feet hit the pavement, I realized my legs were wobbling from the terror of Hattie's driving. "Next time, we take my car."

"Your car is still full of all your belongings because your apartment smells too bad to move into," Hattie pointed out.

"You can hang onto the roof."

"Hah." She barked a laugh at me, then peeled out.

The smell of burned rubber lingered in the air behind her, wrapping around me like a warm blanket of love that needed to be laundered desperately.

I did a quick double-check of the parking lot to make sure Chief Stone's car wasn't anywhere to be seen, but the SUV with the "Police Chief" on the side of it wasn't in sight. Just a few regular police cars, including two SUVs, and three civilian cars.

The police station was a cute, gray, one-story building with white trim and a lush lawn. The parking lot was newly paved, and big floodlights lit it up. There were manicured plantings and landscaping, and the sign was a dark wood with gold lettering.

The front steps were a very pretty bluestone, and they led to a front porch that had two wooden benches, some beautiful pink geraniums, and pristine white pillars.

It was exactly the police station that one would expect from a town that had won Best Lake Town in Maine for eleven years running.

I was kind of surprised, actually. I realized I'd set expectations for Bass Derby based on the decrepit state of my marina. I'd been so busy chasing down murderers and trying to get the stink out of my living quarters that I hadn't taken time to drive around my new town.

If the police station was any indication, it was adorable.

I wanted to live here, not in the marina.

Maybe I should let Chief Stone arrest me after all.

I paused, seriously considering the merits of that idea, until I realized it meant King Tut would be left alone.

Nope. That cat needed me. I would not abandon him.

But I would enjoy every minute inside the charming police station while I was here. It was like the cozy home I'd never had, but always wanted.

Seriously. It was that appealing.

I pulled open the glass door and hurried in. The lobby of the police station was almost as inviting as the outside, with potted plants, armchairs, and nature photographs of loons, baby foxes, and black bears. Guarding the front door at a reception desk was a woman I recognized from Hattie's café. "Angelina?"

The grandma of the hot Greek twins looked up from her phone and waved at me. She was wearing a cheerful yellow cardigan over a white blouse, with gold loon earrings. Her smile was bright and friendly, a perfect welcome for the feel-good vibe of the police station. "Mia! Great to see you! What's going on?"

This was going to be perfect! "I didn't know you worked here." I hurried up to the desk. "I need to pay a fine. Can you do that?"

"You bet." She put down her phone and started tapping on the computer. "Did you bring it with you?"

I grimaced. "No, I forgot."

"No problem. I can look it up."

As she typed on the computer, I had a sudden idea. "Can you look up license plates on that?"

She shook her head. "Nope. I don't have that access. Officer Hunt does though. He's here tonight."

There was no way I was going to ask Devlin for help, not after our incident earlier when he'd basically accused me of protecting a murderer. "No, it's fine." I'd text Griselda later. He'd help me.

"Here it is." She whistled as she read the screen. "That's pretty hefty."

"I didn't kill the sign."

"I know. Hattie told me," she said as she rang it up. "She asked me to let her know if I hear anything about Rex's murder case," she said. "I'd never do that, of course." Then she winked at me, and I realized she would do exactly that.

I grinned. "You gotta do the right thing."

"Always."

Movement to my right caught my eye, and I looked up as Devlin walked past, carrying a brown folder. He was apparently immersed in its contents, because he didn't even notice me. He was wearing jeans and a T-shirt, clearly off-duty, but looking irritatingly attractive.

He went out of sight, then a moment later, he leaned back around the corner, peering at me. "What happened to you?"

"Me?" I put on an innocent face. "Nothing. Why?" Admit to a police officer I'd been involved in a gunfight, a high-speed chase, and then forced two trucks into a ditch? Nope. That didn't feel like a sound plan at all.

"Why?" he echoed. "Because you smell like a brewery, and you look like someone tarred and floured you."

I looked down and saw that I was covered in a thick coat of white powdery paste. For a split second, I had a flashback to that July morning when I found the white powder in my china cabinet. What if it hadn't been flour I'd hurled out the window? What if Hattie was Maine's answer to Stanley? I panicked and licked my arm. Dry, tasteless flour. Rock on. All was well. "Whew. It's only flour."

Devlin was staring at me as if I'd lost my mind. "You're covered in it. How on earth do you not know what it is?'

"I thought it was flour, but then I had a PTSD moment. You know, ex-husband drug runner and stuff."

Angelina coughed, and I grimaced. I'd totally forgotten she was there.

I took a deep breath and tried to wipe my pants off. It didn't work. All I succeeded in doing was grinding the white paste more securely into my jeans. "It's good. I'm good. Everything's good." Flashback was over. All was well.

Devlin still looked confused. "How did you get covered in flour and beer?"

Hmmm… if Hugo and his pals decided to report the flour incident to the police, it might be good to come up with an alternate tale. "Hattie was making beer bread in the café. I wanted to learn, and there was an incident." I had to remember to tell Hattie my cover story. I had no doubt she'd be happy to back me up. I was pretty sure she'd be accommodating about fabricating stories to the police in the interests of moral justice and well-being.

"An *incident*? It looks like a lot more than an incident." He narrowed his eyes. "Is that why you came straight here without changing your clothes? What's happening?" His hand went to the gun on his hip. "Is someone after you?"

I stared at him, startled by his reaction. His hand was literally on the butt of his gun, ready to point it at the hit man that Griselda had warned him about.

Was it weird how much I liked that?

Probably. Maybe I needed to spend some more time having positive self-talks in the mirror. *I live in peace. There are no guns or professional killers in my life. Ohm. Ohm. Ohm.*

Either way, Devlin's eagerness to shoot someone on my behalf made me feel better about him, especially since the last time I'd seen him, he'd been a little irritating about his lack of faith in my moral standards.

Angelina cleared her throat. "Officer Hunt could look up those records for you."

He closed the folder and gave me his full attention. "What records?"

Could I worm the information out of him? Maybe. "I need a quick favor." I noticed his hand was still on his gun. Adorable, wasn't he? He was like a cupcake made of bullets. "Are you free right now?"

He took his hand off his gun. "Maybe."

"I'll take that as a yes."

"I'll buzz you in." Angelina helpfully hit the buzzer, and I scooted in before he could stop me.

I picked a direction and started walking. "Where's your office? This will take only a moment."

"Mia." He sounded tired and irritated, reminding me of Griselda. Was it me or life as a law enforcement agent that created such weariness in them? I was going with their chosen career.

"Oh, look, Chief Stone's office." I peered inside. It looked like the world's most charming living room. His desk was a beautiful wooden table, and there were two upholstered armchairs. White, built-in bookshelves lined the walls. Several flowering plants. Three paintings of the lake. A photograph of a moose. A carved loon was sitting on the windowsill.

Every pen was positioned artistically on the desk, along with an antique letter opener, and a high-end laptop. There wasn't a paper out of place.

In fact, I wasn't sure there were any actual papers in there, let alone signs of actual occupation. "Does he do any work?"

Devlin walked up behind me. "What do you need?"

"We both know he doesn't." I kept walking down the hall. "Oh, look. Your name is on this door. Perfect." I walked into the office. It was neat. Precisely neat. Functional. Organized, but it had the distinct aura of an office in use. Exactly as I would have expected from him.

It looked like the office of a cop who took his job seriously, which really wasn't very surprising.

I sat down at his desk, and I was delighted to see that his computer hadn't locked yet. I moved the mouse around a bit to make sure it stayed unlocked. He had been searching articles on the Derby Moose.

The one currently open on his screen was about the police officer who had been stalked by them, and then found floating in the lake. Chief Stone hadn't been exaggerating, apparently.

Chills crept down my spine.

Had I been only a few feet from Derby Moose tonight? Had the men in those trucks been Derby Moose?

Suddenly, I was very glad Hattie had been our driver tonight when we'd fled from the Ugly Man Tavern. Both because of her mad driving skills and her flour hoarding.

I needed to get this sorted out and quickly. "How do I search for license plate records?" Devlin was a little bossy, controlling, and irritating, exactly like Griselda. I'd learned the best way to handle men like him was to simply do what I wanted and let them step out of my way.

It worked pretty well for the most part, except with Griselda. It had almost never worked with him, but it felt a lot better than begging for favors I wouldn't get anyway.

Devlin walked into the office, propped his shoulder against the doorjamb, folded his arms over his chest, and studied me.

I studied him right back. He was looking mighty delicious with his biceps flexing. And his jeans sat perfectly on his hips. He was as put-together and focused as Griselda, with that same law-enforcement vibe, but, unlike Griselda, he was also, quite clearly, a tempting, intriguing man.

Damn him. I wasn't interested in noticing attractive men right now.

"Why do you need to search license plate records?" he asked.

I leaned back in the seat. "I'm trying to find Rex's murderer."

His eyebrows shot up, and he stiffened. "Don't."

"Why not?"

"Because whoever killed Rex is a murderer."

"Obviously. What's your point?"

"What's my point?" He didn't sound impressed with my question, based on the sarcasm dripping from his words. "Do you really need to ask that? Hawk said you're very, very smart."

A little warm fuzzy settled over me. "Did he really?" He'd never said that to me in person, but it felt good. I'd worked hard for him.

"Yes." Devlin set the folder down on a shelf, walked over, and leaned on the desk with both hands.

"That's a threatening posture," I observed. "Why are you trying to threaten me?"

"You're sitting in my chair." But he did pull back and brace his hands on the back of a chair instead.

"You could have asked me to get up," I pointed out.

He paused, and surprise flickered over his face. "Would you have gotten up?" He sounded like he didn't think there was even a remote possibility I would've relinquished my seat upon request.

I narrowed my eyes. "What exactly did Griselda tell you about me?"

"You have attitude. Sass. You're a pain in the butt."

I sighed. "Such unrequited love. I fear he'll never find another, because every woman will fall short in his eyes."

This time, Devlin couldn't hide his surprise. "Did you and Hawk *date*?"

There was the faintest edge to his voice that made me sit up. "Why?" Because Devlin had been having fantasies about me? Because I would be happy to have fantasies about him.

No. No I wouldn't. I was done with men for at least a few centuries.

"Because if Hawk was sleeping with you, that would force me to look at his request to protect you as a personal favor, instead of a professional courtesy. There's a difference."

Bummer. He wasn't lusting after me.

Which was fine.

I didn't need his lust.

"Oh, okay. That's good to know." Disappointing as well, because what woman doesn't want to be admired as a sexual siren by a very hot police officer willing to pull a gun to save her life? None that I knew of. But I supposed it was all for the good. Fantasies could lead to trouble, and I had very specific life goals to stay out of trouble.

I stood up. "You can have your chair back." I walked around his desk and sat down in the chair he was leaning on.

He didn't move for a moment. Which meant he was looming over me with his chiseled muscles and delicious scent. After-shave? Deodorant? A fresh shower? I wasn't sure, but he smelled amazing.

Which was annoying. Distracting. And dangerous.

"Did you date Hawk?" He didn't sound amused that he'd had to ask again.

"Griselda would have thrown me in front of a tank if it would have helped his chances to nail Stanley." I heard the bitterness in my tone, and I grimaced. I was really trying to get over any negativity about that period in my life, but clearly, I hadn't quite managed it.

He narrowed his eyes. "That doesn't answer my question."

"Of course it does." I raised my brows. "If you know anything about me at all, you would now have all the information you need to figure it out yourself." I surprised myself as I said it. I hadn't actually been intending to be helpful when I'd made the tank comment. But in truth? I would never have dated a man who would throw me in front of a tank for any reason, let alone for his work. I had standards.

Devlin studied me for a moment longer, and then his shoulders relaxed infinitesimally. "You never slept with him." He sounded satisfied, certain he was right.

He was even smart. Could the man get any more irritating? I grumped at him. "Can we look up the license plate now? Hattie will be back in a few minutes to pick me up."

"I need more details." He whistled cheerfully as he strode around the desk and settled into his chair. "Whose license plate do you need and why?"

Of course he would ask for details.

But did I want to give them? I contemplated the scenario if I told him that we'd found a moose costume in Lucy's car, along with receipts from the tavern where it looked like the rest of the Derby Moose were hanging out.

There was no way to prove that the moose costume wasn't hers...or mine, for that matter, since Chief Stone had seen it under my tractor. I doubted that Devlin was the type to simply say "Thanks," and ask no questions if I gave him the plate numbers and told him they might or might not belong to the Derby Moose members.

He would ask questions. If I answered them, how did I know he'd believe that *we* had nothing to do with it?

I didn't know that, seeing as how he was already predisposed toward believing the worst of our charming little gang.

What I did know was that if he was all-in on pinning the murder on Lucy, my story would give him more things to connect her to a crime she didn't commit.

I'd have to find another way to get the info on the plates. Griselda would help me, and it wouldn't risk Lucy.

Devlin leaned forward. "Hawk said that when you got that look on your face, it was usually worth finding out what you were thinking. So, what's going on in that brain of yours, Mia?"

I immediately made my face expressionless. I was a master at cons. There was no way I had a face that told tales. "What face?" I ignored his question.

He shook his head. "I'm not telling, or you'll stop doing it."

Damn Griselda. "Did you guys have a boys' weekend when you spent the entire time discussing me? You two seem to have covered a lot of ground."

"He told me what he thought I would need to know." Devlin drummed his fingers on the table. "Talk to me. I want to solve this case, too. Whose plates?"

"I can't tell you." I stood up. "Never mind. I'll figure it out."

Devlin stood up, too. "Withholding evidence from the police is a crime."

I held out my wrists. "Arrest me, then. I can't sleep at my

apartment without being asphyxiated, so I might as well sleep here."

He ran his hand over his hair in evident frustration. "I don't want to arrest you. I just want to know what you know."

"So you can use it to arrest Lucy? No."

"Mia—"

"*No.*"

He stared at me.

I stared back.

Which meant we were in an alpha-dog staring contest.

Griselda had totally out-alpha'd me, mostly because he'd been holding a genuine threat of imprisonment over me.

Devlin didn't have that leverage. Although, he was definitely hotter, and that got under my skin a little bit.

He finally sighed. "I can't let you pursue a murderer."

"I can't let you arrest Lucy." I would have told Griselda what I'd found. Griselda would have believed me when I said Lucy was innocent. Yes, he'd sent me into the devil's playground without compunction, but he'd believed my innocence every single step of the way. In return, I realized that I'd learned to trust him, at least on a certain level. Not with my life and well-being, but with my integrity? Yes.

Griselda might be irritating and overbearing, but he was predictable and reliable.

I realized suddenly how much I'd learned to count on Griselda's faith in me. I realized it, because of how helpless I felt standing there with Devlin, unable to be honest with him and ask him for the help I needed.

I sighed. "Can you process a credit card, or shall I go back to Angelina? I need to pay my fine."

He stared at me for a long moment, then finally said, "What?"

"Chief Stone came by to arrest me earlier today for failing to pay my fine for destroying the sign I didn't destroy. Can you take my money so I don't get arrested?"

The look on his face was almost comical. "I honestly don't give a damn about the sign or the fine."

I let out a snort of laughter at his outburst. "Chief Stone would not approve."

He gave me a small grin. "No, he wouldn't, would he?"

We grinned at each other, a moment of connection. A day in town, and I already had enough inside info to share a laugh with Devlin. It felt good. It felt like I was starting to belong. "He came at me with handcuffs," I said. "I need help."

He raised his brows. "I'll make a deal."

CHAPTER 22

A DEAL.

The moment Devlin said those words, I had a sudden flashback to that moment in Starbucks, when Griselda had told me he'd make a deal with me: no prison in return for spying on Stanley. I'd had no conception of the degree to which that one little deal would tear apart my entire life or my own sense of safety.

But I knew now.

I couldn't go through that again. Never. Ever again.

"*No.*" I shot to my feet, backing quickly toward the door as fear clamped around my lungs. "I don't make deals with law enforcement anymore."

"Whoa. Wait a sec." Devlin jumped up, bolted around his desk, and got to the door before I made it there, bumping me as he squeezed past me. "Hang on."

The moment our hips met, I put my hand on his waist to push him away. But when I did, I felt his phone in his pocket. Instinctively, my fingers closed around the phone, and I liberated it from his jeans and shoved it in my pocket, backing away as I did so.

If I had to use his phone as leverage for my freedom, I would. Whatever it took.

I was starting to hyperventilate, which caught me completely off guard. I hadn't realized exactly how deeply traumatized I was from the whole experience with Stanley, but the trembling of my hands and my rising need to run to the bathroom and throw up made it clear. "I'm not making a deal with you. I'm leaving."

Did he have leverage on me, enough to force me into a deal? I didn't think so, but what if he did? Oh, God. *What if he could force me?*

He was still blocking my path to the door. "Tell me what you've found out, Mia. Give me the license plates. Let me handle it."

"No." I hit his chest, but he didn't flinch. "Move. I need to get out of here." I felt like the walls of the police station were closing in on me. I needed to get out.

"Mia." He set his hands on my shoulders, and I jumped back, crashed into the chair, and fell into the trash can.

I scrambled to my feet as I held my hands out to block him. "Stop!"

His hands went up in surrender. "It's okay." His voice was soft, like he was trying to sooth a wild animal. "I'm not going to hurt you."

"I know." I was having trouble breathing now. "I need to get out of here." I bent over, bracing my hands on my thighs. "I can't breathe."

Devlin crouched in front of me. "Slow your breathing."

"I can't—"

"Match my breath." He took a long, slow inhale. "Breathe with me."

I closed my eyes and listened to his breath, trying to match it. He exhaled slowly, and I did the same, focusing on the sound of the air leaving his lungs.

Slowly, agonizingly, my breathing calmed, and the panic receded.

Devlin was still crouched in front of me, watching me. "What was that about?" he asked gently.

I closed my eyes. "You said we'd make a deal. When Griselda

said that to me, I didn't have the choice to refuse his offer, and then he ripped my life to shreds."

Devlin swore. "Mia, I didn't mean—"

I shook my head, needing him to understand. "When I was working for Griselda, I would lie in bed beside Stanley at night, wide awake, waiting for him to grab the gun from his nightstand, point it at my head, and pull the trigger. Every night, every moment of every day, I lived in terror that Stanley would discover what I was doing and make an example of me. I was terrified every minute of every day for two years. *Terrified.*"

Devlin swore under his breath. "I'm sorry, Mia."

I looked up at him. "Every time I met with Griselda, I hoped he'd tell me that they had enough evidence. That I didn't have to go back. And every time, he sent me back in there. Every time, I had to walk back into that house and take the chance that Stanley would be waiting for me with a gun, an axe, and a trash bag."

"An axe?"

I nodded. "For chopping me up into little pieces and leaving bits of me all around town as a lesson to anyone who betrayed him."

"*Shit.*"

"I agree." I took a breath and stood up. My legs were still shaking, and when I tried to push my hair out of my face, my fingers shook against my head so badly I couldn't even feel my hair. I folded my arms across my chest instead, trying to hide how much my hands were trembling.

I was so frustrated by my panic attack. I'd worked so hard to move beyond it, to reclaim my sanity. I'd thought I was fine.

Clearly, I wasn't.

I didn't deserve to feel like this. I wasn't the bad guy. I knew it. I'd grown up thinking that I didn't deserve anything good because I was a lowlife criminal, but Stanley had showed me who the real evil was, and it wasn't me. "You guys all see me as a criminal, because of my past with my mom. But I'm not. Stanley, and people like him, are the real criminals."

He nodded. "I know."

I tried again to push my hair out of my face, but it was too stiff from the flour and beer, so I dropped my hand in frustration. "Sleeping next to a man who will murder you in a heartbeat is…" There were no words that could do justice to the level of stress and anxiety I dealt with for those two years.

But Devlin didn't seem to need an explanation. "I get it."

"I did it for two years. I can't do that again. Griselda didn't let me walk away. I'm never, ever putting myself in a situation where I can't walk away again." I stood up and took a deep breath. "No deals with police again. Not ever."

"I don't blame you." Devlin was still in a crouch, looking up at me, a thoughtful expression on his face. I couldn't tell what he was thinking, and honestly, I didn't care.

My trip down memory lane had given me a nice, clear reminder of why my childhood distrust of law enforcement was a valid and excellent lesson I had to always remember. Griselda had had my back, but it had never been about me. It had been about getting his collar.

Devlin and Chief Stone were also law enforcement. They were about getting their murderer, and all signs pointed toward Lucy. They didn't care about the human side of the equation, the fact that Lucy would never have done something like that.

Devlin rose to his feet, moving slowly, as if he were afraid he was going to spook me. "You're a force, Mia. A strong, powerful force."

I rubbed my forehead wearily and found hardened flour paste ground into my skin. "I'm not a force. I'm tired, and I want to go home. So please run that plate for me and take my money for the fine. Can you do that for me?"

I honestly thought he'd take pity on me. I felt like we'd shared a moment. I'd revealed a deep, dark terror that still haunted me. He'd uttered profanities on my behalf and called me a force. Didn't that amount to something?

But for Devlin the Cop, it apparently didn't, because he shook his head without hesitation. "Just because you took down your ex-husband's drug-running operation doesn't mean you're equipped to handle a murderer."

"I know that!" I put my hands on my hips. "I seriously already know that. Do you think I want to be anywhere near this? Look at me!" I held up my hand, which was still shaking. "I know exactly how well I stack up against murderers, but you guys are trying to pin the murder on an innocent person. I can't sit around and let her be arrested." I put my hands on my hips and lifted my chin. This time, I was helping on my own terms, and no one had the right to make me take risks I didn't want to deal with.

His eyes narrowed. "So you *would* protect her."

"She didn't do it!" I was so frustrated I felt like screaming. Why couldn't these law enforcement officers stop doing their job for one minute, long enough to have a little humanity?

He stared at me.

I stared back. Again.

He finally sighed. "Listen, Mia." Devlin's voice was softer now. Gentler. He was definitely trying to manipulate me. "I want to find out the truth. If Lucy didn't do it, then the more evidence I get, the more equipped I will be to find the real murderer."

"Everyone sees the world through their own perspective," I snapped, citing one of the founding principles of con artist success. "People see what they want to see, and what they expect to see. If you want to arrest Lucy, then you'll look at the evidence that way."

He stiffened. "I'm a police officer trying to find out who murdered a resident of my town."

I heard the roar of an engine pull up out front. "Hattie's here. I'm leaving."

"Mia—"

I heard the clicking sound of high heels marching through the lobby, which made me frown. Last time I'd seen Hattie, she'd been wearing boots meant for stomping. I wasn't sure she even owned heels.

"Devlin?" A woman's voice called out. "Are you here? I saw your car out front as I was driving by."

Devlin swore under his breath, and I turned quickly to see a woman striding toward me. She was in her early sixties, with dark brown hair, diamond stud earrings, a black skirt, and heels. Not high heels. More like business-height heels. Her face was pinched in a frown, and her shoulders were tense.

Not exactly what I'd expected to see in Bass Derby's police station at night.

She noticed me, and her eyes widened when she took in my flour-covered appearance. Her mouth dropped open, and I stiffened, preparing the Hattie story, but before I could say anything, her frown morphed instantly into a friendly, delighted smile.

"Well, hello." She held out her hand to shake mine, despite the beer-caked flour on my palm. Her grip was firm, but not too firm. Well-practiced perfection. "My name is Eloise Stone, Mayor of Bass Derby, winner of Best Lake Town in Maine for eleven years running. Welcome to our lovely oasis on Diamond Lake. How may I be of service to you?"

I felt like the sun had just shined its light all over my soul. Eloise Stone was absolutely compelling. No wonder Bass Derby had won eleven years in a row. Who would be able to resist her? She would be incredibly successful as a con artist. Like, top-of-the-line successful.

She was attractive, but not in a threatening way. Put together, but not in an offensive way. She hit every note perfectly to exude charm, welcome, competence, and confidence.

I was impressed.

And, I noted, her son had not learned those skills from his mother.

"Nice to meet you," I said, intentionally not offering my name. I might be a far less accomplished charmer than Eloise, but I had a decent sense of self-preservation. After Lucy's revelation of the hostile family brouhaha, I didn't trust Eloise's warmth even a tiny bit. Her son had his sights on me and my friend, so I was staying off her radar. "I'm all set. I just needed directions." I nodded at Devlin. "Thanks so much for your help, Officer Hunt. I'll let myself out."

He opened his mouth to protest my leaving, then glanced at Eloise and I saw him decide not to say anything about what we'd been discussing. "Have a good night," he said, with just the faintest hint of grumpiness.

How interesting that he was willing to let me trot out of the police station without turning over the license plate info now that the mayor had showed up. Eloise no doubt wanted to get the murder solved. Devlin could have told her I was sitting on information and used her to pressure me. But he hadn't. He'd told her nothing.

Which made me curious.

Curious enough that I continued to stand there for a moment, hoping that they would start to discuss whatever she'd come there to talk about.

They didn't.

They both continued to look at me and wait for me to leave.

Devlin looked resigned and more than a little irritated. At me or her?

Eloise looked like her face was starting to ache from keeping the smile plastered to it, which, of course, made me want to wait there a little longer.

I smiled at them both. "Are there any good places for moose watching around here? I'd really like to see a moose."

Eloise's face stiffened, and Devlin gave me a stoic, not-entertained glare.

The mayor recovered fairly quickly. "If you go south on Route Six for ten minutes and take a left at Peach Tree Farms, they have a field out back that they allow the public to park in for five dollars and watch the moose. The best times of day are late afternoon into early evening."

"Great." It *was* actually great. I'd love to see a moose that wasn't wearing a nylon costume and felt antlers. "I can't wait. I'll check it out tomorrow." I paused, the moose jarring my memory back to a more pressing issue. "Where can I rent Jet Skis around here?"

This time, Eloise's eyes narrowed.

I gave her my most innocent expression and blinked several times.

Finally, Eloise caved. "The Diamond Lake Yacht Club," she said. "It's right downtown."

I blinked in surprise. Holy cow. I hadn't even thought of that. The Jet Skis had to have come from somewhere. But the Yacht Club? The high-end, luxury destination that had won every customer on the lake? How could it possibly be involved in something as lowbrow as a bunch of idiots running around in moose costumes? "Is there anywhere else?"

She shook her head. "The Yacht Club is the only marina on the lake."

Well, I knew for a fact that wasn't true. "Really? It's the *only* marina on the lake?"

"Yes." She intentionally looked at her watch. "If you'll excuse us, I really must speak to Officer Hunt. I have dinner plans with my son that I must be home for. Devlin?" She motioned to his office, basically directing him inside. "Good evening, Ms.—?"

"I'll be on my way." I gave her a winning smile, deciding not to give her my name. "This police station is adorable. If the rest of the town is like this, it will be perfect for the movie."

Eloise's mouth dropped open. "The movie? What movie? Are you scouting a location for a movie?"

"Oops." I pretended to lock my lips and throw away the key. "Mum's the word. I didn't just say that. Bye." I trotted down the hall before Eloise could say anything else, grinning as I heard her grilling Devlin on who I was and what movie I was scouting for.

I didn't wait to see if Devlin gave me up.

I just escaped while I had the chance.

The place had jail cells, after all. I had a feeling Eloise would have been very happy to put the sign-killer behind bars and make an example out of me.

The woman scared me, so I was relieved to pay my fine to Angelina on the way out, ending Chief Stone's leverage over me. When I climbed into Hattie's waiting truck, it felt like coming home as I filled her in on everything.

Girl time made everything better. I couldn't believe I'd gone my whole life without it.

CHAPTER 23

After Hattie dropped me off, I made quick work of getting to bed. I hid Wally under my bed of life jackets, both to keep him out of sight and to give myself a little extra cushioning. King Tut was delighted with the new sleeping arrangements, and he'd burrowed through the life jackets to spoon with Wally, purring with deep, feline satisfaction.

So cute, right? I had no idea the joy a cat would give me. Experiencing King Tut's simple basking of life made the stress of being shot at, chased, and having a panic attack fall away.

Was I going to become one of those cat ladies? I might have to.

Grinning, I pulled my phone out of my pocket to take a picture of King Tut and his new bestie, but the phone didn't feel right in my hand. I looked down at it, and my gut sank when I saw what I was holding.

It wasn't my phone. It was Devlin's. I'd forgotten to give it back to him.

He'd kill me if he found out I'd purloined it and *left* with it.

I couldn't take the risk of waiting until morning, so I grabbed my keys and hurried out to my car.

After a quick drive to the station, I parked behind the hardware store down the block, then jogged along the sidewalk, trying to keep my sneakers silent as I ran. I stepped off the sidewalk as I neared the station, ducking into the landscaped bushes that made the lot look so pretty.

I slipped from shadow to shadow, as old skills came rushing back. How many times had I been the one sent in to sneak in or out of a place when I was a kid? Too many to count.

My heart started to pound as I snuck around back, not wanting to be caught by Eloise, Devlin, or Chief Stone. But it was a good pounding. The thrill of adventure. The possibility of discovery. The challenge of pushing myself.

I immediately scowled. This was not my idea of fun anymore. I had to remember that.

I hurried around the back corner of the building and peered around at the lot.

Devlin's SUV was still in the lot, just waiting for me to quietly slide the phone into it. Easy-peasy.

I hurried across the asphalt to Devlin's car, crouching by the back tire as I watched the front door, waiting to see if he was coming out.

The lobby was empty.

Quickly, I snuck up to the driver's door and tried the handle, but it was locked. I bit my lip, trying to decide. If I left the phone on the ground, he would assume he dropped it. Or he wouldn't see it, and would drive over it, which would be a bummer and totally my fault if his phone broke.

I could jimmy the lock and leave it on his seat, but that would probably set off the alarm.

Or, I could do the smartest thing and simply set it on his windshield, and he'd assume someone found it and put it there. He might also assume that someone was me, doing exactly what I'd done.

But he'd never be able to prove it, and I was a great liar.

That felt like the best plan.

I checked the front door of the station again, saw no sign of Devlin, and then I popped up and put the phone on the windshield so he couldn't miss it. But as I turned to leave, movement on the street caught my eye. I ducked behind his SUV as a pickup truck drove past, going very slowly.

It went beneath a streetlight, and the hood was covered with white powder, like, oh, I don't know, a coating of flour? I tensed. It had to be one of the trucks from earlier. Why was it here? Had they somehow followed us? Was it Hugo?

Crud.

The truck paused at the entrance to the lot, its engine revving. Had he seen me? What was he waiting for? I shrank lower, my heart racing. Devlin would never get outside in time to save me if the driver decided to run me down. Hugo had been mad enough to shoot at us for a dominance staring contest, but now that we'd run him off the road?

I didn't feel like we were going to be besties. If he came for me, would I have time to make it to the police station door before he ran me down?

I was pretty sure I wouldn't.

Then, as I watched, another SUV pulled up behind it. It took me all of a tenth of a second to recognize Lucy's Jeep. What was going on? Was she with them?

The driver of the pickup truck got out. As he passed under the light, I saw it was Hugo. Why on earth would he be in front of the police station? That made no sense. Criminals didn't hang out in front of police stations.

He walked over to the driver's window of Lucy's SUV. Her window rolled down, but he was blocking my view of the driver.

I could hear their voices. The driver of Lucy's car was definitely a woman, but I was too far away to identify her voice. I looked for a way to get closer, but the police parking lot was brightly lit. There was no way to approach without being seen, and I had a feeling he'd have no trouble recognizing me.

He patted the roof of the Jeep, and then walked back to his truck.

Lucy's window was already going up, making it impossible for me to see the driver.

Both vehicles moved out, and I sprinted around the back of the station toward my car. I was back to my car in less than two minutes, but by the time I pulled out onto the street, both vehicles were gone.

Had it been Lucy? If she was teaming up with Hugo, did that mean she *had* actually killed Rex? Had *she* been the one driving her own car when it had almost run me down? We'd all assumed it was Rex who had been driving…but had it?

I knew all about being a good liar. I knew there were people with excellent deception skills, but I hadn't thought for even a moment that Lucy was one of them. Had I completely misjudged her?

The thought was shocking.

I needed to know if I'd been wrong.

I drove straight to her house, and, as I'd expected, her Jeep wasn't in the driveway.

But maybe she was home, and someone else was driving her car.

But that wouldn't prove her innocence. She could have loaned her car to someone, knowing full well they were going to meet up with Hugo. Or she could have driven straight home from the police station, beaten me there, and parked it behind the house where I couldn't see it.

I sat in my car, my knee bouncing restlessly as I tried to decide what to do.

I'd met Lucy only a day and a half ago. What if my instincts were wrong about her? I'd been conned with the marina. I'd believed Stanley was a law-abiding nerd for almost six years, and I'd *lived* with him. I'd grown up with a mom who was an expert on making people believe all sorts of lies about who she was, and I'd seen her mastery at work.

What if Lucy was one of those people?

I leaned my head back against the seat and closed my eyes. I'd come here looking for friends, for roots, for community. I'd found murder, deadly moose, a town that refused to acknowledge my marina existed, and the possibility of friendship with two awesome women---who might have been covering up a murder.

I thought of Devlin's question. If I thought Lucy had killed Rex, would I protect her? It had been easy to answer because I'd been so sure of her innocence. Now?

I was doubting myself, and I didn't like that feeling at all.

A light knock suddenly sounded on my window, and I jumped to the side, my heart pounding.

Lucy smiled and waved at me through the glass. "Mia! What are you doing here?" She looked so friendly, with her warm smile, brown eyes, and US Mail sweatshirt. She looked like the same woman I'd believed in. She didn't have the face of a killer. But I'd seen her Jeep at the scene of two things that weren't good.

I looked quickly around, but I still didn't see her vehicle anywhere. Slowly, I rolled down my window. "Hi. Um, where's your Jeep?"

She raised her brows. "I assume in my garage."

"You have a garage?" Even if the Jeep was here, it didn't prove anything. She could have beat me here from the police station. "Where?"

"Behind the house." Her smile faded. "Why? What's wrong?"

Did I get out of my car and walk to her garage to check out her car? Or did I call Devlin and tell him to come get her?

If she were a murderer and realized I was onto her, she could kill me behind the house, because, as I had been repeatedly informed, she was freakishly strong, and I was not.

But if she were innocent, then she needed to know someone had stolen her Jeep and was no doubt planning to implicate her further.

"Mia?" Her smile faded. "You're making me nervous. What's going on?"

I had to decide right then. I had to decide whether to trust my initial instincts or hand her over to the police. Was I so desperate for a life and a home that I'd overlooked her true nature, like I'd done with Stanley? I searched her face, but I simply couldn't find anything there but the funny, irreverent, penis-hacker who had narrowly escaped crazy dudes with me earlier in the evening.

I bit my lip.

"Mia?"

I hedged. "Did you loan your Jeep to anyone tonight?"

She frowned. "No. Why?"

I made my decision.

I was going to trust my instincts. I had to. My mom had always said that our greatest weapon was our instincts. They told us when it was time to run. They'd tell me when an opportunity wasn't right. They'd tell me when it was.

My instincts were telling me Lucy was innocent. I took a breath. "I was at the police station just now, and I saw a woman driving your Jeep. She pulled up behind the truck that we ran off the road earlier. The guy who was driving it got out to talk to her. Then they drove off."

Lucy stared at me. "*My* Jeep? You're sure?"

"Yes." Of that much, I was certain.

Without another word, she turned and ran down her driveway and disappeared around the side of her house.

I put my car in park, jumped out, and raced after her. To my death? To the solidification of a new friendship?

I would know momentarily.

I found Lucy standing in the front of her open garage, her hands on her hips, staring at an empty bay. There was not a fire-place poker to be seen, so I was pretty sure tonight was not my night to be murdered by her.

Yay for my instincts. I huffed my way up next to her and braced my hands on my knees to catch my breath. "Was it here when Hattie dropped you off?"

"I don't know. I didn't check." She sounded stunned, but not remotely winded. "Why would someone steal my car?"

"Because it's pretty?"

She looked over at me. "It is kind of pretty, isn't it? I really love that color blue."

"Me too." I paused to think. "Does anyone else have a set of keys?"

She looked over at me. "Rex did. I never got that set back from him."

I swore under my breath. Anyone he'd known could have them now. "I think you need to report it missing. Right now."

She stared at me. "Why?"

I bit my lip. Once I'd decided Lucy was innocent, there's been only one explanation that made sense. "They're going to do something with it, and make sure people see it's your car."

Her face paled. "To implicate me in something else?"

"It's a good plan." I thought back to the sign incident. "When I was almost run down by Rex, or who we thought was Rex, the Jeep backed up and waited for a moment before taking off. I wonder if the driver was trying to give me a good look at the license plate, so I could report it. I was too afraid of death to be a good witness, though." I paused. "Maybe that's why they were in front of the police station. To make sure your car was seen. I never got a look at the driver, so it could have been you for sure."

Worry flickered across her face, and she pulled out her phone and dialed. It rang and rang, and finally she spoke. "Hi. This is Lucy Grande. I just discovered my Jeep has been stolen out of my garage." She described it, gave the license plate, and then hung up. "It's a recording," she said. "If my car turns up with a dead body in it, I have no proof that I wasn't making the call from my car."

"I'm here. I saw it." But even as I said it, I knew how easy it would be for a jury to decide I was lying to protect my friend, especially with my background. She needed more than just me. "Do you live alone?"

She nodded. "I have no witnesses since Hattie dropped me off."

"Well, you have one for the rest of the night. I won't leave."

Alibis were very important elements of avoiding arrest. I'd been trained in the alibi by the best. "We need Hattie, too. She's solid, right?"

"I can't ask you—"

"It's not an ask. It's automatic. I'll call Hattie." I pulled out my phone, and Hattie answered almost immediately, as if she'd been waiting by the phone.

"What's going on?"

I explained the situation, and Hattie was all business. "Bring Lucy here."

I hesitated. "I think we should stay here. Maybe we can catch them when they return the car."

"They're *murderers,* Mia. You want to be there when they come back?"

She had a point. "No, but they're making me mad by picking on Lucy."

Hattie paused for a moment. "You know, you're right. Let's take those suckers down. I'll come prepared."

Hattie hung up, and I turned to Lucy. "I'll move my car down the street. We'll find a place to hide so we can get some pictures or videos if they come back."

She grinned. "Got it." She gave me a quick hug. "Thank you," she whispered, so heartfelt that my throat tightened.

"No problem. I'll meet you back here in a few." It took me only a few minutes to jog back to my car, move it around the corner, and drive it off the road between some trees. As I was walking back, I saw headlights round the corner. It was too soon for Hattie, but the headlights were high off the ground, indicating a truck or an SUV.

I slid back into the woods, and pulled out my phone and texted Lucy. *They're coming!*

The vehicle neared, its engine loud and roaring as it sped past.

It was a black pickup. Floodlights on the top.

But no flour on the hood.

I let out a breath. *False alarm. Never mind.* I slid my phone back into my pocket.

My nerves were spiking as I ran back down the street to Lucy's.

I tried to jog the rest of the way to her house, but my lungs and legs were mocking my belief in my athleticism, and they forced me to slow to a breathless stagger for the last few hundred yards. By the time I made it to Lucy's yard, she was waiting for me.

With two rifles. "I didn't have flour." She held one out to me.

I didn't take it. "That's a *gun*."

She raised her brows. "It's Maine. Everyone has guns."

"I don't have a gun."

She shoved it in my hand. "Well, you do now."

The gun was cold and hard in my hand. And terrifying. I shoved it back at her. "I'm not a gun girl."

Lucy sighed, did something to dump the bullets out, and then handed it back to me. "There. Use it as a club."

"A club? I don't want to club anyone." Con artists were non-confrontational. We prided ourselves on the subtle art of the game. There was nothing subtle, artistic, or non-confrontational about guns. Or clubs. Hairdryers, however, had a certain amount of creativity to them that I did enjoy.

"Use it as a warning. Most people will freeze if a gun is aimed at them."

I would freeze if someone aimed a gun at me. Or I might hurl bags of flour at them repeatedly. "Seriously, Lucy—"

We both heard the roar of a truck engine at the same time. We stared at each other, and then took off toward the house. I dove behind the bushes, and Lucy hid beside me.

A red pickup truck drove past her house slowly. It wasn't Hugo's truck, but it was driving slowly enough to be suspicious. Or a safety conscious driver, depending on how the night turned out.

"Think we should shoot it?" Lucy asked.

I looked over at her. "You're a little insane. You know that, right?"

She grinned. "I was kidding. I only shoot trucks on Saturdays."

The truck in question surged forward, cruising around the corner and out of sight. I let out a breath. "What's going on with you, Lucy? Why are they targeting you?"

She bit her lip and rested her rifle across her knees. "I don't know. I honestly don't."

I eased my butt onto the ground, leaned against the house, and set my unloaded gun on the ground beside me. "It's looking more and more like you were set up from the start. For the sign. For Rex's murder. Who would have it in for you?"

She sat down beside me and rested her rifle across her knees. "I have no idea. I've lived in town my whole life. My parents own a dock company, and I've installed docks in hundreds of camps over the years. I deliver mail. Nothing that makes enemies."

"What about Ellis? The guy who had your mail route?"

"Ellis?" She shook her head. "I wasn't the reason he got fired. I just took his route after he got booted."

"What about Jillian?"

She raised her brows. "Jillian? We didn't get along, but I hadn't seen her in years before I saw her at Rex's that day. There's no history that could justify all this."

That didn't surprise me. I hadn't gotten a murder vibe from Jillian. Plus, she was so tiny that there was no way she could have killed Rex. She probably wasn't even strong enough to lift a poker, let alone swing it.

I tried another angle. "You said you know secrets about people because of their mail. Can you think of a secret that might be worth killing to protect?"

"No one is trying to kill me. They're just trying to get me sent to prison. I can still talk from there," Lucy pointed out.

"True." We sat in the mulch for a few minutes. "What about Rex?"

"He's dead. I don't think he's trying to set me up for his murder."

"I know, but what if something he was involved in put a target on you? I get that he was a bad guy, but what specifically was he involved in?" A rock was starting to dig into my butt, so I shifted, trying to get a more comfortable position.

She shook her head. "I don't know. He didn't like to talk about what he did when I wasn't with him."

I scanned the empty street, and then asked the question I'd been avoiding asking. "Do you have a history with Ruby Lee?"

"Ruby Lee?" She looked over at me in surprise, her fingers relaxed around her gun. "No. She moved here a couple years ago, and she's not on my route. She used to live in Bugscuffle, so she sells a lot of houses around there still."

I sat up. "Bugscuffle?"

Lucy nodded. "She specializes in luxury lakefront property, and Bugscuffle's lake is much bigger than ours."

"And do the property values rise for the town that wins the Best Lake Town award?"

Lucy drummed her fingers on the rifle. "It makes a huge difference for the economy. There are always people who want to be part of what other people think is the best."

"Yes, there are." I leaned my head back against the shingles. "So, if Bugscuffle won, then Ruby Lee's commission would go up on her Bugscuffle listings, right? More money in her pocket?"

Lucy frowned. "You think she wrecked the sign and resurrected the moose to make Bass Derby look bad? But she sells houses here, too."

"But Bass Derby already has the title, so prices here reflect that. If Bugscuffle won, then those housing prices still have room to move." I rubbed my jaw, contemplating that. "But why would she target you?"

Lucy leaned forward, resting her arms on her knees. "Maybe after Rex signed her up to sell his house, she got to know him and realized that he was a lowlife who would do anything for a little cash, like run down a sign and resurrect the moose. Rex was pissed that I dumped him, so he would've enjoyed getting me busted for the sign."

"And then after Rex was murdered, she had to pin it on someone—"

"And I was already on her radar."

We looked at each other. "And now we have motive for her," I said quietly. I didn't want it to be Ruby Lee. But it was all pointing toward her.

"Wow," Lucy said. "I would never have guessed Ruby Lee."

"I wouldn't have either." I'd thought she was a small-time, non-violent, but this was so different. But money was money, and she was definitely driven by money.

"Do we call Chief Stone?"

I pressed my lips together. "With what? We still don't have any concrete evidence." And something about it just didn't feel right. I wasn't okay with putting another innocent person on the chopping block just to keep Lucy out of prison. "We have to be sure."

"How are we going to do that?"

"I—" My phone buzzed suddenly, and I looked down to see a text from Hattie. *Get over to the marina NOW.*

King Tut. I bolted to my feet. "Come on! We need to go!"

CHAPTER 24

I WAS no Hattie with my driving skills, but I beat my GPS estimate to the marina by three minutes, which was impressive when it was only a ten-minute drive to begin with.

My car skidded out as I turned into the dirt parking lot and pulled up next to Hattie's truck. Her engine was on, but her lights were off. I could see her sitting in the truck.

I threw my car into park and leapt out. "Hattie—"

The sound of a low, haunted singing cut me off.

I spun around toward the water, fear clamping in my gut when I saw six moose on Jet Skis driving in a slow circle in front of my dock.

Singing.

They weren't exactly in sync, so it was impossible to understand the words, but there was no mistaking the off-pitch, melodic attempt.

The Derby Moose were singing to me. Which, under normal circumstances might feel romantic or adoring, but after Chief Stone's story? It was clearly supposed to be my epitaph.

"Holy cow." Lucy came up beside me. "They're going to kill you."

"No way. I refuse to die at the hands of fake moose." I grabbed my phone and called Devlin's cell number. I'd programmed it into my Favorites after he'd given it to me, figuring that if I had an assassin sneaking into my house, efficiency in calling for help would be a good thing.

He didn't answer.

What? Hadn't he said he'd have my back?

Then I remembered his phone was sitting on top of his windshield, not in his pocket. *Damn.* The risks of a life of petty thievery, right? As if I didn't already know them. "Devlin! I'm at my marina. The Derby Moose are singing to me. I don't like death threats, so please get over here now!" I shoved my phone in my pocket, watching as they began to drive faster and faster, the circle getting tighter and tighter. I might not want Devlin's help with Lucy's murder, but with obvious death threats? I'd take all the help I could get.

Water crashed against my dock, the loud swish of the lake clashing with the wood. My docks were already decrepit. Could they withstand a lake assault?

Hattie got out and stood beside me. "Bullies."

"My gun is still loaded," Lucy said, raising her rifle. "I can easily take out an engine from here—"

Hattie snatched the gun out of her hands. "No guns."

"I won't hit one of the moose. Just their Jet Skis."

"Aren't you a top murder suspect right now?" Hattie asked. "Do you really need to add to that? What if one of them jumped in front of the bullet and got himself shot?"

"You're right." Lucy's eyes widened. "That would be so inconvenient."

"It sure would." Hattie lifted the gun. "I, however, am an old woman who no one would suspect—"

"Stop it! We're not shooting them." But as I stood there, flanked by the two women who had turned my life upside down in less than forty-eight hours, I started getting mad.

I'd come here to claim a life of serenity and legality. I was done with bullies, criminals, violence, and PTSD flashbacks of being terrified of getting hacked up into little pieces. "Enough!" I grabbed Lucy's gun and sprinted across the parking lot and down toward the lake. "Get away from my dock!"

"Hey!" Hattie shouted. "Mia! Don't go down there!"

My friends tried to grab me, but they were too slow. I might be the most unathletic person on the property, but anger was a powerful motivator, and I was seriously pissed.

"This is my home," I shouted, shaking the gun at the moose as I ran toward them. "You don't get to mess with it!"

As soon as I reached the dock, there was a shout, and the moose broke formation. The largest moose headed straight for me, clearly trying to scare me.

Screw that. If he wasn't a drug kingpin who slept with an axe and a machine gun, he wasn't going to be able to scare me. "Just try it," I shouted, waving the rifle as I sprinted toward them. "You don't get to—"

I suddenly saw the glint of metal.

A gun? Did he have a gun?

"He has a gun!" Hattie yelled.

The wood by my right foot exploded. *Yikes!*

I took back my claim of bravado immediately. I tried to stop, but my feet slipped on the wet wood, and I went flying. I had a split second to brace myself, and then I went feetfirst over the side of the dock. I hit the water with a splash, but once I was underwater, I turned myself around and immediately swam under the dock. I came up slowly, trying to breathe quietly as the Jet Ski neared.

I scooted backwards, closer to shore, trying to move away from where I'd gone in.

Hattie shouted at them to leave, then I heard his gun fire and the sound of glass shattering. Had he shot at Hattie? I waited to hear Hattie yell again, but there was no sound.

Was she dead? Fear clamped down on me, mixing with my rising anger. Threatening me? Shooting my friends? I needed to do something. Anything. But what? I felt helpless and defenseless, which made me even madder.

The Jet Ski cruised slowly past the dock. I sank lower into the water, hoping for invisibility. The moose bent down, the antler dragging in the water as he tried to see beneath the dock.

I took a breath and submerged. It was so dark, I doubted he'd be able to see under the water.

My lungs started to burn. I closed my eyes, fighting as long as I could to hold my breath, until finally I shot up out of the water, gasping for air.

I opened my eyes to see a moose head upside down, looking right at me, with the barrel of a rifle only six inches from my face.

I froze. I was going to die right now. Killed by a fake moose.

"Bang," he said, in a rough, low voice. "You're dead."

Bang? That was it? *Bang?* Seriously? "What is *wrong* with you?" I shouted. "You don't go around pointing guns at people's heads! You want to shoot me over a stupid sign? Are you insane? What the hell!"

"Close your marina."

His command cut off my rant just as I was getting started. Instead, my mouth dropped open in surprise. "What? My marina? What are you talking about?"

"Shut it down. Sell it. Leave."

"Wait. Hold on a second." I held up my hand, trying to pivot from murder, destroyed signs, and freakishly aggressive fake moose, to my marina. "Is this personal? You don't want *me*, specifically, in town? Or is it about the marina, and it doesn't matter who owns it? Because clarity really helps to solve problems."

The moose stared at me with a surprisingly emotionless expression for an inanimate creature. "I said, 'Bang, you're dead.' Did you not hear that?"

"I heard you, but I'm not dead, and you clearly aren't going to shoot me right now, so I have a few questions. Of course, I could scream at you instead, because I still don't find this remotely funny, but that doesn't feel productive to me."

Did his voice sound familiar? I didn't think so, but his voice was raspy, as if he were trying to disguise it. I looked at the Jet Ski, trying to see any helpful name tags on it with a home address and phone number. It was yellow with stripes with a sticker on the side that said JBN725. Was that a model? A brand? I wasn't making the mistake I made with Lucy's truck. I was paying attention this time.

"No second chances. Next time, you die." Then he sat up, spun the Jet Ski around, and gunned it, streaking across the lake, followed by the others.

I scrambled out from under the dock, trying to catch a glimpse of license plates or other distinguishing features, but they were already too far away.

I clasped my hands over my head, staring after them as I replayed our conversation. He wanted me to close the marina. Why? What was going on?

"Mia!" Lucy's shout drew my attention back to them.

I suddenly remembered them shooting at Hattie and the sound of glass breaking.

Hattie.

I was already running by the time I hit dry land.

CHAPTER 25

It took almost seventy-five yards, all the oxygen I was capable of harvesting, and enough terror to last me a lifetime before I was close enough to see Hattie run out from behind her truck.

"Is everyone okay?" she shouted.

She was alive.

I staggered to a stop, bracing my hands on my thighs as I fought for air. "Don't scare me like that," I gasped. "I can't handle it. Never stop shouting after someone shoots a gun at you again. Do you understand?" Then awareness hit me. "Where's Lucy?"

"Here! I'm here! I'm okay!" Lucy waved her arms as she hurried out of my store. She didn't go through the door. She stepped out over the front window, which now lay in millions of shattered fragments all over the deck and the interior of the store.

Stunned, I went down on my knees, not from shock as much as lack of oxygen, staring at it. "Are you kidding me?"

Hattie rushed over. "Are you dying? Were you shot? We didn't think you were shot!"

"Not shot. I'm fine. Just out of breath." And somewhat devastated that my window had been murdered.

"You have got to start working out, girl. Seriously."

"I know." I waved my hands. "They shot my window? Were they aiming for you guys?"

"I was by my truck," Hattie said. "But Lucy was on the deck."

I looked at Lucy. "How close was the shot?"

She shrugged. "I was in front of the window when it shattered, but I don't know exactly."

I sat back on my heels, looking at the two women. The moose had almost killed Lucy tonight. Whether they'd intended to or not, they'd almost hit her. "What is going on?"

"The sign is a pretty big deal," Hattie said. "It's what they always put on the cover of the magazine when we win."

I dragged myself to my feet. "He didn't mention the sign. He said to close the marina and leave town."

"Really?" Lucy's eyes widened. "You chatted with him?"

"I yelled at him, he threatened me. I'm not sure I'd call it chatting." I stared in dismay at the shattered window. I couldn't sleep there now. It was so unnerving to realize how easy it had been for them to put a bullet in my store from the lake. If any of us had been standing there— "I need to sit down."

I sank down right on the edge of the decks. "They shot my store. What did my store do to them?"

"That therein lies the question." Hattie walked over to her truck and came back with three brooms. Why she had three brooms in her truck, I had no idea. "If this was a marina assault, why?"

I lay down on my back, spread my arms out, and stared at the sky. There were a lot of stars. I wanted to run away and live on one of them, except for the part about being incinerated instantly. "I'm done."

"You're not done," Hattie said. "Get up. We're going to sweep this up and cover the window." She dropped a broom on my chest, then handed one to Lucy. "You, too. I can't have my customers trekking broken glass into the café in the morning."

I gripped the broom like a weapon. Would it work as well as a hairdryer? "I can't live this life anymore. I want peaceful serenity. Not guns. Not bullets. Not creepy moose." A shadow suddenly loomed over the edge of my roof, and I bolted upright, gripping my broom. "Guys? There's something on the roof—"

It launched itself off the roof right at me. I screamed, and then, at the last second, realized it had a tail, ears, and fur. "Oh, *sh—"* King Tut landed right on me, twenty-five pounds of cat right in the chest, knocking me on my back. I gasped for air as he dug his claws into my chest, kneading and purring as he stretched out on his belly.

"You're being attacked by a bobcat!" Lucy swung her broom. "I got this—"

"No!" I put up my hand to shield him, but before she could finish her swing, King Tut shot to his feet, puffed himself out, and unleashed a low, terrifying growl.

Lucy froze. "It's going to kill us all."

I grimaced at the claws digging into my flesh. "Not if you put down the broom."

"I don't think that's a good idea." She lifted it higher, pointing it at him. "Back off, beast."

King Tut puffed out even more, and his tail went stiff. The growl got deeper. The claws went through my ribs nearly to my internal organs, but I didn't dare move him.

I owned a demon.

Hattie started laughing. "I love that cat so much. I wish Chief Stone was here."

"Cat?" Lucy echoed. "You mean bobcat."

"Maine Coon Cat," I said, gritting my teeth against the pain. "His name is King Tut."

Lucy's eyes widened. "He's your *pet?"*

"I think I'm his pet, actually." I was pretty sure his claws were millimeters from puncturing my lungs. "Can you put down the broom? Please?"

"No. I'm pretty sure I can't. I have this unstoppable self-preservation instinct to defend myself at all costs." But she inched backwards slowly. "Aren't you afraid he'll kill you in your sleep? Eat your eyeballs for dinner?"

"I hadn't been thinking that, but thanks for putting it into my mind." I was afraid to move, because King Tut was still watching Lucy like he was going to use her for the scratching post I hadn't gotten for him.

"That growl is going to haunt me for the rest of my life." She made it to the edge of the deck. "I hereby promise I will *never* sneak into your apartment without giving you advance notice."

I was pretty sure I wasn't going to either. I slowly lifted my hand. "Hey, King Tut. It's cool. She's a friend." He didn't launch himself at my hand with bared teeth, so I set my palm gently on his back. His fur was sticking straight up, and his body was taut. He didn't relax as he watched Lucy.

Hattie stopped laughing. "The way he's watching you is kind of creepy."

"I know. Animals usually love me." Lucy went to step off the deck, and King Tut tensed.

"Stop!" I shouted.

She froze, one foot on the deck, and the other on the top step. "What?"

"I think he's about to launch himself at you."

"Tell him not to." Lucy sounded a little stressed, which I agreed might be the appropriate reaction, given the sounds emanating from King Tut's chest.

"He's a cat," Hattie said. "They don't take orders."

"So, what do we do?" Lucy asked.

"I think he's a little strung out from the moose assault." I lightly scratched him behind his ears. "He gets worried when he thinks I'm going to die." I wasn't sure if that was true, but it felt good to believe. Who doesn't want someone to mourn if they die? "I think he thought you were going to kill me with the broom."

"Lucy definitely could do that," Hattie said. "He's an astute cat."

"Putting down the broom might help," I said.

Lucy shook her head. "I don't want to."

"Oh, for heaven's sake." Hattie marched over to Lucy, yanked the broom out of her hand, and tossed it aside, ignoring Lucy's protests. "There. Gone. Satisfied, Cat?"

King Tut relaxed immediately, shifting his growl into a purr as he sank onto my chest and started kneading. I pried his claws out of my flesh and sat up, while Lucy let out her breath—

At that moment, the sheriff's car came screaming down the street, lights flashing and siren on. King Tut sat up, his tail swishing as we all turned to watch.

Behind Chief Stone was Devlin's SUV, a single blue light flashing on the roof, exactly how Griselda used to do with his undercover car.

The two vehicles pulled into the marina, but Chief Stone reached us first. He skidded to a stop in front of us, and leapt out, nearly wiping out when his feet slipped on the broken glass. "What's happening? I got a call about gunshots." He stopped when he saw King Tut in my arms. His eyes narrowed at the cat. "*You.*"

King Tut hissed.

I pointed to the lake as Devlin pulled in behind him. "The Derby Moose were singing to me, and then they shot out my window."

Chief Stone paled and stumbled. "What?"

Devlin got out. "Is everyone all right?"

I took a breath. Devlin might not be Griselda, but having him and Chief Stone there relieved some of my terror. The odds of getting murdered by moose were drastically reduced by having two police officers in my parking lot. For the moment, we were safe. "Lucy was standing in front of my window when they shot it."

Devlin shot a look at Lucy. "You think they were aiming at you, or you got in the way?"

His question froze me. There was an edge to his tone that got my attention. "Now you're blaming Lucy for this, too?"

Chief Stone held up his hand. "I'll handle this, Officer Hunt."

Devlin's brows shot up, but he nodded once, stepping to the side. He folded his arms across his chest and leaned against the corner post to listen.

Chief Stone turned to me. "Tell me what happened."

It took only a few minutes, but by the end, Chief Stone was so pale he looked like he was going to pass out. He was pacing back and forth, muttering under his breath as I answered his questions.

As soon as I finished, Devlin turned away and headed toward his truck.

Chief Stone shouted at him. "Where are you going?"

"To get my boat. I'm going to see if I can find them." He got in his truck and drove off, his wheels spinning out as he hit the gas.

His SUV disappeared from sight within moments. It made sense for him to hit the water and try to find them, but my feeling of safety dissolved as soon as he was gone. Apparently, it hadn't been the presence of two police officers that had made me feel safe. It had been Devlin. Good to know.

Chief Stone appeared to feel the same, because he immediately headed toward his own vehicle, not even trying to pretend he was brave enough to hang around. "I have the info I need. If you have any other incidents, or if they come back, call the station."

"But—"

"And you." He pointed at Lucy. "Don't leave town." His door slammed shut, and he peeled out, leaving us standing in the midst of broken glass, in a dark, shadowy parking lot, our only protection being three brooms, Lucy's soggy rifle somewhere in the lake, and a demon cat.

We stood there silently for a moment, then Lucy spoke. "You think this was about Rex?"

"I don't know." I was so confused. There were so many pieces, and none of them seemed to fit. Even though Ruby Lee seemed to be involved, it just didn't feel right. But she was the only thing that made even a little sense.

Except for the fact that the moose had told me to close the

marina. That didn't fit at all. The marina had been neglected for ten years. No one had cared about it. It didn't make sense for it to suddenly become an issue.

Hattie's phone rang. She glanced at it. "It's Angelina." She answered it. "This is Hattie." She paused for several minutes, listening, then hung up. She looked at us. "She's working at the police station tonight."

I nodded. "I saw her when I went in there."

"She heard your conversation with Devlin, and it got her curious, so she did a little checking once Devlin took off."

I raised my brows. "She searched his office?"

Hattie shook her finger at me. "Don't ask questions you don't want to know the answer to. Let's just say that the initial findings are that the fireplace poker killed Rex. The divot in his head matches the hook on the poker, and there was blood on it."

I nodded. It was what we'd expected.

Hattie wasn't finished. "Chief Stone got fingerprints from the poker and sent them off this morning. It's a thirty-six-hour turnaround."

Lucy sucked in her breath. "My fingerprints are on that. They'll match them."

"Only if they're in the system—"

"My prints *are* in the system. I had to get fingerprinted to work for the USPS."

Oh...*hell.*

"Well, given that they were sent off this morning, that means we have about twenty-five hours to give Chief Stone another suspect, or Lucy's going down for it." Hattie looked at us both. "They won't look further than Lucy. With her fingerprints on the weapon, they have all they need."

I let my breath out in a long exhale, trying to shake the tension mounting inside me. "Which means we have until five o'clock tomorrow to figure this out."

"But how?" Lucy looked worried. A logical response given the situation. "We have no leads."

"We have one. Twenty-two Main Street tomorrow afternoon. Plus, we have a lot of pieces. It's simply a matter of putting them together." "Simply" might be a bit overly optimistic, but it was the truth. That's what all good cons were: a lot of little, apparently insignificant details which could be put together to work miracles. We had the details. We just needed to figure out how they fit together. I picked up a broom. "You guys head back to Lucy's and wait for her Jeep to be returned. See if they show up." I hoped they did. That would make it so easy. I know, life wasn't easy, but why couldn't it be easy? I deserved easy.

"Okay." Lucy nodded. "What are you going to do?"

"Fix my window, find out more about Hugo, and hopefully be here and ready for the Derby Moose to come back. If we figure out the connection between the Derby Moose and Rex, that might be our answer."

Hattie grinned. "I like it. Catch those fleabags when they come back to finish you off."

Lucy didn't move. "I *don't* like it. What if they kill you?"

"He clearly didn't want to shoot me tonight, so I think I'm good." That might be a slightly optimistic evaluation of my safety. He'd made it abundantly clear that he would be willing to knock me off if I didn't vacate.

Guess what. I wasn't going to vacate.

Mostly because it was my home, which I hadn't even had time to claim. But also because people were counting on me. Hattie, Lucy, and King Tut to be specific. Plus, Cargo and the Greek twins would lose their jobs as well. Yes, that was a small crew, but to them, it mattered if I kept this marina going.

Plus, I hated jerks who bullied people, and I was pretty sure the Derby Moose fit into that category.

I'd come to Bass Derby for peace, serenity, and a new life.

Instead, I'd gotten a murder, flying bullets, endangered friends, and most importantly, a gang of furry, gun-toting moose who'd given the proverbial finger at my dream tonight.

I'd *been* scared. But now? I was mad.

CHAPTER 26

As soon as Hattie and Lucy left, I grabbed my hairdryer from my car (aka drive-in closet) and tied it across my upper body like a beauty pageant sash.

No, more like a supply of bullets like in some old Rambo movie.

Yeah. I was totally the caliber of an ex-military black ops operator like Rambo. I was definitely on board with being some ex-war hero who only wanted peace and quiet, but had to take down an entire army of Special Forces before he could sit back on his porch and sip his coffee.

He had machine guns, hunting knives, explosives, and special training.

I had a hairdryer, a monstrous demon cat, and flexible moral standards, according to Devlin.

I was good. We had this.

I looked down at King Tut, who was sitting next to my ankle, his tail swishing as he looked up at me. "You have my permission to kill."

He said nothing, but I was pretty sure he blinked with unbridled glee.

"Let's go." I set off across the parking lot, our footsteps silent with stealth as we headed toward the garage.

Well, King Tut was silent. I was making an admirable attempt. A gold star for effort.

Cargo had locked the door to the garage. For a moment, I considered running back to the marina store to get the keys, but then I decided, screw it. I was already off the wagon, right?

I picked the old lock with a wire I found in the dirt by the door, and let us in. The garage was huge and gloomy in the dark, but then I found the light switch by the door and flipped it.

Then the garage was still huge and gloomy, but I could see the plywood sheets I'd noticed earlier in the day when I'd been taking inventory of the garage.

It took a minor head injury, a scraped shin, an almost fatal accident with an angry cat, and a hand truck, but I finally got the plywood out of the garage and to the front of my store. Another foray into the garage that was much less dramatic left me armed with a hammer, a box of nails, a nail gun, and a layer of dust and grime that I wasn't sure I'd ever get off. But it was a nice accent to the flour paste I'd been wearing earlier, right? All good. My warrior chainmail.

I dropped all the gear on the deck while King Tut took up residence in the corner, watching me with an unblinking yellow gaze that felt a little bit judgy. Keeping an eye on the lake, I pulled out my phone and texted my most and least favorite FBI agent. *Hi, Griselda. It's Mia. If I give you a license plate, can you tell me who it belongs to?*

The three dots appeared shortly. *It's three in the morning.*

Not in England. I owed Griselda so many three a.m. wake-up calls.

I could almost hear his long-suffering sigh. *I'm not in England.*

I grinned. *How would I know that? You never tell me your travel plans anymore. I think we need to break up. See other people. Get a new start in life.*

It's three in the damned morning.

Well, fine. If he wanted to be grumpy, I was happy to skip the social bantering that was such a beautiful part of our relationship. *A guy was murdered in front of me yesterday, and I'm being hunted by some rude, overly aggressive jerks who are threatening to kill me. I need you to run a plate for me.*

My phone rang immediately.

Aww…he cared.

Grinning, I answered. "Hi there. "

He greeted me with love, kindness, and concern that was so typical of our friendship. "What the hell are you talking about?"

Weirdly, a little part of me relaxed at his familiar outburst. It felt like coming home. Griselda was my partner in crime. He was the one who had my back when I did things like find a stash of huge guns in a storage facility, or discover a hidden door that led to a basement full of bad, drug-kingpin stuff.

I let out a breath of relief, wishing I'd called him sooner. "It's a long story, but your pal Devlin wants to arrest a friend of mine for it."

He let out a groan. "Mia. Devlin's good at his job. Let him do it."

"No." His irritated, slightly condescending tone made me pause. "If I give you the license plate, are you going to share it with him?"

"If it helps him solve a murder, yeah."

Why did he have to be so irritating? "I need the information to find out who really killed this guy before Devlin arrests my friend. What if I asked you not to share it with him?"

"Suppress evidence as a personal favor? No chance. You know that."

My jaw tightened. "Seriously?"

"Yes, seriously. What's the plate number?"

I hung up.

I couldn't believe him. I mean, yeah, I guess I could, but it didn't change how it felt to have Griselda once again put his job first. He'd said to reach out if I needed him. Now that our stint with Stanley was over, I'd thought that maybe we were friends, that he was that person I could count on if things got bad enough.

But I couldn't. Just like before, he'd throw me in front of a tank if it would help him with his job.

Stupid men. Stupid law enforcement. Didn't they understand that life wasn't always black and white? That it was a myriad of colors, hues, patterns, and nuances? "Screw you, Agent Straus."

He wasn't even worthy of my affectionate nickname.

Agent Straus called me right back, but I silenced the call and tossed my phone on the deck, anger coiled tight in my chest. "Marry one stupid drug dealer, and you're nothing more than a tool for crime solving and career advancement," I muttered as I grabbed the plywood. "Have one famous con artist mother, and you're haunted for life by your ties to her. It's a bunch of crap—"

"What's a bunch of crap?"

I screamed, flung the plywood aside, and lunged for the hammer—

"Oh, no you don't." He got there first, snatching it out from under my frantic grasp.

So I went for the nail gun instead. I grabbed the cord, whipped the gun part behind me and spun around, swinging it as hard as I could—

And then saw it was Devlin.

It was too late to stop. "Duck!"

His eyes widened, and he swore. He had time only to turn slightly, and the nail gun slammed into his shoulder, throwing him sideways. He stumbled, and his boot came down toward King Tut's head. My precious baby yowled, and Devlin jerked his foot up to avoid crushing him. The quick move threw Devlin off balance, but his weight kept going. His boot came down to the right of King Tut, missing the deck by six inches.

He shot off the edge of the deck, flipped over his head, and thudded to the dirt of the parking lot.

I dropped the nail gun and sprinted to the edge of the deck.

What if he'd broken his neck? Or cracked his head open? Or impaled himself on a rebar stick?

But Devlin, resilient chap that he was, had already rolled to his side with a groan.

He was alive. I let out a shuddering breath of relief. I jumped off the deck, ran over, and went down on my knees beside him. "I'm so sorry. Are you all right?"

He gave me a smoldering glare as he sat up, bracing his hands behind him. His face was pinched in pain, but he channeled his testosterone and didn't acknowledge his injuries. "What the hell was that?"

"Instinct." He wasn't bleeding from anywhere that I could see. Skull in one piece. All his limbs working. "You startled me, then you went for the hammer. Why'd you go for the hammer?"

"Because I thought you were going to attack me with it." He gave me a baleful look. "Apparently, I should have gone for the nail gun instead."

He was grumpy, but he didn't seem in danger of imminent death, thank heavens. I glared at him. "Don't ever scare me again."

"You think?" He rotated his shoulder. "I'm impressed, though. You got some serious momentum with that nail gun."

"Thanks." I sat back on my heels, feeling a little guilty at his grimace of pain. "I'm really sorry. Did I break your shoulder?"

"It's fine." His gaze went to my artillery belt, aka hairdryer. "Is today spa day?"

"It works the same way as the nail gun. It has a great cord. Nicely balanced." I braced myself, waiting for him to yell at me. Or mock me. Or lecture me.

He did none of the above.

All he did was nod. "Ah." He leaned forward, resting his forearms over his knees, clearly not quite up to standing just yet. The deck was only a few feet high, but his dismount hadn't exactly been graceful.

The image of him flailing through the air flashed through my mind, and I had a sudden urge to smile. I doubted Devlin had spent more than a few seconds of his life being out of control. I was glad I got to witness one of them, now that I knew he was all right.

He raised his brows. "You're laughing at me?"

"It's a little funny. I mean, now that you're okay." I grinned. "I had no idea you could be that ungraceful."

His eyes narrowed. "I'm very graceful."

"Except when you catapult off a deck."

"I made a conscious decision not to crush your cat." As he spoke, King Tut wandered over, climbed onto Devlin's lap, and stared at him with unblinking focus.

Devlin stared back at him. "What do you want?" he asked King Tut.

I grinned. "He's thanking you for sacrificing yourself on his behalf. He's very polite. Except when he's not, of course."

Devlin studied the feline for another moment. "You're welcome," he finally said.

King Tut raised a massive paw, tapped Devlin on the cheek, then rose and sauntered off, his tail lofty and arrogant. As we watched, he trotted across the parking lot, down the ramp, and parked himself on the end of the dock near Devlin's boat, which I hadn't even heard arrive.

He must have come while I was wrestling with the plywood and the tools in the garage. The fact I hadn't heard him didn't bode well for my awareness if the moose came back. I really needed to work on my instincts. There was a time when I knew how to be aware of everything.

Not anymore. I was a washed-up petty thief at age twenty-nine. Sigh.

Devlin frowned as King Tut continued to sit at the end of the dock, staring into the water, his tail twitching. "What's he doing?"

At that moment, King Tut vaulted off the dock, diving straight into the water and out of sight. He disappeared briefly, then surfaced, something wiggling in his mouth. "A moonlight swim and a late-night snack," I said. "Isn't that what all cats do?"

Devlin stared at King Tut as the girthy animal swam back toward shore. "I've never seen a cat do that before."

"I know, right?" King Tut was so strange. I loved that cat so much. "He's awesome." I grinned at Devlin. "Thanks for not crushing his little head."

"Anytime. The world needs more cats like him."

A little warmth wrapped around me at Devlin's appreciation of my furry sidekick. "He is pretty spectacular," I agreed. For a moment, we bonded silently as we watched King Tut enjoy his evening. I became aware of the peacefulness of the night, of the serenity surrounding us.

The sky was so dark, I could see millions of stars. The lake was quiet, gently lapping at the shore. Across the water, I could see the lights on at the Yacht Club, but all was serene. There was a sense of the earth breathing deeply, relaxing into itself.

I felt like the power of the earth, of nature, of the lake, was seeping into my soul, easing my stress, inviting me into its magic.

This was why I'd come. To be a part of the gloriousness of the lake. To experience a life away from the grime, bustle, and grittiness of the city. To be here. To be present.

Sitting beside Devlin, it didn't feel like I was trapped with some law enforcement jerk.

It felt nice. I glanced over and saw him watching me. It was too dark to read the expression on his face, but he was definitely studying me, not the lake. "What?"

"I came back to check on you and make sure you were all right," he said. "I guess I didn't need to worry."

I stared at him, surprised by his response. "You came back to check on me?"

"Yeah." He grimaced as he reached across and grasped the shoulder I'd clobbered. "I take it that you're alive? Safe? Recovering all right from the trauma of being shot at?"

"I am." Wow. He'd really come back to check on me. I sat back on my heels, noticing the scrape on his forehead that hadn't been there before I'd attacked him and caused him to plummet to his near death. "Thanks for coming back. For not being mad."

He nodded. "No problem."

Silence fell between us, and I became aware of how close Devlin was. All he'd have to do is lean in and—

My phone rang, interrupting my little fantasy before it could get me into trouble. I turned around to look for my phone. It was in the dirt next to Devlin, probably kicked off the deck during the nail gun incident.

He looked at the screen, where the name Griselda was lit up. "Hawk's calling you at three in the morning?" His tone implied that he could think of only one reason for the FBI agent to be ringing me in the middle of the night, and it involved romantic liaisons that I'd claimed not to be involved in.

My good mood fled, replaced by the grim reminder that my life was not currently about sitting in the moonlight with a ridiculously hot guy watching my cat fish. I had a murderer to ferret out by five o'clock this afternoon, and neither Griselda nor Devlin were there to help me do that. "Griselda's calling me? How odd."

"Are you going to answer it?"

"Nope." The phone stopped ringing. "See? He must have butt dialed me."

At that moment, Devlin's phone rang. He shifted, wincing as he reached for his back pocket. He looked at his phone. "Now he's calling me."

"Is he? That's a bizarre coincidence." I needed to distract him, and fast. "Well, it's been great hanging out, but I need to get this plywood up over this window. Will you help me?"

"Sure. After I take the call." He punched the send button. "Hunt here."

Cursing under my breath, I scrambled to my feet. The plywood was half off the deck now, wedged in the dirt. I crouched down, grabbed the edge, and tried to lift it.

"She did?" His phone tucked between his shoulder and his ear,

Devlin walked over, grabbed the sheet of plywood, and helped me lift it back onto the deck.

I had no doubt Griselda was ratting me out to Devlin. What was I, like five years old? A naughty little kid who needed to be reported on? "Heaven forbid I actually make choices on my own without anyone's approval," I muttered as Devlin and I carried the plywood back to the window and leaned it up against the gaping wound in my poor wall.

The sheet of plywood was wider than the window, but covered only the bottom two-thirds. I was going to have to bring another one out? Sudden exhaustion flooded me, and I braced my hands on the wood. *I can handle this.*

"She's fine," Devlin said into the phone. "No, it's not related to the Stanley Herrera situation." He paused, looking over at me. "Yeah, I'm sure."

Stanley? That's why Griselda had called me so quickly? Not because he was worried about me witnessing a murder, but because he thought it might have to do with Stanley?

Of course that's why he'd called Devlin. Griselda didn't care about my health and well-being. He never had. I jutted my jaw out, stuck a handful of nails into my pocket, and grabbed the hammer. "I got this now. You can leave."

"Yeah, sure, Hawk. I'll let you know if anything changes." Devlin hung up the phone and shoved it in his pocket as he turned to me. "You asked him to run the license plate?"

"Yep. He said he'd tell you what he found, though, so I hung up on him." I refused to explain myself. Devlin was a man and law enforcement, so that was a double strike against him.

Devlin picked up the nail gun and plugged it into an outlet I hadn't even noticed.

Without another word, he hefted the plywood up off the deck, which made his biceps flex so admirably that I decided his arms needed to be illegal. They were much too distracting, especially when I was focused on him being the enemy, an obstacle thrust in my way.

Apparently oblivious to the unrest his sculpted perfection was wreaking, Devlin rested the board on the window frame. That position gave it enough height to cover the entire window, which meant I didn't have to retrieve another one from the garage.

Yay for the small joys in life.

"Lean on it to hold it in place," he said.

I did as instructed, but he didn't say anything more as he ran the nail gun around the perimeter.

He would though. I knew it was coming.

He made it through two and a half sides before he caved. "When did you take my phone?"

I'd totally forgotten about that. "You have a phone?"

He shot me a look. "You're good."

A little smile crept in past my crankiness. Pilfering the phones of law enforcement officials was such a pick-me-up. "I know. I really am."

He shot another nail into the plywood. "When did you get it?"

I grinned at his oh-so-casual question that wasn't casual at all. He was ticked that I'd gotten it, and he wanted details so he could make sure it didn't happen again. See? This was why it was fun. Besting those who were the experts at catching bad guys was deeply satisfying. "I can't give away my trade secrets. If I told you, I'd have to kill you, and then Chief Stone would want to arrest me, and who wants that?"

"No one wants that," he agreed.

"Right?" I grinned. "So, don't ask questions."

"I ask questions. It's what I do." He cocked an eyebrow at me. "I didn't believe Hawk when he told me how good you were at pickpocketing."

My smile vanished. "Heaven forbid Griselda lie about anything."

Devlin shot me a thoughtful look, but he didn't say anything else until the board was secure, the glass was swept up, and we'd piled up our gear on the counter in the store, aka my temporary bedroom.

Devlin glanced at my bed and nightstand, also known as inflatable rafts and a crate with a battery powered lantern on it. A soggy King Tut was already curled up in the middle of it, his nose tucked in his tail. "You're sleeping down here?"

"I am. I can't get the smell out upstairs. It's really bad. I have a cleaning service coming Thursday, though, so hopefully that will take care of it." I knew he wanted that license plate, and he wasn't going to walk away without making another attempt. I was ready, waiting for him to circle back to the topic hanging between us. "Did you find the moose when you went out on the lake after them?"

He shook his head. "I couldn't find any sign of them. But I will."

That meant they were still out there. Somewhere. Able to return. I put my hand on the hairdryer draped around me. "Well, thanks for the help."

"No problem." He nodded at the nail gun. "Good work with that."

I winced with guilt. "I'm sorry about that. I really am."

He shot me a grin. "It's fine. It's my fault for underestimating an unplugged nail gun." He started to leave, then paused on the threshold and turned to face me.

And here it came.

I put my hands on my hips, raised my chin, and braced myself. He might have injured himself keeping my cat safe, stayed to put up plywood, and possess illegal biceps, but that didn't mean he was going to get past my emotional shields.

I was too jaded, bitter, and wise for that.

He leaned against the doorframe, propping his uninjured shoulder against the chipped paint. He studied me for a moment, as if he were considering how to approach the topic of license plates.

I waited, steeling my resolve.

"I grew up in a gang in New York," he finally said. "I spent time in juvie for stealing cars."

I blinked, startled by his unexpected announcement. "What?"

"I got two years for riding along with my cousin in a car he stole." He met my gaze with a steadiness that told me he was telling me the truth. "Police were the enemy. I learned early on never to trust them, under any circumstances. To run from them if I saw them coming. To solve my own problems instead of going to them for help."

I shifted uncomfortably. I knew about that.

"Some law enforcement officers suck." His voice was quiet.

I looked up at him.

He met my gaze without flinching. "But some are good people you can trust."

I pressed my lips together. Griselda had proven repeatedly that my well-being was not as high on his list of priorities as I would have liked it to be, but at the end of the day, there was some trust there. Not all-in, but yeah, a decent man under certain circumstances. But he was the only one on my list. So far. "And you're which kind?"

Devlin cocked an eyebrow. "Does my answer even matter? You need to decide for yourself that I'm worth trusting. I know that."

I let out my breath. He was right. I didn't like that he'd pegged me, but at the same time, it was a relief not to have him spout all sorts of nonsense to try to win me over. I was far too jaded and skeptical for that to work.

"But I will tell you one thing. I want Rex's killer locked up before he or she can hurt anyone else." He met my gaze. "Including you."

My heart warmed at his inclusion of me in his bubble of protection, but it was quickly chased away by frustration. "It's not Lucy."

"I follow the facts. Give me facts to follow, and I'll hunt them down. I swear it." He waited. "If you know something I don't, tell me."

I said nothing. Would he really be willing to look past the obvious answer of Lucy? Or even Ruby Lee?

"If I need to lock you up to get the information, I will," he warned.

And there we go. I had the answer I needed about who he was and what mattered to him. "Good to know. I'll keep that in mind."

He sighed. "I'll give you twenty-four hours. You have my number."

I lifted my chin. "Yes, I do."

He met my gaze for a long moment. "Don't risk your life, Mia. Rex was murdered. The person who killed him is still out there and doesn't want to get caught. Don't make yourself a target."

I thought of the shattered window we'd just covered up. "I'm already a target."

CHAPTER 27

THE NEXT MORNING, I decided to go on the offensive.

A great idea? Maybe.

A stupid idea caused by a complete lack of sleep? Entirely possible, given that I spent the night sitting up on my raft, gripping the nail gun, leaping to my feet at every sound I heard, ready to defend / attack, depending on the moment.

I'd thought I heard a boat down by the dock, but when I raced outside, there was nothing.

I'd run up to the apartment twice, thinking I'd heard footsteps.

I'd done all the asinine things people do in horror movies, when they run toward the suspicious noises instead of away from it. Why? Because I'd needed to feel some sense of control in my life.

I hadn't squashed an imminent crime, but I hadn't been chopped up either, so I was going with the win. King Tut hadn't moved from the life-jacket pile even once. Occasionally, he'd opened one eye to see what I was doing, but that was all the support I got from him.

Which was fine. He'd almost had his skull smashed. Emotional resilience sometimes requires sleep. Plus, I think he had a crush on Wally and didn't want to miss out on a chance for some private time with him.

Hattie and Lucy had reported that her Jeep was back in the garage when they got home, but Hattie had decided to stay there in case Lucy needed an alibi. They'd searched the car, but found nothing incriminating. Where had those people taken the Jeep?

We hadn't figured it out yet.

Hattie and Lucy were good people. Good friends. I was glad I hadn't decided to hand over the license plate to Griselda or Devlin. Anything that could incriminate Lucy was for our eyes only.

While King Tut and Wally had been bonding after the cat's morning swim, I'd driven by Ruby Lee's real estate office, but it was unoccupied. I'd checked her house, but no one had answered the door. I'd even gone by Rex's house to try to sneak in and see what I could find, but Chief Stone's car had been there, so I'd kept on going.

That meant we were at a dead end until we hit 22 Main Street, which gave me the morning to thumb my nose at the moose who'd told me to leave.

What did I do to stir them up and taunt them into coming back so we could figure out who they were? I cleaned the heck out of the marina, and I hate cleaning. But when a woman needs to make a point of something, sometimes it requires self-sacrifice.

I'd found a power washer in the garage and tackled the front deck, blasting away any last slivers of glass and ten years of dirt. I hadn't expected much of a result, but by the time I was done? Power washing. Is. Magic. Seriously. The boards looked almost brand new.

My biceps had gone on strike, and my forearms were so sore I could barely fix my ponytail, but so worth it.

Cargo's boat had appeared, and he'd left an invoice on the counter for the boat he'd just finished fixing, but the dude was like a ghost. I'd found a cup of steaming coffee in the garage. I'd seen the wrapper from a Hattie's Café sandwich in the trash. His boat had moved to three different slips over the course of the morning.

But my only employee? Invisible.

I'd found four Adirondack chairs in the garage loft. I'd dragged those surprisingly heavy suckers down the ladder (holy cow, that had been a near-death experience) and set two of them up on the deck, and the other two down on the dock.

The canoes had nearly defeated me, but I'd gotten three of them off the risers, across the parking lot, down the ramp, and into the water, tying them up. Then I'd cleaned ten years of dust off them.

I'd found a can of red paint and painted "We are now open!" in huge red letters across the plywood sheet on the front of the store. I'd even discovered a Ford car key in the register. A search of my property had turned up an ancient, light blue, dented pickup truck behind the garage. Eagle's Nest Marina was painted on the driver's door in faded red letters, which I thought was pretty cool.

The keys managed to get it to start, so I'd claimed the vehicle as mine, named it TurboJet (trying to put positive vibes out to the universe on the longevity of it), and moved it to the parking lot so that the letters on the side of it were clearly visible from the lake. I was pretty sure Cargo must have been taking care of it over the last ten years, so I'd thank him when I met him.

If I met him, rather. Because I was beginning to be a little skeptical.

Lastly, I'd nailed the loon from the murdered sign up over the front door, because it was cute, and who was I to turn down a housewarming gift from locals?

All my actions were steps designed to make it clear from the outside that I wasn't going anywhere. The moose had declared war, and I was standing my ground.

The inside of the marina? Still a mess. I really needed to deal with that refrigerated package Lucy had left me and start to organize the interior of the store, but they took second priority to publicly staking a claim to my life.

Next? Power washing Hattie's Café. I'd just unleashed the first jet of water at her shingles when she flung the door open. "Really?"

"You can thank me later." I adjusted my safety goggles. "It's going to look great."

"My customers are complaining. Go do something else."

I turned off the power washer. "Like what? What can I do? We have three hours until Main Street. I'm trying to irritate the Derby Moose so they come back." The Derby Moose weren't the greatest lead, though, and we both knew it. If 22 Main Street didn't turn up something, Lucy was in trouble.

Hattie sighed and stepped outside, pulling the door shut behind her. She looked as worried as I felt. "I don't know." As she spoke, her phone rang. She looked down. "It's Angelina." She answered it on speaker phone. "What's up?"

"Just got into work. Ruby Lee missed a showing today," Angelina said "Opal went to check on her and found her on her kitchen floor unconscious."

"What?" My stomach dropped. I'd been there this morning. Had I unwittingly left Ruby Lee behind when she was hurt? I'd looked in the windows, but I hadn't seen her.

"Ruby Lee?" Hattie asked, sounding slightly shocked. "Is she dead?"

"In a coma. She was hit in the head, just like Rex, with her own fireplace poker."

I felt sick. "Is she going to be okay?"

"I'm not sure. They think she was attacked in the middle of the night. And that's not all." Angelina lowered her voice. "The neighbors swear they saw Lucy's Jeep parked in front of the house last night, during the window of the attack. The mail sign was even on top of it."

Hattie swore.

I stared at Hattie in horror. We all knew that Lucy's alibi with me and Hattie had a gap. There was a window when there was no one to vouch for her that she hadn't been at Ruby Lee's.

"Oh…no." Angelina went silent.

"Oh, no, what?" Hattie gripped the phone. "You can't say 'Oh, no' and then not finish it! What's going on?"

"The report on the fingerprints just came in. Chief Stone and Officer Hunt are in a meeting with Eloise about the Ruby Lee situation, but they'll be out in a half hour and will check the results."

Hattie grimaced. "Thanks." She hung up. "A half hour, Mia. That's all we have until Lucy's fingerprints will be matched to the murder weapon, and there are four eyewitnesses, including two police officers, who identified her at the scene. No jury on earth would let her off. And her car was at Ruby Lee's house!"

We had just hit panic level situation. "We need to call Lucy. Now."

Hattie nodded and got her on speaker phone.

Lucy answered on the second ring. "Hey, Hattie. I'm about two hours ahead of schedule, so I'll be ready to hit 22 Main Street right on time—"

"Ruby Lee Hanrahan was attacked last night and left for dead," she interrupted. "Your car was seen at her house. You're being set up for it."

There was stunned silence for a moment. "What?"

We needed to take action now, and the first thing was keeping Lucy off the radar until we got to 22 Main Street. We needed Lucy with us in case she was the one who would be able to put the pieces together, because somehow, this revolved around her. Although the fact that Ruby Lee was attacked brought it awfully close to my front door as well, since she'd conned me. Was it about both of us?

I grabbed the phone. "It's Mia. The fingerprints came back."

Lucy sucked in her breath. "Already? They know my route. They'll be able to figure out where I am and come get me. But I can't just not deliver the mail."

"You're early today, though, right?"

She paused. "Yes, but everyone knows my vehicle."

My gaze fell on TurboJet. "Come by here. You can take my

spare truck. We'll swap out. It'll give you time. Drive straight into the garage."

"You're my next stop anyway. I'll be there in three minutes."

She hung up, and I looked at Hattie. "I have a café full of customers," she said. "I can't leave Niko and Cris alone for long. You need to handle this."

"No problem." I paused. "If Chief Stone or Devlin stop by while Lucy's here, you need to distract them."

"No problem. I'm on it. Go!"

We parted ways, and I sprinted for TurboJet. The ancient beast started up nicely, and I pulled around toward the garage. I jumped out, dragged the heavy garage door open, and then backed the truck up so it was next to the door.

Lucy peeled around the corner within minutes. I waved her in, and she coasted straight into the garage. I backed in after her, then climbed out when both vehicles were inside. "Load the mail into TurboJet."

She quickly got out of her Jeep, her face pinched with worry. "TurboJet?"

I pointed. "My truck."

She nodded and started unloading mail. I sprinted for the garage door and started to pull it closed. Just as I did, I saw Chief Stone's car driving down the road. I swore under my breath and dragged the door shut, clanging it closed as he pulled into the parking lot. "Chief Stone just drove in."

Lucy froze, a bin of mail clutched in her hands. "Already?"

He must have slipped out of the police station when Angelina wasn't looking. Shoot! "Hattie said she'd stall him. Let's get the stuff moved." I ran over and grabbed a bin, nearly crushing my foot when it hit the ground. "Why do you pack these things so full?"

"They're a reasonable weight. You need to lift some dumbbells or something." Lucy grabbed another bin and sprinted for the truck, shoving the bin into the front seat. "We can get most of the mail up front. We'll do packages in the back. Is there a tarp or something to hold them down?"

I'd seen one in the loft, and I ran for the ladder. What if Chief Stone came back here? What if he'd seen Lucy pull in? *Come on, Hattie.* I found the tarp I'd seen during my Adirondack chair relocation, grabbed it, and tossed it over the railing.

By the time I got back to the truck, Lucy was dripping with sweat, and an impressive amount of the mail was already in TurboJet. "Check if he's still here."

I dropped the tarp next to the truck and ran to the side entrance. I cracked the door slightly, but I couldn't see around to the front of the marina. I stepped out and shut the door, then ran across the parking lot to the side of the marina store. I inched around the corner, enough to see the bumper of his car parked in front of Hattie's Café.

I leaned back against the wall and texted Lucy. *He's still here.*

Cargo's here now. He's helping me move the mail. I'll be ready in a couple minutes. Can you distract him?

Cargo was there? I literally didn't understand that man. *I'll go intervene. Text me when you're clear.*

You bet.

I deleted the texts, clutched my phone in my hand, and then stepped around the corner and ran right into Chief Stone. We crashed into each other hard enough that I gasped and staggered, and he did the same, stumbling backward.

"Where's Lucy?" he snapped. "I saw her headed this way. I know you and Hattie are hiding her."

Mother of pearl. From the corner of my eye, I saw the garage door open. If Chief Stone took even one step, he'd have the angle to see the garage. He could see the driveway from where he was. I had to get him to back up.

"Mia!" Hattie came running. "Chief Stone is accusing us of harboring a fugitive."

"What?" I put my hands on my hips. "I'm completely offended by that accusation."

He glared at me. "Her car must be in the garage. I'm going to check it out."

I looked frantically at Hattie, who gave me a fist pump of encouragement. "The Derby Moose told me that they were going to come back tonight and kill me. I want a bodyguard," I blurted out. "I want to hire you to protect me."

That got his attention. His face paled. "What?"

I repeated the sentence, to make sure he understood all the words correctly. "I want to hire you to protect me from the Derby Moose when they come tonight to kill me."

He took a step back. "I'm not available for private hiring."

Hattie ducked around him and stood beside me, adding herself to the physical barricade keeping him from the garage. "It's a great idea. You'll be here tonight in official capacity anyway, right? To arrest them when they return to kill her." She inched forward, and I did the same.

Chief Stone took another step back. "Tonight?"

"Aren't you going to set up a sting operation?" Hattie asked. "You could hide under the dock and wait for them."

"I have a wetsuit you could use," I added, also inching forward. "Would that work for you?"

He took another step back, succumbing to our stealthy, subversive pressure. "I'm going to have to discuss this with the mayor. We need to allocate resources—" His gaze shot past me right as I heard the roar of an engine that hadn't been serviced in ten years.

He sprinted past me, and we ran after him, rounding the corner just as TurboJet reached the edge of the parking lot. Lucy had a ball cap and hooded sweatshirt on, so it was impossible to identify her.

"Who's that?" He narrowed his eyes, watching the truck with much more astuteness than I would have expected from him.

"Cargo," I said, watching as she put on her right blinker and turned down the road away from us. She was driving with impressive slowness, as if she had no reason at all to be running for her freedom. "He's going to get supplies. Isn't that old truck cool? I named it TurboJet."

"TurboJet?" Hattie raised her brows at me. "Really?"

"You like it, don't you?"

"I want to name my truck TurboJet," she said. "That's fantastic."

"Right? I figure if I believe in its capability, then it'll deliver."

"Self-fulfilling prophecy. Of course."

Chief Stone turned and ran for the garage, ducking past us before we could stop him. For an out-of-shape doughboy, he was impressively fast, beating us to the garage door by ten yards. Granted, he'd outrun only a seventy-something senior citizen and a woman who'd used all her physical ability for the month dragging chairs down a ladder, but still, he was more athletic than I'd hoped for.

I looked over at Hattie as he hauled the door open. When he saw Lucy's vehicle in there, it would take him only a moment before he connected her with TurboJet. "Wait—"

He disappeared into the garage.

We ran in after him, then I stopped in surprise. Lucy's car wasn't there. I looked around the interior of the cavernous workspace, but all I saw were the few boats Cargo had been working on, his cup of coffee, and a lot of boat parts I couldn't identify.

Chief Stone sniffed the coffee.

"Cargo's," Hattie said. "He always has dark chocolate roast."

He shot her a suspicious glare, then walked deeper into the building.

"Do you have a search warrant?" I called out. "I'm not giving you permission to search my garage."

He stopped and looked back at me. "Only guilty people insist on search warrants."

"Oh, for the sake of my great aunt Millie's garden," Hattie scoffed. "That's a bunch of crap. Who wants a cop running through their garage? You need to get out."

At that moment, I heard the sound of tires crunching over the dirt. I backed up a step so I could see out the door. Lucy's SUV was inching across the parking lot about five feet away. Was Cargo driving it?

"Fine." Chief Stone glared at me and headed back toward us. "But I will find her, and you'll be on the hook for harboring a fugitive—"

"No!" Hattie and I both shouted at the same time, leaping away from the open door, startling Chief Stone into stopping before he stepped outside and saw her Jeep.

"It's fine," I said quickly. "Go ahead and search. I don't want any more trouble. I just want to make friends, start my business, and become an upstanding citizen of Bass Derby."

He raised his eyebrows at me suspiciously. "Is that so?"

"Absolutely."

Hattie was standing back by the door, glancing outside periodically.

He narrowed his gaze at me. I smiled back at him.

"Seriously. Go search. I'll wait here—"

"Mia, I need you to help me out in the café," Hattie said suddenly. "She'll be in the café if you need us, Chief Stone." She paused. "Is Cargo working out back? Because I hear a car engine. Maybe that's Lucy."

Chief Stone whirled around, his hand going to his gun, like he was going to shoot Lucy. "How do I get out there?"

"Straight through to the back," I said. "Past the rowboat. There's an exterior door." I wasn't positive there was, but I had a vague memory of seeing one.

He took off without another word, ducking around stacks of paint, barrels of who-knew-what, and engines. He'd barely taken off when Hattie grabbed my arm and hauled me out the door, to where Lucy's SUV was idling. The driver's door was open, and the key was in it. "You need to get this out of here."

"Me?"

She nodded, shoving me toward it. "Cargo brought it around, but you need to get it out of here."

I ran toward it. "Where do I take it?"

"Hide it somewhere. Go!"

I jumped into the car, strapped on my seatbelt, and hit the gas. The tires skidded on the dirt, then caught. I sped toward the parking lot, hit the left blinker, and took off.

CHAPTER 28

I didn't know the town well enough to have any idea where to take Lucy's car. I also didn't really want to be seen driving it, given who had been almost murdered last night.

Ruby Lee had basically stolen my money and misrepresented the marina when she'd brokered the deal. I'd gotten over it, because I loved my new home, but to an outsider?

People had killed for less.

So, I had decent motivation, and now I was driving the car that had been at the scene of the crime.

I needed to ditch it and fast.

I took a bunch of turns, driving way too fast, and having a near panic attack every time someone drove past me. No one ran me off the road, yelling "citizen's arrest!" but I knew my luck was going to run out.

I needed to ditch the car, and then get back to the marina. Technically, Cargo could come get me, but first, I still wasn't sure he actually existed as more than a figment of everyone's imagination. Second, as far as I knew, he had only a green canoe with a motor on the back of it, which meant he could only retrieve me from somewhere on the lake.

I turned right, and suddenly found myself in the middle of a block of cute little shops. The town center. It was only late May, but there were still a lot of people strolling around. I had no idea there were so many stores. Cute ones. Ones that I wanted to pop into.

If, of course, I wasn't driving a vehicle that could get me thrown into prison for murder, along with Lucy. Since it wasn't tourist season yet, and it was Wednesday, I was guessing that everyone milling about was a local. Which meant they would recognize the familiar mail Jeep cruising down the road.

I needed to hide this!

I saw a parking lot ahead on the right. It was crowded, filled with boats up on trailers. Some of the boats were big enough to block even a Jeep. It had to be the Diamond Lake Yacht Club. Perfect. What better place to stash a murder vehicle than in the parking lot of my competitor? A double win for the good guys.

I hit the gas and took a hard right into the lot that might or might not have resulted in squealing tires because I was going much too fast. I didn't slow down, though. I shot across the lot, squeezed between two big ski boats, and hit the brakes so hard that I almost lost control. The Jeep's tires screeched, and then came to a stop.

Twisting around in my seat, I quickly evaluated my hiding spot as the smell of burned rubber drifted through the air. Well-trimmed bushes blocked the front of the Jeep, and the two boats on either side were high enough that I couldn't see over them. The only exposure was the back of the Jeep, but it would be visible only if someone was actually in the lot right behind the vehicle.

It was solid. Not fool-proof, but it was pretty darned impressive.

I wiped my fingerprints off the steering wheel, the gearshift, and everything I'd touched (basic thievery skills returning with disturbing swiftness), leapt out of the Jeep, locked the door, and shoved the key in my pocket as I quickly walked away. I texted Hattie. *I'm at the Yacht Club. Can you have Cargo come pick me up?*

I'll see if I can track him down. Head down to the dock.

Got it.

As I walked out from my hiding place, I whistled, trying to look casual and calm, but my heart was racing with the thrill of the chase.

Trying to stay unobtrusive, I hurried across the lot toward the lake. There were a lot of luxury cars in the parking lot. Some of them had Maine license plates, but there were plenty from New York and Massachusetts as well. The upper echelon clientele. Why were they all in town?

Then I remembered that Memorial Day weekend was this weekend. That's why the boats were out and people were descending. Summertime was about to launch.

Close to twenty huge boats were up on trailers, shiny and bright as they lined up in the lot. About half of them had *For Sale* signs on them. Three of them were being diligently polished by well-groomed people in navy polo shirts, khaki shorts, and white sneakers. The boats were clearly being prepared for their illustrious owners to roll into town after a winter of hibernation.

I could feel the energy and anticipation as the polo-shirt people chatted with each other. I wanted my marina to be like this. Full of excitement and fun. I wanted to be the one who supplied people with the joy of lakeside living.

There were multiple marina buildings stretching out along the parking lot and lake. Like the police station, all the buildings were gray clapboard with white moldings. The buildings on the right housed the marina store and a café, which had beautiful potted geraniums, flower boxes, and outdoor seating with cheerful blue and white striped umbrellas.

On my far left was what appeared to be the mechanics' building, but the outside was the same charming clapboard. It was twice the size of mine, and it was absolutely beautiful. The middle building was a showroom, with gorgeous gleaming boats for sale.

Through the glass window (that had not been replaced with a plywood sheet and spray painted with a welcome message), I could see a salesperson in a navy polo showing a huge pontoon boat to a man and his diamond-laden wife.

They all looked so pretty.

The whole place felt like a beautiful people kind of place. It was the kind of oasis my mom had lied, cheated, and stolen her way into getting us invited to.

The Yacht Club was more than charming.

It was luxury. It was beauty. It was perfect.

Jake's marina was a class act.

There was no way I could ever compete with it. Who would want to come to Eagle's Nest? Even I didn't want to go back there.

Stifling a sigh, I headed around the side of the building down to the docks. Across the lake and to the right, I could see my marina in the distance. More specifically I could see the brown dirt of my parking lot, the gray outline of my little buildings, and the empty slips. The bright red "Open" paint job on the plywood looked like someone had been murdered and left on the wood to bleed out.

I turned my gaze to Jake's docks. It was a vast expanse of ramps and slips, made with some sort of fancy composite instead of wood. Everything was immaculate and clean. There were many big boats, but also a fair number of smaller ones, even a few little boats with tiny motors tacked to the back, which meant every kind of boater used the Yacht Club.

There were about two dozen kayaks and canoes racked along the shore, and more people in navy shirts were strapping people into life jackets and helping them into the boats.

It was busy, vibrant, and alive. I, in comparison, hadn't had a single customer except Bryan, and he'd been there only to see Cargo, gossip, and apparently, hope for a sighting of Hattie.

This wasn't helping me. I needed to focus. I wasn't there as a commercial spy. I was there because a murderer was running around town, dragging Lucy and me into his web. I checked my phone to see if Hattie had texted that Cargo was on his way, but there was no message from her.

I needed to kill time. I couldn't just loiter here suspiciously until Hattie found me a ride home. Someone would figure out I was trouble, and–

"Can I help you?"

I jumped and whirled around. An early twenties-ish guy in a navy polo and khakis was standing behind me, his hands clasped behind his back. His skin was a dark, rich brown. He was lean, wore glasses, and had a friendly smile. He was wearing his hair in short, bleached twists that looked very familiar.

It was Tyrone, the bartender from the Ugly Man. And now he was *here*? What was the connection between all these pieces? I suddenly remembered the Jet Skis, and how Eloise had said the Yacht Club was the only place who rented them. Jet Skis. Jakes. Moose. Rex. Ruby Lee. How did they all come together?

I was standing in a marina that might have clues. "Hi," I said cautiously.

Tyrone gave me a neutral smile, clearly not recognizing me in my soggy clothes and hair, and sunglasses. "My name's Tyrone Evans. How can I direct you?"

I smiled. "I wanted to reserve some Jet Skis for me and some of my friends." I paused to see if he reacted, but his friendly smile remained the same. "Do you have any? I'd like to look at them and see if I want to rent them or not."

"We do. We actually just put them in the water this morning. Follow me, and I'll show you how to get there." He gestured politely toward the maze of docks. "It's a big marina, and they're at the end. It can be confusing."

He was so polite, I felt like I needed to comb my eyebrows just to be worthy of being in his presence. At the Ugly Man, he'd been tense. Now? He seemed like he was locked down behind his starched shirt and ironed khakis.

"That would be great to have an escort. Thanks." I followed him along the brick walkway, my heart pounding. Should I tell him I recognized him? At the Ugly Man, his parting warning that we'd never talked had seemed to be an attempt to cover up that he'd helped us.

I didn't want to get him into trouble, but I sure as heck wanted to ask him a zillion questions.

"Wonderful." He led the way. "We have twenty Jet Skis available for rent. They book up quickly, so I recommend planning ahead to the extent possible."

He answered freely, clearly not trying to hide anything. I'd stumbled into a prime opportunity to engage in some Jet Ski sleuthing. I quickly tried to think of what would be helpful to know. "Where do you store them? Before they go in the water?" Since they'd been put in the lake this morning, that meant that if they were the Derby Moose watercraft, the moose had gone somewhere else to get them last night.

"We have an offsite storage facility," Tyrone explained as we reached the dock ramp. "Watch your step."

"So, that's where they were last night?" I asked, wanting to confirm before I went racing off to Jake's onsite storage facility.

Tyrone shot me an odd look as he led the way down the ramp. "Actually, they've been in the maintenance garage for the last few days. I've been getting them tuned up after the winter."

Excellent. The window of access was getting dialed down. "Does anyone have the key to the garage? I assume you lock it up."

He looked at me more carefully. "We have excellent security here. Too many expensive boats at risk." He pointed to the end of the docks. "They're down at the end."

I saw the cluster of Jet Skis, and my heart rate sped up. I had no idea how much variety there was in Jet Skis, but from a distance, they looked exactly like the ones I'd seen off my dock. White body. Yellow stripes. "So, no one could, for example, have taken six of them in the middle of the night, gone on a little joyride, and brought them back without being caught? If someone took them, they would have had to have a key and access to the security code?" If that was the case, it would be so easy to figure out who had liberated them last night.

Tyrone's smile faded. "What did you say your name was?"

Did I tell him the truth? If he was one of the moose, I'd be in big trouble if he knew I was onto him. He had all the opportunities to be the bad guy: working at the Ugly Man, knowing about Rex's murder, and working at Jake's marina with access to the Jet Skis.

But as I studied him, I didn't see it. I knew how to see lies, shiftiness, and evil, and I simply didn't see it in Tyrone. But was I certain enough to stake my life on it?

No, but I *was* sure that I was almost out of time to get some answers, so I had to take the chance. I took a breath, then stuck out my hand. "My name's Mia. Nice to meet you."

He paused, searching my face, then shook my hand. "Do I know you? You look familiar."

"People tell me I look like movie stars all the time. That's probably it." Total lie, but I'm sure that some movie star somewhere had the same brown hair and ponytail that I was currently sporting. Tyrone's grip was strong and solid. I knew honest when I saw it, and Tyrone had the goods. I was sure of it. Almost. "Do you like working here?" I asked.

He released my hand. "Yes."

Holy cow. He was lying. Why was he lying? "What do you do here?"

"I'm a staff mechanic, but I also fill in when they need help. Rentals. Sometimes I work in the store. But I really like to work on the boats." His face lit up. "I love restoring them. I have my degree in boat restoration, but Jake doesn't like us to do a lot of it. It's what I love, though."

Oh. I really liked him. His face literally glowed when he talked about restoring boats. I could so use some of that positive energy at the Eagle's Nest. "Do you have any interest in working somewhere else?"

His brows shot up. "Like where?"

I pointed across the water to my marina.

We both turned to look at it.

"You're the new owner?" he asked, after a minute.

"I am."

"I'm not working there."

I sighed. "I know it's rundown, but I'm turning it around."

"It's not just that. You've been targeted by the Derby Moose. No one wants to get in their way."

I was surprised by his statement, but also not surprised. Of course the word would spread, right? "Actually, it's kind of fun. We had a nice chat last night. They're harmless." Yeah. Harmless. Just ask my window.

"Harmless?" He snorted. "I'd always thought they were a rumor. That they didn't really exist. I mean, I heard about them growing up, but no one had seen them for years." He eyed me. "What'd you do to bring them back to life?"

I decided not to mention the sign fragments hurled on my dock the first night, in case Tyrone was one of those militant sign worshipers. "My charming personality, I think. It tends to bring out the best in people."

His eyebrows shot up, and I thought I saw the corner of his mouth quirk ever so slightly. I was just about to commend myself for winning him over, when the almost-grin suddenly dropped off his face.

His eyes narrowed in suspicion as he looked back at the Jet Skis, then at my marina, and then back at me. "The Derby Moose," he said. "You think they used *our* Jet Skis when they went after your marina?"

I shrugged. "I thought I'd check them out," I said neutrally. "Some folks are saying that Jake did it to try to eliminate the competition."

"Jake? No way." Tyrone shook his head. "Your marina doesn't even exist on his radar."

Ouch. "So I've heard. Is there anyone here who you think

might have had a grudge against my marina? Someone who might do something like that."

"No." But again, his response was too quick, and I knew he was lying again.

"Tyrone." I lowered my voice. "What's going on here? I know you know something, just like you did at the Ugly Man last night."

Tyrone's brow furrowed, and then his eyes widened as recognition dawned. "Oh, *no.*" He took a step back. "Uh, uh. No chance. I'm out of here—"

"Tyrone—"

"No." He held up his hand. "Absolutely no. I've never met you before, and I will swear to it." He spun around and walked away, not even looking back.

But I knew what I'd seen in his eyes.

Fear. Almost panic.

Tyrone was scared. Not of me.

Of whoever he'd exposed when he'd given us that tip.

Of whoever would come after him if they found out.

Of whoever I was poking at with a big fat stick.

I let out a breath. The danger was real. Not only to Rex, but to innocent people like Tyrone, which meant I was also at risk if I kept going.

I watched him walk away, not stopping him. If he felt he was in danger, I would trust that and not force him to participate. But I was going to find out on my own, for sure.

So I gritted my teeth, took a deep breath, and headed down the ramp toward the Jet Skis, right into the heart of the Diamond Lake Yacht Club.

The closer I got to the Jet Skis, the more nervous I became. What if the Jet Skis were a perfect match? In the movies, it never went well for people when they found the smoking gun and got caught by the bad guy the moment they put it all together.

There were people around. People who would see me trot out to the Jet Skis and start poking around. Lots of people with navy blue shirts and khaki shorts. Any one of them could be the one who had put that fear into Tyrone.

I looked around, half-expecting someone to leap out from between two boats with a fireplace poker. No one did, but I suddenly couldn't stop thinking about Devlin's warning that the person we were hunting was a murderer who would likely be all right with killing again to keep from being caught.

The second kill was always easier, right? Like trying to pop off poor Ruby Lee, for example. What did she do? And what if Rex hadn't been number one? What if he was number twenty? Or thirty? For someone like that, killing me would literally be as insignificant as getting a cup of coffee.

I didn't want to be a serial killer's next cuppa joe. Seriously.

And yet, here I was, sticking myself right smack into the middle of it, trying to appear casual as I strolled right down the dock toward the Jet Skis.

I got increasingly edgy the closer I got to my targets, but no one stopped me, so I kept going. When I reached the ramp that led to them, I sauntered oh-so-casually out onto the dock and crouched next to the first one to inspect it carefully.

My mouth went dry when I saw the sticker on the side of it. JBN028.

It was the same lettering as the one I'd seen last night, but a different number. I looked down the line of the Jet Skis, and I saw each of them had a unique number.

The third one had the same number as the Jet Ski from last night. JBN725.

I froze.

The matching numbers could be a coincidence, right? It could be a common model number or something. It didn't mean it was the machine from last night, where the moose had pointed that gun at my forehead and said, "Bang. You're dead."

"I'm not dead," I said aloud as I inched along the dock, not wanting to look, even as I wanted desperately to look.

I crouched down next to it and peered at it.

At first I saw nothing unusual.

But then I saw a few pieces of debris on the footbeds.

I inched closer and picked a piece up.

It was wood. A splinter of wood. Like from a broken sign.

My heart started to hammer for real. This was it. This was *it.* I'd literally found the smoking gun, if not of a murderer, at least of a gun-toting sociopath who dressed like a moose and death-threatened innocent women.

I scurried along the dock to the next Jet Ski.

Wood on that as well.

Oh, *wow.* My adrenaline jacked up, and I shivered with anticipation. I'd found the lair of the moose. Even Devlin and Chief Stone hadn't found them. It was terrifying, but also deeply satisfying to know I'd done this.

The next Jet Ski was clean. As was the one after that. But four of the next eight had wood splinters on them as well, bringing the total to six.

I sat back on my heels, stunned. The Yacht Club's Jet Skis had been used by the Derby Moose. Someone had snatched them from the garage and put them in the lake, either at Jake's dock, or somewhere else.

No wonder Devlin hadn't been able to locate them. They hadn't been on the water for him to find. They'd been locked up in Jake's garage.

Luxury Jake wasn't the innocent pretty boy I'd thought he was, after all. Was it Jake himself who had crushed Rex's head with that poker? And what did it have to do with me? With the marina? With the sign?

They must have loaded up the sign fragments before heading out, and not noticed that they'd left splinters behind.

Idiots not to notice it, right? Unless they didn't care. If they believed there was no way to trace them, then maybe they were happy to implicate the Yacht Club. Or maybe, Jake and his staff were involved up to the collars of their navy-blue shirts.

"Can I help you?"

I yelped in surprise and spun around. Standing in front of me was probably the most beautiful human being I'd ever seen in my life. His cheeks were chiseled, his jaw had a designer-perfection amount of stubble, and his eyes were a radiant blue. He was over six feet tall, toned, and belonged on the cover of every men's modeling magazine known to humankind.

And on his navy-blue polo shirt was a name tag that said, "Jake Nash, Owner."

CHAPTER 29

I LEAPT to my feet so fast I stumbled and almost fell off the dock. When Jake reached out to catch me, I vaulted sideways, hit a piling with my hip, and bounced back onto the dock with staggering grace.

He raised his brows at me, and I mustered a charming smile as I inspected him for weapons that he might direct at my cute little forehead.

He wasn't aiming a gun at me, so yay that.

I checked his fingers to see if he had dried blood under his fingernails from popping off Rex or taking down poor Ruby Lee.

His fingernails were perfect, clean, and might actually have been subjected to a professional manicure. Was there actually clear nail polish on them? They looked very shiny and flawless. He matched the boats in his showroom and parking lot.

Satisfied that there was nothing lethal currently happening with his beautiful fingers, I pried my gaze off them and inspected his face for shiftiness, deception, or murderous intent.

He smiled at me, a winning smile that was nearly blinding with his impressively large, white teeth. I wondered if he had them bonded. They were unnaturally spectacular. "Welcome to the Diamond Lake Yacht Club," he said. "Can I help you?"

I realized that was the second time he'd asked me that. Clearly, I needed to work on maintaining the appearance of societal niceties while inspecting for threats to my life.

No problem. I could handle this. I cleared my throat. "Um, yes." I gestured vaguely to the Jet Skis behind me. "I was thinking about renting some Jet Skis with some visiting friends this week-end, but there's debris all over them." I watched his face closely for his reaction.

His smile didn't leave his face. "Debris?"

"Debris." I pointed at the nearest one. "It looks like..." I paused, not quite sure I wanted to open this particular door. "...splinters of wood." Okay. I'd opened it.

Jake's smile became slightly plastic. Just a wee little bit, but I was watching for it, so I noticed the moment the corners of his mouth froze, and his lips thinned. "Splinters of wood?" His gaze flicked toward the Jet Skis. "Where?"

I took a step backward, strategically edging away from him as I pointed. "There. Where my feet would go." I really needed to learn boat lingo. "On the foot deck." That sounded plausible as a real boating term.

He crouched down, reached into the Jet Ski, and picked up a fragment. He rolled it between his fingers, and I saw the muscles in his neck tighten.

I became aware that we were alone on the dock. During our chat, the other blue shirts had moved away, and they weren't paying any attention to us. The dock extension we were on was about twenty feet long, but the water was deep enough I couldn't see the bottom of the lake. Jake could probably drop me in the water without anyone noticing, and then hold me down until I sank to my watery death.

Because that was a cheerful thought.

Jake stood up quickly, and I jumped back again. I was almost at the end of the dock now, and the only way back to shore was by squeezing past him.

He gave me another blinding smile. "I do apologize for the

mess," he said. "This is not how we run our business. We keep all our rentals in top condition at all times. I can assure you that the Jet Skis will be pristine for your rental this weekend."

He was pissed. *Super* pissed. It didn't take a genius to see how he was fighting to be polite to me right now. Was he mad because the reputation of his glorious marina had taken a hit? Or was he riled up because he realized a contingent of joyriding moose had pilfered his machines? Or, most ominously, was he mad because he had a Derby Moose costume stashed under his cash register, and he didn't want to get busted?

Maybe he'd sent the Derby Moose after me to get me to shut down the marina before I even started. Hadn't Hattie said he'd driven out Rusty? Was my competitor willing to murder to get me out of the way?

They were his Jet Skis. It was his yacht club. It wasn't a huge cognitive leap to conclude I might be only a few feet from a murderer. I didn't know what the connection was between Rex and Jake, but I knew that Rex had had a moose costume in the Jeep, and Jake had debris from the assault on his machines.

Guess who had just jumped way up on the suspect list? My new bestie, Jake.

I lifted my chin and gave him a haughty look. "I'm not sure I want to rent here," I said. "Is there anywhere else to rent on the lake?"

His smile widened, and I was pretty sure he had a charm dial that he'd just turned up a few notches. "No, but I promise you'll be completely satisfied with your experience. We offer a full refund if we fail to provide a stellar experience."

No? Again, with the no other options on the lake? He hadn't even hesitated. "What about the other marina on the lake. Eagle's Nest?"

Jake didn't even blink. "They're closed. The owner was a criminal, and the police shut him down."

Um, lie! Rusty had moved to Florida with a woman.

He took out a business card and scrawled something on it.

"Here, take this to the office. It's good for a free rental of a Jet Ski for a full day on the lake. It's my promise to you that we will deliver."

I took the card. He was giving away full days of rentals? How could I compete with that? Especially since I hadn't actually seen any Jet Skis for rent in my garage. Where were all my boats? And I was more than a little irritated by the prevailing sentiment in Bass Derby that my marina literally did not exist. It was tough to get past that kind of publicity. But, hey, at least I wasn't associated with any potential murderers, right? So big bonus right there.

"Um, thank you." I paused. "Do you rent at night? We were thinking about going out for a night ride."

"No." Again, he didn't hesitate. "All Jet Skis must be returned thirty minutes before sunset, as they aren't equipped with lights for night driving. Now, what was your name again?"

I paused. "Um—"

"Excuse me. Hello! Yoo-hoo! Mr. Nash! They said you were down here. We need a word with you!"

We both turned to see two women hurrying along the docks toward us. They were maybe in their sixties, but moving with admirable alacrity. One of the women was wearing a long, white flowing skirt, a glittery emerald-green jacket, with a matching silk scarf and high-heeled green boots.

The shorter woman had closely cut gray hair, a denim button-down shirt tucked into high-waisted black pants. The most striking thing about her were her thick-framed, hot pink glasses that appeared to be decorated with rhinestones.

Jake muttered something under his breath, then plastered on his smile. "Good morning, ladies. How may I be of service?"

The taller woman, which wasn't saying much, since neither of them came up to his shoulder, tossed her flowing, emerald scarf dramatically over her shoulder. "My name is Gladys Donovan, and this is Wanda Barnett."

He gave them a high-wattage smile. "Lovely to meet you. How may I help you?"

"We're from the Diamond Lakes Conservation Association," Gladys informed him. "Last June, we booked the yacht club for our fundraising event this Sunday, but the young man at the store just told us that we aren't on the schedule. That some fancy wedding reserved the entire place."

"Ah, yes, the Callahan-Ramos wedding," Jake said. "Lovely people. Quite the celebrities, you know. The bride's family has been coming to the lake for generations. We're delighted to be able to be a part of their big day."

I grinned. For all his charm, Jake was an idiot. Swooning over the Callahan-Ramos wedding party wasn't the best move.

Gladys narrowed her eyes. "We booked the marina a year ago, immediately after our last fundraiser."

"I'm sure we can clear this up," Jake said, quickly realizing that they weren't as impressed with the celebrities who had gotten them booted out of their reservation. "Unfortunately, your organization needs the space donated. We need to prioritize paying customers. The Callahan-Ramos wedding has been booked since last fall. I'm sure we notified you."

"I'm sure you *didn't* notify us," Gladys snapped.

I liked her. Definitely.

Jake tried to blind them with a soothing smile. "I'm sure we can find another date for you. Maybe a weekday when things are quieter would work." He gestured to the store and walked past her. "Let's go check the schedule."

Gladys, to her credit, didn't budge. "We have over a hundred and fifty people registered for *this* Sunday. We can't reschedule."

Jake paused and turned back toward them. "I'm sorry to hear that, ladies. I do wish that I could help, but I've signed a contract with them. If you're willing to change the date, I'm happy to donate my space. If not, then I'm sure you can find somewhere else. The middle school might work. I'm happy to make a call to the principal. He and I are good friends."

I leaned my hip against the piling and folded my arms over my chest. Watching. Listening. Developing a plan.

"It's a *lake* association," Wanda pointed out. "We can't have the fundraiser at the school. We need people to bask in the beauty of the lake, not a parking lot and a soccer field."

Irritation flickered across Jake's face. "Well, then, I'm out of suggestions. If you think of a way I can be of assistance, please let me know. Otherwise, I wish you the best of luck." Then he turned and strode off, leaving the two women sputtering next to the Jet Skis.

I couldn't compete with Jake with money, facilities, beauty, charm, or in a whole lot of other ways.

But I beat him hands down in the most important area: I was a decent human being.

"Excuse me," I said.

Gladys and Wanda turned to look at me.

I smiled. "My name's Mia Murphy. I'm the new owner of the Eagle's Nest Marina. I'd like to offer you my facilities and grounds for free for your fundraiser on Sunday."

If I'd expected them to be impressed, or fall to their knees in appreciation, or tackle me in a huge bear hug, I would have been deeply disappointed with their reaction.

Because they didn't do any of those things.

What they did was look across the lake to my little haven, then they looked back at me, then back across the lake, looking more depressed and dejected each time.

I cleared my throat. "I understand that Rusty was a criminal, and the place has been abandoned and neglected for a long time. But I own it now, and I care about the marina. About the lake. About this town. It might not be much, but there's space, the bathroom works, and it's on the water."

As I said it, I realized I did care. A lot. I wanted to make this my community. I'd come here because of the lake. The town. The people I wanted to make my friends.

"Didn't you destroy the Welcome to Bass Derby sign?" Gladys asked.

I pressed my lips together for a moment, fighting down the

urge to scream my denial. "I was taking a selfie with it and almost got killed when another vehicle careened into it." I was not going to mention whose vehicle it was. "So, anyway, I would love to help you out."

"Give us a moment." Wanda and Gladys turned away, lowered their voices, and frantically whispered.

As I waited, my phone dinged that I had a text message. Hattie! She must have found Cargo. I pulled out my phone and checked. *Cargo's not around. Why don't you swim? It'll help build your strength.*

Seriously? *My strength is fine.*

Is it?

Oh, for heaven's sake. I shoved my phone in my pocket. Swim back to my marina? It wasn't *that* close. But just to confirm, I glanced over at the Eagle's Nest, and saw a boat pulling into my dock.

I knew that boat. I also knew the big, blue letters on the side that said Lake Police. And I also recognized the tall, muscular silhouette and athletic build of the man who got out of the boat and tied it up.

Devlin was at my marina. There could be nothing good about that. He was either hunting Lucy, after me to arrest me for Ruby Lee's attempted murder, or tracking me down to force me to turn over the plate number, even though he said he'd give me twenty-four hours.

I knew Hattie wouldn't rat me out, but he could very well swing by here to do some Jet Ski inspections on his way out. He was a cop, trained to be vigilant. There was no way he wouldn't recognize me standing on the end of the longest dock, right next to the Jet Skis he was coming over to investigate.

I began to inch back toward shore. "I need to get going, ladies, so I'll see you later. Call if you need—"

"Does Cargo still work there?" Wanda asked, blocking my escape.

"Yes." Or so the rumors said.

Both women giggled. "In that case, we'll take it." Gladys beamed at me.

I stopped, startled by her answer. "You'll what?" I really needed to meet Cargo. He was clearly a thing with the ladies. Plus, he was willing to get involved in helping a murder suspect evade the police, and you had to appreciate that in an employee.

Gladys beamed at me. "We'll accept your offer and host our fundraiser at your marina."

I grinned. "Really? That's great." This was a huge break, and I knew it. Yay!

Gladys nodded. "We'd like to have the tent set up by seven on Sunday morning. Then the caterers will be there by eight. It opens for food at two."

Devlin would soon realize I wasn't at the Eagle's Nest. My window to escape was dwindling. I stepped around Gladys and Wanda. "That's great. Let's talk and walk, as I'm running a little late. Whatever you want—"

"Can we stop by there? Talk to Cargo about setting things up?"

"Yeah, sure. Come by. I'd love to stay here and chat, but I have some errands to run. The marina is yours to do with whatever you want." I kept walking, eager to get off the dock before Devlin or Jake decided to join us.

"Oh, wonderful." Gladys and Wanda hurried to catch up to me as I hustled up the dock. "Why don't we come by this afternoon and look around?" Wanda asked.

Technically that was fine. It wasn't as if anything else was happening over there. But I wanted to be there for it. I wanted to build connections with them. "I have to go into Bugscuffle this afternoon. How about tomorrow morning? Is that enough time?"

Wanda shook her head. "It's really not. This is a complete pivot for us, and we need to change things. We can do our assessment without you."

The roar of a boat engine caught my attention, and I looked around quickly. How had Devlin gotten over here so fast?

But the boat that was pulling up to the gas tank we were

walking past wasn't Devlin's boat. It was a gleaming white ski boat with beautiful yellow seats and white awning.

And it was being driven by Ruby Lee's cousin, Hugo. The man who had been with Lucy's Jeep shortly before it had been seen at the site of Ruby Lee's attempted murder.

I ducked down between Gladys and Wanda, trying to stay out of sight. Why was he here?

He cruised to a stop and threw the rope over the piling. It landed literally six inches from my toe.

I didn't look up. I kept my head down.

"Hey," he shouted. Was he yelling at me?

"Why is he yelling at you?" Gladys asked.

"I might or might not have been part of a group of ladies who ran him off the road after he tried to run us down," I whispered.

"What ladies?"

"Hattie and Lucy—"

Gladys clapped her hands, and Wanda broke into a grin. "You're with Hattie and Lucy?"

Oh, yay. Friends of Hattie! "Yes, I'm helping them clear Lucy's name—"

"Well, heck, girl. You need to make these things clear from the start!" Wanda's tone changed to one of delight and purpose as she put her arm around me. "Gladys. You distract him. I'll get Mia out of here."

"What? No, he's dangerous. Don't go back there—" But my protest was too late.

Gladys had already broken away and headed back toward him, while Wanda hustled me down the dock. Gladys shouted at him about getting her shoes wet, and I glanced back over to see her rushing down the dock toward him, swinging her purse like she knew how to use it.

He looked even scarier in the daylight. His face was long and angular, and his right arm seemed to be twitching. His eyes were still focused on me, as he tied his boat up and vaulted out.

Gladys' purse was going to be no match for him. "Gladys! Don't!"

"She'll be fine." Wanda turned me and urged me forward. "This way."

"He might have killed Rex and attacked Ruby Lee. I don't want her to get hurt."

"No one murders old ladies in broad daylight. He won't dare touch her." Wanda didn't sound remotely concerned. "But she'll have his murderous butt in the water in no time."

"That is literally impossible. He's twice her size." I looked frantically around. I saw the kayaks to my right. They were stacked up like brightly colored dominoes. I raced over to them, hit the first one with my shoulder, and then shoved as hard as I could.

For a split second, the orange tie-dye kayak seemed to move in slow motion, the tip of it slowly sliding down to the right. Then gravity won, and it tipped over and knocked the adjacent kayak. Which then fell into a turquoise kayak. And then they all started crashing down to the ground with the loud clunks of massive, heavy plastic colliding with the ground.

They bounced off each other, and then they started bumping and sliding down the bank to the water. They landed in boats. A couple hit the water and started to float away. Another knocked over a stack of life jackets and sent them careening into the lake.

People in navy blue shirts came running, yelling and shouting.

Jake came sprinting down the ramp. "Hey, hey, hey!" he shouted. "What's going on?"

Chaotic perfection. I was impressed with myself. That was almost worthy of the good ol' days with my mom. I'd have to name that move something cool. Like Kayak Paddle #1. Or Operation Kayak Chaos.

Hugo hesitated as people convened around him, because, as everyone knows, killing people when there were a lot of witnesses never goes well for the murderer.

Gladys gave me the thumbs up and started hurrying back toward us.

"Let's go," Wanda said, tugging my arm. "Gladys is on her way."

"I like that plan." I spun around and stepped right onto a life jacket. My foot tangled in the straps, and I fell, landing on a sliding kayak. It hit me in the stomach, and I bounced off, shielding my head as the second row of kayaks came cascading down on me.

Hugo started rushing through the kayaks, trying to get to me as I scrambled to my feet.

I was too slow.

He caught me by the shirt and grabbed me, yanking me back toward him. His face was twisted and terrifying, and I realized he had no awareness there were people all around, watching. He was going to kill me—

"Hugo!" Jake shoved him to the side. "What are you doing?"

My soon-to-be-murderer took his gaze off me long enough to look at Jake.

Then he looked back down at me, his fingers still clenched in my shirt.

Holy cow. Was he going to kill me even with everyone standing there? His breath smelled like beer and cigar smoke, and I was pretty sure he smelled faintly like my apartment, rotting fish and scaly carcass.

Then, suddenly, he pulled me to my feet and released me. "Just wanted to make sure she was all right, boss," he said.

Boss? He worked here? With Tyrone and the Jet Skis? No wonder Tyrone didn't like his job. Who could possibly feel safe working with Hugo?

He smiled at me, a creepy, evil smile that made me want to run away screaming. "Are you all right, ma'am?"

I stared at him, startled by his smile. It was utterly devoid of any warmth or humanity at all. I felt like it was the smile of a sociopath as he was chopping up nice ladies with an axe.

Jake turned to look at me, and his eyes narrowed just a wee bit. "Did you get hurt?"

"No, I'm fine, thanks." I cleared my throat, hoping that no one was going to start shouting that they'd seen me launch myself at the kayaks. There were so many navy shirt people and customers around that someone had to have noticed my shenanigans.

We needed to get away before someone spoke up.

Gladys hurried up and took my arm. "Thank goodness you're all right." She nodded at Jake. "We need to be on our way. Have a nice day."

"Bye!" I hurried away with my two new friends, who were yammering about deadly kayaks and telling Jake they would never have their fundraiser in such a dangerous place. They were loud, obnoxious, and distracting everyone from the carnage of the kayaks and my role in the fiasco.

As we reached the top of the ramp, I glanced back and saw Hugo and Jake in deep conversation. Hugo was listening and nodding, but he was watching every step I took, threat evident in his eyes.

I swallowed. "Let's get out of here."

At that moment, the lake patrol boat pulled up to the dock, its engine roaring. "Mia!" Devlin yelled as he cut the engine. "Wait!"

My gaze shot back to Hugo and Jake, who glanced at Devlin, then back at me.

Hugo smiled. Jake's eyes narrowed.

"Are you going to wait for Officer Hunt?" Gladys asked.

I hesitated, watching as Jake cornered Devlin as he climbed out of the boat.

"Hang on." I quickly pulled out my phone and texted Devlin. *Check Jake's Jet Skis. There looks like debris from the broken sign in them. JBN725 was the same serial number as the moose from last night who had the gun.*

I hit send and waited.

Devlin pulled his phone out of his pocket and looked at it. He looked up at me, and I gave him a thumbs up.

There were three dots on my phone, and then he texted back. *Get down here. I need to talk to you.*

I ignored his request. *Lucy's fingerprints were on that poker because the murderer threw it at her. She's innocent. You know that.*

"Mia?" Wanda asked. "Are you going to talk to Devlin?"

"Nope. Time to go." I shoved my phone back in my pocket, and then I realized that my only transportation was Lucy's Jeep, which I wasn't about to touch with Devlin down at the docks. "Any chance I can bum a ride off you back to the marina?"

Wanda grinned. "For a partner in crime of Hattie's? It would be our honor."

"I'm not a partner in crime." Seriously. That was about the last reputation I wanted to have.

"Sure. Okay." Wanda winked, and I knew that neither of them believed me.

As I followed them up the ramp, my phone beeped. Figuring it was another text from Devlin, I sped up as I glanced down at the screen.

But it wasn't from him.

It was from Hattie. *Angelina just called. There's an arrest warrant out for Lucy for Rex's murder. We're out of time.*

CHAPTER 30

Two hours later, after some skillfully evasive work that might or might not have qualified as harboring a fugitive, or something equally illegal, Hattie, Lucy, and I escaped Bass Derby with no one in prison or arrested.

Yet.

I tried to lighten the mood by regaling them with the incident with the kayak, and they both thought it was hilarious. Unfortunately, neither of them had any good info on why Jake might be a murderer or even harass my marina. The truth was, although there were a lot of threads connecting the Derby Moose with Rex's murder, we had no solid connections, no proof, nothing that we could give to the police.

Why had the moose come after me? My marina was really not worth anyone's effort. And I still couldn't believe the sign was. Now that Ruby Lee had been attacked, she was off our suspect list, but that left…no one.

Sure, I wanted it to be Hugo, but we literally had nothing on him other than that he had been in the right place and had anger issues.

Bugscuffle was our last chance, but when we rolled up to 22 Main Street, I thought we'd gotten the address wrong. It wasn't a den of iniquity. It was a cute, two-story wooden building with a front porch, a beautiful lawn, and a charming sign about the same size as the Bass Derby one had been, but it was new, with brown wood and black letters. The sign told us we'd arrived at *Sassy Silver-Bullet Babes*. On the second line, it said "We Never Stop Grooving!"

There were gray-haired seniors knitting outside, a shuffle-board court, and brightly colored Adirondack chairs in the shade.

"I thought we were going to find a meth lab." Hattie sounded distinctly disappointed as she pulled her massive pickup truck into the parking lot. "This is such a let-down."

"Try to stay optimistic. There could be a meth lab on the second floor." Honestly, it didn't really look like a meth lab kind of place, and I was okay with that. StanleyGate had cured me of any need to get involved with drug dealers. A gambling ring on the other hand? That would be perfect. "They might have bingo. That could be dodgy."

"No one murders over bingo," Hattie muttered as she slammed the truck into park.

"Anymore," added Lucy.

Anymore? I kinda wanted to know about that. But we had to focus. Instead of picking up that thread, I peered out the window at *Sassy Silver-Bullet Babes*, an expansive, natural wood building that backed up to a completely adorable movie theatre.

The center looked newish, and it was as charming as the police station in Bass Derby. To the right side of it was the grassy area with gray-haired knitters in Adirondack chairs, several picnic tables, and a Japanese stone garden, beside which ran a small, picturesque river with trees and foliage and a stone wall.

It didn't look nearly as nefarious or sketchy as I'd hoped, given how we'd ended up here. In fact, it didn't look at all disreputable. It looked like gossip, polyester pants, and granny panties, not that there was anything wrong with those, but they didn't usually lead to stampeding murderous moose and dead calendar models.

"It looks boring." Hattie leaned on the steering wheel. "There is literally no way that anything interesting can be associated with this place, especially not murder."

"The sign says 22 Main Street. We're in the right place," I pointed out, although I had to admit I agreed with her.

Lucy leaned over the back seat. "This was it. Our chance." She sounded crushed. "We don't have any more time. Why did we listen to some random stranger?"

I thought back to my encounter with Tyrone. "He was legitimately scared. He knows something."

Hattie put the truck in reverse. "Let's go to Jake's and shake him down, then."

"Wait." I held out my hand. "I want to check it out. He sent us here for a reason." I was afraid Tyrone would be emotionally scarred for life if Hattie decided to subject him to any kind of shake down.

"No." Hattie said. "I'm going to find him and that jerk Hugo at the marina."

"No." I opened the door and jumped out. "I'm going in." Hattie had already let the tires start to roll while I was in the air, and the door almost took me out when I landed. "Hey!"

"Sorry!" Hattie hit the brakes, narrowly missing beheading me. "Get in, Mia. This is a waste of our time—"

"Is it?" I put my hands on my hips. "Don't you always say that you could get away with anything, because no one would ever suspect an old lady?"

"I'm not old," she snapped. "I can kick your butt all day long."

"*I* know that, but you always say that people underestimate you because you don't *look* like you can." Con artist success was based on the fact that people rarely look past the obvious, especially if you give them what they want to see, or expect to see. I jerked my thumb at the adorable center for ladies who liked to play bingo, knit, sew, and get their hair done. "Wouldn't this be a great place to plan a murder? No one would ever come looking here."

Hattie frowned, her gaze going to the building again.

"We can't go back to Bass Derby," I added. "Chief Stone and Devlin are looking for Lucy. The minute we go back to town, they'll arrest her. This is it. We have to make this work."

"Mia has a point. I want to check it out, too." Lucy hopped out of the back seat and scrambled out of the truck. "It really is the perfect location."

Hattie raised her brows, pursing her lips. "It's true. People are prejudiced toadbrains when it comes to respecting the ability of gray-haired goddesses."

"Right?"

She put the truck into drive. "I'll go around back and see what's there. Text if you find anything. Let's rip this sucker wide open." She peeled out before I got the door shut, but the force of her whipping around the parking lot flung the door closed with a bang.

I watched smoke literally rise from her tires. "She's terrifying."

"That's why I buy into your idea that this place could be the perfect cover. Who knows what evil could be lurking behind this innocuous façade?" Lucy put her hands on her hips and turned toward the building. "Let's go. I'm not going to prison today."

I fell in beside her as we headed toward the front door, walking across the grass that was about the most perfectly maintained lawn I'd ever seen. "Let's go with ever, not just today."

She flashed a grin at me. "Or ever," she agreed.

We reached the front door, looked at each other.

"Hang on." I needed someone to know where to look for us if everything went south. I pulled out my phone and texted Devlin. *We're at 22 Main Street in Bugscuffle. If we disappear, start looking here. It's not Lucy. She's being set up. Trust me, please.* I paused, then quickly typed in the license plate information. Hugo was bad news. If we disappeared, someone needed to know about him and look in his direction. As an afterthought, I added, *Ask Jake about Hugo.*

Even though he clearly had information, I couldn't turn Tyrone over to Devlin. I was afraid it would put a target on his head, and

I couldn't live with that. Jake on the other hand? I was okay with that.

Three dots appeared, but I shoved my phone in my pocket, not wanting to deal with questions. Instead, I grabbed the handle and pulled it open. "Let's do this."

She took a breath and nodded. "Let's make this happen, Murph."

I paused. "Murph?"

"Mia sounds too sweet and perky. Murph sounds like Irish mafia, or, better yet, the IRA, which might be what we need. Did you happen to bring any Molotov cocktails with you?"

"I left them with Hattie."

"Perfect. Nothing could possibly go wrong then."

"Exactly. I'm sure explosives in her hands makes the world a safer place." I led the way through the double doors into a large, homey foyer furnished with couches, armchairs, wall-to-wall beige carpet, and a number of older-ish ladies gossiping and sipping coffee. "This is seriously a good cover. No one would track a murder plot to this place."

"Totally."

There was an information desk, but no one was tending it, so we strolled past, whistling innocently. Once past the desk, the hallway widened, extending both to the left and to the right. The corridor was empty, giving the building a quiet, almost eerie feeling. I wondered if everyone had been murdered, and we'd find them in a huge body pile in the bingo room.

Or not. Please not.

We paused at a card table wedged up against the wall. The table was loaded with assorted flyers, clipboards with sign-up sheets, a couple mugs filled with pencils, and an electric pencil sharpener plugged into the wall. Apparently, they expected a run on sign-ups that would overwhelm the capacity of the several dozen yellow pencils they'd provided.

"Which way?" Lucy whispered.

According to a sign taped to the front of the table, to the left was sewing, knitting, and baking. To the right was yoga, ballroom dance classes, bingo, and the main hall. "There's nothing that points to plotting a murder or recruiting people to dress up in moose costumes."

She pointed to the sewing. "Maybe they made the costumes here."

"Oh. Good call."

She frowned. "What if no one's there, and the door's locked?"

I grinned and dug my lock picks out of my back pocket. "I came prepared." I'd shoved them in my pocket at the last second.

Instead of smiling, she frowned and peered at them. "Is that a dead bug on them?"

"A bug?" I looked at the picks. For a moment, I didn't see what she was talking about, but then I saw a brown, fuzzy lump. "No. It looks like hair." I grabbed it and tried to pull it off, but it was stuck. I yanked harder, and it finally came free in my hands. I held it up and inspected it. "It looks like..." I suddenly remembered my lock picks getting stuck in the sweater of the murderer as he'd been exiting Rex's house. "Yarn?"

Lucy peered at it. "It's not yarn. It's fur." She touched it. "Brown, nylon fur."

I stared at her. "Moose fur."

Her eyes widened. "Derby Moose costume fur."

Chills ran down my spine. "Whoever killed Rex was wearing a Derby Moose outfit," I said. "And then he came straight to my marina to throw wood at the dock." There it was. "The missing link connecting Rex's murder to the moose." I let out my breath. A Derby Moose had murdered Rex. And moose had sung to me last night, which, according to local lore, meant that I was supposed to die at their hands tonight.

Fear suddenly congealed in my stomach, and all my bravado vanished. "I don't really want to go down the hall."

Lucy looked around nervously. "Me either."

We stood there for a moment, until I finally spoke. "How scary can they be, right? It's a bunch of ladies who sew."

"Yeah, right? They probably just made the costumes and didn't do the actual murdering. So, it's fine." But Lucy didn't move either.

"Unless the murderer is one of the old ladies," I pointed out. "Hattie could murder someone, no problem."

"That's the truth." Lucy paused. "Or maybe the actual murderer is here right now, cleaning up evidence."

The long hallway suddenly looked even longer and emptier. It would be a long sprint back to safety if we ran into someone who wanted to kill us. I wasn't a fast runner. I would definitely be the one who got caught.

"Hang on." Lucy grabbed one of the clipboards, fisting it between both hands. "The plastic is thick. It's pretty durable. It's not a rifle, but I could do damage with this."

I glanced at the table for a weapon. I didn't want to stab someone in the jugular with a pencil. I'd seen it work in movies, but I was pretty sure that much blood spurting all over me would make me pass out, and then, where would I be? A defenseless victim.

Then my gaze lit on the electric pencil sharpener and its lovely black cord. "I'm kind of an expert at using projectiles with cords." I pulled the cord out of the wall, wrapped it around my hand and swung the sharpener. "It's pretty heavy. Definitely hard. I can work with this."

"Okay, then." Lucy took a deep breath. "Let's go."

"Right." Swinging the electric pencil sharpener unobtrusively by my hip, I fell quiet as we headed down the hall, our sneakers almost silent on the laminate wood floors.

The first room on the left had a sign on the door that said knitting. We peered in as we went by, but it was empty. I was fine with that, because I had a sudden vision of being stabbed with knitting needles. Who needed that? Across the back wall was a bookshelf with cubbies that had different colors of yarn stacked in each one.

"They sell yarn here," Lucy said. "Good to know."

I glanced at her. "Do you knit?"

"Nope, but if I ever decide to, now I know where to go."

The next room on the left was a kitchen. A large one, in fact, with multiple ovens, huge counters, two sinks, and three refrigerators. A smiley woman with a pink apron, curly gray hair, and a very large knife was showing six other women how to chop garlic.

"I hope she's not the murderer," I whispered. "That knife could probably cut through my femur."

"Why does she need such a big knife for garlic?" Lucy asked. "It's super creepy."

"She's probably related to Hattie."

The chef looked up and saw us, so we scooted out of her line of sight before she could call us out for being forty years too young to be in their hallways.

The next two doors on the left also opened to the kitchen. "There are a lot of tables to eat at," Lucy whispered.

I thought of the table that had been in my living room with the plastic tarp and all the sharp knives. "Or to filet people on."

She stopped and looked at me. "Really? What's wrong with your brain?"

"I spied on my ex for two years, only one wrong step from being caught. Drug dealers have a lot of creativity when dealing with traitors. I've imagined pretty much every way to die."

"Wow." Sympathy flashed over her face. "That sounds kind of stressful."

"It really was," I agreed. "I don't recommend it."

"Good to know. I'll give it a pass next time I get an offer to betray hardened criminals." She paused and pointed to the end of the hallway. "Sewing."

"Sewing." I took a tighter grip on the cord of the pencil sharpener, gazing at the closed door. "Well, at least we know where to find knives if we need to save ourselves."

"They probably know where the knives are as well."

I shot her a look. "Not helpful."

"Right. Stay positive. My clipboard and your sharpener are all we need." She shot me a peppy smile. "Shall we?"

"Of course. I've been wanting to learn how to quilt for years now. Maybe we can learn here." I leaned in, pressing my ear against the door, listening. I could hear the bass thud of music, and muffled voices shouting over the noise. "It sounds like female voices." My heart started hammering. I'd really been hoping to find evidence without actually having a face-to-face with the bad guys, but life doesn't always deliver dreams, does it?

Lucy tightened her grip on the clipboard. "We can handle women."

"Can we, really?"

"We can."

"Okay." I took a breath, grabbed the knob, plastered a friendly smile on my face, and opened the door. "Is this the quilting class?"

CHAPTER 31

I HADN'T BEEN sure what to expect from a sewing room, but it wasn't what I found.

Because who would expect a sewing room in a women's senior center in Bugscuffle to be pumping out heavy metal music while a dozen later-in-life women wearing black, heavy-metal T-shirts with skulls, daggers, a deformed grim reaper, a skeletal hand dripping blood, and other fun designs, hammered on their sewing machines.

Most of them had spiked hair. Several of them had a dozen or so earrings all the way around their ears. I saw black leather pants. I saw leather boots with metal spikes on them. Most had donned black lipstick and glittery eye shadow.

"Oh, man," Lucy whispered behind me. "These women have definitely spent time in prison."

"We can totally take them," I whispered back, feeling extremely relieved that we'd stumbled across gray-haired heavy metal fans and not Hugo and his pals. I cleared my throat. "Hello?"

No one noticed me. They were shouting to be heard over the music, yelling about how someone named Madge had done something with a pumpkin that most of them thought should be illegal in the state of Maine.

I waved my arms and shouted. "Hello!"

The one nearest to me finally looked over. Her gray hair was braided into a maze of gorgeousness, sweeping all over her head like a work of art, and her skin was almost the exact same shade as Tyrone's. Her eyes widened, and she grabbed her phone, touched the screen, and the music went off. "This is a private rental time for the room. We have it every Monday, Wednesday, and Friday from two to five."

I cleared my throat. "I can see that." Two to five, eh? That fit with what Tyrone had told us, which meant these women were who he sent us to find.

"What are you doing here?" she asked, in a voice that wasn't all that friendly.

Lucy started to answer, but I had a sudden flashback of the penis-hacking incident, so I interrupted her. "We're here to do an article on senior women who are thumbing their nose at the stereotypes of what it means to be on the better side of sixty." I figured I could have said eighty and been right, but who wants to offend elderly women with metal spikes on their boots? Not me.

The woman with the braids narrowed her eyes at me. "Who gave you our name? We stay off the radar."

I took a gamble. "Tyrone did."

Her face softened. "My grandson Tyrone?"

"Yes!" I let out a sigh of relief. "Yes, your grandson Tyrone. He said you were exactly what we were looking for." There was no way Tyrone was afraid of these women, and why on earth would he report his own grandmother if she was involved in something nefarious? So what had been going on?

She grinned. "Well, if Tyrone sent you, that's all I need to know. You're all right."

I grinned back. "I am all right."

One of the women in the back with bright orange hair yelled at me. "What newspaper? It's not some retiree glossy magazine, is it?"

"No. It's..." I looked at Lucy.

"*O Magazine*," she said immediately.

In unison, their jaws dropped open.

"Oprah is doing a special issue on women in their sixties and above." Lucy pointed at me. "Murphy O'Malley is writing the article. I'm her assistant, Patty McFee." She smiled. "Unless you guys don't want us bothering you during your private sewing session?"

It took less than five seconds for me to be crushed in a throng of overly excited, geriatric, heavy-metal sewing queens.

It took less than ten seconds for Lucy to haul every one of them off, hurl them back to their seats, and shut them all up with a glare. "Did I mention I'm also her bodyguard? No one messes with Murph. Got it?"

They all nodded in acknowledgment, including me. I could now add Lucy to the list of women I was afraid of.

Lucy stepped back and gestured to me. "Ms. O'Malley. You have the floor."

I cleared my throat and stepped up. How many questions did I need to ask before jumping into the moose thing? "So, my first question is…I noticed that you all seem to be a fan of heavy metal. What is it that resonates with you about that music?"

Tyrone's grandma raised her hand.

I nodded to her. "Go ahead. Your name is…?"

"Bootsy Jones. We all hate this music." When she said it, everyone nodded, and people started shouting.

"It's vile!"

"It's just a bunch of screaming and shouldn't even count as music!"

"It's trash!"

"You'd have to be deaf to like it!"

And more choice words that Lucy pretended to write down on her clipboard, while chewing her lower lip and trying not to laugh.

I held up my hand, and the shouts faded. "If you all hate it, why are you listening to it, dressing like it, and sewing quilts out of heavy metal T-shirts?" I felt like that was a valid question. It wasn't likely to help me find Rex's killer, but I really wanted to know.

Bootsy answered again. "Because we're channeling."

"Channeling what?"

"The vibe." One of the women in back held up the quilt section she was working on. It was an assortment of Metallica T-shirts with skulls, poison, people dying, and other fun stuff. "We were hired to create a quilt to sell as a fundraiser for the high school. The senior class voted for a theme of rebellion, so we came up with heavy metal." She pointed to her black lipstick and nose ring. "You really think we walk around like this all the time?"

"Well, I—"

Bootsy stood up. "We're known in these parts as the Seam Rippers. We're master sewers for hire. We're very selective about who we take on. If it doesn't inspire us, we don't touch it, no matter how much money they offer us, or how good the cause is."

The other Seam Rippers raised their fists and shouted their agreement. I kinda wanted to join in. How cool did that sound? What a great way to live.

A woman with fuchsia hair spiked into a mohawk raised her hand. "Sophia Cortez here," she said. "I've been wanting to wear a leather bustier with metal rivets for years." She unzipped her leather vest and showed off cleavage that most twenty-year-olds could only dream of.

"Impressive." Lucy peered over for a better look. "Those are great breasts."

"Right?" Sophia patted her girls. "I love them, they love me, gravity has no chance."

"Love is a powerful force, for sure." As much as I adored admiring other women's cleavage, I needed to stay focused. "So, you always dress up for whatever project you're working on?"

"Damn straight," Bootsy said. "It's half the fun."

"What else have you dressed up as recently?"

"Hookers," shouted one of the women. "That was fantastic when we went out to the bar and—"

"Flower children," added another.

"Swimsuit models," shouted one woman.

"Ninja assassins!"

"Harry Potter!"

"Moose!"

"Old west cowboys!"

"WNBA players!"

I held up my hands, trying not to show my excitement. "Wait a second. Did someone just say *moose*?"

"I did." A woman on the right, who was wearing about fifty gold chains, black leather pants, and stilettos raised her hand. "I'm Shirley Kincaid. The moose were crazy. We had to make our own moose costumes first so we could wear them while we made the moose costumes for our client."

"Those things were so difficult to sew in."

"Right? Those hooves were a bitch."

"And hot. I had to drink three extra margaritas just to stay hydrated, I was sweating so much."

"We were all so tipsy we had to redo those antlers how many times?"

"At least a dozen."

I looked at Lucy, then back at the Seam Rippers. "Who did you make them for?" I asked, trying to keep my voice casual.

There was a moment of silence.

"I don't even know," Sophia finally said. "I was just having so much fun drinking, I didn't even care. Does anyone remember?"

There was a round of discussion, until finally Bootsy clapped her hands. "It was for the fundraiser for the Greater Maine Nature Preserve."

"Fundraiser at the Greater Maine Nature Preserve," Shirley agreed. "Save the moose, right?"

One of the women raised her empty glass. "State Animal of Maine. We believe in our moose."

"Thank God we remembered. I need a drink. Does anyone have any more tequila?"

"Tequila break!"

"Wait, wait, wait!" I held up my hands as tequila bottles, blenders, and mix suddenly appeared on the sewing tables. "Do you know how I can contact someone at the Preserve?"

"Sure. She's coming to pick up the leftover fabric this afternoon. She called me this morning, all worked up about getting that fabric. She's even taking the moose costumes we made for ourselves, which is fine because those things were hot as the devil in a sauna." Bootsy set a huge blender on the desk. "Who's making a run to the kitchen for the ice?"

Sophia and another woman stood up, grabbing for a cooler. "We'll go." Sophia looked over at us. "You guys want in?"

I didn't really feel like now was the time to get hammered. "I'm all set, thanks."

"Me, too," Lucy said. "Do you know when she's coming?"

At that moment, the emergency exit at the back of the room opened. Lucy and I looked over as a woman poked her head in, a woman who we both recognized immediately.

It was Jillian, the waitress from the Ugly Man Tavern. Glitter. It wasn't Lucy's twirling glitter that had been on the costumes. It had been Jillian's.

Holy *cow.* I heard Lucy suck in her breath.

She didn't even notice us. "Hey, Bootsy. Did you bring everything?"

"Sure did, Jillian. Left it by the back door as you asked." Bootsy nodded at us as Jillian hurried over to a stack of bins and lifted the entire pile at once.

What? She weighed about twenty pounds with arms the size of toothpicks. Was she actually strong? Like, strong enough to clock Rex in the head? As a twirler, she knew how to use a hard stick, for sure.

"Is this it?" Jillian asked, her face hidden behind the bins.

"That's all of it, but before you go, we've got some reporters from *O Magazine* who want to talk to you about the moose costumes we did," Bootsy said. "Murphy? Assistant person? This is Jillian, from the Greater Maine Nature Preserve. We made the moose costumes for her."

Jillian pivoted so she could look around the bins. She saw me first and frowned, but alarm didn't creep in until her gaze shifted to Lucy. The moment she saw Lucy, she paled. Horror flashed across her face.

That was such a guilty look. But holy cow. Jillian? She'd seemed legitimately crushed by Rex's death.

Lucy waved the clipboard at her. "Hi, Jillian. So good to see you again," she said with completely non-believable innocence. "I had *no* idea you were involved in moose preservation."

Jillian paled, then turned and bolted out the door, still gripping the bins.

"Hey!" I took off after her, dodging sewing machines and blenders, Lucy hot on my tail.

We got outside just in time to see Jillian disappear around the corner of the building, toward the main street. "Hattie!" I shouted as we took off after her. "We've got her!"

Hattie didn't appear, but we didn't have time to wait. We sprinted around the corner, then stopped. The main street was busy, with people milling about, going into shops. "Where is she?" I shielded my eyes against the bright sun. "Do you see her?"

"No." Lucy scanned as well.

Hattie came panting up behind us. "What's going on? I heard you shout!"

"It's Jillian. Our waitress from the Ugly Man. She's carrying bins of moose costumes." I showed her the fur from my lock picks. "And we figured out that Rex's murderer was wearing a moose costume. This got stuck in my lock picks at Rex's house. Do you see her?"

"No." We all looked around, but she'd disappeared.

"She has to be somewhere," Hattie said as she peered at the fur. "Look at that. I can't believe it's been sitting here all this time, and we never noticed it."

"I know, right?" My bad for trying to pretend I wasn't a thief and putting away the lock picks in total denial of who I was. But I didn't have time for that. Precious time was slipping away. "Let's split up. We need to find her before she leaves!"

"I'll go left." Hattie hurried down the sidewalk.

"I'll take right." Lucy took off.

"I'll go across the street, then." I broke into a run. I dodged a few trucks, then made it to the opposite side of the street without being squashed. But now what? I quickly surveyed the street, trying to figure out how Jillian could have disappeared so quickly.

What did she need for this to be a success? She needed to be unseen and to be able to get away.

Transportation that was out of sight.

I spun around again, this time searching for a place to hide a vehicle. I saw a tiny green sign with a parking lot "P" on it, pointing behind the block of stores I was standing in front of. That was it. I knew it. My childhood instincts flared up, and I knew for certain that was it.

I gripped the cord and swung the pencil sharpener, giving it momentum as I hurried down the alley between the stores. I reached the back of the stores, peered out, and then nearly squawked with terror.

Not five feet from me was the truck that had nearly run us off the road at the Ugly Man Tavern. The one owned by Hugo. Jillian had the back of the truck bed cover open, and she was shoving the bins frantically into it.

Was Hugo around? He terrified me. I needed help.

I ducked back around the corner out of sight. I pulled out my phone to text Hattie and Lucy, and then I saw a new text pop up from Devlin. *Mia. The guy who's driving that truck is wanted in Florida for murdering six people. Get out of that building. I've called the Bugscuffle police. They'll be there in a few minutes.*

My stomach dropped. Murder. Hugo was literally a killer.

Mia. Did you get this? Get out. Get out now. I'm on my way.

I started typing. *I'm out. His truck is across the street from the women's center. Jillian, a waitress at the Ugly Man is loading moose costumes into his truck—*

My phone was snatched out of my hand. "Seriously, Hattie? I —" I looked up.

It wasn't Hattie.

It was Hugo.

CHAPTER 32

MY GUT DROPPED as I stared at Hugo, my phone in his hand. This was the moment I'd feared every second of my undercover time against Stanley. Being caught by the person willing to kill me.

I swallowed my fear and plastered a smile on my face. "Hey, so I was thinking—" Mid-sentence, I whirled around and sprinted back down the alley. Escape was always the first choice in situations like this. Always, always, always. "Help! Help! I'm being attacked—"

Something hit me between the shoulders, and I flew forward, losing my grip on the sharpener as I landed on my face, just like when Joyce had taken me down. I tried to scramble to my feet, but he was on me too fast, clamping his hand over my mouth.

I tried to bite him, but his hand was so large that he was holding my jaw shut while covering my mouth. I fought desperately, but he dragged me back through the alley as if I was nothing more than a second thought.

At the end of the alley, I saw a mom and her little girl walk by, but neither of them looked down the darkened gap. Two teenage boys strolled past, but didn't notice my fight for survival. What the heck? Did no one check alleys anymore? From now on, I was going to inspect every single alley I passed to make sure no one was being dragged to her death.

I slammed my elbow backwards, and I heard an oomph, but he didn't let go. We were almost back to the end of the alley now, where his truck was. I couldn't let him get me in the truck. That was a surefire way to ensure kidnapping, torture, and certain death.

I channeled everything I could remember about what Griselda had taught me in the event Jimmy the Butcher (or someone similar) came for me, but Griselda had never taken into consideration six psychotic feet of antlered death.

I kicked backward. I stomped. I squirmed. I screamed as best I could.

None of it mattered.

Hugo was a beast, and he tossed me effortlessly onto the backseat of his pickup. He wrapped some gross smelling fabric across my mouth, tied my arms behind my back, and threw me on the floor. "Sit on her," he ordered, his forearm still pinning me to the floor. "Now!"

"Let her go," Jillian said. "This is going too far—"

Yes, let her go. Please let her go. I tried to kick him, but totally missed, nearly ripping my groin instead.

"She can connect us to the moose, and the moose connects us to Rex's death. You want that?"

Jillian blanched. "No, but I didn't kill Rex—"

"Sit on her, or you'll die too."

Jillian whimpered, but she quickly climbed into the truck. She sat on my butt, pinning me down. I fought to get her off me, but I couldn't get leverage with my hands behind my back.

Hugo slammed the door closed, the engine roared to life, and then the truck peeled out.

As I tried to get out from under Jillian, I listened for the wail of sirens. For the screech of Hattie's tires. For Lucy's shout.

But there was nothing. No one had seen them grab me.

There was simply the growl of his engine, the grit of the floorboards on my cheek, and the warmth of Jillian's butt on top of me.

Nothing else. No Griselda. No Devlin.

The speed of the truck picked up, and I knew we were out of town.

They were going to be too late.

No one was coming to save me.

I was going to have to save myself.

From a serial killer.

Who had already tied me up.

Odds? Totally in my favor.

I took a deep breath and forced myself to stop fighting. It wasn't working, and I needed a better plan. I did a quick glance under the seat to see if he'd stashed a rifle under there like Hattie did, or a Derby Moose costume with a hole that matched the tuft of fur in my lock picks, but there was nothing in sight but a lot of fast-food trash bags, beer cans, and cigarette butts.

So, apparently, I had no weapons, except my fantastic street smarts and quick thinking. No problem. I got this. *I got this.*

I thought back to Jillian's half-hearted protest about killing me. The truth comes out in times of stress, right? That meant maybe she wasn't all-in on the Murder Mia plan. Maybe I could leverage that.

I hit her with my elbow and twisted my body in ways it wasn't meant to be torqued so I could see her face.

She looked down at me, and to my great joy, she looked worried.

I did a bunch of shifty things with my eyes, to make it look like I was trying to tell her something.

She frowned at me, then looked at Hugo, then back at me. She shook her head once, ever so slightly.

I did a bunch more dramatic eye moments until my eyeballs started to cramp.

After a second, she slid her hand down and tugged the gag out of my mouth.

Holy cow! I could breathe! I sucked in a breath, and then immediately stopped, remembering my lesson from the assassin in the bathroom incident: *stop breathing when being hunted by someone planning to kill you.*

I looked up at her and mouthed, "*He's going to kill us both.*"

She frowned at me and shook her head in lack of comprehension. Or denial of the obvious. I wasn't sure which it was, but neither were acceptable.

Now that I knew about Hugo's serial killing tendencies, I seriously doubted that Jillian had killed Rex or attacked Ruby Lee. I was putting that all on Hugo's shoulders.

She might, however, be sucked too far into Hugo's little game to be thinking clearly. How did I convince her that I wasn't the only one in danger? Because she might not care that much about saving me, but most people were deeply concerned about saving themselves.

An idea came to me, so I hit her with my elbow again. *My phone,* I mouthed to her. I hadn't seen what Hugo had done with it, but I was hoping he'd decided to keep it.

She looked around, then nodded, pointing to the seat beside her.

Yay! We still had it. *Read my text.*

Jillian hesitated, but then picked up my phone. She held it to my face to unlock it and then peered at the screen. I knew Devlin's text about Hugo was the one that was open on the screen.

Her face paled, and she sucked in her breath. Her face turned almost green, and for a horrifying moment I thought she was going to throw up. Not good, even under the best of circumstances, but since she was sitting on me, it was really less than optimal.

Text him, I mouthed. *Tell him where we are.*

Jillian's jaw tightened as she tossed the phone back on the seat. Guilty people don't like to call cops. I knew all about that.

"Can you drop me off at my house?" Jillian spoke up. "I'll grab the rest of the moose costumes that are there, and I'll get rid of them."

Oh, so that was her answer? To bail and leave me to die? Any thought I'd had of becoming besties with her were now dismissed.

"We're not done with the moose," Hugo replied, his voice sending shivers down my spine. I was literally trapped in the back of a truck belonging to a murderous sociopath.

I gritted my jaw. There had to be a way out of this. If I could escape a professional killer with nothing more than a hairdryer and a moldy shower curtain, I could evade this guy, right?

"We *are* done with the moose," Jillian protested. "It was supposed to be about messing with Bass Derby's reputation so it didn't win Best Lake Town again. No one was supposed to die!"

I was so stunned by her protest that I forgot to be panicked for a minute. It really was about that ridiculous contest? I'd nailed that, except I'd put it on Ruby Lee instead of Jillian. Lucy had said that Jillian's mom was the mayor of Bugscuffle, but I'd been so focused on hoping it hadn't been Ruby Lee that I hadn't thought past her to the obvious.

I felt like Jillian and her mom maybe needed to develop a hobby.

Hugo didn't respond, but the truck tilted like he'd turned a corner. Fortunately, I didn't roll over because I had a full-grown woman sitting on me. See? Good things were happening already.

Jillian scooted forward, leaning over the seat, lifting just enough weight off me so I could breathe, and circulation could start to return to my legs. I wiggled slightly and tried to squirm forward a few inches. I wasn't sure what that would accomplish, but no opportunity ever showed up without creating an opening.

"I ran over the sign," Jillian whined. "I let Mia see the plates so Lucy would get in trouble. We used the moose to set up a turf war between Eagle's Nest and the Yacht Club. The *Charming Maine* magazine evaluation team is coming this weekend after I tipped them off. It was enough! But you killed Rex and then—"

Hah. See? I knew it! Sociopath Hugo had killed Rex. But why had he killed him? I still didn't understand.

Hugo hit the brakes so hard that I crashed into the back of the seat, and Jillian did the same.

Ow.

"Seriously? Don't you know how to drive?" she shouted.

The seat squeaked, but I couldn't see what he was doing. "The cost of keeping you alive is getting too high."

The car went silent. I took advantage of my new skill of not breathing when under times of stress and clamped my lips shut. Maybe they would forget I was there, and I could sneak away while they were brawling in the street.

"Did you attack Ruby Lee?" she asked. "When you made me park Lucy's car in the driveway, and you went inside, did you try to kill her? Why would you do that?"

I groaned silently at her idiocy. Honestly. Could she be even more stupid? Who on earth was dumb enough to expose the bad guy while alone with him? The only smart thing to do was to pretend you know nothing and are on their side until you can get away. Then you call the cops. You don't declare to their face that you know what they're doing!

But I was curious as to his answer. Why had he gone after Ruby Lee? That still didn't make sense. I had to admit, I was feeling a whole lot of empathy for Ruby Lee right now. I'd complained my whole life about being related to my mom. Ruby Lee was related to Hugo.

She definitely had it worse.

There was a click. I knew that click. It was the click of a gun.

CHAPTER 33

Jillian tensed, knocking something against my hip. "Don't threaten me. My mother will hunt you down."

"Your mother?" He laughed. "No one hunts me down."

I tended to agree with him. He'd made it all the way from Florida without getting caught. Cagey little turd for sure. Then again, I'd met Eloise. If her counterpart in Bugscuffle was anything like her, Hugo might be in trouble if he hurt her little girl.

But that didn't really help, because throwing Hugo in prison *after* he killed us didn't feel like my favorite plan.

Whatever Jillian had moved was digging into my hip, so while she continued to threaten him with things that would send her faster to a grave, I wiggled my hands around to see what it was.

As soon as my fingers hit the hard, square plastic, I recognized it as the pencil sharpener that I hadn't managed to use for any great defense. Was that what was binding my wrists? The cord from my secret weapon? Oh, the irony, right?

As Jillian shouted at him again, I felt around, following the cord up to my wrists. I was definitely tied up with my weapon, which was unfortunate. The cord was way too difficult to break.

Hugo and Jillian were shouting now, and I could hear the edge in Hugo's voice

She was pushing him too far, he was armed, and we were both going to die.

I had to come up with something. What would a serial killer like Hugo be interested in? There was one thing, a card I'd sworn never to play. But my life was on the line. "Hey!" I yelled. "Don't you even know who I am?"

The car went silent for a minute.

Then Jillian looked down at me. "You own the marina."

"Why isn't she gagged?"

I had only seconds until I was out of chances. "Stanley Herrera. Drug king? Recently sent to prison until the end of time?"

"So what?" Of course Hugo knew who he was. People like Hugo would probably admire Stanley.

"I'm his wife." Ugh. That felt terrible to say. "The one who turned him in. The one who hid most of the drug money from the feds. The one who is taking over the business." Oh…I hadn't even thought of that last sentence before I'd said it. That would be impressive to a guy like Hugo, right?

There was silence.

Then Jillian looked down at me. "You're the drug lord wife?"

Was it only days ago when I'd cringed at that reference? Ah, how time changes things. "I am. Look me up."

Into the ominous silence of the cab came the sound of fingers typing on a phone keyboard, then Jillian gasped. "It *is* her."

Hugo swore. "I knew she was dirty. I said to push her on the drug thing, but no one listens to me. Get her up."

Yay for being worth money! And, um, why had he thought I was dirty? And who had he told to push me? Had he already known about my past with Stanley? Ruby Lee must have told him. Seriously, that woman needed to stop gossiping about me!

Jillian scrambled off me, and Hugo reached over the seat with his monstrously long arms, grabbed my forearms, and dragged me off the floor of his truck. He threw me onto the seat beside Jillian, which gave me a clear view of the gun he had aimed at my face. It also sat my cute little fanny right smack dab on something hard and smallish, like hey, my phone? Who knew Jillian's dismissive toss of it would wind up being so convenient?

"Where's the money? Where are the drugs?" Hugo demanded, adding in a few choice profanities that I chose not to process. Mostly because he was scaring the living daylights out of me, and I was mere moments from passing out in terror.

Where was the money I'd just claimed to have hidden from the feds? That was such a great question. I glared at him, trying not to focus obsessively on the gun, while I fished my phone unobtrusively out from under my butt. "Do you think I took over the most powerful drug empire in New England by ratting out to worms like you?" My voice wasn't shaking, which was so impressive. Two decades of lying under pressure, thanks to my wonderful childhood.

He pressed the gun against my forehead. "Bang. You're dead."

Hmm. Where had I heard that before? Maybe from a sociopathic moose last night before he'd shot out my window? I now had pretty clear confirmation that Hugo was one of the moose. And with the fur in my lock picks, we had proof that one of the moose had killed Rex. Yay for connecting the dots.

"If you shoot me, I take the money and the business to the grave." I was so scared that I could barely think, but I managed to see a road sign behind him. Hiding my phone behind my back, which conveniently was where my bound hands were, I made a valiant attempt to text the street name to Devlin. Then I texted that I'd been kidnapped by Hugo, we were about to die, and to find me now. I hoped autocorrect helped me out, and Devlin wasn't currently reading a text about daisies, unicorns, and poison ivy.

All I knew was that Devlin, Hattie, and Lucy were in Bugscuffle looking for me, which meant I had to get there.

"The money," Hugo said, pressing the gun against my nose. "Now."

What would a drug kingpin do? Not crumble under the

pressure.

I took a deep breath, and then summoned my inner drug lord. "Look," I snapped. "You don't get to shoot me. You don't get my money. But I do need people willing to kill for me. I pay very well. Drugs. Money. Whatever makes you happy."

He narrowed his eyes, and I stared him down. My heart was pounding so hard I was sure he could hear it, but I didn't back down. I'd learned how to fake it, and I was calling on every single skill and strength I'd spent the last decade trying to forget. "You will die a death worse than you could ever imagine if you so much as breathe on me the wrong way," I said, keeping my voice low with menace. "I took down Stanley. I'm unstoppable. And if you work for me, you will be, too. I protect what's mine."

He still didn't lower the gun.

I leaned forward. "I'll clear your record." I waved my fingers, not that he could see them, but hey, gotta live the part, right? "Poof. Gone. A free man."

He narrowed his eyes. "I don't want a job. I want the money and the drugs."

I stared at him, frantically trying to decide the best way to handle him. Continue to be hard core, or let him think he could get free money from me? He was a loner sociopath. Money would matter more than a job. I had to pivot. I hoped it wasn't too late.

"I have money and some product in Bugscuffle." I decided to pretend I was stupid. I had a feeling Hugo would believe me. "Then, once we're there, you can have half of the money and drugs, and I'll take the rest, and you let me go." Because that always worked, right? I forced myself to sit back. "Otherwise, shoot me now and forget about your chance for ten million dollars in cash and twenty million dollars in cocaine."

Hugo's eyes widened, and he looked down at his phone again, no doubt double-checking the reports in the paper about Stanley's worth.

Jillian glared at me. "You're a bad person."

I gaped at her. "*I'm* the bad person? You literally hired a serial killer so your mom could win Best Lake Town."

"I didn't hire a serial killer," she retorted. "Rex did!"

"Rex was working for you, so that makes you responsible!"

"He wasn't working for me! He did it because he was my *boyfriend!"*

I stared at her. "What?"

"I was at his dad's house, helping him go through stuff, and we found the Derby Moose outfit. Rex thought it would be hilarious to resurrect the moose, and we started talking about how we could screw with Bass Derby's win. Then Lucy showed up, and I hate her so much, so it was perfect! Set her up, win the prize, and have fun. That was it! No one was supposed to die!" She shouted the last part, her face red, and tears glistening in her eyes.

I really wished I'd recorded that. I realized that Jillian was probably the woman that Rex had been schtupping while he was dating Lucy. All the pieces were coming together now. "And your mom let you do this?" I asked.

"She didn't know! It was supposed to be a birthday present!"

I blinked. "Wow. That's a really creative present."

"I know. I'm an awesome daughter. Unlike you. You're just a—"

"Hey!" Hugo interrupted, waving the gun at my face again before I could enjoy Jillian's well-founded opinion of me. "You have a deal." The smug look on his face made it clear he was going to pop me as soon as he had the money. Which was fine, because there was no money, so hah on him.

"Great." Understatement of the year. If I could get back to Hattie, Lucy, and Devlin, I felt like I had at least a slim chance of living. "Head back toward Bugscuffle."

Jillian folded her arms over her chest and stared out the window, her jaw clenched.

Hugo slammed his truck into reverse, and it shot backwards so fast that I fell forward and smashed my face against the back of the seat.

"You brought it with you?" he asked as he shifted into drive and hit the gas, throwing me back against the seat so hard that I fell over and, sadly, lost my grip on my phone. It clattered down beside the seat.

"Why do you think we were meeting with the Seam Rippers?" I wiggled myself back into an upright position, flexing my face to see if my cheekbone had been shattered. "You think they just sew things? Those old ladies are the best dealers in New England. Who suspects old ladies?"

"The Seam Rippers are drug dealers?" Jillian whipped around to look at me. "Seriously? I hired drug dealers to make my costumes?"

"How can that possibly surprise you? Why do you think they run around dressed like that? It's called a cover." I rolled my eyes at Hugo. "She's so naïve."

Jillian's eyes narrowed. "You are truly evil. Corrupting those poor old ladies. Is Hattie in on it? And Lucy? You destroyed them all, bringing your drug trash into our community."

I gave her the classic "don't even start with me" glare. I wanted to shout at her that I didn't bring any drug trash anywhere with me, but seeing as how I'd just claimed to do exactly that, I couldn't get all holier-than-thou on that one. But the Seam Rippers and Hattie? They were a treat all on their own. "Don't blame me for them. Give them a little credit for making their own life choices."

Jillian looked pissed now. "Tyrone said his grandmother could make the outfits. He didn't say she was a drug dealer! What if it got out that I'd hired drug dealers?"

And now…the connection. Tyrone must have overheard Jillian and Rex talking about getting moose costumes made when they were at the Ugly Man, and he'd offered up the Seam Rippers, not realizing it was for the Derby Moose until it was too late.

Poor kid. Do one nice favor for the scrawny waitress, and you get sucked into a murder battle with a serial killer. Murder addicts and bitter twirlers. Never trust either of them. I wondered if Tyrone had accidentally caught Hugo doing something illegal, and that was how Rex had gotten the chance to save his life. I was grateful to Rex. Tyrone was a good kid, and his grandma was hardcore.

I focused on Jillian, who I wasn't feeling quite as warm and fuzzy toward. "Well, I'm sure you didn't tell Tyrone that the costumes were going to be used to harass people and murder Rex, did you? So I think my assessment is pretty fair, honestly."

"Do the Seam Rippers have the drugs and the money?" Hugo asked, his voice just terrifying enough to make me realize he would be happy to knock off every one of them to get his money.

Oh, *no.* He was targeting *them* now? I needed to get them off his radar and fast. "No, not yet, because Jillian showed up and then someone *kidnapped* me." I glared at him. "My team is waiting for me to close the deal, but they have specific instructions to disappear and dispose of all evidence in the event I get caught by the police. Or kidnapped by an asshat," I added, because what self-respecting drug lord would miss an opportunity to insult an idiot who tried to kidnap them?

I didn't know the roads well enough to have any idea if we were heading back toward Bugscuffle, but Hugo was driving almost as enthusiastically as Hattie liked to do, so I felt optimistic that my plan was unfolding perfectly. "What time is it?"

"It's almost five," Jillian said. "Why?"

I swore loudly. "They're going to trash the stash at five. How far away are we?"

"Five minutes," Hugo said, taking a turn at a terrifying speed. Had our right tires just come off the ground? I barely trusted Hattie to keep me alive at this speed. I certainly had no faith in this sociopath.

"Cutting it close," I said, bracing myself as I slid into Jillian. "I think I should text them. Let them know I'm on my way." Could he be stupid enough to let me text them? Doubtful, but it was always best not to underestimate people.

Hugo hit the brakes, skidding to a stop at a stoplight as a group of teenagers stepped out in front of him, showing that he was a serial killer with a strong ethical line that prevented him from driving through a crowd of innocent people. So, a good guy, on some levels. "Get her phone," he ordered Jillian. "Text her people that she's on the way."

"No! You both are horrible human beings!" Jillian flung the door open, launched herself out of the truck, and took off running down the sidewalk, moving incredibly fast as she hauled butt down a street lined with cute shops and yellow and white striped awnings

That was *such* a good idea. How had I not thought of that? "I'll get her!" I yelled as I dove for the open door.

Hugo lunged for me, but since I'd executed a perfect dive, I was too low for him to reach. I skated just under his monstrous hands, crashing shoulder-first onto the pavement, landing in an explosion of pain. For a split second, I was too stunned to move. My shoulder felt like I'd broken it, and my jaw hurt so much I could barely think.

Through my haze of pain, I saw the teenagers turn to look at me.

"Help!" I gasped. "I'm being kidnapped. Call 9-1-1! Save me!"

They did not call 9-1-1. Instead, they all pulled out their phones and started taking pictures. Or videoing. Either way, not the helpful good Samaritans I'd been hoping for. Freaking teenagers.

With my arms still tied behind my back, I bit my lip against the pain and tried to scramble away, but Hugo leapt out of the truck, grabbed my arm, and yanked me to my feet.

Staggering pain shot through me, and I screamed with agony and fury. "Enough!" I whirled around, twisting my shoulders and torso with as much force as I could muster. The sharpener, which was still attached to my wrists, flung around. I gave a hard twist with my hips for extra momentum, and it plowed him right in his crotch.

It wasn't a hard hit, but as they say in real estate, location, location, location.

His eyes widened, and for a split second of terror, I thought he was too insane to feel pain.

Then he dropped to the ground, clutching his crotch and shouting all the ways he was going to kill me.

I stumbled, gasping as the pain flooded back into me with devastating force. I tried to run, and my legs gave out. I landed on my knees and tried to crawl to the curb. "Call the police," I shouted at the teenagers still recording me. "Call the police!"

I suddenly saw their eyes widen as they looked behind me toward Hugo. "He has a gun!" They took off screaming, scattering in all directions, leaving me there to die.

Again, freaking teenagers.

I fell over the curb and rolled onto my side so I could see Hugo. He was still on the ground, but he'd pulled out his gun. "You don't get to take me down," he snarled, as he managed to get himself onto his knees.

I logrolled over the curb onto the sidewalk, but he was already on his feet. Still hunched over, he raised his arm and pointed the gun at me. "Bang. You're—"

Hattie's pickup truck slammed into him, sending him careening through the air like a three-point shot in a championship basketball game.

I shrieked as she hit the brakes, the tires screeching and smoking as she fought for control as the truck skidded right toward me. I scrunched my eyes closed and braced myself for impact.

But it didn't come.

"Mia!" Hattie's shout jerked me back from the edge of certain death. I opened my eyes to see the grill of her truck less than a foot from my face, but it was no longer moving.

Hurrah! Hattie jumped out of the driver's seat, and I could hear Lucy yelling my name.

I twisted around, trying to see where Hugo was. At first I couldn't find him, but then I noticed a vast expanse of sociopathic human on top of a striped yellow and white awning, sliding slowly down it.

He fell off the edge and thudded to the ground next to me.

His gaze met mine as he lay on the sidewalk, not moving, but clearly not dead either, unfortunately. "Bitch," he snarled.

"Maybe. But you're no prize either." Then I rolled away from him because, well, who wants to stay that near a murderer who clearly wasn't close enough to dead for my comfort.

Then the police cars rolled up, sirens blasting. Hattie and Lucy tackled me in a hug that made me yelp with pain, and then I saw Devlin sprinting toward me, his gun out. He was running hard, his gaze locked on me, his corded arms pumping hard as he raced all out toward us. "Mia!"

Hattie looked over at him. "He looks worried. I think he has a crush on you."

"Hah." I knew about law enforcement. "He just doesn't want to get in trouble with Griselda. It's all about the career for guys like them."

"Maybe." Hattie looked speculative. "Or maybe not."

"No." I shook my head. "Don't start with me on that. I can't. I really can't."

Devlin had almost reached us, and the other cops had already pounced on Hugo, shouting about how dangerous he was.

"By the way," I said to Hattie and Lucy. "You guys need to know. I'm officially a drug lord taking over Stanley's business, you two are my enforcers, and the Seam Rippers are our dealers."

Hattie raised her brows. "Okay."

Lucy grinned. "Sounds fun. I'm in."

I loved them so much.

Devlin reached me. He went down on one knee by my side, but he kept his gun and his attention on Hugo. "Mia. Are you all right?"

My arms were still bound behind my back. My shoulder was probably broken. My cheekbone was most likely crushed. "Fantastic." I paused. "Did anyone find Jillian?"

Devlin nodded. "The Bugscuffle police picked her up down the street. She's already talking as fast as she can, trying to get a deal." He cocked an eyebrow. "Apparently, you're a drug kingpin, and there's a stash of money and cocaine in Hattie's truck."

"Feel free to search it." I grinned, ignoring how much it hurt to smile. "Did she mention Hugo?"

"She said he killed Rex."

I grinned. "So, Lucy's off the hook?"

He glanced at Lucy and then nodded. "I expect so."

Hattie and Lucy let out cheers, and I grinned. "I told you she was innocent."

One of the Bugscuffle police shouted for Devlin to join them, but he ignored them. He leaned over me and unwrapped my wrists. "If you'd trusted me with the license plate info sooner, you might not have had to almost die." His voice was rough.

I gasped with relief as he released my wrists, nearly sobbing in pain as my shoulders were allowed to return to the position they were meant to be in. "If you'd trusted me," I shot back, "you might not have wasted so much time looking in the wrong direction, and then I might not have had to almost die to prove Lucy's innocence. So really, my almost-death is on you."

He met my gaze. "I'm the cop, Mia."

"I know that, thanks."

For a long moment, we stared at each other. How many times had Griselda and I had a showdown between his need for job success and my need for personal well-being? So many times, and it had never made a bit of difference to him.

But as I stared at Devlin, I felt something else simmering beneath the surface between us. I wasn't sure what it was, but it made me pause.

Then the paramedics arrived, and the moment was gone.

Devlin turned away to deal with Hugo, and Lucy and Hattie pulled me into the best hug I'd had in a long, long time.

Maybe ever.

No one in my life had ever been much of a hugger.

Until now.

CHAPTER 34

It was almost midnight by the time Hattie pulled up to my marina to drop me off. It had taken quite a long time to sort everything out with the police. Particularly tricky to navigate had been Hattie's attempted murder of Hugo with her truck, and the drug lord accusations that Jillian had ignited. Fortunately, Devlin had gotten Griselda on the phone, and the two of them had worked together to crush any attempt to throw us in prison.

I appreciated the boys working together on my behalf. I would have said I was touched, but I knew better than to think it was out of any concern for my well-being. More importantly, it was worrisome. I had a feeling that my life would go better if Griselda and Devlin didn't team up.

Once Devlin and Griselda had secured our freedom, Lucy and Hattie had taken me to the hospital to get checked out. It turned out I hadn't broken anything. It didn't lessen the pain, but it did make me feel kind of like a badass. We'd stopped by to see Ruby Lee, but she was asleep. Apparently, she'd woken up from her coma very quickly and was keeping the staff running around, so she was going to be fine, which made me happy.

I apologized to her inert form for thinking that she was a

murderer. The fact that Hugo had taken her down made it clear she wasn't a killer. Except, I still didn't understand why Hugo had gone after her. The whole thing still seemed to be complete overkill for the title of Best Lake Town, but Hattie and Lucy had assured me it made complete sense, and that I'd understand after I'd lived there longer.

As Hattie put the car in park, I turned stiffly to grin at them. "We took down a sociopathic serial killer today. Not bad, right?"

They both grinned.

"Feels good," Hattie said. "It was fun."

"I'm so grateful to both of you," Lucy added. "That was close, much too close."

I waved my hand dismissively. "No need for thanks," I said, meaning it. "I couldn't have let you take the rap." I shrugged. "It's not how I'm wired."

Hattie beamed at me. "Does that mean that next time, you're not going to pretend to resist at first? It'll save a lot of time if we can just move forward."

"Next time?" Genuine horror flashed across Lucy's face. "Can we not have there be a next time?"

"I'm with Lucy," I said as I opened the door. "No next time."

"You two young 'uns are so innocent." Hattie looked back and forth between us, amused empathy on her face. "There's *always* a next time."

"No." I stepped back and put my hand on the door while Lucy climbed into the front seat. "Not for me. This was it. I have a fundraiser to host on Sunday, and a marina to resurrect."

"And a lake police hottie to seduce," Hattie said with a grin.

My cheeks heated up. "Triple no to that one."

Hattie and Lucy exchanged knowing glances, but they were smart enough not to pursue it. "How about a celebratory lunch tomorrow?" Hattie asked. "Can you at least manage that?"

Lucy clapped her hands. "I'm in. Mia?"

I looked at the two women staring at me expectantly. Women who had some idea about who I was, and liked me anyway. I'd never had friends before, but I was pretty sure I might be on my way. "I wouldn't miss it."

Hattie honked her good-bye, and I stood and waved as they drove out. Lucy was leaning out the window shouting about freedom and murderers, and Hattie's horn would have woken all my neighbors, if I had any.

The truck skidded out as she launched the vehicle out of the parking lot, making me laugh.

"Crazy women. They're both insane." But I was still grinning as I limped up the deck, swinging my newly acquired pencil sharper gently.

The police had let me keep it, so I was going to add it to my arsenal of the hairdryer and the nail gun. Heavy things attached to cords were everywhere. I could literally find a weapon anywhere I was, now that I knew where my talents were.

It was such a reassuring feeling.

King Tut bounded over as I reached the door, meowing fiercely. My heart swelled up. See? I'd stayed alive for him, and he was happy about it. I couldn't believe how good it felt to come home to someone who cared that I was there and safe.

"Hey, sweetie." I crouched down to hug him, but he raced right past me, across the parking lot, down the dock, and took a flying leap into the water with a loud splash.

"Right." I stood up. "That's fine. I know you have trouble expressing your emotions."

I rotated my shoulder as I opened the front door. The hospital had given me a prescription for pain meds, but I'd tossed it. There wasn't a chance I was touching anything even distantly related to controlled substances.

I paused inside the store to survey my little haven. How was I going to redeem the good name of the marina now that my secret life with Stanley was out? And the rumors that I was taking over his business? I doubted it would take long for that rumor to get around. Jillian would make sure of it.

Yes, Jillian wasn't exactly the most trustworthy source of

gossip, but she was drama, and people loved to feed on drama. They'd be all over whatever stories she started telling about me, regardless of whether they were true or not. I had a feeling Jillian was going to get to skip out on prison in exchange for testifying, since Hugo was the guy they wanted, which meant she'd be liberated to ruin my good name, what little there was.

I could have done without the added challenge, but I didn't regret what I'd done. It was better to be seen as a drug dealer than to be dead, so I was calling it a win.

I wanted nothing more than to collapse onto the lifejackets and inflatable rafts, but I was still covered in dirt, gravel, and the stench of terror that had bled through my rigid control during that fun trip in Hugo's truck.

My shower was in my apartment, which was never a fun place to venture into, seeing as how I hadn't yet managed to defeat the dead fish stench. The cleaning service was coming tomorrow, so I had high hopes that life was heading in the right direction.

I could handle the smell long enough to shower. All I had to do was sprint through the living room area and leap into the bathroom. If I kept the door closed and the window open in the bathroom, it wasn't that bad, since most of the stench seemed to be emanating from the living room. I could breathe through my mouth for five minutes for the sake of a shower.

I set my sharpener on the display case and gave it a loving pat. My phone dinged, and I grinned when I saw a text from Hattie telling me how badass I was.

Maybe I was. Even thinking about it felt good. I'd lived afraid for a long time during my undercover stint, and it felt good to be regaining some of that confidence I'd honed to perfection as a kid.

I propped the front door open for King Tut, grabbed sweatpants, fuzzy socks, and a T-shirt, and jogged up the stairs to my stinky home.

When I reached the top, I noticed that the door was slightly ajar.

I stopped, my smile fading. I always kept it shut. I was certain of it, because I didn't want the stench to drift down into the store.

But it was definitely open a couple inches.

Fear gripped me before I was able to catch myself. Hugo was sitting behind bars right now. Jillian wasn't a killer. It was over.

Granted, Hugo had refused to identify the names of any of the other Derby Moose, and he hadn't confessed to killing Rex or attacking Ruby Lee. He hadn't even admitted that he was the one who'd gotten the Jet Skis from the Yacht Club, even though Jake had confirmed he'd hired him a couple months ago to work on the engines with Tyrone and a few others. Hugo's code had been used to open the garage the night the Jet Skis were stolen, so it was a clear win for the good guys, despite his denial.

However, until he revealed the names of the other moose, there were still five unaccounted for.

I stared at my door. Were the other moose coming to get me?

No. It was over, right? Best Lake Town was pretty much wrapped up for Bugscuffle at this point, and that was the reason for the moose.

Besides, Hugo was the leader. Without Hugo, they wouldn't come after me, right? Jillian had said Rex was the leader, and then Hugo had taken over after he'd killed Rex, kind of a situation of accidentally unleashing the beast.

And the Jet Skis were now locked up tightly at the Yacht Club.

I took a breath. It was fine. Fine.

But I reached for my phone to text Devlin. Just because.

When my fingers hit my empty pocket, I remembered I'd left it on the counter downstairs.

No problem. I hadn't wanted to go upstairs anyway. Not with the open door. I quickly turned around and jogged down the stairs, stepped out into the store, and then screamed when I saw the silhouette of a man in the doorway.

"Get out!" I shouted as I scrambled back into the stairwell. "I have a gun!" I yanked the door shut and slammed the deadbolt. "The police are on their way!" I yelled. "I already called them!"

"Mia?"

I paused halfway up the stairs when I heard the familiar voice. It took me a split second to recognize the voice of Bryan, my only customer, and Hattie's devoted admirer. I was so relieved that my legs actually gave out, and I sat down on the stairs with a thump, holding my hands to my face, as I tried to catch my breath.

He knocked lightly on the door. "Mia? Are you all right?"

"Fine. Thanks." I was such a wreck, I could barely think. The last thing I wanted to do was be sociable, but Bryan was literally my only customer, my one link into the community of boaters. "What do you need?"

"Bait."

I blinked. "Bait?"

"Yeah. Cargo usually leaves the door unlocked for me so I can come get it before I head out for fishing. I didn't mean to scare you."

I pressed my forehead to my hands. "Fishing? It's midnight."

"The best time to catch the big ones." He paused. "I noticed that you locked the cooler. Any chance I could get the key so I can grab it?"

"I don't have bait."

"Didn't you get a box from Rusty? One that was refrigerated? He sends me special bait I can't get anywhere up here."

Oh. That box. I was too tired to deal with this, but as my only customer, this man was my future.

I dragged myself to my feet, unbolted the door, and opened it. Bryan was standing in the middle of the store, wearing jeans, the same plaid shirt he'd been wearing that early morning, and a pair of black boots. I'd forgotten how tall the older man was. Not as tall as psycho Hugo, but still a solid foot taller than I was.

Unease crept down my spine, which I found completely irritating. Was I now adding tall men to my list of things that I was terrified of? "I put it in the cooler. But it was already smelling."

"It'll be fine. It holds okay." He held out his hand. "I can grab it if you just give me the keys."

"Fine. Keys." I mustered a customer-worthy smile at him as I navigated around the life jackets on the floor. "I'm surprised you dared to come here tonight. The Derby Moose sang to me last night. They're supposed to murder me tonight, I think."

Good gravy. Why had I said that? I didn't need to add to the creep factor.

His bushy gray eyebrows shot up. "Did they?"

His tone of voice caught my attention, and I glanced over at him as I reached the display counter. "You heard about it?"

"Everyone did. Word gets around."

"I guess." I crouched down behind the counter, scanning for the keys. I was pretty sure I'd stashed them under there, but there was a lot of crap still under there that I hadn't sorted through yet. "Hang on." I moved some papers, and then frowned when I saw the sheets I'd seen the first day, with the lists of numbers and dates. This one had Bryan's name on it and some numbers.

Was it his tab? That would be great if he owed me money.

I pulled it over and scanned it more closely. There were dates and numbers on it. Other numbers. Names. As I scanned it, a cold dread clamped around my chest.

I'd seen a list like that before.

I'd seen a list like that many times before.

I'd seen lists like that in Stanley's desk.

It was a shipment list. Tracking numbers. Weight amounts. Names and initials that were a distribution plan.

It didn't have to be drugs, right? It could be bait, right?

Except that Rusty had moved to Florida, and anyone who watches television knows that lots and lots of drugs come into Florida.

Rusty shipping in the drugs. Bryan distributing it. *No. Please tell me no.*

The dates started fifteen years ago. They stopped ten years ago, when Rusty had left town. Rusty's notes. So maybe it was over.

Or not. Maybe there were no more notes because Rusty wasn't around to write notes to himself anymore.

I suddenly remembered that Bryan had arrived at my dock only moments after the moose had left the first time, and yet he hadn't seen six Jet Skis rushing away. He'd offered to help me clean the marina. He'd been at the Ugly Man, where Rex and Hugo hung out. He'd asked Lucy if she was going to keep the mail route, or if Ellis was getting it back. Ellis, who had been fired for package tampering.

Holy cow. Rusty and Bryan must have been shipping in drugs through the marina, and Ellis had been in on it. And Rex? Rex's dad, who had a lot of money and went on trips to Florida, had been friends with Rusty. What had Rex found in the house? Had he wanted in on it and been killed to shut him up?

Leave the marina, Hugo the Moose had said.

It hadn't been me specifically. It had been the marina, because my presence cut off the supply chain from Rusty to Bryan.

Killing Ruby Lee because she'd sold the marina to me? Or because she knew too much. Or because she was a smart, morally flexible woman who had realized what her cousin was involved in, and she'd wanted in, or threatened to report them.

Or maybe I was imagining it. Maybe Bryan was just an old man who fished. We already knew that Jillian had orchestrated everything for the title. There was no place for Bryan to fit into what had happened.

But I also knew that Rex's murder and the attack on Ruby Lee didn't make sense...until I added in the drug factor.

I knew that list. I knew what it meant. And I suddenly remembered that first conversation with Bryan, when he'd asked me if I was going to take over Stanley's business. Was that why Rusty had approved me to purchase the marina? Because they thought I'd help? Hugo had said he'd told them to pressure me. Had he told Bryan?

Of course it was. It all made sense now. Ruby Lee had told me she'd told Rusty about my background, and Hattie had told me that Rusty had turned down a bunch of buyers. Until me. Until the ex-wife of a drug lord who could help them with their business.

Crud.

"Mia?"

I jumped, hitting my head on the cabinet. I stood up, gripping the keys, trying to plaster a smile on my face. "Found them." My legs were shaking as I tossed the keys at him. I wasn't stupid enough to confront him. All I wanted was for him to leave, and then I would call Devlin.

He caught them easily, but he was watching me carefully. "You okay?"

"'Yeah, sure. Just had a tough day is all." I swallowed. "Help yourself. I'm heading over to Hattie's for girls' night, so lock up when you're done." I needed to get out of there. Maybe I was wrong. Maybe the list was for bait. But I knew too much about the willingness of drug dealers to kill, so I was turning this right over to Devlin.

I reached for my phone, sliding my hand across the glass. My fingers brushed the edge of it, then suddenly, I heard an all-too-familiar click.

"Don't touch that."

I jerked my gaze off my phone to see Bryan pointing a gun at me.

Because I hadn't had enough of that in my life lately.

CHAPTER 35

I FROZE. "WHAT?" I tried to sound completely confused, befuddled, and harmless. "What are you doing?"

Bryan watched my face carefully "You figured it out, didn't you?"

"Figured what out?" I wondered if he could hear my heart pounding. That would totally clue him in that I was lying like a teenage boy out past curfew. "What's going on?"

"What did you find under the counter?"

I blinked with the wide-eyed innocence of my five-year-old adorable self. "Nothing. Keys."

"Back up." He gestured with his gun for me to retreat so he could search under the counter.

I shuffled back, burdened with the grim truth that, apparently, innocence is much easier to fake when one is a cute five-year-old than when one is a drug lord ex-wife.

Bryan reached over and grabbed the paper. He scanned it, swore, then crumpled it and shoved it in his pocket. "I liked you, Mia. When you said you weren't continuing the business, I respected that. I didn't want you involved. All you needed to do was to leave the door unlocked so I could get this shipment. And then you needed to leave town. That was it. It's Maine. No one locks doors. Instead, I had to wait until you got home tonight."

"You sent the moose after me," I pointed out. "It freaked me out. How was I supposed to leave the door unlocked after a death threat?"

"All right. I concede that point." He held up his hand. "I acknowledge that may have been a strategic error on my part. Put your hands on your head."

I did as he instructed, watching helplessly as he unlocked the cooler and pulled the box out. "You know what, Bryan? I don't care what you do. Take the bait and leave, and we'll call it even, okay?"

He hefted the box onto the raft that was my bed. "I'm not leaving yet."

"But Officer Hunt is on his way."

"Is he?" Bryan grinned at me. "I don't think he is." He jerked the gun at me. "Upstairs."

I felt like that was a very bad idea. "Why?"

"I need to get the product out of the fish."

I stared at him. "The fish? It's stuffed in fish?" Awareness dawned. "So you *have* been cleaning fish in my living room? And taking drugs out of them?" That was wrong on so many levels. "I'm pretty sure you said you hadn't cleaned any fish in there."

"I lied. These things happen." He flipped the muzzle of the gun toward the stairs. "Go."

I thought of being upstairs with him in Stink Central while he pulled out that terrifying filet knife. Nope. I couldn't think of a reason why I needed to be involved with that. "I'm fine to wait here."

"Upstairs. Now." He raised the gun. "You first."

If I made a break for the door, he'd shoot me long before I made it to safety. He was too far away for a hairdryer attack. I literally had no way out. "You like me, remember?" I set my hand on the counter, trying to inchworm my fingers toward my phone. "I like you, too. You're my only customer. Take the bait and go. No one needs to know, and we both get what we want." Me, alive. Him, drugs.

Drugs. He wanted to sell drugs.

I hated people who sold drugs. How could I let him walk out with a payload of it?

And how could I justify dying trying to stop him?

He leveled the gun at me, and I froze, my fingers less than a millimeter from my phone. "Up. The. Stairs."

"Right. Okay." I moved slowly, nearly sobbing as I left my phone and weapon behind. How on earth could this end well? I really was at the end of my coping capacity. "Hugo got arrested today," I said. "He'll probably tell everyone about you, so it's best if you bail from town quickly."

"Hugo doesn't know my name or my face."

I looked over my shoulder at him in surprise. "How is that possible?"

"I was at the Ugly Man when Rex was recruiting for the Derby Moose. He talked too much, yammering about how he and Jillian wanted Lucy to get blamed for destroying the sign and resurrecting the Derby Moose. That was perfect for me. A few days in jail would get her off the mail route. Her predecessor and I had an understanding, but she wasn't so flexible."

I recalled Lucy saying that the guy who had the route before her used to let packages slip by. Obviously, he gave Bryan his bait. No one kept track of the marina because it was basically abandoned. All had gone well until Lucy had taken over the route and I'd shown up.

My shin hit the bottom step, and I started inching my way up the stairs. I had a sudden, terrible thought. "Did you kill Rex?"

Bryan shrugged. "He found notes in his dad's house about our little program. When I stopped by to pick him up for the Derby Moose run that night, he confronted me. He wanted to take over his dad's role. When I said no, he threatened to expose us. He knew my face, so I shut him down. Had to be done. I was going to set Hugo up for his murder, but you guys showed up. Made it easy."

"You were the one wearing the moose outfit when you killed him, not Hugo?"

He grinned. "That was a great disguise. I'm pretty pleased about that one."

My mouth went dry. "What about Ruby Lee?"

"She figured out what was going on."

"Did she want in?" I would be so sad if Ruby Lee wanted to be a drug dealer. That crossed the line in my book.

But Bryan shook his head. "She got it out of Rex when he changed his mind about selling his house, so he could stay here and run drugs. She said she was going to Chief Stone, so I sent Hugo to shut her down, though he wasn't as effective at that as I would have expected." He laughed. "You can't tell me you weren't happy about that one. She sold you this dump for more than it was worth."

"I wasn't happy that she was almost killed. I don't murder people who con me."

"Well, you should rethink that." We reached the top of the stairs, and he gestured for me to open the door. "You got rid of my table. That was an excellent filet table."

"I'm happy to run outside and bring it back in for you."

He pointed to the corner. "Sit."

I slid down the wall. He'd admitted that he'd killed Rex and contracted for Ruby Lee's murder. That meant I wasn't going to live. No bad guy ever admits his crime if he's planning to let someone go. Was he going to hack me up and leave me in sixteen different forests in New England? Drown me and hold my body down with cement? Or leave me floating in the lake for all the town to see in the morning?

None of those felt like a good way for me to die.

I frantically looked around, searching for a weapon, but there was nothing, because I hadn't moved anything in yet. All I had were my toiletries, which were too far away to do any good.

Bryan dropped the box on the floor, grabbed the knife from where I'd left it on the counter, and ripped the box open with a fierceness that suggested a skill with the knife that was far beyond what I'd hoped.

The moment he opened the box, the smell of old fish filled the apartment. I gagged and covered my face. "Really?"

"Lost my sense of smell during the war. Doesn't bother me." He sliced through the plastic. "Too bad your husband's hit man found you all the way up in Maine. Took you right out."

Oh...so that was his plan. It was actually a good one. People always saw what they expected to see, and having one of Stanley's hitters come after me would make perfect sense. "Look, Bryan, you don't need to kill me—"

"I do, actually. You've made it very clear where you stand on this kind of thing." He looked over at me. "I like you, but I don't trust you. When I get this product out of the fish, you're going to be found floating in the lake with some cocaine on you. Everyone will think you kept your ex's business going, and it came back to bite you."

I lifted my chin. "Griselda won't believe it." I was pretty sure I was telling the truth on that one, but not totally certain.

He peered into the box. "Griselda?"

"Agent Straus. The one on Stanley's case. He won't believe it. He'll know something else went down." I thought I did a pretty good job sounding absolutely positive I was correct. Yay me.

Bryan grinned. "Even if he does, he'll track it back to Stanley's business, not mine. There's no way he'll think that an old Maine fisherman is capable of it. I'll just fade away, and no one will know."

He was right. Not that Griselda's avenging my death would help me anyway, given that I would already be dead.

I had to do something, and do it fast. But what?

I saw a shadow appear in the window behind him, and I sucked in my breath when I saw a familiar, massive Maine Coon cat appear. Drawn by the scent of the fish? *Yes.*

I tensed, readying myself. Bryan pulled out a fish as King Tut leapt silently down to the floor. The cat went into a crouch, and then began to stalk him.

The cat glided across the floor, one menacing step at a time, as Bryan opened the first fish and removed a small baggie of white powder.

White powder. Again. Sudden anger hit me like a cannonball, a fierce, furious anger. That day in July in my dining room, I'd been scared. Freaking out, even. But now? I'd been through too much. Seeing that baggie ignited something inside me.

I was not letting my life get screwed up again. I wasn't losing my home again. This time, it was ending my way. I shifted, pulling my feet under me, preparing to move.

Bryan went to grab another fish, but as he lifted it, King Tut shot through the air with an earsplitting yowl. Bryan jumped and spun around as King Tut snatched the fish out of his hand and took off down the stairs.

Bryan howled with fury and sprinted after him, racing toward the stairs, past where I was sitting.

I stuck my foot out at the last minute. Unheroic, I know, but I'd never claimed to be a hero.

His boot caught on my ankle, and he pitched headfirst down the stairs. As he thudded and bounced down the twisted, narrow steps, I scrambled up, sprinted across the room, and dove out the window onto the roof. I thought I'd be able to stop, but my momentum carried me much too fast. I slid across the shingles, frantically scrambling for grip, but I had no chance on the slanted roof.

I shot off the roof, yelping as I shot through the air. I was suspended for what felt like an eternity, and then I crashed down, landing on something that went flying as soon as I hit it, tangling around me like a web.

I catapulted across the parking lot, but somehow, my head was shielded, and something was wrapped around me, absorbing the impact. We finally skidded to a stop, and I lay there, trying to catch my breath, waiting for the pain of broken bones.

It didn't come.

I was all right.

"Mia? You okay?"

I opened my eyes to find Devlin beside me, breathing hard. I gaped at him, confused. "What are you doing?"

"Catching you. Obviously. Are you all right?"

I couldn't wrap my stunned brain around what was happening. "That doesn't even make sense."

"Sure it does." There was a loud thud from the store, and he shot to his feet, and pulled out his gun. "The Derby Moose sang to you last night, which meant tonight was the night you were going to be murdered. Some of the Derby Moose are still unaccounted for. I wasn't about to leave you to die. I didn't think I was going to get to you in time when I saw you shoot across your roof, but it worked out."

"It did." I propped myself up on my elbows, still trying to process. "You really came back to save me?"

He was watching the store now, his gun aimed at my door. "Yep."

He'd found his murderer. He'd tied up all his loose ends. And yet, he'd still come back, just in case? My throat tightened. "That was nice of you."

"I know." He shot a glance at me as he began to work his way toward my store. "Who came to murder you?"

I was so glad that everything had turned out well enough that he could ask that question while grinning. "Bryan. He fell down the stairs when I escaped. He's a drug dealer." I sighed. "My store has been used to process drugs, apparently."

Devlin raised his brows at me as he moved farther away. "Hawk was right."

I stiffened at the mention of Griselda. "About what?"

"You're excellent at breaking up drug rings." He got to the deck and peered in the door.

"I don't break up drug rings," I protested. "I own a marina. That's all I do."

He looked back at me. "It's not all you do, Mia. It'll never be all you do." Then he disappeared into the store, shouting at Bryan to freeze or whatever it was cops yelled these days.

I didn't get up.

Instead, I laid down in the parking lot, crossed my ankles, and clasped my hands behind my head, staring up at the sky. "I refuse to have this be my life," I informed the universe. "I no longer attract crime, murder, drugs, or anything else like that into my life. It's over. I'm done."

The universe said nothing.

"I'm serious," I shouted. "This has to stop now!"

Again, no response.

I sighed and rested my forearms across my face. My reputation was never going to recover. Not mine, and not the marina's. Did I give up now? Or did I fight it out all the way until the ugly, soggy, infamous death of my dream?

Something settled on my chest, and I opened my eyes to find King Tut sitting on me. He was dripping wet, purring, and twitching his tail as he fixed his eyes on me.

I stared back at him. "What?"

He continued to purr.

I smiled. "You did good tonight, kitty cat."

He purred louder.

I scratched his head as I heard sirens in the distance, heading toward the marina. "If you stay with me, I can't promise a peaceful life," I told him. "I was born a criminal. I was raised by a criminal. I married a criminal. I bought a marina from a criminal. Hattie and Devlin might be right. It might follow me everywhere I go. You sure you want that?"

King Tut stared at me for a long moment, then he stood up.

"Wow." Rejected by my cat. "Okay, then. I get that—"

He did a little circle on my chest, curled up into a tiny ball, buried his nose in his tail, and closed his eyes. Staking his claim.

Staying put. Staying with me. Not believing that life with me would be so bad.

Tears burned in my eyes, and I buried my fingers in his thick fur. "Thanks," I whispered.

He wasn't giving up on me. On us. On the marina.

I didn't want to either.

I wanted to stick around. I felt like maybe, just maybe, this place was weird enough that I could find a little corner of it to occupy. Friends. Roots. A home.

Honestly, what were the odds of getting tangled up in another murder? Of running into more hardened criminals? This was Bass Derby, winner of the Best Lake Town in Maine title for eleven years running, not a hotbed of criminal activity.

I let out a deep breath.

No more murders. No more death threats.

Just a marina. A girl. And a cat.

But where did I even start?

I turned my head to look at the Eagle's Nest. My marina. My home. My chance for the life I wanted. It was then that I saw the racks and racks of rental tables and chairs that were piled up next to the building.

I'd forgotten about Wanda and Gladys's fundraiser on Sunday.

I smiled. "That's our chance," I told the sleeping feline. "The fundraiser is our chance to prove to the town that they can trust me."

The fundraiser was my opportunity. No murders. No drugs. Just me, getting to know my town.

What could possibly go wrong?

THANK you so much for reading *Double Twist*. I hope you enjoyed Mia's first foray into the world! **For more Mia, you can do any of the following**:

- Order *Top Notch (Mia Murphy*, Book Two) right now!
- Skip ahead to read a sneak peek of *Top Notch*.
- Skip ahead to read *The FBI & the New Year's Eve Mishap* by Mia Murphy (A sneak peek of Stephanie's newsletter, which Mia sometimes hijacks, much to the delight of all the recipients).

What to read next?

If you loved *Double Twist*, hop on over and preorder *Top Notch* (*Mia Murphy*, Book 2), coming in September, 2022! While you're waiting, if you're up for that same fun and you enjoy some magic with your humor, try my *Immortally Sexy* romantic comedy series (it has some hilarious sexy times in it, so be forewarned!) or the *Guardian of Magic* paranormal mystery (contains some clever profanity, so also be forewarned! No sexy times, though!).

SNEAK PEEK: TOP NOTCH (MIA MURPHY, BOOK 2)

AVAILABLE SEPT. 20, 2022

CHAPTER ONE

The night was the kind of dark that was every assassin's dream, which meant that it wasn't exactly the perfect kind of night for me.

The rain was hammering so loudly on the metal roof of my marina that even an entire army of drug dealers firing assault weapons could have snuck up on me without me hearing them.

I'd been outside checking for assassins for almost twenty minutes, which was more than enough time to get absolutely drenched, thoroughly chilled, a little freaked out, and up to my ankles in mud and puddles.

And yet, I couldn't remember the last time I'd been so happy. If ever.

Whistling cheerfully, I sloshed through the flooded parking lot behind the marina, finishing up my nightly pre-bedtime property check for assassins. As had been the case for all four nights since I'd arrived in Bass Derby, Maine, there were no professional killers lying in wait to pop me.

Witness protection? Who needs witness protection? Hah. No one would bother to follow me here.

Sure, I'd had a couple amateur murderers pointing guns at my face this week, but I was alive and they were in jail, so yay for me. More importantly, they'd had nothing to do with my ex-husband's drug empire, the one I'd spied on for two years and then testified against, in a move that had made me all sorts of popular with his slightly bitter and vengeful family. My former in-laws hadn't followed me to Bass Derby (so far), so I was calling my decision to move here a win.

Equally delighted to be traipsing around in a cold downpour was King Tut, my massive rescued/purloined Maine Coon cat. He was trotting happily beside me, his ears nearly flattened to the side of his head from the rain.

I grinned down at him as we rounded the corner on the backside of the deck that stretched across the entire front of the marina. "Pretty great, right?"

He didn't answer me. Instead, he froze in place, one paw raised mid-step. His body went stiff. His tail went still, except for a tiny flick at the end, and the fur on his back went up, his gaze fixed on the latticework lining the backside of the deck.

I shined my flashlight in the direction he was looking, and I saw a hole in the lattice work that I hadn't noticed before. A gap big enough for a human.

Alarm shot through me, and the hair on the back of my neck stood up. Had that been there since I'd moved in? Or had someone made that hole tonight?

Fear started slithering down my spine, and I scowled. I was so over being scared. "I'm sure it's fine," I said aloud. "What are the odds that someone came here to kill me?"

Low. The odds were super low.

But not zero.

Which meant I needed to check it out. Discovering an assassin while I was awake and only a few feet from my car gave me marginally better survival odds than discovering an assassin while I was asleep in my bed.

When it came to death, I needed any additional edge I could

squeeze out. "If someone explodes out of there with a gun, you kill him."

King Tut ignored me. In fact, he still hadn't moved from his stiff-legged, puffed-out-fur stance, which was really creeping me out. Was he in predator mode or defender mode? I really hoped there was some creepy crawly under there that King Tut was going to have for dinner, and not an assassin who was going to dump my precious body in a gully somewhere.

I took a breath. An assassin hired to kill me wouldn't bother to lie in wait. I had no skills. They'd just walk up, pop me in the head, and collect their paycheck. So it was probably fine. If it wasn't, I'd be dead already.

But I still had to check. Because, you know, in case I was wrong.

"It'll be fine. I'm very good at evading being murdered." My voice sounded confident, but my heart starting pounding as I crouched down and shined my light under the deck, keeping my weight balanced so I could leap up and bolt for my car if I needed to.

The beam illuminated an old wooden barrel on its side, tucked up close to the entrance, blocking my view under the rest of the deck. It was wet from the rain, making the beam of the flashlight reflect back at me.

I grimaced and bent lower, angling my light to the sides to try to see around the barrel. There were several cement blocks, old boards, a couple canoe paddles, a half-buried keg, and other abandoned junk that was impossible to identify in the dark night.

What I could tell, however, was that there was plenty of space for a hit man to squeeze past the barrel and retreat into the shadowy recesses of the 100-ish-foot-long deck. The puddles obscured any possible footprints, leaving me with no way to tell if someone had recently crawled under there.

I tried to listen for movement, but all I could hear was the hammering of the rain on the wooden deck slats, against the metal roof of the marina maintenance building, and into the puddles surrounding me.

Short of crawling through the mud to the back of the deck, I had no way of knowing if a professional killer was hiding under there in waterproof pants, waiting for me to nod off to sleep.

Crawling under there didn't feel like the best choice at this time. Or any time, for that matter.

King Tut crept past me and slithered past the keg. His feet disappeared into the puddles, but he didn't make so much as a ripple, despite his snowshoe-sized paws. He suddenly lifted his head, his body tense as he stared into the dark underbelly of the deck. He went utterly still again, except for the twitching of the tip of his tail.

I knew that stance. He was about to launch. Fear shot through me. "Wait, don't—"

He hissed and shot under the deck and out of sight. I could hear scuffling and yowling. And…was that a curse? Had someone just *cursed?* The hair on my arms stood up—

A hand came down on my shoulder. "Mia."

I screamed and leapt up, cracking the back of my head on the underside of the deck. I hurled the flashlight at my assailant and ran, racing for my car as I tried to get my keys out of my pocket—

"Mia! It's me!"

I knew that voice. "Hattie?" I stumbled to a stop and whirled around.

The silhouette of Hattie Lawless, the seventy-something race car driver who leased space in the marina for her local eatery, Hattie's Café, loomed in the darkness. She held up her hands. "It's just me. Relax."

"Relax? I've had four people try to kill me in the last three weeks." I put my hands on my knees, bending over as I tried to catch my breath. "I thought we decided you weren't going to surprise me like that anymore."

King Tut shot out from under the deck and sprinted past me into the marina store, carrying something in his mouth. A dead animal? Crud. I hoped he didn't put in my bed. But yay for a dead animal and not a murderer. Unless it was my potential murderer's hand. King Tut could definitely take off a hand.

"We didn't agree I wouldn't surprise you." Hattie sloshed through the puddles as she headed toward me. "We agreed you wouldn't try to kill me if I did. There's a difference, and I'm pretty sure that hurling a metal flashlight at my head violates our pact."

"I don't think that's what our agreement was, and you're well aware that I'm a little jumpy when people sneak up on me." I'd kept my pickpocketing, con-artist childhood hidden from Hattie, but she'd recognized me from the news as the ex-wife of a Stanley Herrera, drug kingpin.

I'd spent two very stressful years as a spy for the FBI gathering evidence on him, and now that he was in prison, I was trying to pretend I had a chance at a normal life. I was on day four as the new owner of the Eagle's Nest Marina in Bass Derby, Maine, seizing my chance for the friends, home, and the life I'd never had.

So far, Hattie and my mail carrier, Lucy Grande, had helped with the friend goal. The law-abiding life? Not so much. Murder will do that. But I was hoping day five would be the charm. Or I had been, until Hattie had snuck up on me, mostly because I couldn't think of a single innocuous reason for her to be in my parking lot at midnight in the middle of a storm.

She held out my flashlight. "Either way, you have terrible aim. My head thanks you."

"I have great aim when it counts." Like when an assassin, or a hot police officer (oops), was sneaking up on me. I tucked the flashlight in my pocket, no longer needed now that we were under the floodlights from the marina. "What's up?"

"We have a situation."

"We do?" I tensed. We'd had a lot of situations in the last few days, but I'd thought they were over. "What happened?"

"I'll tell you on the way. Hop in." She pointed at her truck, which was idling, headlights on, in my parking lot. Attached to her truck was a boat trailer, which was half-submerged in the lake. Lucy, fresh off almost being arrested for murder, was strapping a small, worn-out motorboat to the metal struts.

Apparently, they'd been busy while I'd been sneaking around my property checking for professional killers. Good to know that the rain on my metal roof could drown out that much noise. That made me feel safe.

Lucy waved enthusiastically. I narrowed my eyes in suspicion, but waved back.

They were both way too cheerful for being in my parking lot in a storm in the middle of the night. Something was definitely up. I was getting a bad feeling about this situation. "Is that my boat on your trailer?"

"Yes, mine are too big. Let's go." Hattie started heading toward the truck.

I put my hands on my hips and made no attempt to move. "That boat has a leak. It's been sinking all week."

Hattie sighed and turned to face me. It was raining so hard that her jacket was glistening, and her cheeks looked like they were coated in glass. "The boat's not sinking. It just has a month's worth of rain it, because you haven't bailed it out. It'll be fine."

I folded my arms over my chest. "Fine for what, exactly?" I might have known them for only a few days, but I already knew better than to blindly trust any of Hattie's plans.

Hattie set her hands on her hips, looking impatient. "A little trip to Dead Man's Pond."

Going to a place called Dead Man's Pond at night during a storm in a sinking boat sounded like a fantastic idea. "Why would we be doing that?"

She blinked as the rain hammered her cheeks. "We're going to rescue some old ladies."

"Seriously?" I wasn't sure I believed her. Hattie already knew me well enough to know there was no chance I'd refuse to help rescue some senior citizens from a storm. "Who needs rescuing?"

"You remember Bootsy Jones and Shirley Kincaid?"

"Of course I remember them." Bootsy and Shirley were part of a group of senior sewers-for-hire called the Seam Rippers. Last I'd seen them, they were dressed up in leather, blasting rap music, and drinking margaritas. They were absolute spitfires, and there was no way I could snuggle down and sleep while they were stranded somewhere. *If* they really were stranded. "Why are they out on the lake? Were they camping?"

Maybe they weren't really in trouble. Maybe this was a front for going out drinking with the ladies...or something more nefarious that she was hiding from me.

"They were hunting a ghost."

I stared at her. "Ghost? Did you just say *ghost?*"

Hattie nodded. "The ghost of the man that Dead Man's Pond was named after. Jack the Ripper."

Jack the Ripper? Because that was charming, innocuous nickname. "Was he a serial killer?"

"Never proven."

I looked over at Lucy as she jogged up. "Is she serious?"

"Totally. It was never proven." She grinned. "According to Hattie, the Seam Rippers got hired to make a fundraiser quilt for the Halloween fest in October, so a few of them decided they needed to get in the spirit. It's difficult to channel proper Halloween mojo when it's Memorial Day. "

Ohh... I could see where this was heading. "They decided to commune with a ghost? And they chose a serial killer's ghost?"

"It's for Halloween," Lucy said, with just a wee bit of sarcasm that my highly tuned senses were able to pick up. "What good are *friendly* ghosts?"

"No good," I agreed, with equally subtle sarcasm. "Deep, debilitating terror is the only way to channel Halloween. Or even just everyday living. Fear is such a great motivator."

"Right?" Hattie nodded. "See, Lucy? Mia gets it."

Lucy raised her brows at me. "Does she?"

I grinned at her wise skepticism. "Of course. I love fear. It's super fun."

"You young 'uns are such wimps. You're lucky to have me around to toughen you up." Hattie gestured impatiently. "They hired Glory Starr, a ghost whisperer from Portland, to take them out tonight. Bootsy texted that they're stranded. They've been out there for hours, but they're running out of tequila, so Bootsy called for a rescue."

Lucy and I exchanged knowing glances.

"So, basically, they waited until midnight to call for help because they were having too much fun until now." It wasn't surprising. I'd met the Seam Rippers. Why abandon fun if you don't need to?

"Pretty much." Hattie grinned. "When that alcohol wears off, there are going to be four very cold, very wet, close-to-death old ladies on that pond, unless we go save them."

I believed her now. Given what I knew about the Seam Rippers, it made sense. But... "You want to rescue them in a sinking, old boat? Why not call Devlin?" Devlin Hunt was a local police officer who also carried the honor of being Lake Patrol. He was capable, charming, and distractingly attractive. "Saving people on lakes is literally what he's paid to do."

"Why delegate when we can do it ourselves?" Hattie asked.

"A lot of reasons, actually."

Lucy tucked her hand around my elbow and leaned on my shoulder. "Come with us, Mia. It'll be fun."

"You'll be the hero that you long to be," Hattie said.

I eyed the blue-haired senior. "I don't long to be a hero."

"Yeah, me either, but sometimes we get what we get." She started toward her truck, sloshing through the puddles that were getting deeper by the moment. "Let's do this. The girls are waiting."

I glanced at Lucy. "You realize there's no way this little adventure is going to turn out fine, right?"

She grinned, despite the rain dripping off her hood onto her cheeks. "It involves Hattie. What could possibly go wrong?"

Hattie started honking her horn at us and flashing her high beams.

I sighed. "A lot. Definitely, a lot."

Lucy raised her brows. "And you'd want to miss that?"

"Yes. Absolutely." But as I said it, I started walking toward Hattie's truck. Because who was I kidding? I totally wanted to go. Lucy and Hattie was already becoming friends, and, although I was committed to a law-abiding life, I'd never been able to shake the need for adventure that had been trained into me by my infamous, con-artist mom.

Lucy laughed. "Me, too." She slung her arm over my shoulder. "Have I told you how happy I am that you moved to Bass Derby?"

I pulled open the door as Hattie yelled at us to hurry up. "Me, too." I paused before climbing into the truck. "One promise, though."

Hattie raised her brows as Lucy squeezed into the back seat. "What's that?"

"No murder. No dead bodies. Nothing illegal." That last one was critical. I was desperate to leave the world of crime far behind me.

Hattie grinned. "That's an easy one. Nothing fun like that is on the agenda. A murder would be great, right?"

"No!" Lucy and I spoke at the same time.

I shook my head as I climbed in. "What's wrong with you, Hattie? Seriously."

"Nothing. I'm flawlessly fantastic. As always." She hit the gas before I'd even gotten the door closed, leaving me dangling out of the truck for a terrifying moment before I got the door yanked shut.

Yep, this was definitely going to go well. I had a good feeling about it. Really, I did.

Want to read *Top Notch*? Treat yourself to a copy today!

THE FBI & THE NEW YEAR'S EVE MISHAP

(THE ONE THAT ALMOST KILLED ME)

Are you hankering for some more Mia, and wishing that you didn't have to wait so freaking long for the next book? Well, yearn no more! Stephanie (and often Mia) send out a weekly (usually) email, and sometimes Mia does a guest post. For example, check out Mia's New Year's Eve newsletter below for an inside scoop on what you get! If it's your thing, and then zip on over to www.stephanierowe.com and sign up so you don't miss out on any Mia shenanigans!

Mia's Newsletter Hijacking: THE FBI & THE NEW YEAR'S EVE MISHAP By Mia Murphy

Once again, this email isn't from Stephanie. It's from me, Mia Murphy, the incredibly delightful heroine of Stephanie's AWESOMELY FUN mystery *Double Twist*.

You guys are the best! So many love notes to Steph about me, and now she's turned over the reins once again so I can tell you about my best, and worst, New Year's Eve ever. It involves the FBI, a sweaty silk dress, and a wire gone burning-breast crazy.

For my whole life, my New Year's Eve has been overrated. As a kid, because it always involved my mom and I conning our way into another Hollywood bash so that we could score an Aspen ski trip invite or two. Then, after I ditched my mom, it was because I was doing my best to overcompensate for my criminal childhood by feeding the homeless (well, honestly, the homeless I was feeding was myself at first, but that was the best I could do, so let's take that as a win, right?)

But then two years ago…yikes.

It was my second New Year's Eve since I'd anonymously reported my nerdy husband, Stanley, to the FBI after I'd found out he might be a massive drug dealer. As you know, the feds loved my tip so much that they'd forced me into going undercover against him.

As it turns out, it's actually incredibly stressful to wear a wire and spy on your hubs and his heavily armed mercenary besties. Go figure, right?

On that New Year's Eve, Griselda (my pet name for my FBI

handler, Agent Straus, who isn't nearly as amused by the nickname as I am) informed me that some big brouhaha was going down at the house, and I had to be front and center.

Because who doesn't want to be front and center at a drug dealer convention, right? It's a bucket list item for pretty much everyone.

So there I was, super relaxed and happy to be on the stage in my slinky red gown and the matching stilettos that would make it impossible for me to sprint for my life, when feedback happened.

You know feedback, right? That's when the microphone squeals and everyone looks around to figure out what's causing it. In this particularly delightful moment, I realized that the feedback had been triggered by the FBI wire that was playing footsie with my left breast. The wire that got fried because of all the terror-induced sweat cascading down my chest.

Instantly, all these hotties wearing tuxedoes, knives, and guns got all jacked up, pointing the their weapons all over the place, trying to figure out who the spy was. My hubs was standing next to me, ordering all the doors to be locked until they could search everyone.

Like me. Like searching the gal standing next to him who was, actually, the spy in question.

Because my awesome spy work had made it clear to me and my FBI pals that my nerdy hubs was a paranoid, amoral drug lord who'd definitely chop up his beloved if she were caught doing something like…oh…wearing a wire for the FBI.

While Stanley was shouting for his peeps to start disrobing everyone at the party, the wire started sizzling, that little hissing sound when things aren't going well for electrical wires. You can picture that, right?

Stanley knew that noise.

He literally shouted at the room to shut up and held up his hand for silence.

When a drug lord demands silence, he gets it.

In that gun-filled silence, I was sweating, burning, and freaking out, while the whole room was waiting for that stupid wire to hiss again.

One hiss, and I was dead. And not a fast dead. It would be the kind of suffering, tortured, slow-to-die dead that serves as an example for all the other drug lord wives who are contemplating calling the FBI hotline.

Sure, it's great to be the kind of woman who paves the way for other women, but I really wasn't feeling that this was my calling. At least not, yet. I mean, maybe when I was a hundred and ten, it might be fun to be assassinated.

But I was only twenty-seven, and it wasn't one of my New Year's resolutions.

There was nothing I could do except wait to die.

But here's the thing. My mom might have been a con artist and a criminal, but she was a big believer that there was always a way, no matter what. She was all about girl power, innovation, and creative problem-solving, using whatever tools you had, and she'd ruthlessly drilled that into me for seventeen years, until I'd bailed on her to launch a law-abiding life (and yes, the irony of who I'd unwittingly married is not lost on me).

My old skills came back in a whirlwind hurry.

Standing on that stage, I had only a second, maybe two, but my mind was moving so fast that it felt like an eternity. I scanned that stage and the room so quickly, assessing every detail, like my mom and I used to do at those parties in the Hamptons, when she was figuring out who to hit up for an invite for the summer.

I didn't have a weapon. I didn't have an exit. But I had my special skill that I was particularly awesome at, the one skill that I'd kept up, because it was so fun for me.

I was, and always had been, a master pickpocket.

Use what you have, my mom always said. Without time to plan much of anything, I leapt backwards, pretended to trip on a speaker, and fell. The speaker clattered to the floor, and the nearest tuxedo-clad mercenary grabbed me and yanked me to my feet before his boss could yell at him.

While he was doing that, I snagged his phone, tripped on his foot, fell into a tray of champagne glasses, and typed in the constantly changing code that I'd just checked on before the speeches.

A split second later, the house alarms were blaring, lights were flashing, and all heck broke loose. Why? Because the alarm to the gun safe had been triggered. *innocent blink*

I got the phone back in his pocket before he managed to take off, got my hand inside my dress, and ripped out that wire. A childhood of training kicked in, and I wiped off my fingerprints,

DNA, and sweat, and then jammed it into the pocket of another gun-toting muscle-head as he was racing past.

Then I frantically looked around to see if anyone had noticed.

But the distraction had worked, exactly as it had so many times with my mom when I was a kid.

No one was paying any attention to me.

It wasn't my night to die.

Best. Feeling. Ever.

There you go: my worst New Year's ever. And also my best, because I got to escape death (it's amazing how that puts things in perspective) and because Griselda had to apologize for the faulty equipment.

Happy New Year's to you. May it not involve assassins, faulty FBI equipment, and mercenaries. Small goals, right?

Smooches,

Mia

Want more fun like this delivered to your inbox for free? Sign up for Steph's newsletter at www.stephanierowe.com.

A QUICK FAVOR

Hey there, my friend!

It's Mia! Tell me, tell me! What did you think of *Double Twist?*

I hope you loved it, and my suffering wasn't for naught.

Just kidding. No suffering here! I love my life. And my hairdryer. And my cat. And my friends. And… well… the list goes on and on. And just wait until my next book, *Top Notch*, comes out. More fun on the way!

I hope I gave you some feel-good entertainment in these pages! If I did, it would rock if you'd do me a favor and help get the word out, so that other folks can find their way here.

Tell a friend. Tell an enemy. Leave a note for your barista.

Reviews are also incredibly helpful to encourage new readers to make that leap and try a new book. It would be super fab if you'd consider taking a couple minutes and jotting one or two sentences on the etailer and/or Goodreads telling everyone how freaking amazing I am. Or King Tut. Because we all know that he's the best. Even the short reviews really make an impact!

Thank you again for reading my story! I can't wait for you to see what happens next!

Smooches,

Mia

BOOKS BY STEPHANIE ROWE

MYSTERY

Mia Murphy series

Double Twist

Top Notch (Sept. 2022)

ROMANCE

CONTEMPORARY ROMANCE

Wyoming Rebels series

(Contemporary Western Romance)

A Real Cowboy Never Says No

A Real Cowboy Knows How to Kiss

A Real Cowboy Rides a Motorcycle

A Real Cowboy Never Walks Away

A Real Cowboy Loves Forever

A Real Cowboy for Christmas

A Real Cowboy Always Trusts His Heart

A Real Cowboy Always Protects

A Real Cowboy for the Holidays

A Real Cowboy Always Comes Home (May 2022)

The Hart Ranch Billionaires series
(Contemporary Western Romance)
A Rogue Cowboy's Second Chance

Linked to the Hart Ranch Billionaires Series
(Contemporary Western Romance)
Her Rebel Cowboy

Birch Crossing series
(Small-town Contemporary Romance)
Unexpectedly Mine
Accidentally Mine
Unintentionally Mine
Irresistibly Mine

Mystic Island series
(Small-town Contemporary Romance)
Wrapped Up in You (A Christmas novella)

Canine Cupids series
(Romantic Comedy)
Paws for a Kiss
Pawfectly in Love
Paws Up for Love

Single Title
(ChickLit / Romantic Comedy)
One More Kiss

PARANORMAL

Order of the Blade series
(Paranormal Romance)
Darkness Awakened
Darkness Seduced
Darkness Surrendered
Forever in Darkness
Darkness Reborn
Darkness Arisen
Darkness Unleashed
Inferno of Darkness
Darkness Possessed
Shadows of Darkness
Hunt the Darkness
Darkness Awakened: Reimagined

***Immortally Sexy* series**
(Funny Paranormal Romance)
To Date an Immortal
To Date a Dragon
Devilishly Dating
To Kiss a Demon

Heart of the Shifter series
(Paranormal Romance)
Dark Wolf Rising
Dark Wolf Unbound

Shadow Guardians series
(Paranormal Romance)
Leopard's Kiss

NightHunter series
(Paranormal Romance)
Not Quite Dead

***Noble as Hell* series**
(Funny Urban Fantasy)
Guardian of Magic

***The Magical Elite* series**
(Funny Paranormal Romance)
The Demon You Trust

***Devilishly Sexy* series**
(Funny Paranormal Romance)
Not Quite a Devil

ROMANTIC SUSPENSE

Alaska Heat Series
(Romantic Suspense)
Ice
Chill
Ghost
Burn
Hunt

For a complete list of Stephanie's books, go to www.stephanierowe.com

ABOUT THE AUTHOR

New York Times and *USA Today* bestselling author Stephanie Rowe is the author of more than fifty published novels. Notably, she is a Vivian® Award nominee, and a RITA® Award winner and a five-time nominee. She loves her puppies, tennis, and being as as sassy and irreverent as her heroines. She's pretty sure dead bodies are better in fiction than real life, but hey, never say never, right? She has a pretty fantastic newsletter thing happening, so if you want in some good entertainment, you can join the fun over at www.stephanierowe.com.

Made in United States
Orlando, FL
03 June 2022

18447916R00214